Futures

FREDA BRIGHT, who was born in Boston and largely educated there, had a long and successful career as an advertising consultant to the film industry before switching to novel-writing. Her first book, *Options*, was written in London where she lived for ten years. She now lives in New York with her teenage daughter.

Futures is Freda Bright's second novel, and she has just completed her third.

FREDA BRIGHT

Futures

FONTANA/Collins

First published in the USA by Poseidon Press 1983
First published in Great Britain by
William Collins Sons & Co. Ltd 1983
First issued in Fontana Paperbacks 1984

Copyright © Freda Reaser 1983

Made and printed in Great Britain by
William Collins Sons and Co. Ltd, Glasgow

To the dearest of friends, Katie Evens,
and the dearest of daughters, Vicki.

1

Nervous? That was hardly the word for it. For one nightmare moment she was afraid she might faint.

The closeness of the room, the merciless lighting, the short, stocky official behind the stand with his glinting bifocals and neatly clipped moustache – the whole place was so stifling. So oppressive.

She wiped her hand on her dress – the hand that had written up so many six-figure deals without a tremor – a hand that was shaky now and damp with sweat.

The man adjusted his glasses and peered at her. She shut her eyes – the eyes that could on occasion stare down the toughest corporate chief without flinching – unable to return his glance.

'Are we ready to begin?' he said.

She opened her mouth – the mouth that had talked its way through a hundred high-powered meetings – and no sound came out.

'Yes, sir!' A rich masculine voice boomed in her ear. 'We're ready.'

The official dropped his gaze to the docket before him.

'Please step forward.'

She couldn't move. She was frozen with fear and might have stayed rooted to the spot forever had not a firm arm encircled her waist, propelling her gently to the lectern.

The official checked his papers, cleared his throat, then began.

'Do you Thomas Darius take Caroline Harmsworth to be your lawful wedded wife. . . .'

She swivelled her head and stared hard at the man standing beside her. Was that Tom?

He certainly looked like Tom. Had Tom's thick dark hair. Tom's eyes, his nose. Was even wearing Tom's blazer. Yes. . . .

7

it was definitely Tom and no one else. That at least was reassuring. But something still nagged at her, something wrong and alien.

It was the tie, she realized. The tie had thrown her off.

'A tie!'

Those had been Tom's first words when he crawled out of bed that very morning. 'Jesus Christ, honey. I don't have a tie.'

'I shouldn't think you'd need one,' she murmured from the depths of the pillow. 'It's not Westminster Abbey, after all – just City Hall.'

'Well, this is going to be some classy wedding,' Tom shrugged. 'The bride wore white and the groom wore best jeans.'

'I'm not wearing white' – she rubbed the sleep from her eyes – 'just a nice silk dress, and you'll look perfectly fine in a polo-neck. I think the only thing they insist on is the licence.'

She watched him riffle through his clothes – a tall well-built familiar figure moving as always with consummate grace. Watched him, and thought with a sense of wonder that they had just made unmarried love for the last time. Next time it would be as husband and wife.

'The last time. . . .' Was Tom reading her mind? But no, he was following some drift of his own. 'The last time I wore a tie was when they took my picture for the High School yearbook. It was one of those wide jobbies and I remember burning it that summer at Woodstock. Good old Woodstock. There was everyone else smoking grass, getting laid . . . and there was me, lighting a bonfire and burning my tie. The big symbolic gesture. How was I to know' – he withdrew a cashmere polo-neck from the dresser – 'that I'd be wanting it some day to get married in? So much for male emancipation.'

With that he went off to shave, while Caro, feeling faintly disorientated, got up and made coffee.

It was decidedly odd, a funny feeling, being at home well past nine on a business morning. Like playing hooky. But everything today seemed subtly different, unfamiliar – the angle of the sun on the kitchen counter, the muffled street sounds now that rush hour was over. Without warning, her stomach muscles tightened in spasm.

8

Dammit, she was nervous.

Idiotic, she admonished herself. What on earth is there to be scared about? People get married every day of the week, and it wasn't as if she and Tom were a couple of kids rushing into matrimony on the basis of a half-dozen kisses in the moonlight. They were mature sensible people, fully-fledged adults who knew each other well and cared for each other deeply. Two people who had rid themselves of outmoded traditions and foolish illusions.

For she was the New Woman, he the New Man – and between them they would create the New Marriage. *Real* marriage – flexible and dynamic. Not mastery on the one hand and submission on the other; not the coupling of superior male to manipulative female. Simply the equal partnership of two smart, independent and consenting adults.

Who happened to love each other very, very much.

It would be as Tom had promised, resolving all her doubts. Nothing between them would change except for the better. Marriage was just a formality after all, a public affirmation of private love and trust. And the wedding itself would be a modest, no-fuss occasion. 'We won't come out of there two different people,' he assured her. 'What's to change? You're not even changing your name.'

Nor was she. She had been Caroline Harmsworth for twenty-eight years and would continue to be – certainly in business circles. She'd worked too long and too hard to make that name count for something merely to scrap it on one day's notice.

No, she'd be the same person, she reassured herself. And so would Tom – wonderful Tom who now popped into the kitchen, freshly shaved, looking very handsome and confident in his best twill trousers and navy blazer. And – characteristically – tieless.

'Terrific!' she beamed up at him. 'You look just great. My bet is we'll be the snappiest couple down at City Hall, necktie or no.'

But twenty minutes later on their way downtown, Tom stopped the taxi on impulse and with a 'Wait for me' jumped out and dashed into Wallach's. When he emerged a few minutes later, he was wearing a white shirt and waving a blue silk tie like a trophy.

'Just so I don't make waves,' he explained getting into the cab. But buying it was one thing, tying it another; and while the taxi was fighting its way through East Side traffic, Tom too was locked in mortal combat with the tie.

'Here, darling' – he handed it to her in disgust. 'Have a whack at it. You're good at that sort of thing.' And Caro, who was indeed good at that sort of thing, slid it deftly under his collar and managed a passable imitation of a Windsor knot.

'Not too tight, is it?' she asked, patting it flat.

'It's fine, sweetie. You know, I always thought tying a tie was one of those things you never forget . . . like riding a bike.' He looked down at his new acquisition, then over to her. 'I guess I'm a little bit nervous. How about you, Caro?'

Yes, she confessed. She was a little bit nervous too.

'. . . to love, honour and keep her with you (the official voice droned on) as long as you both shall live?'

There was a moment's pause. Then

'I DO.'

Tom's response rang out like a cannon. He *did*. He actually did. Caro turned to him in the numbness of fear to find him radiant with joy and love. He gripped her hand, and suddenly she could feel his joy passing through her fingertips, suffusing every cell in her body with the reality of his warmth and his happiness and his commitment.

How marvellous! How utterly unutterably marvellous that Tom! – wonderful loving clever sexy funny tender warm good-looking good-natured passionate sensitive fair-minded high-minded wonderful wonderful Tom – should love her so much that he would pledge her a lifetime. From this moment on.

The fears were gone now. The doubts, the near-hysteria. Everything gone but the reality of their love. And in that moment when Tom had touched her hand, she knew herself to be the happiest woman in the world.

And so it was that Caroline Martha Harmsworth took Thomas Stearns Darius to be her lawfully wedded husband in the state of matrimony; to love, honour and keep him with her as long as they both shall live.

With one sure deft motion, Tom placed a slim gold band around her finger and at precisely 10.44 Eastern Standard Time, a shortish man wearing bifocals exercised the authority vested in him according to the laws of the State of New York and pronounced them husband and wife.

Tom's first act as a married man was to loosen his tie.

2

Caroline Harmsworth had not been raised to marry. She had been raised to achieve.

In her mother's lexicon, the words *marriage* and *career* were not merely incompatible; they were diametrically opposed. In short, Augusta 'Gusty' Harmsworth had failed at the former and succeeded brilliantly at the latter.

To the current generation of film-makers, her television documentaries stand supreme as models of the genre. Among them *The Child Brides of India*; the classic *Couvade: Shared Birth-Rites of Africa*; and, of course, her ground-breaking *Behind the Veil – the Women of Islam*.

'I like to think' – she once wrote in *Life* – 'that through the medium of film, I am able to blend the world of art with the world of anthropology.' A network chief put it rather more crassly. 'Gusty figured out a way to show tits on TV.'

To Gusty Harmsworth, the camera was no mere assemblage of metal, glass and leather; it was an instrument of power and freedom. The means of escape from mediocrity.

She was born Augusta Frink into a large family in a small town whose principal products she later described as 'beer and boredom'. Her mother ran a boarding house, and conceivably Gusty might have followed in her footsteps had not fate intervened in the shape of a departing lodger who – in those cash-poor days of the Depression – left an aging Graflex behind in lieu of payment.

'Well, of all the useless . . .' sighed Mrs Frink, but the ten-year-old Gusty was mesmerized. Even years later she could recall the impact of that first tentative glimpse through the viewfinder.

It was magic! You could make big people small, stop time in its tracks, edit everything around you to your own requirements. Here was the world controlled and controllable, a world with no smell of boarding-house cabbage about it.

The day she left home and boarded the train to Chicago – a short, compact sixteen-year-old still wearing bobby sox and loafers – she possessed little more than her camera and a one-way ticket. In her heart she knew there would be no turning back.

Even then, everything about her generated electricity, from the wiry blonde hair to the piercing blue eyes to the stubby, restless fingers. She found a job in a newspaper dark room ('Kid Dynamite' the staff used to call her), learned her craft, saved her pennies, then spent the next several years barnstorming through the Midwest photographing everything from state fairs to fires and plane crashes.

There had been (and perhaps still was) a Mr Harmsworth encountered somewhere along the line and briefly married.

On those few occasions when she had cause to refer to him, it was as 'the face on the cutting-room floor'. What had induced the then young, but promising, photographer to succumb, however momentarily, to the lure of marriage and suburbia, no one could ever explain. Not even Gusty, except to say 'I think everyone should try everything once.'

The marriage was destined to fail. In a matter of months, the view from the picture window had so thoroughly palled, the threshold of boredom had been so fully reached and surpassed that when the chance for an assignment in Algeria suddenly materialized, Gusty didn't think twice. She simply packed her cameras and took the next plane out, leaving behind her winter clothes, her wedding ring and a one-page note for the unsuspecting Harmsworth. In it she informed him that he was free to sue for divorce and no hard feelings.

What she didn't mention – then or ever – was that she was three months pregnant at the time.

And so in due course, Caroline Harmsworth was born in the French Hospital of Oran. Trade gossip has it that Gusty entered the labour room clutching her Hasselblad, determined to photograph herself in the actual process of birth.

In any event, her Algerian flight left her with more to show than just a baby daughter ('After all, any woman can have a baby.') It also produced her first film documentary: *Behind the Veil*. To Western eyes, the film was a revelation, touching as it did upon the hitherto unphotographed life of the *hareem*, and it quickly established Gusty in the front rank of documentary film-makers. It was a revelation for her, too, for she discovered that in a field proverbially dominated by men, her sex for once proved an advantage, not a drawback. As a woman she was free to venture into those precincts forbidden to mere males. Free to record through the camera's eye that no-man's-land of exotic childbirth customs and puberty rites and pre-nuptial mysteries never photographed before. Nothing fazed Gusty in the pursuit of her quarry – not even the ever-present language barrier. 'Women communicate with women,' she told an interviewer. 'And we don't need words to do it.' Although she could, when pressed, muster the odd phrase or necessary curse in anything from Urdu to Swahili, in fact Gusty was at home in only one language. Film was her mother tongue. Of the North African sojourn that had given birth to Caro and *Behind the Veil*, Gusty would say 'That was the year I found my *metier*.'

And by *metier* she did not mean motherhood.

'Oran, Calcutta, Quito, Nairobi, Baghdad. . . .' Caro once amused Tom by reeling off the scenes of her childhood, and Tom had envied her. He relished hearing of the places she'd been, the celebrities she'd met, the romance of those early years. 'Sure beats the hell out of growing up in Morristown, New Jersey,' he laughed. And Caro was pleased that her stories had pleased him. Yet in that recounting years later, her childhood gained a lustre she had not felt at the time. She was reluctant to dispel the glamour she had earned in Tom's eyes, but privately she remembered those years with anguish.

'There's no such thing as a free lunch,' Gusty once said. 'God says take what you want, but pay for it.' That Gusty herself had taken what she'd wanted most from life was undeniable. She had achieved fame, status and a fair measure of financial independence. Her address book bulged with the names – and the nicknames – of the mighty. She was invited everywhere. Respected. Admired, if not always loved. As for the price of that success, she felt she had paid her dues fully – in hard work, in chronic insecurity, in the physical hardships of a life perennially on the move. 'I've paid,' she'd say, 'God knows I've paid.' But she had not footed the bill alone, and inevitably a large share of the cost was borne by Caro.

In her memories of childhood it was always Moving Day. Sadness at one end – the packing, the closing of a house, the rounds of flurried goodbyes – and excitement at the other. Immediately upon arrival in a new country (there were to be a over a dozen in all), Gusty would plunge into a frenzy of activity. In a matter of weeks, she would have rented a house, hired domestic help and made arrangements for whichever local school catered to the children of the international community. Once Caro was settled, Gusty was off on assignment, usually for months at a time.

Caro would await her mother's eventual return with a mixture of fear and longing. These reunions were brief but intense. They exploded the orderly routine of her life. Overnight, the once-quiet house would be filled with people and film cans and extravagant gifts and marvellous tales of Maharajahs or Maori tribesmen. Gusty's excitement was contagious and it would have been a dull child indeed who did not live those moments to the full. 'Little Gusty's no gust,' an overworked assistant once grumbled. 'She's a fucking hurricane.' When she was home, no detail of Caro's life escaped her practised eye. When she was gone, no detail of it troubled her. She *was* like a hurricane, arriving abruptly and as hastily departing, leaving only silence in her wake. Caro would kiss her goodbye with mingled relief and regret. And then settle down yet again to her routine.

Gusty's entourage invariably included a lover, some reasonably attractive young man who came and departed with her, for although she had sworn off marriage, she was fond of men and always had one on call. They were largely interchangeable, and on those rare occasions when one defected he was quickly forgotten, and a replacement found on short order. Their tenure was determined only by the length of Gusty's stay. They were expendable.

'Caro,' she would say, 'I'd like you to meet Jack (or Eric or

Teddy), who's going to be with us for a while. You can call him Uncle if you like.'

Caro never did, however. Real uncles surely lasted from one year to the next; they were not left behind at every move, along with the ethnic rugs and native pottery. Caro liked some more than others, detested one or two. But there was one she fell madly in love with.

His name was Nigel. He was a tall fair Englishman with a perpetual sunburn who lived a few doors away from them in Calcutta and managed investments for an Anglo-Indian bank. She would have gone to the stake for him happily. For, whether it was out of neighbourliness or good nature or genuine affection, Nigel was unique among Gusty's lovers in that his interest in Caro was independent of her mother's comings and goings.

No matter that Gusty was away for long stretches. Nigel would invite Caro around for tea. Or take her to a local cricket match. Or drop in casually after work, bearing loads of bank rubbish. But it was not rubbish to Caro – it was heaven. Great sheets of graph paper. Rolls of adding machine tape. Stamps from places with unpronounceable names. Stock certificates from long-defunct companies, all lovely whorls and swirls.

One evening he brought an over-sized cheque book that dated back to the days of the Raj. He explained very simply what a cheque book was and how it worked. 'You could use it to practise your handwriting.'

'You mean,' Caro asked, 'I could write a cheque for one million rupees?'

'You could write it,' he laughed. 'Of course no one would honour it. But why not? Go ahead . . . give it a try.'

'There are lots and lots of noughts in a million rupees, aren't there?'

'There are precisely six,' he handed her his pen. 'So put down the figure 1 and then six noughts.'

Caro laboured for a minute or two then passed him the results of her handiwork.

Pay to the order of NIGEL PRYCE-JONES
In the amount of 1,000,000 rupees

Caroline Harmsworth

'Thank you,' Nigel said gravely. He folded it with a show

16

of ceremony and placed it in his pocket. 'And shame on you too. Your handwriting is absolutely appalling.' For he was also unique among Gusty's lovers in that he nagged at her about everything from her table manners to the condition of her fingernails. She adored him all the more for it.

'Why don't you marry Gusty?' she asked him one day over tea.

'You'll have to ask your mother that.'

So upon Gusty's next return, Caro posed the question.

'Why don't you marry Nigel?' – she could hear her heart beat.

Gusty scrutinized her coolly for a moment. 'Don't let yourself get too attached to him,' came the answer, which to Caro was no answer at all. And a few weeks later she informed her daughter that they would be moving to Ecuador within a month. 'You'll love it, darling. New language . . . new friends. I've always wanted to go to South America.'

'Is Nigel coming with us?'

'Why no, honey. He has his work and I have mine. You'll understand when you're grown up with a career of your own. Anyhow, men come and men go in this life.'

Yet that particular Moving Day would remain fixed in Caro's memory as the blackest moment of her childhood. She was eight years old. And she had loved and lost.

The rootless quality of life was something Caro never questioned. Among people she knew, it was the norm. Her schoolmates, like herself, were the children of the mobile: of oilmen, journalists, diplomats, technicians – that band of international nomads who slip around the globe with the ease and weightlessness of clouds. Like most children of that community, she was highly adaptable, accepting the style and colouration of each new environment with the rapidity of a chameleon. She learned to speak fluent French, idiomatic Spanish and that curiously unaccented English that linguists define as 'Mid-Atlantic'. Experience taught her how to cope with electrical failures, drunken cooks, squat plumbing, customs officials, beggars, insects and long unbroken periods of solitude.

But above all she learned the art of making friendships

swiftly rather than deeply; friendships that could be just as swiftly dissolved. For beneath each budding relationship there lay on both sides the tacit understanding that it would be only for a year or so. Until the next transfer, the next posting, the next assignment. The goodbye that ended each school year was most frequently a goodbye forever. And nobody cried.

In one regard only did she differ from her schoolmates: she alone had no visible father. They were where they were – those other children – precisely because of their fathers: urbane and vigorous men whose absences, though sometimes prolonged, were never permanent. The irregularity of her own circumstances had not struck her in early childhood; it was only after Calcutta and Nigel had been left behind that Caro became aware of that third dimension lacking from her life, like a board game in which a crucial piece had been lost at the outset. A chess set without a king.

Among the free spirits who wheeled in and out of Gusty's circle, the matter was never mentioned. Everyone understood the exigencies of Gusty's career and took it for granted that her mother was, so to speak, a one-man band. Indeed it was often a matter for congratulations. 'What a lucky girl you are,' Caro heard time and again, 'having such a brilliant woman for a mother.'

Yet she knew other children usually identified themselves in the light of their father's achievements. 'We're Army,' they'd say at first encounter. Or 'We're Exxon' ... 'We're State Department'. To which Caro would reply 'My mother is Augusta Harmsworth,' with a mixture of pride and defensiveness.

When she was sixteen, her mother suddenly called a halt to their wanderings and, with typical Augustan dispatch, bought a spacious apartment overlooking Central Park and enrolled Caro in a good private school. The burdens of raising a pretty teenager in the flea-bitten corners of the Third World had finally proved too much even for the indomitable Gusty. 'We have to think about your future right now,' she said, 'That is, if you're ever going to amount to anything.'

Actually, there was little question in either of their minds but that Caro would amount to something, for success was her birthright, a substance ingested from infancy in lieu of mother's milk. She did well in high school ('Caroline is an achiever,' it said in every report), then went on to spend four busy and gregarious years at Midwestern U. At twenty-one, for reasons she herself would only comprehend much later, Caro entered Harvard Business School.

3

'All my life,' she told Tom the day they married, 'I have been marking time, although I never really knew it. I think I must have been waiting for you.'

'And me for you. We should have met years ago,' he murmured. 'Just think if we'd known each other back when we were both going to Harvard. All that time from then to now we could have loved each other. Funny isn't it? . . . you and I just across the river from each other, never meeting, never even knowing the other person existed. . . .'

'Maybe it's just as well,' she pushed the thick tangle of hair from his forehead and kissed the well-loved brow. 'I'm glad you didn't know me then: You would have hated me.'

'I could never hate you, darling. Under no conceivable circumstance.'

'Well, you certainly wouldn't have loved me,' she said thoughtfully. 'I didn't even love myself in those days.'

ABOLISH THE B SCHOOL ran the graffiti in Harvard Yard, to which another scribbler had appended BEFORE IT ABOLISHES YOU. Every morning Caro passed the sign on her way to class and muttered a fervent 'Amen'.

She had had a vision of Harvard as a warm and lively place teeming with scholars, wits, bawdy medical students, future statesmen. The Harvard of *Lampoon* and the Hasty Pudding Club and the football team, fondly remembered by its alumni as 'the lousiest in the Ivy League'.

She had looked forward to Business School – or B School as it was known in the jargon – as a kind of super-college; an exciting extension of what Midwestern had been, only the classes would be more stimulating, the environment livelier, the men that much more interesting. If the world was her oyster, surely

Harvard was its pearl, and she arrived in Cambridge with every confidence – a confidence born of good marks, good nature and good looks.

'You're no picture-book beauty,' Gusty once summed her up, 'but the bone structure's first class. You'll do.' Few people seeing the two together would have taken them for mother and daughter. Where Gusty was small and bouncy and fiercely blonde (one might have said cute if the woman hadn't been so formidable), Caro was modelled of a different clay. She had inherited Gusty's quickness of mind, her wide blue eyes and little else. A full head taller than her mother, she was at once willowy and athletic, with glossy brown hair (rather too much of it), vivid high colour and a smile that could melt the heart of a statue. There was about her a quality that an earlier, more sentimental generation might have characterized as sweetness, although sweetness was not a fashionable concept in these brisker times. Certainly, if anyone had called her 'sweet' she would have blushed (she had an annoying tendency to turn beet-red when flustered). And if anyone had told her she was blushing, she would have turned an even deeper shade of crimson, for she loathed the idea of being thought vulnerable.

Men usually liked her. Women, too – for she was not so much of a beauty as to constitute a threat. Therefore, all things considered, she had reasonable expectations on finding at Harvard that blend of easy friendships and pleasant love affairs that had lightened the undergraduate years at Midwestern. But the Harvard that greeted her paid no homage to her private dreams.

There existed, to be sure, that ivied and traditional campus so celebrated in American lore; but it lay across the river, remote and separate from the B School. They were different worlds, inhabited by different beings.

If B-School students regarded the older campus with cold eyes as a playground for dilettantes and fuzzy-minded idealists, they in turn were regarded with a mixture of fear and contempt. B School was, according to its critics, an assembly line for zombies, a factory that spewed out martinets in pin-stripe suits, automatons lacking both in soul and heart. Competition hung in the air like the scent of blood. It was explicit in every classroom problem; implicit in every personal relationship. *Push* was the message. *Shove. Outwit. Outmanoeuvre.* But above all *Win* – for winning is all.

From Day One, Caro hated the place. The workload was staggering, the pressure more relentless than she'd been led to expect, allowing virtually no time for leisure.

From High School on she had sung in school choirs and among the attractions at Cambridge had been the prospect of joining the Harvard-Radcliffe Chorale. But singing – like tennis, chess and just plain fooling around – now gave way to the exigencies of the B-School schedule.

Fun was a low priority item.

Occasionally she wondered if the workload was meant to be a test of physical stamina, like the training undergone by Marines at boot camp: a programme cunningly designed to separate the men from the boys. The men from the women, too.

Well, stamina she had. And ambition and 'smarts'. And she felt she would have borne up well, had there been other consolations. Had there been about the place any air of friendship, of warmth and casual affection. There was, of course, the occasional laugh, but it was usually at a colleague's expense. Certainly nothing like that easy beer-and-pretzels camaraderie she'd enjoyed in college.

'You'll have a ball,' her roomate at Midwestern had teased her, 'with ten guys to every girl. Let's hope you manage to get some work done while you're there.' And Caro had been worried that, given the man-woman ratio of the place, she might fritter her opportunities away for the blandishments of social life. She had a dread of being seen merely as a sex object. It never occurred to her that she would be seen as an intruder. And in some cases wouldn't be seen at all.

The brightest of the men were yawningly indifferent, tuned in to some frequency she could not hear. Most were older, many were married, and the ones who weren't saw themselves as prize commodities – the answer to a rich maiden's prayer. They had their pick of Boston society and dated with a Dun & Bradstreet in hand. As for the lesser lights, the ones who (like Caro) were off to a floundering start, they often treated her with

22

outright hostility. The handful of women were not warmly welcomed – even by each other. Time and again, Caro had the sensation of making an astute point in class only to have it fall on deaf ears. Yet minutes later a male student would make the same point, and all would sit up and take notice.

She thought, given her cosmopolitan background, she might make friends among the foreign students, but they proved equally aloof – quiet, serious men, dreaming only of the day when they would go home to assume command of a Middle East refinery or a Swiss merchant bank. There was one, a beautiful young Japanese with anxious eyes and a long, forgettable name (people called him 'Mitsi' for short) for whom she felt particular sympathy. He seemed even lonelier than she, poor bastard. She asked him around for coffee a couple of times, and once suggested they study together. He always smiled politely and declined. She gave up asking.

Her first months at Cambridge were marked by insomnia and nervous indigestion. Long gruelling days of classwork in the lecture halls alternated with long gruelling nights of homework in a bleak furnished room.

By mid-term, she nearly succumbed to a case of 'the quits' over an incident at once typical and trivial.

She had been working that morning in the library on the last lap of an assignment. It had been a particularly thorny problem: the case history of a hypothetical company on the verge of bankruptcy and she'd been grappling with it all week long. But now, little by little, she could see the strands coming together, chart the patterns falling into place. See the light at the end of the tunnel, so to speak.

Towards noon, feeling terribly pleased with herself, she stepped outside for a whiff of air; then, invigorated, returned to the library.

Her books lay where she'd left them, her pencils and slide rule undisturbed. Her notes were gone.

For a moment, Caro's heart stopped. There had to be some mistake. She looked around. At the next table, half obscured by a stack of books, sat one of the men from her section. He seemed lost in thought.

'Hey, Burt,' she asked in her library whisper. 'Did you see

23

anybody go over to where I was sitting? My notes seem to have vanished.'

'Huh?' He raised his eyes and peered at her over steel-rimmed bifocals.

'My notes,' she repeated. 'There was a whole bunch of pages on yellow legal paper, plus some diagrams. . . . Did you notice anyone going by?'

'Nope.' He shook his head. 'Sorry.'

'Oh Christ!' Her voice began to tremble. 'It's all my work on the Alpha assignment. Shit! That stuff's due tomorrow. What am I going to do?'

'Listen, honey,' came the cool reply. 'Don't come to me with your problems. If you can't hack the work here, go teach nursery school instead.'

With that he turned back to his books. But there was something stubborn, stony, in the set of his shoulders, and in that moment she was certain he had taken them.

In her ears, the blood started pounding.

'You . . . You. . . .' she addressed the back of his neck, then suddenly burst aloud 'You pig!' From neighbouring tables came hushes, smiles and curious stares while Caro stood there, helpless with rage. Then she turned on her heels, walked out of the library and took the next shuttle to New York.

'Well, what would *you* have done, Gusty?' Caro wanted to know.

'I'll tell you one thing I wouldn't have done. I wouldn't have turned tail and walked out. Nope,' she considered. 'I think I would have grabbed the guy's briefcase without so much as a by-your-leave, and gone through the contents then and there. My bet is, you'd have caught him dead to rights.'

'Oh, Gusty,' Caro sighed. 'This was the Baker Library at Harvard, not some shoot-out at the OK Corral. Ah, what the hell. . . I just don't think it's worth it. Maybe I'll simply quit that goddam place and' – she gave a bitter snort – 'and get a job teaching nursery school. It's not just the one incident, it's the whole atmosphere up there. There's one professor, for instance, in economics. Now I'm pretty good in economics, but every time I open my mouth he looks right through me, like I'm invisible. What do I have to do – get a microphone?'

'Not such a bad idea, you know. Seriously, Caro, it's not as if you're at a garden party. You have to fight your own battles in this world, because if you don't, no one else will. If the guy doesn't listen, then raise your voice – all the way to the top if necessary.'

'You mean I should get into a shouting match? Oh come on, Gusty, that's not my style.'

'Why not, if it's the only way of being heard? Good Lord, men holler at each other all the time, and I do some pretty good shouting myself when I have to. If someone hassles you, hassle back. My God, when I think of the crap I took when I was starting out in the business. . . .' And Gusty went off in a trail of reminiscences, tales of rebuffs and insults, of wild-goose chases and misappropriated credits. ' . . . but no more. Not now. Now I give as good as I get. You know what your problem is?' she added thoughtfully. 'You want it both ways. You want to play the lady and win yourself a place in the sun. Well, it doesn't work like that . . . and where do you think I'd be now if I went through life with white gloves? Right back in Nowheresville, Indiana.'

There was more in the same vein: pep talks mixed with gentle chivvying, rousing battlecries alternating with down-to-earth advice. Yet throughout the long afternoon, Caro discerned a constant though subtle refrain: *I did it. Why can't you?*

'And now,' Gusty concluded, 'you're going to go right back there and make me proud of you.'

Caro boarded the Boston plane feeling both determined and depressed, as she often did after tête-a-têtes with Gusty. Not that her mother had laughed at her, or humiliated her in any manner. Gusty had gone to great pains to offer counsel. Yet Caro would have traded all that good advice and example for one spontaneous and all-embracing hug. She wanted more than advice; she had sought the assurance that, no matter what the outcome at Harvard, she would be secure and still welcome in her mother's affection. At heart, she had wished that Gusty might be a little more of a mother, a little less of a mentor – but that was not the great woman's style.

'Make me proud of you.' The words rang in Caro's ear, and she could only conclude that her mother was not very proud of her. Not yet, at any rate. And that Caro – although provided with advantages her mother had never known – nonetheless threatened to fall short of the mark.

'Look at me,' Gusty had said at one point, and surely by way of encouragement. 'Look what I've made of myself . . . from nowhere, out of nothing. And I never even finished high school.'

All true, all true. Caro had enjoyed the best of everything – good schools, good clothes, good connections. The works. Yet she laboured under one handicap with which Gusty had never contended: Caro was the daughter of a famous woman.

All her life people had said to her 'Aren't you the lucky girl!', the implication being that given her mother's achievements, her mother's contacts, her mother's talent coursing through her veins, Caro could be anything she set her mind to.

But the one thing she could not be was Gusty.

Even in childhood she had shrunk from anything that smacked of the photographer's art, loth to do as much as take a snapshot with a Brownie. Because how – she wondered – do you compete with a giant?

If you did well, you could expect, the knowing wink, the dubious accolade 'her mother's daughter'. And if you did poorly – God forbid – shame, shame. One of the appealing things about B School, indeed about the world of finance, was that in those environs the name of Augusta Harmsworth carried no weight. Here at least she was free of her mother's shadow. Good or bad, succeed or fail, whatever the upshot, it would be Caro's own doing.

Yet it remained to be seen whether the final results would give Gusty grounds for pride. Caro brooded about it constantly. She had the uneasy feeling that she was expected to become as pre-eminent in her chosen field as Gusty was in her own. Anything less would be perceived as failure.

She did not even have the margin for error that Gusty herself had once enjoyed. Had the young Augusta Frink wound up as a tenth-rate photographer on a provincial paper, had she settled down with the mysterious Harmsworth into a life of surburban anonymity, had she even returned home – tail between her legs – to run the family boarding house, no alibis would have been necessary. Who needed alibis in those days when expectations were so low? 'It's a man's world' was excuse enough for any failure.

Above all, Gusty had no Gusty of her own to account to.

But for Caro the margin of error had vanished and she wondered, for the first time, if things hadn't been in some ways easier in those days when on the surface they seemed spectacularly harder.

But of course Caro lived in these days, not those; and as the plane began the descent into Logan, she thought about the course before her. Everything her mother had told her – be tough, be loud, be aggressive – went instinctively against her grain. Caro was not a pushy person by nature.

Yet common sense told her Gusty was right, and by the time the plane landed, she had made a resolution to be – if not more blatantly aggressive, then certainly a good deal more assertive in the future. And, if possible, work that much harder. Hard work never killed anybody, as her mother was fond of saying.

Yes. Gusty would be proud of her yet!

To Caro's unbounded relief, she passed the next set of exams easily. Not only passed, but scored in the top ten per cent. The day the results were posted, she strode over to Aldrich Hall in a state of euphoria, wearing a smile that said 'Hey, you guys – look at me!' But all she got for her smiles was a cool nod, and it struck her that a taut, quirky mood was pervading the building that day. Men were clustered in bunches, making dark and muted sounds; not a beam of sunshine anywhere. Christ, she thought, looking at the clumps of dour faces, they can't *all* have flunked.

'What's up, Howie?' she collared one of the men from her section. 'This place looks like a funeral parlour.'

'You mean you haven't heard?'

'Heard what?'

'About the Japanese guy, Mitsiyashami . . . or whatever his

name was. He went and killed himself yesterday. Can you believe it? Not even hara-kiri or anything fancy. Just took a Saturday Night special and blew his brains out. Over an exam . . . one lousy exam. . . .'

But Caro took in only the key words.

Mitsi. Killed. Brains. Exam.

And each of those words penetrated her own brain like a bullet. Then she could bear to hear no more, could only stumble out of the building, half-blind with tears of rage and grief.

Hard work never killed anybody. Oh, but it had, it had. It had killed Mitsi. She had a piercing vision of that classically beautiful face, those troubled eyes now reduced to shattered tissue. And for what? Over an exam, Howie had said. One lousy exam! Was any failure, any success, worth that price? She stared back at the Hall, but now the dull faceless building loomed on the horizon like a charnel house, a breeding ground of plague and suffering.

What am I doing in this place? she wanted to scream. And what is this place doing to me? She leaned against the railing of the bridge, adding her tears to the water of the Charles. In the distance, she could hear someone running, shouting. Heard her name 'Carooooo . . . wait!'

Howie Bernstein was still panting when he caught up with her. 'Are you OK, Caro? Is everything OK?'

She nodded.

'Whew' – he breathed a sigh of relief. 'For a moment I thought you were going to jump.'

She shook her head.

'Jesus, Caro, I'm sorry. I didn't mean to break it like that. Please don't cry . . . Caro, please.'

She wiped her eyes on the handkerchief he gave her – 'I'm OK, it's just that I can't believe it' – then burst into another round of tears.

'Come on, cookie. I'll walk you home.'

He escorted her back to her room, made her some tea, then, comforted her in the way that men have comforted women since the dawn of time.

'I guess I needed that,' she said later, pulling on her robe. Funny to think of sex as an antidote to death.

'Yeah, we all need it from time to time. Were you very friendly with him?'

'With Mitsi?' – suddenly the nickname sounded childish and absurd. 'No, not really. Is anybody very friendly with anybody here?'

'No,' he replied. 'Not really.'

A few days later, he asked if she'd be interested in sharing an apartment in Cambridge. He'd seen a place over on Brattle Street, but couldn't swing the rent alone. 'We could go fifty/fifty on expenses,' he said. 'Nothing heavy, though. I mean between you and me.'

'Why not? And nothing heavy.'

The apartment proved to be a scruffy affair: Salvation Army furniture, a view of an alley full of dustbins and an ancient refrigerator much given to asthmatic fits and starts.

'Not exactly the Ritz,' Howie commented, but Caro was quick to see the possibilities.

'You know, with a little white paint, some curtains, maybe a window box to hide the view and this could be a very cute place. That ought to be kind of fun. . . . I've never fixed up a place before. My guess is a couple of hundred bucks each would do the job. What do you say, Howie?'

'Fine with me,' he assented, 'but the decorating stuff is your department.'

They moved in next day, and during the first weeks of their tenancy, Caro devoted every free moment to making the place habitable. She was up early, up late, painting, polishing, lining shelves, rooting happily in the bargain basements for sheets and housewares, lugging plants home from the local flower market. One afternoon she arrived triumphant with a big box of white net curtains.

'These are my treat, Howie,' she announced. 'Swiss cotton . . . aren't they lovely? I think they'll brighten up the place no end.'

And though she never did get to sing in the Harvard-Radcliffe Chorale, she was singing now, standing atop a kitchen chair with an armful of curtains while Howie lounged on the bed, reading Peter Drucker and munching biscuits.

After a while he put down his book and watched her work. Then he mumbled something.

'What's that, Howie?' she called from her perch.

'I said "nesting instinct",' the notion clearly amused him. 'Never met a woman who didn't have it, B-School or no.'

'Don't be absurd!' She flushed like a burglar caught in mid-felony. 'Just because I for one don't care to live in a sty. . . . Listen, Bernstein — instead of lying there making sexist remarks, how about getting off your duff and helping me. You live here too, you know.'

'Yeah. Yeah.' He shambled over to lend her a hand, a wry smile still on his lips.

Next morning she woke before the alarm went off and looked about her with half-shut eyes. The sun trickled through the curtains, dappling the plants, striking sparks on the freshly painted moulding. She lay unmoving for an unconscionable time, surveying her kingdom with satisfaction.

Howie had been right about that 'nesting instinct' business — although she wouldn't dream of admitting it to him.

Still. . . ! She looked about the tiny flat with pleasure and a profound sense of achievement. Everything was so fresh, so bright and immaculate. So intensely personal. For this was not a bedroom in her mother's apartment done up by an overpaid decorator, nor some anonymous room in a college dorm furnished exactly like the one next door. This place was *hers* – well, hers and Howie's – part of her own personality. A lifetime's longing had expressed itself in paint and cotton and brass polish, and she felt a pang of regret that the job was now completed. She'd relished every minute of it, even those push-and-shove forays in the bargain basement.

She felt a deep and peaceful sense of order, the comforting sensation of putting down roots.

'What a creature of habit you are!' her mother used to chide, eyes rolled heavenward in wonder.

Yes, Caro supposed she was – or would have been, if life

permitted. During the gypsy years of her childhood, her first act on moving into a new house was to arrange her possessions into as precise a replica as possible of the place left behind. The little night table here, her alarm clock just there. Painted dresser in the right-hand corner. Pictures on the wall just so. Those annual uprootings had been harsh, jangling; the only security lay in the continuity of familiar things. When the decision was finally made to settle in New York, Gusty scrapped all the cheap furniture. 'We're going to get rid of this rubbish once and for all. I'll have a decorator do up the new apartment stem to stern.'

And Caro's protests had been buried beneath her mother's firmer will.

But the desire for order, for routine persisted, governing her life in various ways.

In elementary school hers was the tidiest desk, the neatest handwriting. Chaos distressed her, and as she grew older this craving for order manifested itself in her hobbies. She loved to fix things – whether a dripping tap or a broken hair dryer. One summer she had taken a course in watch-making, and had found an exquisite pleasure in fitting the tiny wheels and bits together precisely until they meshed into a working timepiece. She was very good with her hands.

Her mind too was orderly, disciplined. Problem-solving of all types delighted her: chess problems, maths problems, crypto-grams, crosswords, and lately the intricate business problems of B School.

There was nothing so gratifying, she found, as putting pieces together, making them work, seeing things run smoothly.

Even this dinky apartment.

She looked about her again with undisguised pleasure. No, it wasn't the Ritz, but for all its modesty it bore some semblance of an orderly home – warm and intimate. She'd even managed to silence the grumble in the refrigerator, and now the only sound to disturb the morning quiet was Howie's light and rhythmic snore.

That too seemed part of the order.

He was scrunched beneath the covers, peaceful, sleeping, his dark hair tousled against the bright stripes of the pillow-case. A

31

picture of utter domesticity. And yet there was a rightness about it.

It was very nice, very comforting to wake up each morning as she had done for the last month and find the same face, the same familiar body beside her. The world had never before seemed so cosy, so benign. She watched him for a while with a fond private glow, contemplated cuddling up and going back to sleep, but it was getting late.

'Hey, honey,' Caro brushed her lips against his cheek. 'We've got a nine o'clock class this morning. Get up and I'll make you breakfast.'

Howie Bernstein proved to be a sweet if sloppy roomate, his own domestic arrangements running largly to salami sandwiches and unmade beds. Some days it seemed to Caro she spent half her time picking up after him – he left his socks all over the place. But on the plus side he was good-natured and fairly attractive with bright clever eyes. Above all, he seemed free of that killer-shark instinct that spooked the corridors at B School. Lucky Howard – his future was assured, for Bernstein Senior owned a shoe factory in nearby Brockton and Howie planned to head back into the family firm the moment his MBA was in hand.

He went home odd weekends, and Caro occasionally wondered if he had a girl there. She suspected he had, but to be fair it was none of her business. Nothing heavy. That had been the understanding from the start.

Moreover, living with Howie paid fringe benefits. For the first time since her arrival at Cambridge, she seemed to be fitting in. The men in her section became noticeably friendlier, as though the knowledge that she was getting laid regularly by one of their brethren had made her suddenly visible. She existed for them now, she realized, simply because she existed in relation to Howie.

'I don't understand the guys at school,' she told him one evening. 'You know you were the only one who ever showed any interest in me. I used to be pretty popular at college, believe it or not. But here. . . ! What do women have to do to get your attention . . . stand naked in Harvard Yard?'

'Oh you've got our attention all right,' came the answer. 'Always have had. Why, way back in September, we voted you the best legs in B School.'

'Really!' she was astonished. 'And where did this little caucus take place . . . in the men's room?' He laughed and said no, and she was certain she'd hit it right on the button. 'Go on, Howie, tell me more. Who else got voted what?'

Well, she wormed it out of him. Caro was best legs, Anne Petersen best knockers, Susie Jacobs best ass, Charmian Briggs the most plastic. Evvie Harper the most biodegradable. . . . He paused.

'Don't stop now, Howie, this is fascinating.'

'Well, some of the others aren't so complimentary.'

Complimentary? Biodegradable is *complimentary?*

'I won't tell, I promise.' She crossed the best legs in B School. 'Cross my legs and hope to die.'

There was Janie Woycinscki, he went on, the ten-foot Pole you wouldn't want to touch it with. Liz Wakeman, the poor man's Martha Mitchell. Helen Fishbein, The Beast from 20,000 Fathoms. Linda Kearney, winner of the Hans Brinker Award.

'The Hans Brinker Award,' Caro said. 'Don't tell me, let me guess. Something to do with putting fingers into dikes. Ye Gods, Howie! I never heard anything so sophomoric. And it's not even as if you were sophomores. You're all graduate students for Chrissakes. Why is it you guys have to reduce us all to meat?'

'We were only joking.' Howie clearly regretted having breached the all-male wall of silence.

'Jokes have their reasons,' she retorted. 'That's what you always tell me, especially when other people make Jewish jokes.'

'Well yes,' he conceded with reluctance. 'I suppose it's not very funny. It's what the Germans call gallows-humour . . . when you make fun of the thing you're really afraid of. The condemned man's last laugh, so to speak.'

'And you're afraid of us, Howie? Is that what you're saying?' She was incredulous.

'Don't you know? You women scare us shitless.'

'Why?'

'Why! You threaten our jobs, you threaten our privacy, you threaten . . . our manhood. And you ask me why?'

'In other words, I'm a ball-breaker.'

'Why do you always have to be so subjective? I'm not talking about you personally, I'm not talking about me personally. Just a general statement.'

'Oh fine! So I personally don't scare you shitless.' She was very upset, close to tears.

'Aw c'mon, honey. You know I'm fond of you. Why else would I live with you?'

'I don't know,' she shook her head. 'I'm no different from those other girls, really. Yet you never dated any of them.'

'You're different.'

'How? Tell me.'

'I'll try and explain and please don't take it amiss.' He placed his hands on her shoulder. 'I used to look at you in class and I'd think . . . well, she's attractive, smart as a whip, but kind of cold. Then, it was the day that Japanese kid killed himself and you were all broken up. Weeping. So soft, all of a sudden and . . . you know, vulnerable. I just wanted to put my arms around you then and there.'

'Because I was crying.'

'Yeah,' he put his arms around her now. 'I guess it was because I saw you cry.'

She didn't know how to take Howie's admission. She forgave him, for she had always been a sucker for compassion. Yet it rankled that his affection for her had been rooted in her tears.

'How'd you like to meet one of the ten most beautiful girls in New York?' she asked Howie one evening. 'I just had a call from an old friend who's passing through town tomorrow and she suggested we all have dinner together.'

'Sure . . . why not? Is she really that beautiful?'

'Beautiful,' Caro said. 'And rich. And a genuine sweetie. What else do you want to know about her?'

'Only her name,' Howie laughed.

Her name was Thea Jessup. And she was, if not one of the top ten beauties in New York, certainly well up in the running – with the figure of a fashion model and a face that bore a startling resemblance to Botticelli's 'Birth of Venus'.

She had inherited her wealth from her father and her looks from her mother, who had been acclaimed Deb of the Year back in the early forties and remained a fixture on the 'Ten Best Dressed' list ever since.

The two girls had met in high school and locked instantly into a warm and gratifying friendship. 'We'll be like sisters,' Thea had enthused, for they were both only children, lonely children, both eager for confidantes.

To Caro, fresh from abroad and feeling very much the outsider, here was the intimate she had always yearned for, and Thea had been quick to perceive the newcomer's sense of isolation. Isolation was something she understood first hand.

For despite all her beauty and incipient chic (or more precisely because of it), Theo never fitted in the mainstream of school life. The other girls feared and resented her, the boys – those who weren't intimidated – were perpetually on the make, and few thought to look behind the façade. Gossip followed in her wake, and it was said that she drank, smoked dope, went to wild parties. That she had slept with John Lennon – or maybe it was Ringo Starr. All this at sweet sixteen.

'If only it were true,' she giggled, but the rumours had wounded her for she was, at heart, the most conventional of girls.

All she wanted, she told Caro, was to finish high school, put in a couple of obligatory years at college, then get married.

Caro laughed the first time Thea stated her ambition.

'What's so funny, Caro? Don't you want to get married, too?'

'Oh, I don't know. Maybe some day when I'm already successful, but first I'd want to have a career, although I haven't decided in what exactly. But whatever,' Caro affirmed, 'it's going to be exciting, important. I want to make a name for myself. Be the kind of somebody people look up to.'

'Like your mother,' Thea nodded. 'Well, I wish I could say I'm ambitious too, but I'm not. I'd like to have a good time for a couple of years, do some travelling. But what I really want is to meet someone absolutely super and get married.'

'Like *your* mother,' Caro returned.

'Not quite. Mom's on husband number three already, whereas with me it's going to be once-and-for-all. Yup,' she grinned, 'I plan to fall in love, have a big wedding and raise the regulation 2.8 children – just like it says in the Census.'

'I'll look for your picture on the society page,' Caro teased.

'And I'll look for yours on the cover of *Time*.'

When Caro left for college, Thea enrolled in Barnard, attending courses sporadically, but essentially just killing time. Over the years Caro would hear that her friend was skiing in Gstaad, or sailing off Newport, or developing a tan in the Bahamas.

Or – in this case – would be passing through Boston tomorrow. Not alone, however. 'I'll make a reservation for four at Locke Ober's,' she cautioned, 'so bring a date, because I'll be bringing someone special. See you there.'

Thea arrived in a cloud of fun furs and perfume with a dashing young man on one hand and an immense solitaire on the other. Living proof, Howie later remarked, that the rich always marry the rich. She could hardly wait for the drinks to arrive before she signalled to Caro and the two women escaped to the Ladies Room.

'Beautiful, isn't it?' Thea rotated the diamond slowly to catch the light and her face reflected its radiance.

'Beautiful!' Caro nodded with enthusiasm.

'So what do you think, Caro?'

'Well, I don't know the first thing about diamonds. . .'

'No, silly. I mean, about Brooks.'

'But I've just met him! He certainly strikes me as very bright. But it's what *you* think that counts.'

'What I think. . .' was not that Brooks Talbot was merely bright and handsome (any fool could see that), but dynamic, gifted, sensitive, thoughtful. He had bought a partnership in a Chicago advertising agency and they were going to look for houses soon in Lake Forest. Meanwhile, Thea's mother was raiding the linen shop at Saks 'buying a dozen dozen of everything'. Which was not to say that she and Brooks were merely another rich couple getting married. Because Brooks was different. Brooks was bright, dynamic, gifted, sensitive . . .

she began to repeat the litany, then burst out laughing. 'The hell with adjectives. What I'm trying to say is . . . I'm crazy about him.'

'I can see that,' Caro squeezed her hand. 'Best wishes. And may you always be as happy as you are right now.'

All the next day, Thea's happiness haunted her. How radiant she had looked, how full of life and joy!

'What did you think of my friend, Howie?' she asked that evening.

'A beautiful girl.'

'Yes, isn't she! And that was some ring she had on. Did you notice?'

Howie chewed his lip for a moment, then said thoughtfully, 'Don't get any ideas, Caro.'

'Oh for God's sake, Howie!' She went red with humiliation. 'It was just a remark. Anyhow, have you seen my slide rule around anywhere?'

The rest of the term passed without incident in the usual flurry of studies and exams. There were, thank God, no more suicides; and when June rolled around Caro was undecided whether to stay on in Cambridge or take a summer job in Wall Street. Howie was heading back to Brockton.

'If you don't want the apartment next year,' he asked her in the midst of his packing, 'would you mind letting me have it? I can keep it on by myself.'

'What do you mean?'

'Well, I thought you might prefer a place of your own.'

'Why, Howie!' – he seemed reluctant to meet her glance – 'I thought this was such a good arrangement. Why don't we just go on as we were?'

'Well, the thing is, Caro . . .' His voice was muffled, his head buried deep in a packing case and Caro could smell what was coming.

'You don't have to play ostrich with me, Bernstein. OK, out with it.'

'Well, the thing is . . .' he sat down and folded his arms – 'I'm getting married next month. I'm sorry.' The clever brown eyes were penitent.

'If you're sorry,' she was stunned, 'then why are you getting married?'

'I don't mean I'm sorry I'm getting married. Just . . . I'm sorry if I'm hurting your feelings.'

She could feel the rage forming somewhere down in her toes, then gradually shooting its way up through her body. She gulped down a mouthful of it.

'How long have you been engaged, Howie?'

'Since March.'

'Tell me, didn't it bother you just a teentsie weentsie bit . . . sleeping with me five nights a week, then nipping off to see your girl at weekends?'

'Oh come off it, Caro!' – he was growing cross. 'I never poked my nose into your business. That was always our understanding.'

'She's Jewish, I suppose.'

'Naturally.'

Naturally. Well screw you, Howard Bernstein. 'Well, you sure had me fooled, Howie,' she taunted him. 'All these months together and I never once guessed that you were a man of such deep religious feeling. Only yesterday I cooked you bacon for breakfast.'

'Cut the crap' – he was livid with anger – 'We had an understanding from the word go, you and I. Nothing heavy. So lay off and just tell me in plain English . . . you want the apartment? You don't want the apartment? What?'

'Take the goddam place,' she screamed. 'And take the kitchen stuff, that's my wedding present. How are you set for sheets? Pillowcases? Take 'em all and . . . oh yeah! there's half a salami in the refrigerator. Take that, too, why don't you?'

'I'll come back when you're done with the histrionics.'

'Fine,' she shouted 'because I won't be here.'

He slammed out of the apartment and she was too stunned to do anything but stand there rigid, staring blankly at the door.

She had meant nothing to him! A colleague. A roomate. Somebody to screw on those nights he was feeling horny. She had been a convenience – nothing more.

We had an understanding. His words reverberated in the empty room. And so they had. Convenience had been the very basis of their relationship. Yet somewhere along the line Caro had come to a different understanding. For the first time in her life, Caro had made a home, created an environment of warmth and intimacy. Surely she and Howie had been more than roomates! They had gotten along so well, so very well. The arrangement had proved such a happy and comfortable one that Caro had presumed it would continue indefinitely. They would live together. Graduate together. And then. . . .

And then?

Never in all those months had she asked herself if she were in love with Howie; nonetheless, she now forced the painful admission, she had indeed cherished notions that this was permanent. That the months would stretch into years. That her life would be an unbroken stream of waking up next to Howie while the sun streamed through the curtains. Other curtains, perhaps. Other houses. Here. In Brockton. Wherever. But always with the security of Howie there beside her.

Yes! She realized to her own amazement – she had expected Howie to marry her. And the knowledge that she had come to count on him so heavily, to care for him so deeply now twisted like a knife in her bowels. Christ! – what a fool she had been. And she could only thank God that she had never articulated the smallest part of her fantasies, had spared herself that humiliation at least. But even if she were guilty of nothing more than bad judgement, he had no right to leave her like that.

Sonofabitch!

Gusty was right. Life was treacherous, unstable, a revolving door of hellos and goodbyes and you were a fool to count on anyone but yourself. Playing house – that's all she and Howie had been up to. Kid stuff. And if having a place of her own meant that much, having a few knicknacks and potted plants – fine. One of these days she'd maybe earn a pile on Wall Street and get herself a big fat penthouse on the Upper East Side. Something a damn sight better than Brattle Street or crummy Brockton – so fuck you, Howie Bernstein.

Because Gusty had been right about that too. Men come and men go. Good riddance.

She never went near the Brattle Street apartment again, nor could she face the loneliness of another furnished room. At the start of the new academic year, she rented the top floor in a rambling frame house belonging to one of her more extraordinary classmates.

Even among the B-School hustlers, Walter Lorencz was unique. He had arrived there aged thirty, boasting one credential few other candidates could match: he had already made and lost his first million.

He also arrived with 'the briefcase', as unique in its way as was Walter.

Before the war, the story went, the Lorenczes had been people of substance, prominent in banking circles of Budapest. Then came Hitler, then Stalin, then the Hungarian Revolution with its tragic aftermath until, one midnight, the family had fled leaving behind everything but this one relic of bygone riches: the briefcase. There wasn't another like it in existence: a huge and thoroughly disreputable affair of mottled leather that might have been black when the century was young, but that time and travel had transformed into an effulgent green. Walter kept it with him always as a constant reminder, he said, of the transitory nature of wealth.

'You understand,' he told Caro when she answered his notice on the bulletin board, 'I don't normally make a practice of renting rooms but I'm up against it this year. I should warn you you'll be sharing a house with three small kids. But on the plus side, my wife's a good cook.'

'I don't mind as long as the space is OK. Anyhow, I'm kind of fond of kids.'

Nonetheless it took her some weeks to get used to the constant bustle of the Lorencz household: the sounds of children babbling, of saucepans clattering, of Walter himself who seemed incapable of performing even such a modest act as sneezing at anything less than maximum force.

Yet the arrangement turned out better than anticipated. The attic was large and airy, and there was a certain comfort in the hum and hubbub of the house, definitely better than the sterile quiet of a furnished room.

As for Walter, he proved to be an amiable landlord. His

attitude toward Caro was avuncular, his energy contagious. Almost daily he would burst into the house with some extravagant scheme that was destined to get the Lorencz family 'out of the frying pan and into the *Fortune 500*'. He was as improvident as he was flamboyant, yet for all his quirks, Caro found him endearing. He was a devoted family man, a generous friend and an incurable optimist.

Like many another naturalized American, Walter had fallen in love with baseball terminology. In his vocabulary smart deals were 'squeeze plays', short-range tactics were 'bunts'. He himself was always waiting for the 'grand slam home run'. And from the history of baseball, he had culled the expression 'Nice guys finish last.'

'You know, Caro,' he once remarked, 'they ought to make that the official Harvard motto. It's a hell of a lot more a propos than *Veritas*.'

Her final year at B School went smoothly. The work seemed to flow with a self-propelling energy, goals became more sharply defined. Her social life, too, was proving pleasant if not intense, punctuated by a sprinkling of casual affairs that made no demands on either her heart or her schedule.

From the vantage point of seniority, she now watched the stricken faces of the newcomers, anxious and insecure as she herself had once been. Well, let them learn – just as she had learned – that winning was all. Or if not all, then certainly very, very important. More important by far than picking Howie Bernstein's dirty socks up off the floor.

The violence of her anger had abated; she could even bring herself to nod to him in the corridors. Yet the memory of their last day together, the realization that she had cared for Howie so much more than he for her still lingered on like a bad taste in her mouth. Next time she wouldn't give more than she got. That was a sucker's game. Nice guys do finish last, as Walter said. And if, along the way to the finish line, certain values got submerged – those gentler values still nourished 'across the river' – that was regrettable. Regrettable but necessary.

From January on, the phrase on everyone's lips was 'the fast track'. It was the buzzword, the B-School shorthand for the path that led most swiftly to the heights. Overnight the campus was swarming with emissaries from America's greatest, most powerful corporations, and the students responded with a ferocity that made the previous scrambling look like child's play.

One afternoon, Walter stopped Caro in the corridor.

'You going for the fast track?' he asked her.

'You bet your ass. Just show me where it is.'

'Well, if I were you I'd trot over and see the head-hunter from PAGIT . . . you know, Pacific & General Investment Trust. I hear they're looking for a woman in their starting line-up. Seems like Wall Street's finest is about to be clobbered on a sex discrimination charge.'

'That's a hell of a reason to be hired, though.'

'What do you care?' came the rejoinder. 'You've got the stuff and you'd be a damn fool not to take advantage. They're offering twenty-five thou for openers.'

Three days later the job was hers.

'Well, Pete, I made the fast track,' she announced to a cordially detested classmate. Letting him know she'd crowded him out for the job gave her an almost malicious pleasure. Serve him right, the bastard, for having treated her with such hostility from the start.

'Fast track, my ass!' he snarled back. 'You fucking women have the inside track.'

4

New York had changed in the six years since she had graduated from high school; Caro could scarcely believe how much.

Gone was the unwashed, unbuttoned, anything-goes mood of the Sixties. Flowers no longer decorated foreheads and Volkswagens; the sweet smell of pot had given way to headier fumes – the sweet smell of success.

The first person Caro looked up on her return to Manhattan was her old roomate at Midwestern. At twenty-four, Sally Klein was already a rising star at NBC News.

'Don't shake it, make it. That's my motto these days,' Sally said and ushered Caro into her white-on-white apartment.

'Pretty posh,' Caro nodded approvingly. 'I practically had to take a blood test to get past the doorman. And you're looking pretty posh yourself, Sal.'

'I've come a long way, baby,' came Sally's grateful laugh. She certainly had.

During her four years at college, Sally Klein had made her mark in every campus activity except the competition for Saturday night dates. Men usually gave Sally a wide berth. She was intense, serious, verging on the dumpy, with the wry, bright features of a chipmunk. She herself was the first to admit that whatever success would come her way, it would not be based on sex appeal. In fact, she was lucky in everything but love.

Almost immediately upon arrival at Midwestern, she had fallen head over heels for a professor. He was married with three children and the affair ended predictably in a classic finale: tears, scenes, suicide threats and a messy back-street abortion. Yet Sally could say of it in retrospect 'It was the best thing that ever happened to me. It forced me to rethink my priorities.' All she wanted from here on out, she said, was money, fame, and her own prime-time television show. Her burning ambition was to become 'the blind man's Barbara Walters'.

Already she was well on her way. 'The new improved model', as Sally now termed herself, was the result of countless hours devoted to the business of wardrobe, hair, nails, teeth, waistline – for if beauty still eluded her, chic did not. Caro marvelled at the transition.

'So, where are you staying?' Sally asked once the preliminaries were out of the way.

'Actually, I'm looking for an apartment. My mother's closed up shop and gone off to Australia for a while.'

'You're welcome to stay here while you're looking,' Sally said. 'Next question – how's the new job?'

'Shaping up nicely, I'm happy to say. Not exactly the fast track I was promised, but it's interesting and my new boss is a pussycat. You know, I'm the first woman that company's ever hired at a managerial level, and I thought I'd hit a lot of resistance. But it turns out the natives are friendly.'

Every woman starting out in business needs a mentor. For Caro, Barney Baker filled the role. He was, she once kidded him, 'the only man in Wall Street who can maintain an even growth of five o'clock shadow throughout the entire working day'. Everything about him was faintly worn and easy – hardly what she'd expected from the manager of PAGIT's Mutual Fund department. He wore elastic arm bands on his shirt sleeves, like a city editor in a Thirties movie.

'So, Caroline. . . .' – he greeted her on her first day there.

'Most people call me Caro.'

'Then Caro it is. So tell me, Caro . . . what are your theories about the stock market?'

Caro promptly launched into a monologue larded with B School jargon, but halfway through her piece, she noticed the photos on his desk: two girls in college mortarboards.

Hell, she thought, he has daughters just about my age, so who am I to tell him? She cut her speech short. 'The only thing I'm sure about is that I know very little. I'd much rather know what approach you subscribe to.'

He leaned back and lit a cigar. Clearly, she had hit upon a pet subject. 'There are theories galore in this racket, Caro, and you can pretty much take your pick. For instance. . .'

There was the 'sunspot' theory – very popular in the 50's – which claimed that the market was governed by atmospheric disturbances on the surface of the sun. 'Great, if you've got a degree on astrophysics.' Then, there was the 'hemline' theory that found a correlation between the length of women's skirts and the ups and downs of stocks. When hemlines rise, the market soars; when they're low, the market plunges. 'Nice thing about that theory is, you don't have to do your homework. All you need is the latest copy of *Vogue*.' Then there was the 'dartboard' theory, the beauty of which was that it could be employed by anyone with admirable simplicity. You simply tack the Stock Exchange listings up on a wall and throw a dozen darts at random. 'Kind of like pinning the tail on the donkey.' And when Caro giggled, he quickly informed her that it worked just as well as any other approach.

'But yours, Mr Baker?'

'Call me Barney, everyone does. Well, if you really want to know, I go by the Pepto-Bismol System.'

'Pepto-Bismol?'

'Yeah . . . you know that pink stuff that comes in bottles. You can buy it at any chemist, it's for stomach distress.'

She was astonished to see he was only half-joking. 'I'm afraid I don't understand.'

'It's like this,' he explained. 'A lot of investment possibilities cross this desk, and the problem is always one of decisions. We're an essentially conservative fund – maybe not the "fast track" you were hoping for – and our customers are mostly small investors, widows and orphans to coin a cliché. In any event, not Wall Street pros, and for me that makes a moral obligation. There's always an element of risk involved, but I don't like losing other people's money. So . . . suppose I have x amount of dollars to invest – their dollars, mind you – and I've got to choose between stock A and stock B. Now they both look OK on paper, not a lot to choose between 'em. But there's something about stock B. . . I don't know what, yet every time I think of it, my stomach gets tied up in knots and I'm reaching for the Pepto-Bismol. It's not logic . . . sheer gut reaction. But I never invest when my stomach says no.'

'In other words, you play hunches.' She was appalled.

'Hunches, instincts. Yeah . . . when all else fails, I suppose I do.'

'And does it work?'

'About as well as any other system,' he replied. 'No better, no worse. And at least I don't suffer from chronic indigestion. Listen, Caro' – he turned thoughtful – 'when it comes to predicting the future, all these theories don't amount to a bucketful of spit. All you can know about a stock, about anything in life, I suppose, is how it's performed in the past. But tomorrow? . . . who knows. There isn't a trader in Wall Street who wouldn't give his eye teeth for just a peek at tomorrow's closing prices. Just that one little peek, and you can chuck all the theories and retire to the Bahamas. Trouble is, you never get that peek.'

'And all my B-School education?'

'Use it,' he was emphatic. 'That's what we hired you for. By all means, use every bit of knowledge and research and common sense you can muster. As long as you never forget that in the last analysis, the future is always a gamble. Unknowable. Which is why you may as well trust to your instincts as to anything else.'

He put her in the bullpen as part of a team specializing in public utilities stocks. 'Grunt work', a fellow recruit called it, and indeed Caro didn't have the leeway she'd anticipated. Most of her time was spent doing research and mid-level analysis for those senior traders who actually made the decisions. But, as Barney pointed out, she was there to learn as well as earn. It was no picnic, the workload was too great for that; but she could breathe without feeling others breathing down her neck. As she'd told Sally, the natives were friendly.

The roomate chemistry that had worked so well at college was souring slightly now that they were back in New York. As always, Sally proved to be a goldmine of useful information: where to buy knitwear wholesale, how to find a cab on a rainy night, what to look out for in office politics. She had a real grasp of how to operate in a man's world; she had not gotten where she was, she said, without climbing over a number of more seasoned heads. 'And seasoned bodies,' she added with a laugh.

For there was no doubt but that Sally's bold, new elegance was paying unexpected dividends. She rarely spent a night alone. Nor did Caro begrudge her this sudden onrush of men – poor Sally had waited long enough. What disturbed Caro was the crass utilitarianism in her friend's affairs. Sally was relentless in her pursuit of those men she felt would be helpful: network executives, rising celebrities, potential news sources. The fact that most of them were married troubled Caro a good deal more than it did Sally. 'Married men don't shoot their mouths off ' – was Sally's rationale – 'and if you were a bit less choosey, you could have a ball.'

'I don't like sharing,' Caro said tartly.

'Spare me your moral superiority,' Sally retorted, 'because in case you haven't noticed, this town isn't exactly crawling with eligible bachelors. You're always saying you're not really interested in marriage, so what's the big deal? Anyhow,' she summed up 'there's always a reason when husbands screw around and as far as I'm concerned, that's their wives' lookout – not mine.'

In fact, Caro didn't consider herself a moralist. She simply harboured a native distaste for affairs involving married men, and Sally's indiscriminate behaviour continued to annoy her. She let the matter drop, however, feeling it wasn't worth sacrificing a long-term friendship for. Within a couple of weeks, she'd found a place of her own – a neat little apartment in a brownstone – and moved out. To both girls' relief, their friendship slid quickly back on the tracks. For the two women shared many things: aspirations, anxieties, and that sky's-the-limit feeling that they were moving up up up in a man's world.

'Well, that's that!' Thea summed up the demise of her marriage. 'I feel like the Jews after Auschwitz – never again.'

The dynamic, gifted, sensitive Brooks had turned out, on closer inspection, to be a compulsive Don Juan. For two years, Thea had lived with him in blissful ignorance, incapable of believing all the rumours she'd heard. She herself had once been the victim of gossip; she knew how tongues wagged. 'And you know how I found out?' Thea, eyes brimming, now told Caro. 'I caught syphilis from him. I was so dumb, I didn't even realize what had happened.' It had taken her another year full of scenes and tumultuous reconciliations before she worked up the strength to leave him. But now she was back in New York, maiden name resumed, and in the process of fixing up a huge loft in SoHo.

'So what will you do now?' Caro wanted to know.

'Beats me.' Thea shook her great mane of hair. 'My mother thinks I should trot on down to Palm Beach and start rounding up husband number two – but no way. I suppose I should get a job of some kind, just to keep busy, but I don't have any skills. I was raised to do just one thing – get married. Well, I've served my time!'

'Why don't you go back to college?' Caro suggested. 'And this time really buckle down.'

'Yeah, I've been toying with the idea off and on. . . .'

'Don't toy with it, Thea. Do it. You're too bright just to sit back and let life roll over you.'

'Well,' Thea considered, 'maybe I will. Take a degree in Art History. You know, I've become very interested in Women's Art lately.'

'Women's Art?'

'That's right. It's always struck me, Caro . . . you go to the Met, or any museum really, and you look at room after room of paintings – paintings of women. There are madonnas and saints and nudes and nymphs . . . Lautrec's can-can dancers, Degas' ballerinas, Picasso's umpteen-hundred mistresses – paintings about how men perceive women. All very idealized. What interests me is how women perceive themselves. You, for instance. How do you perceive yourself, Caro?'

'I really hadn't thought about it.'

'Think about it. We used to play this game at dinner parties,' Thea mused. 'The guests always loved it – it was such an ego trip. What you had to do was, you had to pick out three words that you felt best identified you, then rank them in order of importance. Like, say, *actress*, *wife*, *mother*. Or *male*, *professor*,

Jewish. Brooks' three, as I recall, were *rich, successful, swinger.* What would your three words be?'

'Well . . . *woman*, of course.' Caro answered, thinking privately it was an awful question. 'Then I suppose, *business* or *Wall Street* or whatever. . . .'

'And third?'

Caro's mind went blank. To save her soul, she couldn't think of another term that would characterize her life thus far. *Wife mother lover* – none of those applied. *American New Yorker brunette* – not very profound identifications. '*Woman . . . Wall Street*,' she repeated. Then, simply to fill in the blank – '*twenty-six.*'

'What's that, your age? Well, I suppose that's an identity of sorts.' And the two women laughed.

But thinking it over that evening, Thea's little parlour game troubled her. Was her life so empty, so devoid of meaning that she couldn't even find three words to sum it up? But her life wasn't empty. It was goddam busy.

After two years apprenticeship, her work was affording her real satisfaction. She was making good money, moving up through the system, starting to trade on her own. Recently Barney had given her considerable leeway, and although she wasn't yet dealing in the six big zeroes, she had scored a number of coups, committed no real gaffes and in the area of utilities stocks, had amassed a formidable amount of expertise.

It was gratifying to know that her performance had paved the way for several other young women, so that now, the great financial conglomerate was a mere decade behind the times, rather than a whole generation. Gratifying, too, to be singled out as the most senior woman, the most highly-paid woman, The First Woman Who . . . no mean accomplishment, that. *Woman. Wall Street.* And yet, and yet.

And yet the trinity was incomplete. For though she had every reason to be pleased, it nagged at her like a low-grade toothache that despite success, despite a lovely apartment and a wardrobe bulging with designer labels, despite good friends and her fair share of lovers, her life was two-dimensional. She felt she was incapable of forming lasting relationships with men. For a long time she attributed this failure to the nomadic quality of her childhood; yet other women from more settled backgrounds confessed to the same sentiment, this sense of walking on constantly shifting sands. It was a staple topic of the women in her Tuesday night discussion group. And while it was one thing to philosophize, as Gusty did, to say that 'men come and go', it was quite another to see them go before she had a chance to explore her own feelings. Before she had a chance to go beyond laughter and sex into those deeper realms of love and true affection. With increasing frequency she found herself saying 'Yes' to first-date propositions. How could you say 'No', she reasoned? You couldn't wait until you'd sorted out all your emotions before getting into bed with a man: the men simply didn't hang around that long. She often wondered if life hadn't been easier a generation ago, when there was at least a presumption of virginity, whether based on fact or not. When a refusal didn't have to be an insult. Still, she felt, if she liked a man well enough to go out with him (and she considered herself selective), she usually liked him well enough to sleep with him. Bed was where you got to know men better.

Besides which, sex was fun.

Yet those few times when she was poised on the brink of caring, something always went awry. There was one man, a most attractive banker, who was a superb lover and a splendid companion. Caro was certain their relationship was bound to lead to something substantial, even long range, until one night when he took her out to dinner. With no more flourish than if he were offering an after-dinner brandy, he asked her if she would go with him to Dionysus East.

'That's a sex club, isn't it?'

'Swingers' club is the preferred term. You don't have to join in if you don't want to.'

She leaned back and stared at him with death in her eyes. They had been going together for over two months; he had been such an attentive lover; she believed they had shared something special. 'You mean you're willing to go there and watch me fuck somebody else? And that you wouldn't mind my watching you?'

'You might like it, Caro. It would help loosen you up.'

'Go to hell, Richard.' And that was that.

A few months later she became interested, really interested, in a history lecturer who taught at the New School. He had not been over-hasty with the hands and the tongue, rather too much of a gentleman in fact; and it was only after several dates that Caro managed to convey the idea that yes, she was willing. The two climbed into bed with great gusto, but after a sweated half hour of preliminaries, he pulled away. 'I'm sorry. I'm afraid I can't get it up.'

'Is it something I've done?' Caro was perturbed.

'It's not you,' he said reaching for his pants. 'Well, I guess it is in a way. Thing is, I just can't get it out of my mind that you're probably earning twice as much money as me – and that's a real downer. Sorry.'

And that was that, too. She related this seemingly astonishing story to the women in her discussion group, all of them professionals like herself, and was even more astonished to find that hers was not a unique experience.

And so they came and went, the men, in obedience to the law of diminishing returns. Looking back, she could actually view her four months with Howie at B School as some kind of long-distance record, a figure worthy of the *Guinness Book of Records*.

Woman. Wall Street. What?

New York was sweltering in the grip of a heat wave and Caro was working late on reports about natural gas resources in Alaska. *Cheap Heat for the Millions* one report was entitled. Cheap heat! Outside, the temperature registered a torrid 91°. All the heat you could want for free.

The office was deserted, an air-conditioned tomb, and a little after seven, she decided to call it a day. She packed her briefcase, rang for the elevator and when it came, routinely peered inside for potential muggers or rapists. Years in New York had made defensive living second nature. But the sole occupant was a businessman with a briefcase.

'Ground floor?'

'Please,' she said. He pushed the button, and they began to descend, wrapped in their mutual cocoons, staring at the blankness of the door from opposite, neutral corners. The Muzak was playing an old Beatles tune, *Strawberry Fields*.

And then the world went black.

'What the hell?'

They stood, the two of them, in stunned silence for several moments, for the music had stopped as abruptly as the motion.

'Oh shit,' the man said, and Caro felt a tremor of panic.

'What do you think's happened . . . any idea?'

'Looks like Con Edison's done it again.'

'What do you mean?'

'Power cut. The heatwave, all that air-conditioning going full blast. Another blackout like in '65. Anyhow, that's my bet.'

'Oh shit!' It was Caro's turn to curse. 'What do we do now?'

'Find the alarm button pronto. I think the panel's right next to the door. You got a match . . . a lighter?'

'I don't smoke.'

'I mean so I could see what I'm doing,' he said irritably. But she had nothing, and it was no good waiting for her eyes to adjust to the dark, for the blackness was total. Profound. No ray of light anywhere, except for the red pinpoint of the man's digital watch.'

'I'll find it,' he said. She could sense him groping around for the buttons. His hand brushed her breast. 'Sorry.' She stepped back. Suddenly the silence was shattered by a raucous clang. He rang non-stop for what seemed like an eternity, shouted, banged on the door. Nobody came. Perhaps there was nobody in the building to come.

'Well,' he said, 'that's that.' There was a thump from his corner. Had he fainted?

'No, just making myself comfortable on the floor.' The digital watch described a faint semicircle. 'Damn,' he said. 'There goes the 7.28 to Westport. My wife's gonna be madder than hell.'

She felt suddenly foolish, standing erect in the dark and gingerly lowered herself onto the floor. The vinyl felt good, cool against her bare legs, for the air-conditioning had died with the light. She took off her shoes, placed them atop her briefcase. Cautiously. She was totally disorientated. They exchanged a few cryptic sentences. She was worried they might suffocate.

'No,' he sounded authoritative. 'There's air coming in. These things have to be ventilated by law.'

'You an engineer?'

'Bond salesman.'

'I'm in mutual funds.'

That subject seemingly exhausted, they spent the next minutes in silence. Then:

'Listen,' his disembodied voice floated over to her. 'I'm starved. You wouldn't by any chance have something to eat on you.'

'I think I've got a Hershey Bar in my bag.'

'Do you mind?' he asked. 'We could go halves.'

'It's all yours.' She fished around in her bag, found it, then groped in the dark for his fingers. Slid the bar carefully into a waiting palm. 'Thanks.' She heard the crinkling of the wrapper, the crumbling of the foil. The chocolate smelled pungent. All her senses had been sharpened by the darkness.

'Hey . . . um. You don't happen to have the other kind . . . do you? The kind that has the almonds in it.'

'Where the hell do you think you are!' she snapped. 'In the supermarket?' And suddenly they both burst out laughing.

'Well, here we are,' he said. 'So what do you want to do till the Mounties come?'

Caro considered. 'We could play word games. G-H-O-S-T maybe . . . or how about Twenty Questions?'

He was quiet for a moment. Then he said 'Let's screw.'

'Let's screw.' And the moment he had said it, a sudden onrush of desire swept the breath out of her body. It was inevitable. The heat. The dark. The touch of her bare legs against the slickness of the floor. The erotic sense of isolation, of being suspended in time, trapped in space, shut off from everything but her own desires. She sat speechless with fantasy while inside her a hundred tiny motors started whirring.

He must have taken her gasp for refusal. 'It was just a suggestion' – then decided to give it one last try. 'We could be stuck in here all night, you know, and it's a great way to pass the time. Besides, who would ever find out?'

'What happens when the power comes back on?'

He sucked in his breath. Clearly, a man who recognized a 'yes' when he heard it. 'We just push the Stop button . . . and vamp till ready. Christ, honey, there's no one in the building but us!'

No one in the building. In the world. In the universe. Her mouth was dry with desire.

'I don't know what you look like,' she said.

'What can I tell you? I'm male, Caucasian, thirty-six, about five-ten. . . . Listen, even if I looked like Dracula, what difference would it make in these circumstances?'

'I've never made love with somebody I've never seen.'

'Blind people do it all the time.'

She laughed. It was as if they had signed a pact to partake of a glorious erotic game, divorced from all familiar boundaries of time and space and common sense.

'Do you want to know what I look like?' she asked.

'I saw you when you got in the elevator. You looked OK.' His voice was closer now.

'Don't you want to know my name, even?'

'Nope.'

Good. She didn't want to know his name either.

The digital watch wove a broken line through the darkness. She inched toward it. Flesh touched flesh.

'What's that?' he asked.

'My knee.'

'Left or right?'

'You'll have to find out for yourself.'

It was so black, unrelieved black. Blacker than any bedroom she'd ever known, blacker than sleep. She had no idea where in the blackness any part of his body was except that hand on her knee. Then the glow of the watch disappeared, the unseen hand snaked up her thigh, unfamiliar fingers explored a path through pubic hair. 'Now I know where I am.' The fingers slid inside her; cufflinks rubbed gently against her inner thigh. Back and forth. Back and forth. She said nothing, sat there blind and breathless, the only noise was the soft lubricious lapping of her flesh beneath his fingers. She began to move with the rhythm, lay back to afford him deeper access.

'Oh Christ!' The pain made her jump.

'What happened?' He withdrew his hand abruptly. 'Did I hurt you?'

'No, not you,' she massaged her ribs gently. 'I backed into something. Must have been the edge of the goddam briefcase.'

'You know, this place is like a minefield,' he said. 'Why don't we just undress and stow everything off in one corner?'

That made sense, she thought, reaching for her zipper.

Then, 'Listen,' he said. 'I've a better idea. Why don't we undress each other? It could be kind of fun in the dark.'

Fun! It was wildly erotic, incredibly complicated: the fumbling for zippers, the untying of ties, the groping for armholes, for hooks, for buttons. How many buttons on a man's shirt anyhow? Every movement brought unexpected encounters, strange juxtapositions of nipple against cufflink, penis against palm. Men's clothes were so much more intricate than women's. There was no way of judging distances in that darkness; there was only touch and taste. And by the time they lay naked she knew that body – its smell, its feel, its every hollow, every hair – knew it better than the body of any other man.

Then bathed in sweat, creeping cautiously on hands and knees, they swept the floor of all encumbrances. Clothes, briefcases, shoes, keys, cufflinks – they piled everything off in one corner. He placed his watch atop the pile – a faint lighthouse to steer them away from the shoals. 'Now,' he said, 'let's you and I *really* screw.'

It must have been a hundred degrees in there. The vinyl floor was slippery with their sweat. She was lying where? Against a wall? Against a door? There was no point of reference – no street noises, no trickle of light to tell her if her eyes were open or shut. Only the base of a palm kneading the base of her spine.

'Listen,' he said. He had a habit of prefacing every request with *Listen*. 'Did you see *Last Tango in Paris*? You know, that picture with Marlon Brando and what's-her-name.'

She knew. And knew exactly what he had in mind. 'I've never done that before.'

'Me neither. But doesn't the idea kind of turn you on?'

'I don't know.' They'd used butter in the movie, hadn't they? Still . . . yes. It turned her on. Everything in this sweat box turned her on.

'Listen,' she said. She noticed she was picking up his speech mannerisms. 'You don't happen to have any butter on you, do you?'

'Where do you think you are?' he laughed softly. 'In the supermarket?'

'Listen,' he said later. 'Let's play that game of yours . . . animal, mineral or vegetable. What's it called . . . Twenty Questions?'

So OK! He was tired. Well, she was tired too. Wiped out. Her head throbbed where she'd bumped it against a wall, her joints ached, she probably wouldn't be able to sit down for a week. She would have given her soul for something to drink. Water. Coke. Anything. The place reeked with the stench of sweat and sex. And he wanted to play Twenty Questions!

'If you're tired, go to sleep,' she mumbled. 'I don't want to play word games.'

'Who's tired?' He placed a hand on her breast and began massaging her nipple. Incredible how quickly they could find each other now, as if – like bats – they had developed sonar in the dark. He had good hands. 'You'll like the way we're going to play it,' he whispered in her ear. Her nipple peaked beneath the motion of his palm. 'The rules are very simple.'

You had twenty questions, he told her, in which to guess the other person's most secret fantasy. Really secret. Something never before articulated. Perhaps something you even feared.

'And if you don't guess the other person's fantasy,' she asked, 'if you lose . . . then what? Are there penalties?'

'Then,' he sighed, 'the winner has his wish come true.'

It was just short of midnight when the lights went on, more blinding than the darkness it erased. They staggered to their feet – two strangers who had done almost everything that a man and woman can do to each other – and dressed exchanging neither word nor glance. Within five minutes they were out on Wall Street.

He found her a taxi. 'Can I drop you at Grand Central?' she asked, hoping he'd say no. He shook his head. 'I'll take the subway. It's faster.'

But handing her into the cab, he paused. 'Are you sure you'll be OK?' For the first time that night, he spoke with genuine concern. For the first time that night, she looked into his face.

56

'I'll be OK,' she said. He took her hand and shook it – two business acquaintances at the end of a long, tiring meeting. 'It's been . . .' – he was suddenly awkward – 'it's been nice knowing you.'

Her last glimpse was of a figure in a crumpled business suit, disappearing down the steps of the subway.

I dreamt it.

That was the first thing that crossed her mind next morning, though her aching body offered confirmation enough. She dressed – long sleeves, dark stockings and plenty of makeup – and made her way down to the office. The same elevator was there waiting, and she entered half-expecting to find it awash with pools of sweat and semen; but the air-conditioning had done its task well, had dried up the juices, sucked away the stench. The only witness to that extraordinary night was a crushed Hershey Bar wrapper in a corner.

For days the memory lodged in her guts like an unexploded bomb. She felt a burning need to confide it. Finally, one night over coffee in a little expresso house, she poured out the story to Sally. 'I had to tell somebody,' she said.

Sally was goggle-eyed.

'Well, that's quite a story. So what happens now? Are you still seeing him?'

'I see him all the time. He works in my building. We nod, like casual acquaintances.'

'I meant . . . seeing him socially.'

'Are you kidding?' Caro gave a short bitter laugh. 'After that night, what could we do for an encore?'

'Tell me, what does he look like? Is he attractive?'

'He's all-right looking, I suppose. Hell, Sally . . . he's just a man. Just an ordinary married man! With a very vivid fantasy life. My bet is the whole thing was as weird for him as it was for me.'

'Frankly,' Sally said, 'I don't see why you're so uptight about it. You had this fantastic experience. Best sex ever – you said so yourself. No strings, no social diseases. So what's the problem? Tell you one thing, though. Next Con Ed blackout, I'm heading straight for your elevator. Now why don't you just chalk the whole bit up to experience and forget it?'

'I can't,' Caro made a grimace of distaste. 'It was so . . . so abstract, so anonymous, so completely devoid of any affection. In the four hours or so we were in there, we hardly talked. Oh, a little light banter at first, and . . . you know, technical instructions. Then toward the end, we didn't talk at all. It bothers me that sex could be so great with a man I didn't give a damn about. I don't like what that whole experience tells me about myself. There was no kindness in it, no real cruelty either. But cruelty at least would have been personal. It was so dehumanizing – that's the word. Like he could have been anybody, I could have been anybody. That's how prostitutes feel, I imagine.'

'You're wrong there,' Sally corrected. 'At least according to my research. I did a programme on hookers a few months back, and apparently you enjoyed yourself a helluva lot more than they do. Anyhow, what does it matter in the long run?'

' "In the long run we are all dead." '

'Say, that's a good line,' Sally picked up on it, always on the alert for something quotable. 'You just make it up?'

'No,' Caro changed the subject with relief, now that she'd told all she cared to tell. 'Actually, I was quoting John Maynard Keynes . . . you know, the great British economist. Father of Macroeconomics and all that jazz. We used to read him like the Bible at B School. Anyhow, seems someone once asked him what a particular stock was going to do in the long run, and that was Keynes' answer. In the long run we are all dead.'

'Good line!' Sally reached into her bag for a notebook. 'I'll just jot it down for future reference. How do you spell the name?'

Caro spelled it, Sally duly wrote it down.

'Well,' she snapped her bag shut, 'Maynard baby was right. What does it matter in the long run? Besides which, as your Phantom Lover said . . . who's ever to know what happened?'

'I know,' Caro said miserably. 'For that matter, so do you.'

'Yeah . . . well, I'm not going to say anything. You can count on that.' Sally rose to go. 'Jesus, it's not exactly the kind of story you want to get around.'

'It certainly isn't,' Caro sighed.

Yet the memory persisted. Haunted her. Mortified her. Refused to be exorcised, like Thea's parlour game of the year before. The three definitions. *Woman. Wall Street. What?*

What indeed had she gained in the meanwhile? A greater measure of professional success? A greater measure of personal failure? What could she add to her earlier summary?

Woman. Wall Street. Whore?

God forbid!

When she met Tom Darius a short time later, she was emotionally primed for the real thing.

He was lounging against the far wall of the court, looking for all the world like a man badly in need of a tennis partner. Fine with her.

Caro came to the Kips Bay Racquet Club most Saturdays, where she had a court regularly reserved. She loved the game. Always had. And after the long week's confinement at the office, she found the best way of defusing her frustrations was to whack the hell out of an uncomplaining tennis ball. Most Saturdays, she managed to scrounge up a game among the regulars, but today the courts were empty of everyone she knew. That left only him – a tall, nice-looking fellow tapping amiably on the aluminium racket.

'Hi there,' she approached him with a smile, 'You want to play some tennis?' Yes indeed, came the answer. That's why he was here.

'Fine. I've got a court already reserved, so why don't we just go to it?'

They began with a few easy volleys, but after he had taken her measure he began bearing down in earnest.

'Let's keep score, shall we?'

They were well matched. He had the advantage of height and power, she had the virtue of finesse. Soon the game assumed a life of its own. She could feel her body grow limber in response to the rhythm of his play, though they exchanged no words other than the necessary ones.

'Your serve.' 'Net ball.' 'Six four.' 'My serve.' As the hour drew to a close, Caro felt a surge of adrenalin. Never in her life had she played so well. Victory was all and now seemed within her grasp, when suddenly – with a barrage of strokes that left her panting and breathless – her opponent smashed his way to a narrow win.

'Well done!' He bounded across the court to pump her hand, flushed and glistening from the heat of play. 'You have one helluva good backhand, by the way.'

'Not good enough,' she mopped the sweat from her brow, 'but thanks anyway. It was fun.'

'And thank you very much for the game,' he handed her back the ball with a flourish.

'You don't give a girl much quarter, though, do you?'

'You don't need it, pretty lady. You play a good game of tennis. Better than most guys. Now may the winner buy the loser a drink?'

She liked him. Liked the way the thick black hair fell across his forehead. Liked the way the tennis whites set off his tan. Liked the grace with which he had tempered her defeat, making it almost seem like victory.

'I'd like that very much,' she said. 'Meet you in the bar in ten minutes.'

His name was Tom Darius, he told her over long cool gin and tonics.

'And all the time I thought it was Bjorn Borg.'

He laughed. A warm easy laugh that curled around the edges. 'Only in my dreams, I'm afraid.'

'And in the real world . . . what do you do?' It was the standard New York question: not *who are you?* or *where are you from?* but always *what do you do?*

'In the real world I edit a magazine called *Ecology Today* and I'll bet you another gin and tonic you never heard of it . . . not unless your taste in centre spreads runs to whales.'

Whales. She recollected browsing through an article about the humpback whale, remembered the feel of the thick grainy stock. 'Aaah,' she said. 'You're the people who print on recycled paper . . . all that stuff about endangered species.'

'That's us' – he waved for another round of drinks – 'although sometimes I think our magazine's the most endangered species of all. Comes as a shock to meet someone who actually reads it. Are you a subscriber by any chance?'

'No . . . I picked it up in the dentist's office.'

'The story of our life,' he sighed. 'We're not much on the news-stands but by God . . . we're the mainstay of the dentist's waiting room. No root canal complete without *Ecology Today*. I'm told it has the same effect on nerve endings as a shot of novocaine.'

'Not at all. I quite enjoyed the piece on humpback whales.'

'I could kiss you for that.' He leaned across the table and for one fleeting moment, she thought he really was going to kiss her out of sheer exuberance. 'You see, I wrote that piece. It was a labour of love all the way. They're delightful creatures,' he grinned, and she couldn't help smiling back, pleased that such a simple compliment could elicit such a warm response. Next time he leaned across the table, maybe he *would* kiss her. She wouldn't mind a bit.

He wasn't conventionally handsome. He was better than that – he was appealing. And if he lacked the cool good looks of the menswear ads in the *Sunday Times* magazine, he had something incalculably more attractive going for him. A warmth, a vitality, a rumpled joy that set him apart from most men she had known. His eyes smiled when he talked – something she'd often read about but never seen. And as he spoke about his work, she found herself listening to his voice rather than his words. There was, in his tone, that same indulgent affection a fond father might lavish on his children. Only Tom's children were whales and golden eagles and the Great Crested Newt. Rare, marvellous creatures threatened with extinction from hunters and polluters and moneygrubbers. And he had taken them all under his broad protective arm.

He spoke, she thought, with the kind of ardour most people she knew reserved for the making of money.

'Good God!' – he stopped in mid-sentence – 'I'm as bad as an actor, all this talk about my brilliant career. I'd much rather hear about you, Caro. What do you do, when you're not tolerating bores like me?'

Caro flushed. She'd enjoyed hearing him rattle on, and was wary of turning him off. Experience had taught her that men her age were frequently resentful of her status, particularly if they suspected that she was out-earning them substantially. 'I work on Wall Street,' she would say non-commitally, and they would usually reply, 'Oh, you're a secretary.'

'I work on Wall Street,' she told Tom.

'Oh, you're a stockbroker,' he responded.

'No,' she felt gratified, 'but pretty close. I buy and sell stocks for a mutual fund.'

He was impressed but not intimidated – a nice balance, she thought. 'That sounds like great fun. Me, I don't know the difference between the bulls and the bears except in the zoological sense, but I've always felt Wall Street must be very challenging. And potentially creative, too. Listen, Caro . . .' his enthusiasm for his own work had spilled over onto hers – 'just let me make a phone call and rearrange a few things and then you'll tell me about it over lunch.'

She watched his tall retreating figure as he went to find a phone. So strong, so easy, so manly. So nice. A breath of fresh air. If he turns around and smiles at me, she thought, I'll go to bed with him. He turned. Smiled. And mouthed the words 'wait for me,' holding up two fingers to indicate how long.

A couple of minutes later, he was back all in smiles.

'I hope I haven't fouled up your day,' she said.

'Fouled it up? You've made it. Now where would you like to eat.'

'You're a vegetarian, I suppose.'

'Why?' he laughed. 'Because I like animals? Well, I'm not, so how about some Szechuan food?'

'Fine,' she nodded, making a mental note to be sure and go easy on the garlic.

He proved to be a wonderful listener. Not that selfish show of attention with which men bided the time until they could prepare their comeback. He *responded* rather than wisecracked. Over the soup she told him about her childhood – he turned out to be a great admirer of Gusty's work. Over the dumplings, she talked about B School – they discovered they'd both taken their Masters the same year at Harvard, only he was 'across the river', of course. Over the beef and sesame, she opened up about her work at PAGIT – 'I'm afraid with all this utilities stuff, you'll think me on the other side of the ecological fence.'

He laughed, and called for the menu. 'What would you like for dessert, Caro?'

'You,' she said. 'I'd like you for dessert.' And the light that was never very far behind his eyes shone out like a beacon. 'I'll call for the bill,' he whispered.

When it came, she reached for it too. 'Let's split it fifty/fifty,' she said glancing at it. 'After all, we're both working people.'

'No way!' he was firm. 'I'm the one who asked you to lunch.' He dove into his wallet before she could stop him and put some ten-dollar bills on the table.

'You know you ought to call back the waiter,' she remarked. 'He charged us for the chicken and we never got it.'

'Big deal,' said Tom. 'It's not worth making a fuss about.' He chucked her under the chin and smiled. 'Let's go, shall we?'

He was a tender yet passionate lover, as much concerned with the giving of pleasure as receiving it. 'Tell me what you like, Caro,' he had murmured at the height of their lovemaking, 'I only want to make you happy.'

He did make her happy. Everything about him made her happy. Not just the strong, well-formed body, not merely the mechanics of sex – for she had known men of considerable virtuosity – but the way that he brought to the act of love that same intimacy, that lively curiosity that informed his every action. She in turn was overwhelmed by the desire to please him.

'Can I get you something?' she asked as they lounged in bed. 'Coffee? Wine? I think I have some Mouton Cadet cooling off in the refrigerator . . . it's a nice dry white. Or how about something to eat? You never did get your dessert,' she remembered.

He kissed the back of her neck. 'I've had my dessert, but I wouldn't say no to some wine.'

When she came back with a bottle and two glasses on a tray,

she found him poking through her bookcase.

'You a big Germaine Greer fan?' – He had picked out a well-thumbed copy of *The Female Eunuch* and was leafing through it. Caro felt a slight *frisson*. The very last thing she wanted was to get into a divisive confrontation with this attractive and lovable man – let alone on the subject of sexual politics.

'Greer's OK, I guess,' she answered non-commitally.

Tom replaced the book. 'I'm not nutty about her style as a writer,' he remarked, 'but she makes an awful lot of sense now and then.' He poured the wine. 'Here's to us, Caro.' They clinked their glasses and drank.

'You know' – Caro was grateful for the conversational opening that his commendation of Greer provided – 'All afternoon, I've been wondering, worrying really in case you thought I was too aggressive. Back there in the restaurant, my wanting you for dessert. Tell me, do women often ask you to make love to them at first meeting?'

'Not often enough,' he laughed. 'Anyhow, you only beat me to the punch by a couple of minutes. What difference does it make, really – who asks who? After all, men are out there pitching women all the time, and in terms that are a whole lot blunter. I'm glad you asked me. I'm glad to be here. I love making love with you, Caro.'

'Then,' she wound her arms about him, 'can I ask you to make love to me again?'

They spent the night together, talking, sleeping, loving, eating Ritz crackers, drinking Mouton Cadet, learning something of each other's pasts and hopes and dreams. Exchanging pleasures. Exchanging confidences. Caring.

In the morning, Tom went down to get a few things for breakfast, and returned loaded with croissants, bagels, cream cheese, smoked salmon, French apricot jam, some strange Greek goat cheese she'd never heard of but that proved to be fatally delicious – plus two copies of the *Sunday Times*. 'One for you, one for me.'

In the afternoon, they went for a long leisurely stroll in Central Park. Before they left, Tom took a few rolls and put them in a paper bag. 'No reason the ducks shouldn't share in the goodies.' They walked, talked, went to the zoo, had some tea at an outdoor cafe. The afternoon melted away.

'Would you believe it's five o'clock already?' – he said, tossing the last bit of croissant to a greedy duck. 'I'm afraid I must be on my way.'

'Must you? Couldn't you spend the night?'

'Wish I could,' he sighed, 'but I've got a barrel of work waiting for me at home.'

'Well, come back for coffee, anyhow. Besides, you've still got your tennis stuff in my apartment.'

'Just a fast one, and then I really have to go.'

'And when will I see you again, Tom? Tomorrow? You busy?' No, not tomorrow, he said – suddenly diffident. No, Tuesday was no good either. Then it hit her like an arrow to the heart.

'You're married, aren't you?'

'Married!' he dropped the paper bag in astonishment. 'Good Lord, no, Caro. What kind of man do you take me for? Please, please don't cry,' He fished into his pocket and retrieved a crumpled handkerchief. 'No, I'm not married. It's just that . . . well, I have to arrange a couple of things, that's all.'

She wiped her eyes, confused yet relieved.

'In other words, you have some other commitment.' Well of course. He would. New York wasn't exactly teeming with attractive single men free of all attachments. It figured. A man like him would have his pick of beautiful and willing women.

'No, it's not a commitment,' he sounded very earnest. 'Just a girl I've been going with. I don't live with her, if that's what you're thinking. Not all that serious. Still . . . I don't want to act like a total swine and dump her in sixty seconds flat. God, Caro,' he put his arm around her, 'can't you see I'm absolutely bananas about you? Just give me a few days to get out of it gracefully. Give me till Thursday, OK?'

'OK.' She dried her eyes and handed him back his handkerchief. 'Till Thursday.'

He came back on Thursday, radiant as a bridegroom, and swept her up into his life.

5

One lunch hour she popped in on Thea to find her friend looking indecently cheerful in paint-splattered overalls and bandana, a far cry from the pearl-and-cashmered debutante of old.

'Excuse my dust,' came the apology, 'but I've been putting up bookshelves all morning.'

The loft was gradually taking shape, smart and modern, if faintly austere. The walls were hung with contemporary graphics, the floor stacked high with art books. One corner had been converted into a work area with a large desk and industrial lighting.

'You look like you mean business,' was Caro's respectful comment.

Thea did indeed. She had returned to college with a vigour that had been singularly absent in her husband-hunting days, and the interest in art which Caro had presumed a passing fancy was turning into a serious commitment. To her surprise and delight, Thea found that school was more than consolation for a broken marriage, was gratifying in itself.

'Of course I have to work twice as hard as anyone else,' she explained, 'the general sentiment being that beautiful is dumb. But enough about me, Caro. Grab a chair somewhere while I pour us some wine and then you can tell me who he is. And don't tell me there's no one, because it's written all over your face. You look like you've just won the Irish Sweepstakes.'

'Well, maybe I have,' Caro beamed. 'Maybe I've done just that.'

The two friends toasted each other in California red, then Caro sang the praises of Tom.

'He's fantastic,' she crooned. 'A real change of pace. You'll like him too, sweetie. Everyone does. He's not the least bit like those broker types I usually go with. With those guys it's either screwing or shop talk – and usually both simultaneously. Like you wake up in the morning and the big scramble is who gets out of the door first for a crack at the financial pages. And so competitive. But Tom. . . .'

Her voice trailed off. How to describe him, to express her own fondness? – except to say that for the first time since her freshman days at college, she felt her life was being enriched, stretched, deepened. 'You know why he majored in biology, Thea? Because he loves life so much. And he's so . . . so spontaneous, so much fun to be with. Like last weekend, for instance. I came home from the office after a really rotten week. I mean by Friday I was drained, and Tom comes up with this crazy idea. We should pack a weekend bag and go out to Kennedy and get on the first flight available anywhere. As long as we could be back at work Monday morning. We wound up – would you believe – in Kansas City. And it was absolutely great. There's a marvellous museum there, you know . . . we went to the stock car races. It was terrific! I guess that's why I haven't been around for so long. My apologies. It's only that right now, I want to spend as much time as I can with him. Enjoy it for as long as it lasts. However long that is,' she added wryly.

'And you think it might last?' Thea probed gently.

'Who knows?' Caro shrugged. It was a question she asked herself a dozen times each day. 'How long do any of 'em last, for that matter? I think my track record was those four months with Howie Bernstein. I don't know why I should expect this one to be any different.'

Even to her own ears, her tone sounded dour, the words as cynical as a self-fulfilling prophecy. But was it cynical to see the end in each beginning, or was she simply being realistic?

'That sounds like I'm bad-mouthing him, doesn't it? I don't mean to. He really is someone out of the ordinary. I mean there's none of this woman's role, man's role bullshit between us. Everything's so open, so free and easy. No . . . the problem isn't with him. It's with me. I'm so . . .' she hesitated, then burst out 'I'm so fucking afraid of getting dumped again.'

'Aren't we all?' Thea agreed. 'But whatever happens, we

survive somehow . . . even manage to bounce back. You especially, Caro. I always think of you as a real winner, the way you pulled yourself together after that Howie business, then zoomed right on through Harvard. And on and on and on. Not like me, putting all my eggs in one basket. Last year when Brooks and I were splitting up, I thought of you a lot and in a way it helped me to make the break.'

'Really!' Caro was astonished.

'Yes, really. I thought of you so independent, successful, not beholden to any man and said to myself, if Caro can do it . . . so can I. So here we are, both in New York, both doing our damnedest. The only difference is I'm still a college junior and you're a big deal on Wall Street.'

'Speaking of which,' Caro glanced at her watch. 'I've got to be going.'

As she went for her coat, Thea darted in to the bedroom.

'Do you like Opium? Not to smoke, I mean the St Laurent perfume. Brooks gave me a gigantic bottle of the stuff last year as penance for one of his escapades, and I just can't bring myself to wear it. Here . . . take it. I'm sure your Tom will like it on you. And tell him for me that he's a lucky guy.'

She spent the night at Tom's, cooking spaghetti and making love. 'Mmmm . . . you smell delicious,' he said. 'Is that a new perfume you're wearing?'

'Glad you like it. A friend of mine gave it to me at lunch today.'

'A boyfriend?' His voice was unexpectedly sharp.

'No, a girlfriend. Someone I've known for donkey's years.' The sour note of her earlier scepticism suddenly intruded. 'And if it had been a boyfriend, would you have really minded?'

'I'd have minded,' he said softly. 'I'd have minded very much. I guess what I'm saying is that I'm in love with you.'

'I love you too, Tom.'

'You know what advice my father gave me when I left home to go to college?' Tom said next morning, '"Son," he told me, "if you find yourself in bed with some little chippie, remember two things. First, always wear a condom. Second, never under any circumstances tell her your real name".'

'So . . .' she giggled – 'your real name isn't Tom Darius after all. It's actually. . . .'

'John Doe,' he completed the sentence. 'Just think, Caro, you've just been making love to John Doe.'

'But why do you call me Caro?' – she teased. 'My real name is Jane.'

For a while, it was a running gag between them. Then, the secret code name by which they could communicate at parties. 'Hey, Jane,' he had only to say, and she knew it was a signal that he was eager to leave, hungry to be alone with her. Ultimately, 'John Doe' and 'Jane' entered their growing repertory of pet names, an ironic symbol of their increasing frankness with each other.

Their early months together were, in some ways, one long confessional. He told her about the girls he had cared for – high school crushes, Harvard flings. About one long and painful affair with a married woman that had ended only when her husband was transferred abroad. Even now, they occasionally kept in touch. 'We're still friends enough to exchange Christmas cards.' And Caro, following his lead, gradually confided her own affairs and disappointments – something she had never done with other men.

'Your Howie sounds like quite a shit,' Tom commented. 'I'm surprised you could care for someone like that.'

'But I did,' she confirmed. 'Are you jealous?'

'How can I be jealous of some guy you knew before you met me?' came his answer.

He was right. What did it matter? After all, everything until now was curtain raisers to the main drama of her life.

Tom Darius was the most amiable of men. Outgoing. Easygoing. Amiable.

He had that sweetness of temper found only in those fortunate people for whom nothing much in life had ever gone wrong. Not that Tom ever stopped to think of himself as fortunate or otherwise; if he had to summarize his background and upbringing in a single word, he would simply have shrugged and said 'ordinary'. 'The only extraordinary thing that's ever happened to me,' he told Caro, 'is you.'

His father was an ordinary G.P. ('not even a specialist'), who enjoyed a comfortable suburban practice. His mother was an ordinary housewife with a weakness for Barraccini chocolates and a tendency to underbid her bridge hands. He was raised in an ordinary home: four bedrooms, two-car garage, one dog, no swimming pool.

But just as he was the son of Everett and Grace Darius, he was as much the child of his generation. The winds of change that had swept across America in the mid-sixties – stirring the campuses, rousing even the Supreme Court – blew rather more gently into the tree-lined streets of Morristown, New Jersey. But blow they did – brushing away cobwebs, bringing with them bracing whiffs of a new and high-minded society, an invigorating sense of wonder and freedom, a fresh belief that anything in life was possible. That self-fulfillment was no longer an idle dream. It was a necessity. Almost a duty.

By the time Tom was ready to enter college, he could look back on his ordinary home and family with a mixture of contempt and affection.

'Be sure to wear earmuffs,' were his mother's parting words. 'Those Massachusetts winters are awful.' While his father, in a whispered aside, outlined the early-warning signals of VD. Tom thanked them both for the well-meant advice, and managed to keep a straight face. His parents were what they were – and he loved them dearly. But he was going to be something else.

At Harvard, he majored in biology graduating *magna cum laude* and stayed on to take his masters degree. However, a talent for writing, a gift for the trim and memorable phrase, led him to feel he was uniquely situated to bridge the widening gap between the scientific world and the layman. He hoped, he told Caro, to do for biology what Carl Sagan was doing for astronomy. Make it popular, comprehensible, exciting. And when Caro commented that Sagan had made a fortune, Tom protested vehemently. Money-grubbing was the furthest thing from his mind. What appealed to him was the freedom of the work, the friendships, the chance to make a meaningful contribution. Psychic income, he called it. And though he could have had his pick of high-paying jobs – in government or with the pharmaceuticals – he had chosen to join the staff of *Ecology Today*.

He had cheerfully exchanged the microscope for the typewriter, the suburban promise for a Village walk-up. Sacrificed the dream of security for the dream of self-fulfillment. It was a choice he had never once regretted.

He was, in short, a happy and amiable man, doing the work he loved best. Everything interested him: books and theatre and ballet and baseball and politics and science and music. He had a project in hand for every waking moment. With Tom the days were never long enough, the nights far too short. And his enthusiasms were contagious, spilling over onto friends, colleagues and above all, onto Caro.

If Tom had a failing (and Caro was too much of a realist to credit anyone with perfection), it was, perhaps, this very amiability. Tom liked to be liked. It was the lynch-pin of his personality. And, indeed, he was eminently likeable for he had a great capacity for warmth, a patient ear for other people's troubles. He could tolerate bores and cranks with unruffled aplomb and although he might poke fun at them privately, it was always with affection. But it was this very quality, this eagerness to please that sometimes troubled Caro. Occasionally struck her as a softness. A reluctance. An inability to say no when called for. The kind that sticks. And hurts. And loses friends.

He would, she had already noticed, rather pay an inflated bill in a restaurant than make a scene with a waiter. He complained frequently about buying articles for the magazine that failed to meet his standards. 'I couldn't hurt the guy's feelings,' Tom would grumble later to her. Or else 'the poor sonofabitch needs the money'. Inevitably, he wound up either rewriting the piece from scratch, or burying it – paid for but unpublished – in the bottom drawer of his desk. Caro thought this very unbusinesslike, yet she knew that when he erred it was out of kindness rather than any miserliness of spirit.

What the hell, she felt. The world was full enough of tough bastards. And if Tom wasn't the perfect human being, he was – at least – a very human human being.

6

'You're looking very chipper these days, Caro.' Her boss motioned her to a seat across his desk.

'Thank you, Barney. No complaints.'

'And you'll be a lot more chipper when I tell you the news. How'd you like to go to the head of the class?'

Instant euphoria! She could see the squib now in the next issue of *Institutional Investor*. Nothing fancy. Maybe just

'Ms. Caroline Harmsworth, MBA Harvard, has been
appointed to the post of Assistant Manager to
Bernard Baker, PAGIT Mutual Fund.'

Plus a picture maybe.

Or maybe even something bigger. Perhaps a small fund of her own. Utilities probably. Why not? She'd been bucking for more elbow room all year.

'Actually,' Barney amplified. 'It's more than a promotion. A quantum leap you might call it – and a chance at the big bucks. Of course it'll be quite a change from mutual funds. . .'

Caro straightened up abruptly. 'Not working here then? Not in this division?'

'No, not even in this building. You're being transferred to corporate headquarters over on Broad Street, which should offer you plenty of scope. You know our department's considered pretty stodgy by the powers that be, although on the whole we've done pretty well. Still . . . when you came here you told me you were looking for the fast track. Well . . . here's your chance.'

A new fund was being formed, as yet untitled, but tentatively known as the V.C. Fund: Venture Capital-risk money that PAGIT itself would be putting up, creamed off from the company's profits. 'Quite frankly, you'll be at the top end of the risk business. So you can kiss goodbye to the widows and orphans. But remember, the bigger the gamble, the bigger the rewards. You could be making six figures in a couple of years.'

Everything about the group was going to be new – its premise, its personnel, above all the financial superstar who had been brought in to head it.

For openers, Caro could count on an extra $10,000, but that was just an appetizer. For beyond the basic salary lay the promise of real money, yearly bonuses related to performance. 'Of course,' Barney said, 'it won't be the usual stocks and bonds. As I hear it, you'll be handling new business investments, company acquisitions, unregistered securities. I understand this guy they've brought in is willing to take a shot at anything that flies.'

Without warning, Caro's stomach churned. For a moment, she wondered if there hadn't been some mistake.

'Jesus, Barney . . . venture capital, company acquisitions . . . from where I stand it's a whole new ball game. My claim to fame, such as it is, is based on one specialized area of the stockmarket. Why me?'

Barney shrugged and rolled his eyes in the direction of Broad Street.

'Do I know their reasoning in that *meshuggenah* place? The point is, you were picked for it, kiddo – so somebody up there likes you. And why not! You've done a first-class job in this department.'

First class. Nice words, those. But a number of her colleagues had done a 'first class' job, so someone up there more than liked her. Someone had singled her out above all others for a chance to catch the brass ring. She wavered between the soaring ego-high of success and the nagging weasel-low of anxiety.

'It's a terrific challenge, Barney, and I'm very flattered but I'd like to think about it for a couple of days.'

'Sure, but let me give you a piece of advice.'

Over the years, Barney had given her a good deal of advice, most of it apt. She listened willingly now.

'You know why so few women make it to the top, Caro? No . . . it's not all a male conspiracy. If you ask me, it's a failure of nerve. They get to a certain level and settle in. They want to be dragged up the ladder under protest. Don't sell yourself short –

that's what I keep telling my daughters, and the same advice goes for you. You know, I've spent my life studying big corporations and I'll tell you one thing. When anybody – male or female has to be courted and coaxed . . . worse yet, when anyone chickens out on a major promotion, that person gets written off the books psychologically. Not fired, mind you . . . there's always room at the middle. But they cease to figure in company planning. Big corporations don't like folks who say no. That's not how the game is played. Maybe you're planning to chuck it all and get married . . .' – and when Caro shook her head no, he concluded – 'Well, if you're talking career I'll lay it on the line. There isn't a man in my department who wouldn't jump at the opportunity. And nobody would have to ask him twice.'

'You're telling me to take the job or get lost in the shuffle, in other words.'

'I'm telling you the facts. You'll have to make up your own mind, of course.'

Caro rose to leave. 'Thanks for the straight talk, Barney. I appreciate your candour. I'd still like a few days to think it over.'

'You're crazy,' Sally Klein told her over lunch. 'Crazy to even consider turning it down. You may never get another chance.'

'The thing is,' Caro felt defensive, 'I'm comfortable where I am. I enjoy the job, I get along OK with the guys and I really feel secure in my field.'

'Secure!' Sally snorted. 'What kind of crap is that? If you wanted security you should have married an undertaker and moved to Queens. That's secure! Come on, Caro . . . where's the old B-School chutzpah? If they didn't think you could handle the job, they wouldn't have offered. They're not running a charity, you know. So what's bugging you . . . you afraid your boyfriend is going to disapprove?'

'Oh, no!' Caro protested. 'Tom's always very supportive.' And then, because she'd rather talk about Tom than the business in hand, rather talk about Tom than anything – 'You know he's dying to meet you, he loved the interview you did with Bella Abzug. Why just the other day we were watching you on TV and Tom was saying we should all get together. Maybe go out and eat Szechuan one evening soon . . . how about this Friday?'

'Yeah, sure, fine.' Sally refused to be distracted. 'Now let's get back to the issue. Even putting your self-interest aside for a moment, the point is, if you cop out Caro, you'll just be fucking it up for the next woman. Let's face it, Wall Street's the last male enclave, and PAGIT is the worst of the bunch. Turn 'em down and you're playing right into their hands. Then all they have to say is . . . well, we tried to get a woman for that post, but we couldn't find one who had the guts. That's what they're hoping for is my bet.'

'You're probably right,' Caro brooded, 'and I'll probably take it, but I get the feeling that I'm being set up.'

That night, the probably became a definitely as Tom managed to get in his congratulations even before Caro had a chance to voice her doubts.

'Goddam marvellous, darling!' He swept her up in a bear hug. 'I can't tell you how proud I am of you. What say we celebrate with dinner at the Plaza. Best jeans and lots of calories.'

'But Tom . . .' – she hated to squelch his enthusiasm. 'I haven't made up my mind whether to take it.'

'What's holding you back, Caro?' He was nonplussed. 'Do you think they're trying to scam you on the money?'

'What do you mean?'

'Trying to get off cheap because you're a woman.'

'No . . . that's not it. In fact, the money angle is one of the things that troubles me. I mean . . .' – she tried not to make it sound crass, but there were just so many ways of stating a fact – 'the thing is, I'll be earning a lot more than you from now on. I was worried that that might bother you.'

'Why should it bother me? Because you're a woman and I'm a man? Don't be an asshole, darling. If it were the other way around, I came home with a whopping big raise . . . would that bother you?'

'Of course not, but. . . .'

'No buts about it. We're independent people with independent careers. We agreed on that from the word go. I'd feel like

75

an absolute shit if you turned the job down because of me. Might as well label me a chauvinist pig.'

That settled it, of course. The following morning she told Barney she accepted the job 'with pleasure' and by the end of the week, found herself looking forward to the challenge. She would start in two weeks.

'You think your friend will like me?' Tom asked as they were on their way to meet Sally Klein.

'She'll like you, honey,' – it was such a typical Tom question – 'I just hope you like her.'

'I like her on television, she's terrific, although it's always been a mystery to me that such a plain-looking girl ever got past the auditions. Usually the women on TV are such lookers.'

'Funny story about that, Tom. I'll tell you in the taxi.'

In the girls' final year at Midwestern, campus peace had been shattered by a series of rapes. From the first attack on, the dorms were in an uproar. Security was doubled, redoubled, but to no avail. As for the police, they offered nothing but advice: women should lock their rooms, avoid poorly lit paths, only venture out in groups after dark.

Sally in particular was outraged by the police directive. 'How dare they tell us where we can or can't go!' In protest she organized a torchlight parade that would take the marchers down the very paths where the rapist had struck. Despite a bone-drenching drizzle – some three thousand women joined the march with Sally at their helm. There were the usual wisecracks from the usual jocks, but no question – the evening was a triumph.

The following week, the campus humour magazine ran a picture of Sally on its cover. It was a candid shot, snapped in the glare of a flashbulb, and there for all the world to see was Sally Klein – hair streaming and dishevelled, glasses askew, looking like a drowned water rat. The caption read

Would You Rape This Woman?

Sally demanded a retraction, and when the editor refused she decided to bring the matter to a head. She wrote to the newspapers, hounded public officials and before long her story was arousing both laughter and indignation throughout the state. Inevitably she was asked to appear on a public affairs programme on local TV. 'This is it!' she told Caro and prepared for her debut like a bride getting ready for a wedding.

It was only a five-minute spot, but it was enough. Caro, for one, could hardly believe her eyes. The Sally on the screen was a total stranger: hair coiffed, clothes immaculate, horn-rims shelved in favour of contact lenses. She was absolutely compelling – a born television personality – and before the week was out, she had signed with NBC.

To her relief, Tom and Sally hit it off. Tom had set himself out to be charming (which for him was no effort at all) and as they were leaving the restaurant, Sally whispered 'He's an absolute prince.' 'Well,' Caro beamed, 'first I had to kiss a lot of frogs.'

'You were marvellous with Sally,' she told Tom when they were in bed. 'You've earned the Good Housekeeping Seal of Approval.'

'Yeah, well I liked her too. Very bright. Very articulate, very . . . um. . . .' He licked Caro's ear, then murmured into it . . . 'But my God, would you want to rape this woman?'

'You rat,' Caro giggled. 'You're absolutely horrible. I never should have told you that story.' And the two of them dissolved into laughter and love.

Almost from the start, Tom had pressed her to move in with him. He had a long dingy railroad flat on the edge of Greenwich Village. 'It's scruffy,' he admitted, 'but it's convenient to Wall Street and we could fix it up. New curtains . . . a fresh coat of paint. . .'

'You've got cockroaches.'

'Everyone's got roaches in this city, Caro. The mayor's got roaches over in Gracie Mansion, only his wear buttons saying *I Love New York*.'

'I don't have roaches,' she said.

'That's because you don't do any cooking.'

'Is that a criticism?'

'Nope, just an observation.'

She had countered with the offer that he move in with her, knowing it was out of the question. His books alone would consume three-quarters of her living space, and Tom had a thing about physical confinement. Even phone booths made him fidgety. Tom needed space.

In fact, he spent most nights at her place but invariably there was something he'd left at home – fresh underwear, papers needed in the office – always something to pull him out of bed at a grumpy 6 a.m. to make the long subway ride down to the Village. 'If only you'd be a little more organized,' Caro would say. 'If only you'd be a little more pliable,' he'd complain. The whole business of living arrangements was gradually turning into a bone of contention.

'I've had the exterminator around,' he said, walking her home after the theatre one evening. 'The place has been certified 99 44/100 per cent pure. So how about it?'

'We've been through all this before, Tom, and the answer's still no.'

'Why not? My address isn't fancy enough for you, Caro?' – he sounded testy. 'Are you all that hung-up about status symbols?'

'It's not that, Tom. I've lived in some pretty crummy places – more than you have, I bet. Believe me, darling, it's not that. It's . . .'

'You're right,' he cut her off. 'It's not that!' His tone precluded any response. They walked the rest of the way in silence but when they came to her brownstone, he stepped back. 'I won't come up tonight, I've got a big day tomorrow.' His face was hard and strained in the lamplight. Then, without warning he lashed out. 'You really like to play it cool, don't you, Caro? Never show your hand, never shoot the moon. God forbid you should take a chance. Your favourite position is sitting on the fence . . . in bed, in business – in everything!' He strode off leaving her open-mouthed. It was as if the bottom had fallen out of her world.

She stumbled up the stairs drunk with fear and let herself in, all the while the voice within her grieving 'Tom Tom Tom! What do you want from my life?' She could not believe that he found her so cold and uncaring. She had told him what she had never told any man – that she loved him. Yet even this had not been sufficient. How could he have so misread her? Or was it possible – the thought began forming – that she had misread herself?

She looked around the apartment that had been her home these past few years. Until tonight it had seemed so cosy everything so compact and efficient, so snugly in its proper place. Yet now the very walls seemed to speak of a crammed self-satisfaction, for despite the homey touches – the plants, the French fashion prints, the little shelf of Bristol glass – it was not a welcoming place. Everything in it proclaimed *I me mine*. She walked through the rooms seeing them with new eyes. With Tom's eyes. The bedroom. How many times had he complained about his feet sticking out of the covers. 'Why don't you break down and get a bigger bed?' And she had come back with the jokey reply that she'd never counted on having a six-foot-three lover. 'Besides the room's so small.' Yet she knew the choice had been deliberate; the single bed a tacit announcement that the men who came here were on sufferance. This was her turf.

The kitchenette. All she really needed, a small counter and two high wooden stools. No invitation here to linger over coffee, to sit and talk into the small hours of morning.

The living room. There were iron bars across the windows, a necessity in these burglar-haunted streets. Yet now those bars assumed a different meaning. *Do Not Enter* they said to friend and foe alike. What had only hours earlier seemed so cosy and intimate now struck her as a tight little fortress. Her defence against the rest of the world. But a fortress can become a prison.

Tom had seen all this, had read the message implicit in every stick of furniture, and now he has gone. The idea was unbearable. What had she gained by her inflexibility? She had won back her home, her privacy, her precious freedom. The freedom to eat crackers in bed. To leave pantyhose soaking in the sink. To play the radio at three in the morning. Big deal. And for this freedom, she must be willing to revert to what she had been only a few months earlier – a woman both unloving and unloved.

No. Tom Darius was the best thing that had ever happened to her. It was unthinkable that she should destroy a relationship with so much future, so much promise, in a squabble over petty details. Yet she could not bring herself to make all the concessions. With the innate wariness born of experience – of Howie, of Richard, of half-forgotten one-night stands – she

79

determined Tom must make concessions too. After hours of agonizing, she called him up at home. It was three in the morning.

'I love you Tom and I want to live with you. Let's both of us work out a compromise.'

'I love you too, Caro' – he sounded so relieved. 'I'll be over in twenty minutes.'

The solution was simple. They'd both give up their apartments and take a new place together. It made sense in every way. Economically. Logistically. Emotionally. On the basis of two good salaries they could afford something quite splendid – and Xanadu Towers was certainly that.

'The epitome of apartment dwelling' the brochure stated proudly, and the rent was commensurate. 'But when you consider the amenities' – the agent crooned – 'you'll find it's really very economical.' There was a swimming club on the roof, a subterranean garage, and a fleet of round-the-clock doormen whose uniforms would have done credit to a banana republic. And the apartment itself was superb, as young and as fresh as their love.

Two spacious bedrooms – Tom's books would eat up one; a living room all floor-to-ceiling windows; a terrace high above the East River (Caro had images of cool drinks on hot nights); a kitchen and two baths that were the last word in gadgetry. They walked about it, silent and goggle-eyed.

'Well, Jane?' Tom whispered, and she gave a mute nod.

'We'll take it,' they said in unison. But the evening before they were to sign the lease, Caro came down with a case of cold feet.

'Three years is such a long time, Tom. Suppose it doesn't work out. Suppose we wind up at each other's throats.' Emotionally, she couldn't envisage such a turn of events, yet common sense told her it was always a possibility. She had a lingering fear that deep down in every man there lurked a Howie, ready to abandon ship at any moment. 'I'm sure it won't happen, sweetie, but what if it does? What then?'

'We're two civilized people, Caro, and if things don't work out, we can always settle up reasonably. Roomates co-sign leases every day of the week, and anyhow, leases were made to be broken.'

'But all the stuff we're planning to buy . . . furniture, curtains, carpeting. How will we know what's whose?'

'Would you feel better if we drew up a contract?'

Caro mulled it over for a few minutes, then – hating herself for the admission – answered 'Yes, Tom, I would. I don't want to sound cold-blooded and businesslike, especially since I'm nuts about you. But. . .'

'Say no more,' he broke in. 'I understand completely and I think it's a helluva good idea.'

They spent most of the night working out the details, planning for every contingency. Once a month, each of them would deposit a fixed portion of their incomes into a joint account to cover household expenses and entertainment. They'd alternate chores on a day-to-day basis – everything, including cooking. Clothing, lunches, books, medical and personal expenses (Tom's cigarettes, Caro's yoga class) were to be paid by the person who incurred them. By midnight, they had a five-page document that covered every eventuality from hair in the sink to the apportioning of phone bills.

'Now what about pets?' Caro asked.

'Pets?'

'Well, you know, honey, I've always wanted a dog, and when I was a kid we moved about too much. Anyhow, I see it's allowed in my lease, and with two of us, it wouldn't be much of a hassle.'

'Oh, Jesus!' Tom groaned. 'You're only saying that because you never owned one. They tie you down like a ball and chain. Walking 'em is bad enough, but what about weekends when we want to go away? Vacations, that sort of thing?'

'Put him in a kennel.'

'Yeah . . . that means we'd have to plan everything ahead. Tell you one thing, honey, with a dog on our hands, there'll be no more screwball flights to Kansas City. Will you settle for a cat? They're no bother.'

'I'm allergic to cats.'

'How about some goldfish?'

'Oh, fuck it!' She threw up her hands. It wasn't worth

arguing about. 'Why don't we just get some nice houseplants and the cleaning woman can water them when we're away.'

'That's very sensible, pet. Now we come to the sticky bit . . . in the event of dissolution.'

'In the event of dissolution,' she echoed. Then sighed. It was not an attractive turn of phrase. 'Well, suppose we write in that this contract can be voided by either party on thirty days' notice. That would give either of us ample time to buy the other person out . . . or else we could simply sell off the joint property and split the proceeds.'

'Write that down,' Tom said. 'Sounds good.'

The document finally arrived at was a careful and sensible work, but all Caro could say when she re-read it was 'that's a very heartless bunch of papers.'

It was more than that, her sinking spirits told her. It was a monument to the impermanence of love. Tom saw her moue of distaste. 'Do you want me to tear it up, Caro?' He was waiting for her lead.

'Oh, I don't know.' She wound her arms around him. 'It covers everything except how we feel about each other. What do you think?'

'I can't make up your mind for you, sweetie. And you were the one with cold feet.'

'Right.' She stood up crisply. 'Let's sign it and forget it, then go to bed so I can get my feet warm again.'

They notarized the contract the following morning and co-signed the lease that afternoon. The following Saturday they blew $2000 on a sofa, and as Caro sat in the furniture show-room, riffling through swatches of upholsterer's silks, she couldn't help smiling. In just a matter of weeks her whole life had changed: new apartment, new job, new love.

Glass, chrome, steel. Glass, chrome, steel. Every surface was as hard as a diamond. Even the air seemed thinner on the twenty-fifth floor of the executive building. Almost alpine. But if the new surroundings exhibited none of the frowstiness Caro was used to, on closer inspection she noticed the difference was one of tone, rather than facilities.

The carpeting was thicker, the desks more modern and widely spaced. Waist-high dividers marked territorial boundaries. Yet no matter what the decorators called it, it was still the bullpen – a rambling open-floor plan dominated by a single, large private office at the end of the hall. The lettering on the office door looked barely dry, a crisp gleaming black against mahogany.

D. R. CATLETT III

The door was closed. Ominous. Barney had always kept his door open. There was about the place an air of empty expectancy, like a hospital operating theatre awaiting the first incision of the day. She walked back to the desk that had her name on it and unfolded her *Wall Street Journal*. It had been a long time since she had been in this situation, set down to work among a group of total strangers, at the mercy of first impressions. She had dressed that morning with particular care, discarding this outfit as a little too sexy, that suit as a little too severe, settling finally on a soft beige wool by Ted Lapidus that struck a nice balance: elegant without being obtrusive. That decision behind her, she'd arrived on the stroke of nine, in the hope of settling into the surroundings and familiarizing herself with new names and faces. But the men who drifted in one by one exercised no reciprocal curiosity. She finished the *Journal* and switched to *The Times* and at the end of an hour's empty waiting, all she'd accomplished was getting newsprint all over her hands. She walked out in the hall to look for the Ladies Room. Couldn't find it. Returned to her desk.

A little after ten, a slim figure in a velvet-collared overcoat whipped past her into the executive suite, looking neither right nor left. Himself III, no doubt. And some minutes later, a middle-aged woman emerged from the sanctum and began buzzing her way from desk to desk.

'Miss Harmsworth? I'm Stella Gibbs.' She spoke briskly, but in such a low, sombre tone that Caro wondered if someone had died. 'I'm Mr Catlett's secretary. He asked to see everyone in the conference room for an introductory meeting, 10.30 sharp.'

'Thank you, Miss Gibbs,' Caro whispered back. 'But before you vanish, I'd like to ask you a question.'

'Certainly.'

'Well . . . I know this sounds ridiculous, but I've been here since nine, looking around a bit . . . and . . . umm . . . I haven't found a Ladies Room on this floor.'

'I'm afraid there isn't one, or on the next two floors either. You'll have to take the elevator down to Twenty Two where the typing pool is.' Unexpectedly, the elder woman smiled. 'Welcome to the clubhouse.'

'Hello, I'm Dan Catlett.'

He stood in the doorway of the conference room, thin and sleek as a whippet, greeting each new arrival with a handshake, a smile, then a gesture indicating that they take a seat anywhere. Anywhere, of course, except the high-backed director's chair that dominated the long oval table.

'Hello, I'm Dan Catlett.'

'How do you do. I'm Caroline Harmsworth.' She grasped the outstretched hand, returned the smile and went to seat herself as the others had done. Suddenly, she realized that Catlett had slipped around behind her and was now preceding her down the length of the table. His intention was unmistakeable. He was going to pull out a chair for her, like a host at a dinner party. Caro panicked. It would be instant disaster, she knew. For by the mere acceptance of that social courtesy, she would be singled out. Marked. Irreversibly detached from every man in the group. With a swift brusque motion, Caro snatched the nearest free chair and sat down before Catlett could complete his ritual. He stared at her for a moment, then trooped back to his station to greet the last of the arrivals. It had been a graceless bit of business, and Caro still felt awkward and flustered when he finally assumed his own chair at the head of the table.

'Gentlemen' – the voice was Southern and so soft she had to strain for every word – 'and *lady*.'

She felt the blood rush to her cheeks. This was no way to begin. She missed Barney Baker's 'OK, folks' – so casual and clearly unisex.

'We have a great deal of ground to cover today. I'll be discussing my concept for this fund, my long-term goals and how, with your assistance, I plan to achieve these goals.'

My concept. *My* goals.

My God, Caro thought. So much for democracy.

'However,' he drawled. 'First things first. Since some of you don't know me and most of you don't know each other, we'll begin by going around the table and each of you can introduce yourself in turn. Tell us about your background, special areas of interest and anything else you think may be pertinent. Tony?' He nodded to the man on his right who began 'I'm Tony Marcusson. I've been with Lazard Frères the last couple of years. . . .'

But Caro was only half-listening. She was busy taking in the group as a whole and not caring much for what she saw. There were a dozen of them in all – gunslinger types, every man-jack of them, with big-buck hunger written large in their faces. Older than her. More seasoned. Mostly in their thirties was her guess. Catlett, so clearly the senior member, didn't look to be much over forty. Covertly, her glance came to rest at the head of the table.

He was perfect. Right out of central casting. He resembled nothing so much as a photograph in *Fortune*, all glossy black and white. Not a detail amiss, from the beautifully-cut black pin-stripe suit to the immaculate white shirt to the starched French cuffs that showed the requisite number of millimetres beyond the coat sleeve. You could have sliced a salami with the edge of those cuffs. Or cut a throat. Black and white, black and white – relieved only by occasional touches of gold. The watch, the cufflinks, the slim gold wedding band.

My compliments, Caro doffed a mental hat, to your tailor, your jeweller and to the no doubt equally perfect Mrs D. R. Catlett III for doing such a nice line in laundry.

He smiled easily and often, displaying even white teeth that looked as if they had just come back from the cleaners. But the eyes above the smile were cool and grey, scanning the length of the table like a radar screen. Restless. Alert for any outbreak of enemy activity.

And then it was Caro's turn to say her piece.

'My name is Caroline Harmsworth. I'm Harvard Business School, class of. . . .'

'Excuse me,' the soft patrician voice interrupted, then went on to something Caro couldn't catch.

'I'm sorry, I didn't hear you.'

'I asked you if that was Miss or Mrs.'

She froze. There was an insolent, almost baiting quality in his tone, and for one tumultuous second she felt like telling him that her marital status was none of his goddam business. Great! Terrific! Do it and she'd be a five-minute heroine in the Tuesday night women's group, and be signing up for unemployment on Wednesday.

'It's Ms.' – she enunciated with all the *sangfroid* she could muster.

'Aaaah . . . 'Mizz!' he savoured it. Considered it. Then repeated it – 'Mizz' – like a stage darky in an old-time minstrel show. Then folded his arms and studied her as closely as if she were a specimen on a slide. 'Well, I have never called anyone Mizz in all my life, not even Jimmy Carter's mother – and I assure you, I am not about to start now. I expect we shall all have to address you simply as Harmsworth. You, on the other hand, may call me *Mister* Catlett.' He gave her a tight smile. 'You may continue.'

Caro stumbled through the rest of her potted resume, ceding her place in the spotlight with relief.

On closer observation the group proved to be more of a mixed bag than had appeared at first glance. As expected, some of the men had come from brokerages and investment banks. But there was also a Princeton-trained economist, two men with engineering degrees, one who held a Ph.D. in nuclear physics, a management consultant. They all seemed to have heavy credentials. Catlett himself had been a corporation lawyer before he 'discovered where the action was'.

It was noon before the introductions were complete and he got down to business.

The fund, he said, would furnish risk capital to fledgling companies, those enterprises considered too young or too hazardous to attract the usual run of banks and institutional investors. He was looking for companies that were unique in both premise and promise. Companies with futures – that was the key word. Futures. 'I'm not interested in tomorrow's Wall

Street closings, dipping in and out of the market like fireflies. I'm thinking beyond that. To next year and next year and the year after that. My long range goal is that this fund will not only finance, but control and eventually underwrite those firms that offer the greatest futures. My personal target is a fifty per cent annual return on capital, which I hope we can achieve by next year.'

Crazy, Caro thought. Sheer fantasy, in view of the current economic climate. Didn't he know there was a recession underway . . . with new businesses going bust right and left?

Everyone was looking for capital, he went on – crackpot inventors, failing businesses, hustlers, and mixed in among them a sprinkling of enterprises that had real merit. They could expect hundreds of proposals to pour into the office, most of them hopeless. Yet each would have to be sifted and evaluated in the hopes of discovering the next Apple or Atari, the Xeroxes and Polaroids of the coming decade. You never knew where the next great idea would originate. In his own experience, however, he'd found many of the best investments were the ones you dug up for yourself – through the grapevine, on the golf course, at the alumni association. In short, the old boy network.

'This means,' he continued, 'that I expect everyone here to go all out for performance at all times. There will be no such thing as "office hours".'

He had a list of investment possibilities to be explored; these would be assigned either to individuals or small working groups. He expected comprehensive research and analysis and 'of course your personal recommendations for investing'. Final decisions would be his alone – until such time as the individual people present had proved their capacities; at which point they would have a line of discretionary capital. Bonuses. Probably none this year. Conceivably big ones next year, again based on individual performance. 'That's the broad outline. Beyond that, I expect you to use your own initiative at all times, develop projects on your own, keep your eyes wide open and your ear to the ground for new companies that might be of interest. In short, I expect to make this fund the most aggressive in the financial community. Bar none.'

'You keep talking about The Fund, Dan' – someone interpolated. 'Does this baby have a name?'

'Well,' Catlett smiled. 'I've considered calling it the Rumpelstilstkin Fund. Those of you who once were children may recall that he was a gentleman of rather dwarfish appearance who had the capacity to turn straw into gold. An admirable quality – and I trust we shall all emulate his example.'

A mild wave of laughter rippled down the table. 'However, since some of you apparently feel that this name lacks the dignity due a multi-million dollar enterprise, I've decided to call it The Carolina Fund' – Caro flushed a burning crimson – 'in honour of my native state.'

Lunch was sent in from the executive dining room. After that they got down to specifics. To Caro's dismay, most of the men had come well-prepared, their briefcases bursting with detailed projects of their own. She felt exposed and empty handed, like a kid who'd forgotten her homework – except that no one had informed her about the nature of the assignment.

Next, Catlett began parcelling out his own projects. A small toy company in Weehawken fell to her lot, and she cast a quick glimpse at the proposal in the wild hope that here indeed might be another Atari.

Yoyos! Some guy had patented a battery-powered yoyo, for Chrissakes. She looked up at Catlett to see if this was some sort of practical joke, but his face was expressionless. Yet as the afternoon wore on, she could not escape the conclusion that the plums were going to others in the group, the lemons were reserved for her.

Towards six he said 'Better call your wives and tell them you'll be late for dinner.' Caro placed a hurried call to Tom, then made her way back to the conference room. Catlett, she noticed, had taken advantage of the break to change his shirt and provision himself with a fresh pack of Dunhills. Everyone else looked slightly wilted. The meeting then continued without pause till well after ten, at which point he stood up, said 'Thank you, gentlemen,' and departed. They had been at that table for almost twelve hours.

'How'd it go?' Tom greeted her at the door. 'And oh, by the way, the sofa arrived. I had them put it by the window. Is that where you wanted it?'

'The only place I want that sofa is under my aching back.' She walked into the living room and there it was, all in a pale lilac silk. Worth every penny they paid for it. 'Beautiful.' She kicked off her shoes, and collapsed full length. 'Wow! What a day!'

'I gather,' Tom said. 'How's the new boss?'

'Pour me a drink and I'll tell you. No . . . nothing to eat, darling, just a little scotch or something.' He poured her a stiff measure of Chivas Regal and brought it over. 'My new boss . . .' she said between sips. 'Mr D. R. Catlett the Third. Well . . . what can I tell you? He looks a bit like John Dean, you know that pale bloodless type with all the heart and soul of a computer. Yeah . . . really warm and lovable. Oh hell, Tom' – she burst out suddenly, 'I'm not sure I can hack it. All these guys are out of my league – older, more experienced – and as for boss-man, he's made it clear that women are second-class citizens.'

'You sure you're not being hyper-sensitive?'

'No, honey, I'm not. Like he's got a secretary old enough to be my mother. You know what he calls her? "My girl". Patronizing bastard. "Ah will have mah girl send raound the papuhs",' she mimicked. 'Oh, shit. I could never do southern accents. I'm making him sound like a red-neck. Actually ne's a very slick number and brighter than hell. Thing is, I could tolerate all this chauvinist crap. I don't imagine I'll be working with him that closely. But the guy at the top always sets the tone . . . that was certainly my experience working with Barney. Let's drop it for now and you tell me about your day instead.' But in fact she was too tired to do more than give lip service.

'Sally called,' he remembered when they were getting ready for bed. 'Wants to know if you're interested in appearing on her programme. Hot-shot woman on Wall Street, that kind of thing.'

'Just what I don't need,' Caro grimaced. 'I plan to keep a low profile for a while, at least till I get my act together.'

She fell into bed bone-weary, but sleep wouldn't come. She

lay there, watching the clock unfold the minutes of the night, slicing away the time before she had to go back to 'that place'.

'Are you awake, Tom?' she tapped him gently.

'I am now. What's the matter? Can't you sleep?'

'Let's make love.' But when he touched her breast, she started and pulled back. 'Why you're nervous as a cat, poor baby. Now you just relax and leave everything to me. Doctor Feelgood at your service.'

He spread her legs gently and nestled his head between her thighs, yet even as his tongue entered her – now soothing now arousing – that tongue that had pleasured her so many times before, even now with Tom's love deep inside her, images of the day kept parading before her in a kind of instant replay. It was a long, sweated time before fulfilment came, and when it came it was all the sweeter.

'You're wonderful, Tom' – she kissed the lips that tasted of her body – 'I don't know what I would do without you. And I hate to think of that place as ruining our sex life.'

'It won't, honey.' He pulled up the covers and cuddled close. 'Just give it a chance. I think you were simply suffering from a case of first-night nerves. And if there's anything I can do to help you . . . in bed or out. . . .'

'Yeah,' she said, her mind tracking back relentlessly to the office. 'There is. Get me copies of *Business Week* and *Forbes* and the *Wall Street Journal*, only make sure they're dated a year from today. Barring that, how about the name of a good fortune-teller.'

A few days later, Tom gave her a crystal ball. The genuine article. When Thea heard about it, she sent over a companion piece – rather more modest but just as much to the point. It was a painted wooden eight ball, direct, she said, from the local pool hall, a sign that Caro was one of the boys.

Caro placed them side by side on her desk, where they became known as 'Harmsworth's balls'.

Barney Baker sent over a little something too.

It was a bottle of Pepto-Bismol.

'Call me Gusty,' the little woman pumped Tom's hand vigorously. 'Everyone does, even my daughter. Isn't that right,

Caro? You see, we've always had a very mature and independent relationship.'

Even at fifty, Gusty Harmsworth was a wonder. The flattest tummy under the tightest jeans. The sexy St Laurent shirt, top buttons left boldly undone. The silver jewellery that set off the weathered tan to perfection. And if the face was beginning to show faint traces of too many tropical suns, too many desert sandstorms, the eyes were as bright and blue as a baby's. 'Now, Tom, why don't you give me the grand tour of the apartment while Caro makes us margaritas. Not too much ice, honey . . . you know how I like it, and just a touch of rock salt around the rim.'

'I'll have the same,' Tom said.

Caro went into the kitchen with a smile of relief. They certainly seemed to be hitting it off, those two, if the snatches of conversations drifting in were any indication. 'New Guinea . . . absolutely marvellous! . . . oh, you know about the cargo cults then . . . wound up spending the night in an outrigger . . .' and then Tom's warm laughter.

He'd been apprehensive all week long. 'Are you sure your mother will like me? After all, here I am "living in sin", so to speak, with her only daughter. You really think she won't mind?'

'She won't mind,' Caro kept reassuring him. 'My mother is a very liberated woman.' Yet Tom's anxiety had been infectious and now she made a point of mixing the drinks slowly – two margaritas and her own scotch and water – giving the two of them a chance to get acquainted. '. . . what Carl Sagan is doing for astronomy . . .' she heard Tom say, heard Gusty's 'Mmmmm' of approval. She smiled. Tom was wooing her mother as he had wooed her a few months earlier, and she felt a warm glow, a basking in love, that the two people she cared for most in the world had taken so quickly to each other.

Tom popped in the kitchen to help her with the drinks. 'She's like a breath of fresh air,' he whispered. 'Absolutely charming.'

And Gusty had approved. Approved of the margaritas, of the apartment, of Caro's new job, of the sofa with reservations ('not a very practical colour, darling') and above all, approved of Tom. 'Now drink up,' she commanded, 'and I'm going to take you kids out to dinner. Ever eaten Albanian food, Tom?'

'No,' Tom was intrigued, for he considered himself something of a gourmet. 'I've had Greek, Armenian, Turkish . . . but nope, never Albanian.'

'Then you're in for a treat.'

Gusty knew a place. Wilds of Brooklyn. Absolute find. Owner a personal friend. None of your boring shish kebabs. Customers all Albanians. Need a car to get there. No car, Tom? Pity. Take a taxi instead. Get my coat, please. Waiting for you, Caro.

If the place was such a find, Caro reflected, why the hell was the cab driver having such a time trying to find it. The ride was interminable, down every back alley in Brooklyn, and Caro – wedged between Tom and Gusty – found herself in the middle of a verbal ping-pong match. Both Tom and her mother shared an enthusiasm for the natural world, an enthusiasm coupled with knowledge, and there was little she could contribute to the conversations that criss-crossed her. Gusty was indulging in a bout of name-dropping: naturalists, intellectuals, names for the most part meaningless to her, but apparently impressing Tom no end. She heard the name Levi-Strauss. Ah . . . now they were trespassing into her territory. 'Their stock has been doing very well lately,' Caro piped up. Gusty gave a short sharp laugh. 'Not Levi Strauss, the blue-jeans people, darling. I was talking about the French anthropologist.'

The 'find' was eventually found. It proved to be a dank crowded basement, decorated with outcroppings of plastic grapes. All else, however, appeared as authentic as Gusty had claimed. The waiters looked like bandits. The clientele – all-male – sported black, soup-laden moustaches, except for a couple of fair young men at a corner table. Caro presumed they were restaurant scouts for the *New York Times*. Gusty ordered with abandon. Cucumber soup. Raki. Little sausages spiced with anise. 'And for the main course . . .' Gusty held a hasty conference with the waiter, while Tom gave Caro a conspiratorial wink . . . 'Yes. Will you make that for three please.'

'What did you order?' Tom wanted to know. 'Aaah . . .' Gusty rubbed her hands in anticipation – 'a real Albanian delicacy, speciality of the house. Just you wait and see.'

The dish arrived hot and pungent, smothered in fresh herbs. Tom sniffed appreciatively. 'What are they . . . some kind of meatballs?' Gusty gave a whoop of laughter.

'They're lamb's testicles,' she said. 'Go ahead kids, dig in.'

'None for me please,' Caro covered her plate with her hand.

'Don't be silly, darling. It's just a mental prejudice.'

'I don't want any, Gusty.'

'Do me a favour and just try one before you say no.' Gusty speared a testicle and sliced it with surgical precision, then dangled the morsel on a fork in front of Caro. It looked moist and slimy. 'After all, how do you know you won't like it if you've never tried it?'

'I. Am. Not. Eating. Lamb's. Testicles.' Caro felt a swift surge of anger and waved the waiter over. 'Would you bring me a shish kebab, please?'

'Well, really, Caro,' Gusty sighed. 'We didn't traipse half-way across Brooklyn just to have shish kebab. Tom's enjoying his, aren't you Tom?' And in fact, Tom seemed to be downing them with gusto.

They were halfway through before her shish kebab arrived. It was tough and blood-raw – the chef's revenge, Caro suspected, for her intractability. The worst of it was that the goddam balls smelled delicious, but there was no back-tracking now and Caro swallowed her kebab with a great show of relish, washing it down with full tumblers of arak. Liquid fire.

Inevitably, the conversation turned to food. 'You must have eaten some pretty exotic stuff in your travels, Gusty.'

'Oh, I have, Tom. I have . . .' – and she began recounting feasts of monkey meat, locusts, duck-foot webbing. And then, of course, came the story of the sheep's eyeball, one of Gusty's favourite anecdotes. How she'd been invited to a state banquet by the Bey of Dahomey 'and there it was, all alone on the plate, same size as a golf ball. And the thing is, you're supposed to swallow it whole. What could I do? I was the guest of honour . . .' Caro poured herself another tumbler of arak while her mother went through the familiar paces. The kebabs were sitting in her stomach like an anchor. ' . . . passed through my system completely intact, as it happens. And when I went to flush the toilet, I nearly fainted. Imagine finding that staring up at you first thing in the morning! Now . . . what shall we have for dessert?'

After a while, Tom excused himself to go to the men's room. Caro wondered if he were perhaps disgorging himself of the speciality of the house. She herself was feeling very queasy. 'Well, Caro,' Gusty smiled. 'You really picked a winner this time . . . he's just delightful. Cultured. Intelligent,' – she leaned over and patted her daughter's hand – 'Just delightful. Lucky for you I didn't see him first.'

Inside, Caro was steaming. Why did her mother have to do this every time? Why this compulsion to grab the limelight, this need to prove herself the brightest, liveliest, youngest spirit in every gathering? Why did she have to be so goddam competitive? Caro was her daughter, for Chrissakes, not some rival photographer trying to beat her out of a big exclusive. It was as if, having climbed her way to the top, Gusty had lost the power of retracting her claws. Even after all these years, she was still striving for conquests, for petty triumphs. Had the woman no sense of dignity?

It was cheap and humiliating, and for one impulsive moment, Caro was tempted to walk out and simply leave the two of them behind. Yes, Tom too. For the worst of it was that he seemed enchanted, had roared at Gusty's tales and listened to her exploits with rapt attention.

But what would Caro's stalking out accomplish except to leave her mother in full possession of the field, chalking up yet another victory? There was no way she could win in a confrontation with Gusty – experience had shown that – and Caro would simply wind up looking the bigger fool.

So she didn't leave. She poured herself another arak. And then another.

The dessert arrived: a rich confection of honey and nuts and the cloying sweet coffee of the Balkans. The room was thick with the fumes of charcoal and cigarette smoke. She was going to be sick.

'Do you mind if we go now? I'm not feeling very well.'

'Of course, darling. Just as soon as I finish my coffee.'

And suddenly, Caro couldn't wait. Just bolted out of her chair and rushed up the steps, praying she'd make it out of there in time. When Tom caught up with her, she was leaning over the kerb, vomiting violently. 'Poor Caro,' he held his hand on her forehead. 'Poor, darling Caro' while she spewed up kebab and arak. When Gusty finally emerged, he explained 'Caro's had some kind of stomach bug lately.'

'I told her she shouldn't have had that kebab,' Gusty chirped. 'Me, I've got the constitution of an ox.'

Gusty dropped them off in a cab, and Tom helped her into bed. He was very sweet, as always very tender. By the time she was under the covers, she was feeling better. 'I'm sorry I ruined your evening Tom, and it was very nice of you to say it was my stomach. Fact is, I had too much to drink, that's all. By the way, how were the testicles?'

'Not bad,' Tom said, and then gave a low laugh. 'Actually they were pretty awful.'

'Well, I sure got the impression you enjoyed them,' Caro said with some surprise. 'You were wolfing 'em down like peanuts.'

'What else could I do?' Tom gave a good-natured laugh. 'I didn't want to disappoint your mother.'

In fact, Caro's stomach had been giving her a good deal of trouble lately, and the Pepto-Bismol bottle that Barney had sent as a joke had been replaced a dozen times over. She kept a bottle on permanent call in the bottom drawer of her desk.

The cramps usually started right after breakfast – and she'd tried everything: eating good breakfasts, light breakfasts, no breakfast at all. Yet inevitably, by the time she entered the lobby at PAGIT, her stomach was tied up in a granny knot. 'Maybe you've got an ulcer,' Tom said, 'or could be some kind of food allergy,' and insisted she see a doctor. The doctor gave her a clean bill of health.

But it was an allergy, as she knew perfectly well. She was allergic to 'that place'.

The job was proving onerous without offering the rewards that hard work usually brought, and each day confirmed her assessment that Catlett had earmarked her for all the bottom-of-the-barrel projects. She was on the road constantly, and every business she scouted seemed to be located a hard hour's drive from a tenth-rate airport.

The American backwoods were teeming with wild-eyed inventors and impractical idealists, with 'me too' companies hoping to ride the crest of someone else's innovations, with ailing manufacturers on the edge of bankruptcy – all of them desperate for capital, all of them losers.

Caro approached each with an open mind, appraised their proposals thoroughly and honestly, then returned to work up her report. Her summations were, in fact, models of clarity and business acumen and, if nothing else, at least earned her the grudging respect of her colleagues. All, that is, but Catlett.

Reports didn't impress him. Results did – for he was, as he said repeatedly, only interested in the 'bottom line'. And bottom line, there was nothing of value in her files, nor could there be from the leads she'd been given. It was a vicious circle.

She had guessed correctly that she would not be seeing much of Catlett on a day-to-day basis. Nor, despite his threat, did he address her simply by her surname, but always with scrupulous formality as 'Miss Harmsworth' – presumably having checked out her marital status from the records. The other men were more informal; they called her Caro. There were, she noticed, certain intricacies of nomenclature. Men were referred to on a last-name basis when they were absent, on a first-name basis when present. 'Where's Healy? Oh, there you are, Jim.' She wondered if she were ever referred to as 'Harmsworth'. 'Harmsworth's looking into that matter.' She hoped so, for it would have been an admission that she was part of the team.

For the first time since B School, she felt herself at a disadvantage. The pressure was always on to dig up new investments, operate on every conceivable front. The liveliest opportunities did indeed come, as Catlett had foreseen, from connections in the old boy network. 'This fellow I roomed with at Deerfield is starting up a gene-splicing outfit,' she would hear. Or 'I was playing squash with this guy at the Downtown Athletic Club who . . .'

There was no equivalent old girl network. And if the men were moderately friendly to her, they were friendly to each other in different ways. In spite of all their intense competitiveness, the perpetual vying for available monies, they were remarkably cohesive, always forming and re-forming into tight little groups based on work or some other criteria. They laughed a lot, and meetings were often punctuated by little 'in-jokes' that smacked of the locker room. She noticed, too, that they were very tactile with each other, constantly touching: the hand on the sleeve, the pat on the back, the slap on the knee – but there was nothing sexual about it. It was unconscious. She alone was excluded from this easy contact, and she wondered if her presence made them self-conscious, if they were afraid she might translate a friendly pat as somehow sexist or provocative.

She mentioned their behaviour to Tom one night, and he spotted the pattern at once. 'Men and their games,' he said. 'I think it's left over from all those contact sports we used to play when we were boys. Maybe girls don't play in quite the same way. Myself, I find it all pretty macho, that clubhouse atmosphere. In fact, the whole jockstrap world turns me off. I suppose it's why I prefer tennis to baseball.'

She thought back to the day they met on the courts. 'Well, I'm awfully glad you do,' she smiled.

But Tom's appraisal was right on the button. It was, she recognized 'men and their games' that pervaded the office. And the biggest game of all was 'close to Dan'.

That was her name for it anyhow. It consisted of a subtle courting, a quiet jockeying for position to see who could get in closest to the one man who was the ultimate source of power and favour. That Catlett was aware of this jockeying, Caro never doubted, for nothing escaped those radar-screen eyes. Yet he seemed to accept it as his due, actually encouraged it in all its trivial manifestations.

He had a characteristic style of dress – black pinstripe suits and white shirts with French cuffs. She came to think of it as his uniform. Within a month most of the men had adopted it. Ed Griffin had gone one better. He must have smoked out Catlett's tailor, for he turned up one crisp November morning sporting an exact duplicate of the boss's distinctive velvet-collared overcoat. Caro was curious how the great man would react to this blatant form of imitation, but Catlett's reaction was a wry smile and a pat on the shoulder. 'You're looking good, Ed.'

The grand prize in the 'close to Dan' sweepstakes was having the man himself sit next to you at meetings. The full-staff assemblies in the conference room were set pieces, like formal dinner parties; the more usual instrument of business was a small working-party meeting in his private office. The men would cruise around and pick their spots carefully on either of the long white sofas, for the office was furnished in opulent contrast to the spartan arrangements of the bullpen. They always left the place next to them vacant. Once everyone else was seated, Catlett would amble across the soft Kerman carpet, pause briefly and ultimately settle down next to whoever had the hottest projects going. He never sat next to Caro.

At first in keeping with her low-profile tactics, Caro made a point of never being either first or last into his office, of never appearing either to pander or to push. She had needed a breathing space, a chance to reconnoitre the new terrain and gain confidence. But now she had it. She knew herself to be the equal of the men, capable of handling any project.

Perhaps, to give Catlett the benefit of the doubt, he had loaded her with dead-end assignments, not out of sexism or antipathy, but simply because he doubted her ability. If so, he had had a chance to take her measure and grade the quality of her judgments. Surely, the time had come for him to put some meat on her plate.

Accordingly, she decided to turn up early for the next meeting and at the first tactful opening state her case.

He was at his desk when she came in and for a moment looked uncertain whether he should rise or not. But he remained seated and motioned her into a chair. For a long minute neither of them said a word, and then he broke the silence.

'Are you interested in porcelain, Miss Harmsworth?'

It was just the opening she'd been waiting for. Maybe there was a china factory he wanted her to look into for him, or some retail outlet ripe for investment. She sniffed something substantial in the air. The smart thing was to show enthusiasm.

'I'm very much interested in porcelain, Mr Catlett.'

'Really!' Her response had pleased him. He opened a small fitted box that was resting on his desk top and withdrew a little Chinese vase. 'Then you should be interested in this. It's a beauty, isn't it?' he purred. 'I got it at Parke-Bernet this morning.' He swivelled around and held it up against the light, rotating it slowly in all directions.

'Peachbloom. K'ang Hsi period,' he was aglow with the joy of acquisition. 'Absolutely flawless, isn't it?'

It was breathtakingly beautiful and Caro could just picture it on the end table in her living room. That, however, was hardly the point, nor was it the conversational opening she had sought. Determined to bring the conversation back on the track – after all, he was first and foremost a businessman – she said 'Porcelain is an excellent long-range investment. I've always considered it a good inflation hedge.'

He turned and stared at her with undisguised contempt, then carefully replaced the vase in its box. 'Is that what they teach you at Harvard Business School?' he said finally. He didn't speak to her the rest of the day.

'Oh shit,' Caro came home seething. 'Every time I open my mouth with that bastard, I put my foot right into it. Why doesn't he just can me and get it over with? That's what the motherfucker really wants.'

'Jesus, Caro!' Tom looked worried. 'I hope you don't use language like that in the office.'

'No,' – she felt very depressed by the incident. 'I'm the original Goodie-Two-Shoes up there. Maybe that's been my mistake all along. Oh what the hell. Let's forget it.'

But the incident rankled, and in the days that followed, Catlett became – if possible – even more aloof. She was convinced he sneered at her privately – she felt it in her bones – but his public manner remained unbendingly correct. Indeed his control only fed her resentment, and the situation was becoming intolerable.

She stopped in one morning to visit an employment agency, but the only jobs the interviewer could offer would mean a whopping cut in salary. 'Times are tough,' he told her. 'A lot of companies are laying off.' So in the end, she decided to stay put, bowing to the wisdom of Tom's counsel that she grin and bear it, at least for the time being.

And for the time being, money was pouring out at an alarming rate. Furnishing the apartment had eaten up a lot of their capital and now with Christmas just around the corner, they needed every penny of their combined salaries. True, they had solemnly promised not to buy each other Christmas presents – it seemed the prudent thing to do – but Caro was certain Tom hadn't kept his pledge. And she for one had no intention of keeping hers. The brightest spot of her day were the lunch hours she spent scouting around for the ideal gift. She finally struck paydirt at a Second Avenue bookdealers. It was an early edition, each plate lovingly hand-tinted, of Audubon's *Birds of America*. It weighed a ton, cost a fortune – the most beautiful folio imaginable. Caro made a special trip home at midday just to stash it away at the bottom of her underwear drawer. And every morning when she reached inside, she would feel its bulk beneath the softness of her lingerie. It was all she could do to smother a smile. How happy it would make him – dear, sweet Tom – on their very first Christmas together.

A couple of days before the holiday, she was at her desk when Tony Marcusson ambled over. He looked awful.

'Hey Caro,' he asked. 'Do you have any of that stuff you're always taking for your stomach?' She pulled out the bottle of Pepto-Bismol. 'Be my guest.' He poured some into a plastic cup, then swallowed it in one gulp. 'Christ, my mouth feels like the bottom of a birdcage this morning.'

'Must have been some party, Tony, by the looks of it – that is, if I'm any judge of hangovers.'

'Yeah . . . well you should have seen the other guys.'

The other guys. Something clicked. Where the hell were the other guys this morning? She scanned the bullpen. It was deserted except for Bill Jennings with his head buried deep in the *Wall Street Journal*. Bill looked pretty hungover, too.

'The other guys,' Caro murmured, 'speaking of whom. . . .'

'Well, thanks for the Pepto-Bismol . . .' Tony started heading back to his desk.

'Wait a minute!' – Caro clapped a hand on his arm. 'Not so fast, my friend. What the hell was everybody doing last night?'

Tony looked suddenly wary. 'Nothing much . . . just a few of the boys . . . a little Yuletide jollity.'

'Looks to me like it was all of the boys considering the mortality rate. What was it, Tony? The office Christmas party?'

'Nothing like that . . . just . . . uh, Catlett took the guys out for a blast. He always does. It's a sort of Christmas tradition with him. Look, Caro' – he saw the direction in which she was heading, and didn't like it. 'I wouldn't make an issue of it if I were you. It was just a stag evening with too much booze. You wouldn't have enjoyed it anyhow.'

'Just tell me one thing, Tony' – she released his arm – 'Was everybody there except me?' She looked at his face. 'No, you don't have to answer. I wouldn't want you to incriminate yourself.'

She stewed at her desk for the next ten minutes, all the anger, the injustices, the petty neglects of the last months welling up inside her till it could no longer be borne. *She* was one of the staff, goddam it! *She* worked here. *She* had equal standing with every one of those men. How dare he! How dare Catlett add this deliberate insult to all the snubs she'd already endured.

She kicked her desk drawer shut with a bang and stormed into his sanctum, sweeping past the astonished Miss Gibbs. He was lounging behind his desk eating pistachio nuts out of a brown paper bag.

'I want to talk to you . . .'

He looked up bleary eyed. 'Oh, it's you. Sit down. You want some pistachio nuts?' He pushed the bag across the desk toward her. 'They're nice and fresh. I get 'em at a special place in the Village.'

'No, I don't want any pistachio nuts. . . .' her voice turned shrill.

'Do you mind lowering the volume, Miss Harmsworth. I have a bit of a headache this morning.'

'Well you'll have more of a headache when I'm finished saying my piece' – she went up an octave – 'I want to know why I was deliberately excluded from the office party last night. I happen to work here too, remember?'

He suddenly shot up ramrod-straight, his face taut and haggard in the thin December light. 'Of all the goddam nonsense. . . . However, since you seem to feel I owe you an explanation, let me tell you that it was an all-male party. . . .'

'Correction,' she interrupted. 'It was an all-staff party!'

'. . . An all-male party,' he droned on, 'at the Metropolitan Club which happens to be an all-male club, and if it's any comfort to you' – he nodded in the direction of the outer office – 'I didn't invite my girl either.'

That did it. ' "My girl!" ' Caro snorted. 'By that, I imagine you mean Miss Gibbs. Well, how patronizing can you get! But that's not the point. The point is, Miss Gibbs is only a secretary here and I'm a member of the management staff.'

'Oh, aren't we the little snob,' he mocked. 'Too grand to hobnob with secretaries.'

'And aren't we the chauvinist pig,' she shot back. 'Well, I am sick and tired of being discriminated against. There are laws in this country against that sort of thing.' He tensed like a cobra ready to strike, his knuckles bone-white with rage. 'Listen, Harmsworth,' – he hissed – 'Don't you presume to tell me how I may or may not spend my private time. You come barging into this office with some paranoid nonsense that is frankly none of your business. My personal life is just that – *personal*, and believe me, I couldn't care less about yours. But if you think you've got the makings of a lawsuit, go right ahead. Call in one of your loud-mouthed women's lib lawyers and bring me up on charges. Well, I'm a pretty good lawyer myself and I'll tell you one thing – any judge will laugh you out of court. And I'll tell you another thing while I'm about it' – he lit a cigarette in an effort to keep control, but his hands were trembling with pent-up fury – 'My "Miss Gibbs" as you insist I call her, has been with me for over ten years, and I value her services a helluva lot more than I do yours. You have produced less than any other person in this office, male or female, while earning a very considerable salary. However – if you're so hard up that a free meal means all that much to you, allow me to make amends.' He fumbled in his coat pocket and pulled out a bill. 'Here!' He flicked it toward her 'Here's a hundred dollars. Now go buy yourself a dinner and we're even.'

'You bastard!' She snatched the bill, tears of rage welling in her eyes. Then she grabbed his lighter with her other hand. 'Here's what you can do with your rotten money!' She held the money high above his head and set it alight. It flared up briefly, then plummeted down in a column of flame. It was burning still when it landed on the desk and Catlett jumped up to blow out the last of the sparks. One hundred dollars worth of fine white ash scattered over the dark of his suit. For once in his life he didn't look immaculate. He looked shocked. But Caro didn't wait around to find out if it was the depth of her rage or the mindless destruction of money that had left him so stunned. She turned on her heels and fled.

'Well, that's that,' she told Tom when he got home. 'Guess I'll be signing up for unemployment.'

He was nonplussed. 'For Chrissakes, what got into you, Caro? I don't mean just the bit about the money. . . I mean, the whole scene. What a damnfool thing to make an issue about – being left out of a stag party. You should be thankful.'

'Who's side are you on anyhow, Tom?' she asked resentfully. She had replayed the scene a hundred times in her head that afternoon, yet deep down there was the nagging suspicion that Tom was probably right.

'I'm on your side, honey. You know that. And I've no doubt the guy is a prick. It's just . . . you picked one helluva time to make a grandstand gesture, when we're up to our eyeballs in bills. Are you absolutely sure he's going to fire you?'

'What else can he do? I acted like a crazy. So there you are . . . fifty grand a year right out the window, to say nothing of the extra hundred bucks. Just hope this story doesn't get around the Street. I could wind up on some kind of blacklist. Professional Troublemaker. Handle with Caution. Well, Tom' – she made a feeble joke – 'it looks like you're going to have to support me.' But poor Tom looked so wretched, she almost had to laugh. 'Oh come on, love, I was only kidding. Something will turn up.'

Something did turn up within the hour – a special messenger with a package for her. She looked at the return address and made a face. 'That's it,' she said tearing open the wrapper. 'I bet he's sent my stuff home from the office.'

But inside was a spray of white orchids, some variety she had never seen, and a hand-written note on creamy bond paper.

'Dear Miss Harmsworth,' she read. 'Please accept my sincere apologies. My behaviour was boorish in the extreme. May I, however, plead extenuating circumstances – too much liquor and too little sleep. Merry Christmas. D. R. Catlett.'

She and Tom discussed this latest turn of events. Had she scared him by threatening to bring suit? Or was this the cue for Caro herself to apologize? If so, she didn't think she could bring herself to do it. They finally agreed that the most tactful response would be for Caro to wear the flowers to the office next day, like a white flag of truce. She did. But Catlett wasn't there to see them. Instead, she would wear them the next day, when she went out to meet Tom's family.

The din was terrific. 'Cast of thousands,' Tom had warned her, 'inlaws, outlaws, the whole catastrophe.' In fact, there were hardly over twenty, not counting the grandchildren who were mercifully being given a separate table in the sunroom. Not counting the ancient labrador retriever who kept getting underfoot. 'A genuine gathering of the clan,' Grace Darius counted heads, then wrung her plump little hands with pleasure.

'This is my brother Michael, honey' – Tom guided her from group to group '. . . my sister-in-law. I'd like you to meet my grandmother, Mrs Fenner. Grannie, this is Caro' – he shouted into the ear of a fragile old lady who nodded with gleeful incomprehension – 'my favourite Aunt Jennie . . . Uncle Max . . . you met my brother Paul in New York. . .'

There was much shaking of hands and exchanging of kisses, much honing of knives, clattering of silver, much parading of sisters and aunts and, indeed, all female hands in and out of the kitchen. 'Can I do anything to help?' Caro asked at one point. 'Oh no, dear, you're a guest.'

And guest she was. The sole outsider. Here to be inspected, wondered over and, for all she knew, judged. She'd promised in advance to limit herself to two drinks precisely (there would be no repeat of the Albanian restaurant fiasco), but her precautions proved unnecessary. For nursing the one drink granted her by Everett Darius – a very weak scotch-and-soda – she realized that the excesses of the household ran, not to alcohol, but to furnishings and the consumption of food.

'I made everything myself,' Grace Darius boasted. 'Three kinds of pies, all the relishes. Here, take a taste of this. It's Ev's favourite.' Caro dutifully licked a spoon and murmured 'Mmmm . . . delicious.'

'That's my Pennsylvania apple butter. I'll send you the recipe and then you can make it for Tom.'

The long table was filling up – baked ham, roast goose, three kinds of potatoes, sauceboats, side dishes, the traditional seven sweet and sour relishes. Silver platters piled high with baking-powder biscuits. But the main course in this banquet, the *pièce de resistance*, had got to be Miss Caroline Harmsworth. For despite the conventional courtesies, Tom's parents were eaten up with curiosity and at a loss to define their son's new relationship.

'How shall I introduce her to people?' Mrs Darius whispered in an anxious aside. 'She has a name, mother,' Tom answered patiently.

Of course the business of introductions had come up before. Among close friends, there was no need for explanations. 'This is Tom . . . This is Caro. We're living together.' But not all situations were so easily dealt with, and the question bothered Tom, particularly. 'What should I call you?' – he reviewed the possibilities. 'My girlfriend? Too juvenile. My roomate? Too absurd. My lover? Too intimate? My mistress? Too *too*!' And for lack of a word that summed up their relationship, he fell to saying 'This is "Caro"' – with unspoken quotes around her name, in the hope that the slight pause, the faint emphasis would say all.

His parents knew that Tom was living with someone, for Mrs Darius would call up once or twice a week. As a rule, Caro avoided answering the phone when she suspected family business, and on the few occasions when she did pick it up to hear Mrs Darius' hesitant 'Is Tom there?', she handed him the receiver like a hot potato.

But today Grace Darius was not a voice on the other end of a telephone. She was a face. They all had faces. And seated at the Darius family table, eating their food, Caro felt a flush of embarrassment. They were conventional people, Tom's parents, and their youngest son was the apple of their eye. Who was 'this woman our Tom is living with'? It was the unspoken question behind every civility.

'My son tells me you're on Wall Street,' Dr Darius said.

'That's right,' Caro grasped at the straw and began chatting cheerfully about the state of the market.

'And your father, Caro?' came the relentless follow-up. 'What does he do?'

'I never met my father,' she answered unthinkingly, then turned a flustered crimson. What a crude, rude answer to give a family gathering. But what could she say? *My mother dumped my father before I was born and I wouldn't know the man if I stepped on him?* Everyone was watching, listening. They must have thought her illegitimate at worst, or at the very least boorish and Bohemian. Poor Tom! He was probably undergoing enough flak already! This he didn't need.

'What I mean is,' she began improvising wildly, 'that I never knew my father. He died shortly before I was born.'

'He must have been a very young man,' Dr Darius said. 'What did he die of . . . heart?'

And Caro, hoping to forestall further questions – they might think she'd inherited a congenital disease – replied 'He was shot down over Korea.'

There was a murmur of compassion.

'Your poor mother,' Mrs Darius said in a lugubrious tone. 'I hope she remarried.' At which point Tom jumped in. 'Caro's mother is Augusta Harmsworth. She does those documentaries on TV.'

'So that's your mother.' Mrs Darius was impressed. 'Why I heard her lecture last year. I think it was something about cannibals. She was wonderful.'

'That's my mother.'

Dinner over, Dr Darius drew Caro into his study – 'something I'd like you to see' – and when she emerged, she was grinning. More guests arrived. Neighbours. Cousins. Still more cousins. From across the room thick with smoke and noise, she could see Tom mouthing a desperate 'Hey, Jane!' She knew her cue. 'Do you mind,' she asked her hostess, 'if I sneak out for a little walk? Have to work off some of those calories.'

'I'll go with you,' Tom leapt up. 'It's suffocating in here.'
Suffocating.

As they walked down the drive, ice crunching beneath their

feet, Tom kept filling his lungs with great gulps of air. 'Suffocating.' He stopped and kissed Caro in the moonlight. 'Thanks for rescuing me. And how are you holding up, sweetie?'

'Me? Oh just fine, Tom. They're really awfully nice people, very friendly, though God knows what they made of me. That dumb remark about my war-hero father.'

'Fast thinking,' Tom said. 'And speaking of fathers, what did my old man want of you? That little pow-wow in his study, I mean.'

'Oh that,' Caro laughed. 'I thought he was going to show me your baby pictures, something like that, but all he wanted was my opinion of his stock portfolio.'

'Well, you got off light.'

His Aunt Jennie had cornered him first. 'Your mother is very upset about this, Tom.' She tapped his chest with a judgmental finger.

'What's she upset about? Caro's a terrific girl.'

'You know what I mean, Tom. They've always been so proud of you.'

'Come on, Jen. We're not living in the Middle Ages.'

His mother had been a bit more circuitous. 'She's a very nice girl, Tom . . . the sweetest smile. . .' and then had rambled on for some minutes about Caro's sweetness. Eventually, she came back to Square One. 'The problem is, Tom, I find this all very embarrassing. Everyone keeps asking about you – what you're doing, where you're living, and what am I supposed to tell them? Can I at least say that you're engaged?'

'But we're not engaged, mother. Caro and I have no plans to get married and that's that.'

'I don't understand you young people,' she sighed.

His father's attitude was summed up in a single drawn-out word.

'Soooo. . . ?'

'So what, dad?'

'Soooo . . . what's it going to be, Tom? You going to marry the girl?' And when Tom shook his head, Dr Darius frowned. 'I'm not happy about this at all, Tom – and neither is your mother. How do you think we feel knowing our son is shacking up with some girl in Manhattan.'

'Shacking up!' Tom bristled. 'That's a vulgar way of putting it. You make it sound as if Caro were some kind of tramp.'

'If she were, there'd be no problem. I'd put it down to wild oats, although I think twenty-eight's a bit old for that sort of thing. But she is a nice girl, I can see that. A nice girl with a respectable job and I don't like the way you're treating her.'

'I treat Caro very well,' Tom huffed. 'And she treats me very well too. We love each other, we respect each other, and we're perfectly happy just as we are. So don't try to drag us to the altar. Times have changed, Dad. Things are different these days.'

'Some things never change,' his father retorted.

'So that's what I've been going through all day long.' Tom seated himself on the garden bench and lit a cigarette. For the past month he'd been trying to give up smoking, but today had been a strain. 'I don't know. Maybe it would take some of the pressure off if I said we were engaged. What do you think, honey?'

'I'm not going to marry you just to please your parents, Tom.'

'Who said anything about marriage?'

'Well, one thing leads to another.' For an uneasy moment, Caro wondered if that wasn't what he really wanted. To plunk her down in the suburbs. To have her in the kitchen making the seven sweets and sours. God knows, he liked his creature comforts. 'And I am certainly not about to do the suburban housewife number.'

'For Chrissakes, Caro. That's the last thing in the world I want. Look at them,' he turned his head back toward the house. 'You know, my mother won't wipe her nose until she's checked it out with the old man. It's Ev this and Ev that. Ev doesn't like carrots in his vegetable soup. Ev thinks Reagan will make a wonderful president. She quotes him like he was God, no mind of her own. Lord knows how he stands it, her leaning on him all the time.' He ground his cigarette out in the snow. 'Come on, honey. I guess we better go back and face the music before they send out a search party.'

They were staying overnight. Tom's mother put them up in separate bedrooms and for the first time in months, they slept apart. Clearly, hanky-panky might be tolerated in mid-Manhattan, but there was to be no shacking up in Morristown.

7

Now that the storm with Catlett had blown over, the situation snapped back to *status quo ante*. Caro did her work, drew her pay and, to show that there were no hard feelings (which of course there were) managed a perfunctory smile when Catlett made his royal progress through the bullpen. Occasionally she was rewarded with the faintest of nods. In short, nothing had changed. The work remained unfulfilling, the environment remained resolutely clubhouse, and her sole consolation was the time she spent with Tom.

Whenever she could, she'd pick up Tom at his office, hang around for a bit (the place had a casual, homey atmosphere) and then they'd go out for drinks and dinner. For in spite of all their good intentions of cooking in and saving money, they were neither of them domestic, and New York was a goldmine of good restaurants. Tom loved food. He had a knack of discovering good eating places, and each discovery was ample cause for calling up half a dozen people and making a night of it. His circle of friends was immense – far larger than hers, and when they were home the phone never stopped ringing. There was always somebody organizing a theatre party here, a piano bar there, a ski weekend in Vermont. 'I never see you alone,' she complained tongue-in-cheek, and to her surprise, he took the comment seriously.

They talked it out and decided that after that they would take each Sunday off and spend it exclusively with and on each other. Invariably it proved to be the best day of the week. They'd take the phone off the hook first thing Sunday morning and spend most of the day making love, and picnicking from the bedside table. After a while, they began preparing for their 'love feasts' as Tom called them, sometimes days in advance. Tom would scour the gourmet food shops for delicacies – quail's eggs, almond-stuffed olives, Concord grapes, chocolate truffles – anything that didn't leave crumbs. He came home one day with a supply of pot and a copy of the Kama Sutra. That had been a Sunday. One week, Caro popped into Bendel's and bought a black lace negligée that might have come from a Jean Harlow movie. 'Don't ever put that on for anyone but me,' Tom said when he saw it. They experimented a couple of times with a vibrator, then forgot about it, for they were sufficient to each other.

Ultimately those Sundays became a ritual, and Caro shifted her pill-taking schedule, changing her menstrual cycle so it was always over by 'the day'. Tom was a sensual man, she was a sensual woman, and there was nothing they could not ask each other.

Yet every now and then, she would find herself pulling back, emotionally if not sexually, stopping just short of surrender. For love him though she did, she was still dogged by the fear that their lives might become so thoroughly entwined, so hopelessly enmeshed that they would lose something of themselves along the way. She tried explaining this to Tom one evening, and to her relief he understood. 'We're two separate people,' he said, 'and I wouldn't want you to lose your sense of self. I don't want to take over your life, Caro.'

'Nor I yours, Tom.'

So, just as they had their Sundays together, they had their Tuesdays apart. It was the one night they didn't see each other; and though the understanding was implicit that they might follow their own fancies on that evening – and no questions asked – in fact the Tuesdays fell into a kind of routine. Tom played squash or attended a lecture. Caro went to a meeting of her group.

W.E.B. was a newly-formed national organization dedicated to furthering the goals of professional women. The initials stood for Women Executives in Business. The original acronym was W.E.I.B., until someone pointed out that *weib* was the German word for wife, and therefore hardly consonant with the urbane professionalism of its members. Among the women in Caro's branch were two lawyers, an insurance broker, several of Sally

Klein's colleagues from the media, a management consultant, an industrial psychologist – in short, a cross-section of women who, like Caro, were moving into levels that had been until recently the exclusive domain of men.

W.E.B. was not, its members insisted, a bitching session; nor even a Consciousness Raising Group of the genre endorsed by feminist magazines. It was simply an informal gathering of achieving women who met to iron out problems common to all. Problems of prejudice, of stress, of legal rights and moral wrongs, of dealing with men both in and out of the office. That much of the discussion should focus on men was inevitable; and when one member complained that the subject was occupying far too much of their time, she was reprimanded with the words: you can't be a fish and not talk about the water.

On the whole the meetings were useful, and on this particular Tuesday, Caro asked to take the floor. 'I have a continuing problem at the office and I'm looking for advice.' She laid out the situation – the whole sorry story from the first catastrophic meeting to the pre-Christmas confrontation to the uneasy truce now reigning. 'What would you do?' she asked.

'I'd flirt a bit,' said the insurance broker. 'I say, use what you've got.'

'Oh no,' Caro groaned. 'That begs the question, besides which he's a married man.'

'If it were me, I'd quit,' said Linda Ashfield, 'and then write a letter to *The Times*.' But this advice was greeted with a chorus of Nos. 'Why should she let the bastard drive her out? That's what he's hoping for. If I were you, Caro, I'd sue.'

'No no, I wouldn't do that,' Felicia Haines interrupted. She was a deep-voiced Texan who headed one of the city's hottest law firms and specialized in civil rights. 'Litigation usually raises more problems than it solves. Besides, there's no case here . . . unless, of course, you're being sexually harassed.'

'Harassed!' Caro rolled her eyes. 'No one there has ever laid a finger on me.'

'Well, I'd call that a form of sexual harassment,' Sally laughed. 'But seriously . . . I think what you ought to do is go in there and come on strong, with a tape recorder hidden in your bag. Then maybe you can get some of that shit down on record.'

'No way,' Caro protested. 'No way I'm going to make another scene. I just want to do my job, that's all.'

She wound up with as many pieces of advice as there were women present, but none of it particularly apt. In the end she decided the most practical solution was simply to invite Catlett to lunch. He couldn't put her off forever and it would provide, she felt, the easiest circumstance for her to state her case. But before making any overtures, she sounded out Tony Marcusson for he, more than any other man in the office, was 'close to Dan'. They'd worked together over a number of years, and she felt Tony could offer some insights.

'What do you think, Tony . . . is it a good idea?'

'Oh yeah . . . he'll probably be delighted that you got him off the hook. I think this whole thing bothers him, you know. He doesn't like dissension in the group.'

'Any tips on the best way to handle him?'

'Well, I wouldn't suggest drinks at the Metropolitan Club,' Tony laughed. 'But if you really want a piece of advice, Caro – keep it low-key. Dan's a very conservative guy in a lot of ways – not in business, but in his personal approach. Manners mean a lot to him. So if he wants to be the Southern gentleman and open a car door for you or pull out a chair' – Caro winced – 'don't make a fuss. Just let him.'

'In other words, I should play the lady.'

'In other words, you should play it smart.'

She poked her head into Catlett's office later that afternoon and he said yes, he'd be free for lunch on Thursday. 'Only allow me to take you.' He smiled with no trace of irony. 'I believe I owe you a meal. Do you like wild duck, by the way?'

'What should I wear, Tom?' she asked on Wednesday night.

'How about that lace negligée? That ought to bring him around.'

'Seriously. . .'

'Seriously . . . this guy must really scare you, hon. You're as jumpy as an actress before an audition. Funny thing is, I know exactly how you feel. You see, I've been there myself. When I was at Harvard there was a biology professor, a real heavyweight . . . they used to talk him up for the Nobel Prize.

And he was merciless with the students, a real son of a bitch. Well, every time I had to speak in his class, I used to freeze. I mean who was I to tell him about biology. In my mind he was ten feet tall. Then one day he was up there lecturing and I noticed that his fly was open. And it struck me – he's just a man after all. He gets up in the morning, he pulls on his pants, just like me. Then I started picturing what he'd look like in his underwear, drinking beer out of a can and maybe watching the Saturday Night fights on TV. I figured he had knobbly knees. And once I'd built up that picture, I couldn't feel scared any more. Fear is like sex, you know. It's all in the head.'

Chez George reeked of money. From the brass fittings to the mahogany panels to the fresh carnations in crystal bowls, it was more of a private dining room than a restaurant. The menu contained no mention of prices. Nor of wild duck either, for that matter.

'I would recommend the salmon mousse,' Catlett said, and Caro who would have preferred the *paté aux truffes*, smiled and nodded. Let the man have his way. 'And then,' he conferred with the waiter, 'we'll have the duck. Do you have any of that white asparagus in yet? And have George send up some of that nice *Montrachet*. He'll know which one. Well, Miss Harmsworth,' he turned to her, 'here we are.' It was, she recognized, her cue to begin but she waited till the wine had arrived, making small talk in the interim, before launching into her piece.

'I'm awfully glad,' she said lifting her glass, 'we're having this opportunity to talk and smooth things over. I'm afraid you and I got off on the wrong foot somewhere along the line.'

'Correction,' he said softly. 'You got off on the wrong foot from the very moment you arrived. That first day in the conference room . . . I remember it precisely. You were wearing a beige wool dress with some kind of silver doodad at the neck. Oh yes, it was a little silver butterfly. . .' (Oh God! she quailed. The man has total recall.) 'We shook hands, I remember, and then I went to do what any gentleman would have done in the circumstances, I went to pull out a chair for you and you acted as though I'd bitten your head off.'

'I'm sorry. Perhaps I was rude and I hope you'll accept my apology, but I was also a little bit nervous and besides' – she felt she should take the bull by the horns – 'you gave me the impression that you didn't like working with women. May I ask if that is the case?'

He averted his gaze and began muttering into his wine-glass. The voice, always soft, was now inaudible; although she could make out the occasional word – *women, constitution, law-abiding* – she couldn't make out the gist. And then it struck her: the obfuscation was deliberate.

'For heaven's sake, Mr Catlett. Do you think I have a tape recorder planted on me somewhere?'

He looked up sharply. 'The thought had crossed my mind.'

'I don't. Scout's honour, I don't.' The absurdity of the situation hit her and she burst out laughing. 'Would you like to look in my bag? Should I take off my jacket?'

'Oh no, no, no,' he protested, clearly relieved. 'I take your word for it. I regret having harboured such suspicions and I'm delighted they weren't justified. I trust we can talk openly from here on out. You have a very good smile, by the way, Miss Harmsworth. You should use it more often.' It was an appraisal, not a compliment. But she used the smile and repeated her question.

'Before I answer that,' he said cautiously, 'let me ask you if *you're* not the one with the prejudice?'

'*Me*?' – she was astonished. 'I'm used to working with men.'

'I meant, perhaps you have a prejudice against Southerners. I've come up against it time and again in this city. You Yankees all seem to think that everyone born south of the Mason Dixon line is a figure of fun. We eat hominy grits and have silly accents and dress up every night in white sheets.'

'But . . . but . . .' she protested. And then stopped just short of falling into his trap. For it was a trap, she recognized. She'd seen him pull it at meetings when someone wanted something of him that he was not prepared to grant. The sudden about-face, the swift counterattack guaranteed to catch his opposite number off balance. He had a knack for putting people on the defensive. Well, she, for one, saw right through it.

'I'm afraid you're mistaken,' she kept her voice assiduously neutral. 'I'm not a Yankee. I was raised abroad. In fact, I never set foot in this country until I was sixteen.' *Score one for Caro*.

'Really?' he shifted ground, seamlessly. 'Your father with one of the multinational corporations?'

'My mother is Augusta Harmsworth,' she said with dignity, and when she saw that the name didn't register, she added 'the film-maker.'

She gave a quick resume of Gusty's grand career, but his attention was wandering. Surreptitiously, he was watching a woman in a green dress eating oysters a few tables away. The woman was very pretty, very feminine. Caro wound up swiftly. 'Well,' he dragged his gaze back reluctantly, 'I'm afraid I don't know one movie actress from another, although I enjoy a good Western now and then.' *Score one for Catlett*.

'You never did answer my question, Mr Catlett' – she was determined to pin him down. 'As I say, I have the impression you don't like women. . .'

'I adore women.'

'I mean in business. But perhaps that's just because you don't know many. I presume your wife is not a career woman.'

He cleared his throat. 'My ex-wife.' And with a jolt, Caro realized he was no longer wearing a wedding band. 'My *ex*-wife, as it happens, is very much a career woman. She's senior vice president and chief of litigation at Zeelon Copper. And when Zeelon moved its headquarters to Arizona last fall, Madeleine went with them. Apparently she preferred her company's company to mine.'

'I'm sorry,' Caro apologized. She had not expected a personal revelation.

'So am I,' he said softly, 'although that's neither here nor there.' For the first time that day, he looked straight into her eyes, and his own eyes were puzzled.

'I don't understand you women any more, Caroline. You don't mind if I call you Caroline?' – he pronounced it with a long *i*. In honour of his native state? she wondered. ' . . . and I hope you'll call me Dan. No, I don't understand why you want to compete with men all the time. Why you're so compelled to storm the ramparts. What is it you women want? Can you tell me?'

It was the moment she'd come prepared for. 'We want the same things men want, Mr Ca. . . I mean, Dan. The freedom to choose what we do with our lives, to express ourselves in work. Just equal opportunity. We don't ask to be treated differently from anyone else. We simply want to be judged on our merits. When I came to the Fund that first day and you went to fetch me a chair, I felt I was being singled out and marked for special treatment. I don't want that. I'm willing to forego the traditional courtesies and be given the same responsibilities, the same opportunities as everybody else.'

He leaned across the table and studied her thoughtfully. 'Let me ask you a hypothetical question. Suppose, instead of sitting here today, you and I were aboard the S.S. *Titanic*, and suddenly we hit an iceberg. The alarm goes off. Abandon ship. And everybody rushes to the lifeboats. Only there aren't enough lifeboats to go around. Should we go back to the old rules? Should it still be "women and children first"?'

'Well, children first, of course. They're so helpless.'

'Agreed. But after that? Would you expect preferential treatment . . . or would I be justified in shoving you out of the way while I grabbed the last seat in the lifeboat for myself? It would be no contest, you know. Physically, I'm much much stronger than you.'

She was nonplussed. 'That's a loaded question, Dan,' she said finally. 'I don't see the application. You're comparing two different things.'

'You haven't answered my question.'

'Well, then, I suppose the women should have priority if only for the reason that they're better equipped to look after the children.'

'But will they be, in this great unisex world that's coming up? They'll probably have forgotten how. I think you women want it both ways, that's what bothers me. You want all the new opportunities without giving up any of the old privileges.'

'By privileges, I gather you mean male protection. Well, I can't see that it's done women a lot of good so far. I've heard that argument before, you know, that a woman's weakness is her greatest strength. I'm sorry, I can't accept that.'

'So your answer would be. . .'

She smiled and sought a tactful solution. 'I never take a boat when I can take a plane.'

'Spoken like a true casuist,' he laughed. 'You should have been a lawyer like my wife. Anyhow ... here comes the duck.'

The food was superb; the duck well-hung and simply served. She'd never tasted one quite like it. It was a rare breed of canvasback, Catlett told her, peculiar to the marshes of Maryland. 'Best duck I've ever eaten,' she said. 'Thank you,' he beamed. 'I shot it myself ' – leaving Caro to wonder if she were lunching on one of the last of Tom's endangered species.

By the time they were halfway through lunch, he had warmed up considerably. 'You know all about the movie business,' he said at one point and she didn't bother to disabuse him. 'How'd you like to handle a major project for me?'

'I'd love to!'

'Good.' There were a couple of young producers, he told her, who were looking around for film financing. Close to a million dollars. If Caro were interested, he'd have 'his girl' send round the script and fill her in on the background. 'It'll be entirely your baby, and I'll look forward to getting your recommendation at the next general meeting.'

'Thank you.' Caro was buoyant. Tom was right. He was a human being after all.

'And now,' he said, helping her to another portion of duck, 'let me ask you another question. This one is not hypothetical, and I'd appreciate an honest answer.'

'Of course, Dan.'

'Are you gunning for my job, Caroline?'

She almost dropped her fork in astonishment. She couldn't believe her ears. Was that what he was really thinking all this time? Was he such a total paranoid? So insecure that he could imagine she constituted a threat already?

'Good lord, no!' – the blood rushed to her cheeks. 'I swear to God it never once entered my mind.'

'No, I can see it didn't.' He smiled at her discomfiture, then folded his arms and leaned back. 'That's what's wrong, you see. You *should* be out for my job. And you would be if you were really one of the boys. Every man in my group is just waiting for me to either move up or fall flat on my face. They're a bunch of hungry bastards at heart.' He said this fondly.

'But doesn't that bother you?'

'Not at all. Quite the opposite. It's a situation I've taken some pains to create. After all, it's a pretty poor executive who has to surround himself with weak sisters. I expect competition. It's how I get top performance from the men. I want them to try and outsmart me, to go for the shrewder deal, the tougher challenge. I expect each and every one of them to have their eye on the director's chair at all times. And the men all understand that, they've been bred to it from birth. The fact is, they love the competition. And that, my dear, is the difference between men and women.'

He ordered coffee for her, none for himself, excusing himself on the grounds that he'd be late for a meeting. She lingered over her espresso with mixed emotions. The lunch had been success-ful, certainly, in that she had gained her objectives: a better relationship with Catlett and at last some responsible work of her own. Yet her satisfaction was far from complete. All well and good for him to say he valued performance, competition. But would he value it from her? She recalled the covert admiration with which he had studied the oyster-eater. That was what he liked in women – softness, suppleness, grace. As for Caro herself, she was damned if she did, damned if she didn't. If she were to be like the men – tough and aggressive – he would despise her for it. That remark of his about his wife's defection ('neither here nor there') was hogwash; it was very much here and there. But if on the other hand, she chose not to be aggressive, he would see her as falling down on the job.

She headed back to the office, stopping en route to pick up a bottle of Courvoisier as a way of saying thanks to Tony.

'On the whole, it went very well,' she told him, 'and I think we've reached some kind of accommodation. But I wish you'd warned me in advance that he'd split with his wife. I really walked right into that.

'I'm surprised he mentioned it,' Tony said. 'That whole business threw him for a loop.'

'Well, I imagine she had good reason. I don't think there are too many women who'd put up with him.'

'As far as I could see,' Tony said, 'Dan was the one who did all the putting up. Frankly, I always thought Madeleine was a bitch of the first water. She just couldn't stand the fact that Dan was the star in the family, like his success was taking bread out of her mouth. Funny thing was, he was absolutely crazy about her.'

'If she was such a bitch, how come he was so crazy about her?'

'Oh, I think just because she was his.'

'That's ridiculous,' Caro said. 'After all, people don't own other people.'

'I wouldn't try telling him that. And thanks for the Courvoisier.'

Caro posed the S.S. *Titanic* conundrum to Sally one day, half-knowing what the answer would be. Sally laughed. 'The answer to that one's easy. Me first! Why the hell do you think I'm taking up karate?'

8

When Frank Jeffries bursts into a lonely motel room to discover his wife in an act of sodomy with a Doberman Pinscher, he goes berserk. Grabbing a fire-axe, he dismembers the faithless woman, then turns on the Doberman. The dog, enraged by the scent of blood, springs at Frank savagely, clawing at his eyes. Screaming in agony, Frank stumbles from the room vowing death to all adulteresses. Hideously scarred, he returns to the scene of the crime whenever the moon is full to wreak his grisly revenge. He has become *The Ghoul of Motel Room 13* (Opening Credits).

'Hey, Tom' – Caro tapped him on the shoulder – 'I bet my bedtime reading's more fun than yours. Try this one on for size.' Tom put down his *Scientific American* and took the xeroxed sheets Caro handed him. She watched him as he read, his eyebrows going up and down at such regular intervals that she could tell when he got to which bit.

'Now don't you wish you could write stuff like that?' she said when he'd finished.

'Fantastic!' – he handed the papers back to her. 'I love that scene where the girl gets her rocks off with a cucumber. What do they call this epic . . . *Valley of the Dills*?'

'And what you've seen is only the synopsis . . . it fails to do the script full justice. I mean this picture has just about every kinky sex act conceivable – mutilation, transvestitism, to say nothing of the scene with the dog and the girl. Yeccch. . .' – she shuddered – 'I can't believe people can get away with making this stuff.'

'Then you haven't been down to 42nd Street lately.'

'As a matter of fact, I have. I was down there all afternoon, meeting the gents who are planning this little SM pastiche. They've got an office tastefully located between a massage parlour and a store that specializes in inflatable rubber sex dolls. How's that for class?'

'Not bad. Did they offer you a part, baby? I can see it now . . . your name up in lights. Caroline Harmsworth starring in *Lassie Came Home*.'

'Yeah, they offered me, but I turned it down. The dog had all the good lines. Guess they'll have to settle for Julie Andrews instead.'

'Well, if she's smart, she'll take it. I understand there's a lot of money in porn.' Tom returned to his magazine.

'Oh, isn't there just!' she murmured.

Oh, wasn't there just! Caro had spent the last ten days studying the blue-movie business, and the figures were nothing short of sensational. 'Sex is a commodity,' one of the producers had said. 'So is violence, same as soy beans or pork belly futures. And right now, the two in combination are the hottest commodity on the market.'

If her own measure of revulsion was anything to go by, then *Motel Room 13* was destined to be a box-office smash with every sadist, deviant, necrophiliac and black-leather freak between here and Hawaii. Which meant, by her calculations, an audience of fifty million movie-goers easy.

In short, it appeared to be a damn good investment, and the two brothers George and Albie Liddell, who owned the property were shrewd cookies – entrepreneurs to their fingertips. Yet the whole proposition troubled Caro, and she didn't relish the prospect of going in tomorrow morning and asking one of Wall Street's oldest, most respected financial houses to put up money for a venture like this. It was so unsavoury.

'What do you think, Tom?' she asked, half-expecting him to read her mind. He looked over to her and chewed his lip thoughtfully.

'I think,' he said putting down his magazine 'that you and I ought to get married.'

'I mean about *Motel Room 13*.'

'I think you and I ought to get married and spend our honeymoon in *Motel Room 13*.'

'Seriously, honey, I've got to make a decision on this.'

'I am serious, Caro' – and his tone confirmed his words –

'and I have been for the last couple of months. I'm serious about you, apparently a good deal more than you are about me. You know, here we are reading in bed just like an old married couple, but there's one big difference – I'm willing to make a commitment and you aren't.'

The idea of marriage that had seemed so outrageous last Christmas had, simply through familiarity, progressed from the ridiculous to the barely possible to the feasible and now – in Tom's mind at least – to the eminently desirable. Caro, however, was ambivalent. 'Why marry?' she'd say when Tom brought it up, to which he'd reply 'Why not?'

She knew he was being subjected to unrelenting family pressure, but although he could resist that, other pressures were building up.

Only last weekend she and Tom had driven to Philadelphia in their newly acquired Porsche, where he would be covering a scientific convention. At the hotel they had registered as Mr and Mrs, something they had often done before for convenience. The convention climaxed with a formal banquet, however, and the guests in the ballroom were not hotel clerks to be fobbed off with little white lies, but government officials, respected academics, members of the scientific establishment. The people she was introduced to automatically assumed that she was Mrs Tom Darius. 'Is your wife an ecologist too?' someone asked Tom, and he had begged the question by saying, 'Caro is an executive with PAGIT.' No last name. It saved embarrassment.

But the incident had bothered him and tonight he started up again. 'It's not social pressure that's getting to me,' he insisted, 'It's something else. You know the only major argument you and I ever had was about this business of living together. You put up such resistance, but confess – I was right. It did work out and we're both all the happier for your having made the commitment. Yet you're willing to go just so far and no farther. You keep saying – and by and large I agree – there's no practical advantage to our getting married. We wouldn't live any differently, we'd still want the same freedom, the same independence. It would just be symbolic. The point is, I'd feel differently. I'd feel you cared enough about me to take a real chance, to make a public statement. I love you, Caro, and it would have given me great pride to introduce you as my wife. That really hit me down in Philly. I get this impression you're always trying to hedge your bets, like it's a business proposition. I guess what I'm saying is I want some reassurance from you, some proof. . . .'

'Proof of what, Tom?'

'That you love me as much as I love you. That you're proud of me too.'

They talked about it long into the night, and Caro promised to think it over. 'Meanwhile, let's let it rest for a bit. I've got a big day tomorrow.'

The staff meetings always fascinated her. They were few and far between, but when they came, they were marathons – and Caro never made dinner engagements on those days.

In theory, each meeting was a forum. Outside consultants were brought in, trial balloons floated and all major investments were reviewed. In fact, they were a one-man show, and that man was D. R. Catlett.

He was like an orchestra conductor, Caro once thought – a Leonard Bernstein of the conference room, always eliciting exactly the performance he desired from each of the players. A little more oboe here, a little less trumpet there, let's hear it from the violins – and though the final result was a seeming harmony, there was no question who called the tune.

Some of the ventures involved technical companies – biogenetics, microchips, engineering – but the scope was broad and Catlett was willing to entertain any proposition, no matter how outlandish. The more outlandish, the more they intrigued him. 'That idea's so screwball,' he'd sometimes say, 'that I'm tempted to take a flier on it personally.'

There was the bottling company that had come up with the bright idea of making carbonated soft drinks out of tea dust. They had sent around a case of the stuff, and the group had spent the morning trying it every which way, including laced with Jack Daniels bourbon. It was unspeakable.

Then there was the Sonic Massage Company, a team of

acoustic engineers who were developing a type of jacuzzi bath that used sound waves instead of water. Catlett went for that one.

Naturally, anything that promised a cure for the energy crunch received the liveliest attention. Gunther Rees, one of the group's several Ph.D.s, had come across a process that allegedly could turn whey cheese into petrol, like Rumpelstiltskin turning straw into gold.

'Now how would that work?' Catlett wanted to know.

'Well,' Gunther began, all set to give a step-by-step rundown. 'First, you get a herd of cows.'

The remark struck Tony Marcusson funny. 'You get this herd of cows,' Tony interjected, 'and you feed 'em on a diet of baked beans and cabbage. Talk about gas. . . !'

'No bull!' was the comeback and after that it was a free-for-all, winding up with Caro asking 'did you hear the one about the Volkswagen that drove all the way to California on a single pound of Kraft Velveeta?'

'OK, OK,' Catlett laughed and threw up his hands. 'We'll let it go for now.' But from that meeting on, 'first, you get a herd of cows,' became a running gag, the by-word for every screwball proposition.

The reasoning behind Catlett's decisions was not always clear to Caro, and if a detail troubled him – no matter how minor – he would hark back to it again and again, driving everybody up the wall in the process. Yet at other times he came to snap decisions, offering no explanation other than 'I like it' or, more frequently 'no way'.

One meeting a couple of metallurgists came in from outside, looking for capital. They had developed a technique that could radically cut down the costs of refining a rare strategic metal. No one knew much about the metal in question, and halfway through the presentation Catlett interrupted 'What do they use this stuff for?'

'Primarily it's used in the manufacture of handguns.'

'I see.'

He made no further comment until the presentation was complete, then simply shook his head no. He didn't amplify and Caro was puzzled whether his decision had been based on moral scruples, surprising in such an avid sportsman, or whether he just wasn't in the mood.

For his moods often determined the tone of the meetings. There had been a brief reign of terror when he had tried to give up smoking, three weeks when nothing made him happy; but this morning, she noted with relief, he had his gold lighter and two packs of Dunhills squared away before him on the table.

'Gentlemen,' he said when everyone was seated, 'Caroline here has been looking into the blue-movie business for us and we await her report with bated breath.'

After the tittering died down, Caro launched into her piece. She was exquisitely prepared: facts, figures, profit margins, market analysis, everything right at her fingertips.

'However,' she said in summing up, 'although this appears to be an attractive investment opportunity on the surface, I have grave reservations. I'm reluctant to recommend that a company like PAGIT should be involved in a project of this nature.'

'Thank you,' Catlett smiled, then addressed the men. 'What Caroline has been saying is that we have on hand a first-class investment, perhaps not to everyone's personal taste. And I certainly agree with her conclusion that we should follow this one through.'

She had said nothing of the sort; he had manipulated her words out of context to harmonize with his foregone conclusion. It was a typical Catlett ploy.

The next morning he called her into his office and pronounced himself satisfied with the work she had done on *Motel Room 13*. The responsibility for following through on the project was hers alone. 'It's your baby,' he said, 'and make sure these people bring the movie in on schedule and within budget. By the way,' he added, 'I've been reviewing your expense account.'

She was not surprised, for during the past week he had called in the other staff one by one and generally taken them over the coals. Certainly, there had been abuses, with some of the men writing off everything from haberdashery to hookers under the guise of business entertaining. As a group they lived it up, and there was a joke that one of their number would charter a jet just to go to the men's room. In this matter, Caro felt secure, even smug. Her expense sheet was a model of probity and caution and as Catlett poked through the chits, she relaxed and waited for her Girl Scout badge.

'I'm afraid this won't do, Caroline' – he tapped the chits with his pencil. 'You're way under budget.'

'I'm what?' – she jerked up in astonishment.

'You're underspending . . . in other words, you're not making enough new contacts. This isn't a thrift shop, you know, and you'd do well to take a cue from your colleagues – get around more, dig up new opportunities. You must have plenty of connections – B School, family, people you meet socially. Use them. Advertise yourself. What I want to see around here,' he dismissed her, 'is a lot more hustle.'

She went back to her desk with a philosophic smile, then called Tom at his office. 'How'd you like me to buy you a bang-up lunch? Name the place.'

'How about "21"?' he said, 'but what's the occasion?'

'The occasion,' she laughed, 'is I'm not spending enough dough, so I may as well spend some on you.'

She was still shaking her head in amazement an hour later over martinis. 'That guy is really a lulu! I think it gives him pleasure to pull the rug out from under me. Go ahead, honey, order the filet mignon . . . how about some caviar just for the hell of it. Why not? I'm entertaining the dynamic editor of an up-and-coming ecology magazine. I'll write it off as official business.'

They settled for the lobster thermidor and a good vintage wine. 'You know,' Tom said after the waiter took their order, 'if you're really that hot about finding offbeat investments, you might throw some money our way. Lord knows we could use it.'

'You're joking, aren't you?' – but she saw he was not. 'Why? Is the magazine in trouble?'

'It could be healthier,' Tom admitted. 'The thing is, right now we're into the banks pretty heavy and last month's issue didn't even cover expenses. My own feeling is that it's temporary, but we could sure use fresh capital meanwhile.'

'Actually,' Caro furrowed her brow, 'we're looking for new businesses, not sick ones. However, I've got some free time over the next few days, so if you'd like me to talk with the accountants and take the temperature of the place so to speak . . . who knows? I doubt if I can get you any financing, but I might have some practical suggestions.'

'Fine,' Tom said, 'I'll set it up.'

Lucinda Burke was publisher, wet-nurse and prime financial backer of *Ecology Today*. From her salt-and-pepper hair to her Indian necklace to the tip of her mud-brown Earth Shoes, she exuded high ideals and natural products, uncorrupted by any whiff of the marketplace. Her father had owned strip mines in Minnesota and upon his death, Lucinda had pledged her inheritance as reparation money. *Ecology Today* would be her clarion, trumpeting out against those who – like Hammon Burke – would loose havoc on the natural world. She was not a crank, however, and described herself simply as a 'caretaker'. She had always been very good to Tom.

On those occasions when Caro had met her socially, she had liked Lucinda. Right now, she wished she hadn't. Indeed, sitting down across Lucinda's battered wooden desk, she felt like an absolute shit. Still . . . business was business.

'It seems to me,' Caro began, 'that you have some fundamental problems here.'

'That's what my banker keeps telling me' – Lucinda fingered her Indian beads like a rosary – 'but Tom thought you might have some suggestions.'

Caro had suggestions in plenty. . . One, stop printing on recycled paper and switch to cheaper stock. 'Oh, but that paper has always been our trademark.' Two, tone down the editorial content and attract a wider range of advertisers. 'But I couldn't accept money from the chemical companies.' Three, trim the staff and spend the money on promotion. 'But these people have been with me for years.' Four. . . But it was hopeless. For every reason why, Lucinda had a reason why not. At the end of an hour, Lucinda thanked her for her trouble. 'You see the magazine merely as a matter of dollars and cents. I see it as more of a trust. Anyhow, I think I'll just soldier on for a while.' Caro left disheartened.

'If I were you,' she told Tom that night, 'I'd start looking for another job.'

'Is it that bad?' he turned pale.

'Well, I think so . . . I've been over everything, honey. I've seen the accountants, talked to the bank. I wish I could find some silver lining, but frankly I think it's only a question of time.'

'Could be you're exaggerating, Caro. You Wall Street people always see the gloomy side. If things were that tough, Lucinda couldn't pay the salaries she's paying. She's always done well by me.'

Caro pursed her lips. 'She's overpaying you, Tom. I don't mean you're not worth every penny you get, simply that the profits don't justify. That place is bleeding her white, you know. There comes a day when the kissing has to stop. I hate to be the bearer of bad news, but I'd be less than honest if I sugar-coated the picture, and we've always been honest with each other. You have to realize it's a tough world out there, magazines are dropping off like flies. Frankly I think you should get out soon, before word gets around. And if what's holding you back is a question of personal loyalty . . . well, I know you feel honour-bound to Lucinda. . . .'

'Loyalty!' Tom exclaimed. 'What has loyalty got to do with it? I have no special ties to Lucinda. What the hell, we're both free agents and I can split any time I want.'

'Why, Tom!' Caro was shocked. 'I thought you were so fond of her.'

'I am fond of her,' he protested, 'but that doesn't mean she owns me. Lucinda's not the issue. Sure, I could quit and probably land a job in industry tomorrow – if I wanted to. Thing is, Caro, I don't want to. I can't see myself as just another cog in some damn corporate wheel, and money isn't everything, you know, no matter what they say on Wall Street. Look at it from my point of view. Here I am, not even thirty, already editor of a national magazine. I'm free to write, free to publish what I want. I go to seminars, conventions, and everybody knows who I am. My voice is heard, my views are respected. I'm a personage, not a corporate cipher. And every month, when I get that first copy hot off the press from the printer, it's . . . well, it's a thrill. I look at each article, each layout and there are the ideas I've nurtured and fussed over from seedlings. My work – for all the world to see. That magazine is *me*, Caro – my identity. Just as your work is you. Surely you understand that.'

She understood his vehemence, certainly. His passion. 'If you're that committed, Tom, then I suppose you should stick it out. It's just. . . .'

'I know, I know,' he interrupted. 'You've done your duty and warned me, and I'll keep what you've said in mind. But you do understand, Caro . . . I have to see it through.'

She understood, though something he had said puzzled her and she returned to it later that evening.

'What did you mean, Tom, about my work being my identity? I'd be exactly the same person if I were doing something else?'

'You mean if you were a lawyer or a banker?'

'Or a waitress or a file clerk. . .'

'Oh come on, Caro! Can you honestly picture yourself as a waitress. . .'

'. . . or even if I didn't work at all. I'd still be the same person, Tom. It's different for you. You have a vocation. All I've got is a career.'

'All you've got is a career!' Tom repeated. 'Ye Gods, you're the top woman in a major company. Okay, you've been going through a bad patch lately, but now with this movie project, things are looking up. What's the matter, hon?' He suddenly attuned to her mood. 'Something at the office bugging you?'

Something had been troubling her all week long.

Hackley Plastics was a small, family-held, firm that had seen better days. At Ira Hackley's death, company ownership had devolved to his widow, a naive but well-intentioned woman whose sole desire was to keep the family name alive and preserve the jobs of employees.

The assets were few. They did, however, include several patents which Gunther Rees believed to be wildly under-valued.

'Mrs Hackley doesn't have an inkling as to the worth of those patents,' he explained at a meeting. 'Neither does her lawyer. They're really babes in the wood.'

He proposed that the group acquire the company, liquidate it, and walk off with clear title to the patents.

'Sounds nasty,' Tom said. 'I gather Mrs Hackley doesn't realize what's in the wind.'

'Not a clue. She's actually grateful that our benign little group is coming to her rescue. The deal went through yesterday.'

'It's legal, I presume.'

'Perfectly legal, technically ethical. And morally it stinks. Now I'm not saying Gunther actually enjoys the prospect of sticking it to the old lady or throwing two hundred people out of work. I don't think it crossed his mind one way or another. He was too busy rubbing his hands with glee.'

'And what did Catlett say?'

'Dan said, as I recall, that it was "a nice piece of business". That's his phrase for any deal that goes straight to the jugular. And you know what, Tom? He was right. It was a nice piece of business. Shrewd, aggressive – the kind of stuff that's expected of smart operators like us. Well, Tom, I don't ever want to have to make a decision like that. I don't want to succeed on the basis of how good I am at sticking it to other people. And the higher I climb, the more of those decisions there are going to be. So if what you say is true . . . I mean about our work being our identity, then I'd probably be better off as a waitress.'

'In which case' – Tom tweaked her nose – 'I'll have a ham and swiss on rye and hold the mayo.'

That Friday, Tom came home walking on air. 'How'd you like to go to London with me?' He'd been invited to deliver a paper at the meeting of the International Whaling Commission. Out of all the biologists, all the nature writers, all the Greenpeaceniks he, Tom Darius, had been asked to represent the views of the entire ecological community. Then after that to Cambridge to conduct a seminar.

'What do you say, Caro . . . why don't you come along? We could combine business with pleasure, take another couple of weeks, rent a car, visit Stonehenge, Stratford, get married in Gretna Green. How about it?'

'It depends. When are you leaving?'

He told her the dates.

'Oh, I wish I could go, darling,' she sighed and shrugged, but there was no way she could take time off right now. The pressure of work, the shooting schedule of *Motel Room 13*, the opportunities just now beginning to open up for her – Tom's bonanza couldn't have come at a more inconvenient time. They finally agreed he'd go alone. After all, she had her career to worry about, too.

He worked late that night in the next room, and through the bedroom wall she could hear the exuberant click click click of his typewriter – a sure sign that ideas were flowing. It was a homey sound. How nice, she thought, her lying in bed while Tom worked in the next room happy and busy. Even the clatter of the typewriter gave her a peculiar feeling of security. She was glad for Tom, yet wished he didn't have to go. Those ten days without him stretched before her like an eternity. Oh, he'd had the occasional business trips before, but never for more than a night or two, and even on those nights she had missed him dreadfully. Had missed everything about him – the warm scent of his sleeping body, the funny way he had of screwing up his face when shaving, his laughter. Even his felt but unseen presence in another room.

And then it hit her. What if Tom went and never came back? She felt the rush of adrenalin. It was absurd, she thought, trying to push the idea out of her mind. Of course he'd be coming back; he had a round-trip ticket to prove it. But what if he didn't? What if a job turned up suddenly in London? What if he were offered a lectureship in Cambridge? He'd always said he'd like to work abroad. What if he met a girl . . . on the plane, at the convention? Of course he would meet girls, plenty of them. He always did. Tom loved to flirt. 'Just joshing,' he'd say and Caro never resented it, because it was so easy-going, so cheerfully democratic. He indulged in mild flirtations with every woman he ever met – including the homely, the elderly, even Gusty. 'The old girls need it,' he used to kid.

But supposing this time he met a girl, a lovely girl . . . someone more yielding, more giving than Caro had been. Ten days was a long time, and Tom was a very ardent man. Yes, he would meet a girl, a pretty English girl with soft blonde hair and cornflower eyes; they'd go to bed and Tom would say to that girl, as he had once said to her 'Just give me a few days to get uninvolved, and after that it will be you and I.'

He'd be well within his rights, for Caro had always made it clear that he was under no obligation to her, nor she to him. He wouldn't be obliged to offer her more than a graceful explanation; she had no hold over him.

Tom would do no such thing, of course, he wasn't a swine – but the point was, he could. All he had ever asked of her was some sign, some symbolic gesture of commitment, and she had refused time and time again. He must have seen her rejection of marriage as a rejection of him. But she didn't reject him – she adored him. And what was so awful, so unthinkable about the kind of marriage Tom offered her? Not a prison, but a partnership, he always said; not dependent and stifling but free and creative, the most exciting adventure of all.

Yes, Tom would go to London. And he would go alone – she couldn't help that. But he would go there as a married man. And when he returned she would be here waiting – his love, his bride, his wife.

She got out of bed and walked naked into the next room, so quietly he didn't hear her enter. He was sitting with his back to her, wearing an old maroon bathrobe, scrunched over a pile of work. She stole up behind him and wound her arms around his neck.

'John Doe, my darling. You win.'

He swung around startled. 'What do I win?'

'You win me, Tom. Let's get married next week.'

For a moment he sat there, uncomprehending, then gave a great whoop of joy. Papers scattered all over the floor.

'Oh, my own sweetheart,' he said between kisses, 'we both win.'

9

No mistaking that shock of go-to-hell hair.

Even across the crowded expanse of the Pan Am terminal, it blazed forth fiery and red-hot as Tabasco sauce. And if the hair wasn't conclusive, consider the briefcase. There wasn't another like it in the world. The last time Caro had seen those items in tandem – hair and briefcase – had been graduation day at B School. So the combination could only belong to. . .

'Hey, Walter!' she shouted at the short stocky figure zooming toward the exit gate. Scurrying, just as he had scurried through the corridors at Harvard – always late, always breathless, always en route to the deal that was going to knock your socks off. And always always with that extraordinary briefcase. 'Hey Walter . . . Walter Lorencz. Wait for me!'

Walter stopped, dropped the briefcase and enveloped Caro in an ebullient bear hug. He smelled of Coppertone and insect repellent.

'Well, I'll be damned. If it isn't the best set of legs in B School. How the hell are you, Harmsworth . . . and what are you doing out at Kennedy? You coming? Going? Can I drop you off somewhere?' Hardly waiting for an answer, he grabbed Caro in one hand, the briefcase in the other and ferried them through the gate and into a waiting Mercedes Benz 600.

The chauffeur snapped to attention. His uniform matched the whipped-cream colour of the upholstery.

'So,' Walter said once they'd settled in the car. 'What have you been up to these days?'

'Well, for one thing I'm married,' she beamed.

'Since when and to whom?'

'Since. . . .' – she checked the gold Patek watch Tom had given her for Christmas – 'since 10.45 yesterday morning, give or take a minute and to the nicest guy in the world. In fact, that was my husband I was just seeing off at the airport.'

'And now you're going home alone?' Walter blinked in astonishment. 'I've heard of married couples taking separate vacations ... but separate honeymoons? That's the lousiest idea since the square wheel' – and when Caro started to explain, he cut her off – 'Business, schmusiness, you can't spend the first full day of married life playing solitaire in a New York apartment.' Instinctively he reached for the car telephone. 'You come back with me to Westport and I'll have Natalie whip up a wedding cake, or maybe cheesecake instead. She makes a terrific cheesecake.'

He rapped out 'Home, James' to the chauffeur, then grinned at Caro. 'I've always wanted to have a chauffeur named James ever since I was a kid. Took me three employment agencies to find one. Now hang on a sec while I make a few calls.'

What the machine gun was to Al Capone, the telephone was to Walter – the perfect instrument of self-expression – and for the next twenty minutes Caro waited out a barrage of phone calls. First his wife, announcing they were on their way and placing an order for cherry cheesecake; then in quick succession his lawyer, his broker, his secretary, his accountant, even his tailor, all of whom seemed to take it as a matter of routine that their Saturday morning leisure should be interrupted in so peremptory a manner. And all the while he was barking orders and lodging complaints, his free hand punched figures on a pocket calculator.

Caro relaxed, lolled back and gave herself over to the pleasures of shameless eavesdropping. The years since graduation had left Walter unchanged. Despite the incipient pot-belly shaping up beneath the custom-made suit, he was still recognizably Go-Go Walter, as they used to call him in Cambridge. The same red-headed, green-eyed, freckled mass of pure energy, the same irrepressible combination of half-cocked ideas and full-blown enthusiasms that had made him a standout even then.

The last she'd seen of him, he had flung himself wholeheartedly into a scheme that offered medical coverage for animals. P.I.P., it was called – Pet Insurance Plan. It was pure chutzpah, pure Walter, and Caro for one had written it off as harebrained, but listening to him now on the phone she concluded that the business, screwball though it was, must have paid off handsomely.

'Well,' she said when he finally surrendered the phone. 'Looks like life has been treating you OK. You still selling policies to dog owners?'

'Oh that!' Walter crinkled a sunburnt nose. 'What a fiasco. We sold plenty of policies all right, but I lost my shirt. People kept poisoning their pets for the benefits. No . . . I'm out of that now. I've been playing the market, a little arbitrage, having some fun in commodities. Made a couple of bucks trading in mangoes a few years back.

'Manganese?' She must have misunderstood.

Nope, mangoes. You know . . . it's that tropical fruit. Natalie uses them for making chutney.' He gave her a wink. 'They're not bad eating. You ought to try them some day.'

Mangoes my foot! There was no market in mangoes that she'd ever heard of; clearly Walter was having his little joke.

'And what are you into these days. . .' – she eyed the bulging briefcase – 'Pomegranates?'

'Right now,' Walter became evasive 'I'm into nothing heavier than relaxation. Just came back from doing a little fishing down in Florida. You know . . . pompano. Red snapper.'

Red herring was more like it. Walter had been fishing all right, with a business suit, a briefcase and a calculator. But for nothing as prosaic as snapper.

'And which part of Florida would that be?'

'The part that's got the most mosquitoes.' He scratched a bite by way of confirmation. 'Pleasure is such a rigorous business these days . . . easier sitting around an office. Still, you know what Onassis used to say: "Keep a tan all year round because, to most people, sun is money"'.

But Caro refused to be put off by so transparent a lie and remembering Catlett's injunction to utilize her contacts on every front, she set the stage for further probing.

'You know, Walter, I'm with a venture capital group these days. . .' then proceeded to give him a hard sell on the company, its assets, its free-wheeling nature. 'So if you're involved in something that might be of interest to us, we're pretty flush with capital at the moment. . .'

'Hey, Caro,' Walter twitted. 'Who's fishing now!'

She let the matter drop, and as they were pulling into his driveway, he remarked: 'You know the other half of Ari's prescription for success? Always live at a good address, even if all you've got is a room in the attic. Here we are.'

Walter's 'attic' proved to be a huge centre-hall colonial house, set in half a dozen acres of woods and greenery, and lavishly endowed with the amenities – stables, tennis court, swimming pool – that bespoke the country gentleman. Not bad for a kid from Budapest! And smack in the centre of that formal centre hall was Natalie, wiping floury hands on an apron.

Ye Gods, Caro thought. There stands Walter's wife in the middle of a million bucks worth of prime Connecticut real estate, and she's still playing Jewish mother.

No, Natalie hadn't changed either.

The day tripped by quickly and pleasantly, or as pleasantly as it can for a new bride with a husband three thousand miles away. After the initial greetings, the obligatory appreciation of the four Lorencz kids (there had only been three last time she'd seen them), she and Walter played a couple of sets of tennis, drank some wine, gossiped about old times and new. As for Walter's wife, she was largely conspicuous by her absence, surfacing now and then to serve up snacks or keep the older children in line. Not until Caro descended into the kitchen did Natalie come into her own. Undeniably a house-proud woman.

'How do you like it?' she pointed to a space-age appliance. 'It's the latest thing in microchip ovens.'

'You mean,' Caro offered politely, 'microwave.'

'Microchip . . . microwave . . . what do I know? I was an art major, not an engineer.'

Microchips, Caro figured. Walter's into microchips. Probably some hush-hush technical breakthrough. Just up Catlett's alley.

Dinner, when they finally sat down to it, was a formal affair, all candlesticks and crystal and uniformed maid, but the moment dessert was over, Walter bolted from the table.

'Just gonna make a few phone calls,' he said, then vanished.

Jesus! Caro felt a flicker of annoyance. Here his wife has knocked herself out preparing this fantastic meal, and he just wolfs it down and takes off. Natalie must have sensed her disapproval for she smiled and shrugged. 'Walter doesn't mean to be rude, Caro. It's just that he's a telephone junkie. If an hour goes by without his making a phone call, he gets withdrawal symptoms. In fact, I don't think we've had an uninterrupted dinner since the mango business.'

'Mangoes!' Then Walter hadn't been kidding.

'Oh, didn't he tell you? Walter cornered the market in mangoes a couple of years back. He made a killing.'

Caro's jaw dropped. How the hell could you make a killing in mangoes? It wasn't as if they were a basic commodity like sugar, say, or livestock. 'I never realized they were such a popular fruit,' she said.

'Oh, Walter's mangoes weren't for eating,' Natalie said, then seeing Caro's puzzled stare . . . 'You know the old joke about the two commodity traders who are dealing in canned sardines? Well, over the years, these two guys – Moe and Joe – keep selling the same consignment of sardines to each other. Back and forth, back and forth, same sardines, only each trade the price goes up. Finally, after the zillionth deal, Moe calls up Joe one night and says "You know those sardines we're trading in? Well, I got hungry and opened a can . . . and they were awful!" At which point his friend says "But Moe, those sardines aren't for eating. They're for buying and selling." Well, Walter's mangoes weren't for eating either. In fact, he bought 'em for the pips.'

A few years earlier, Walter Lorencz had come across an article in a popular magazine by two doctors who claimed they had found the cure for cancer. The secret lay, so they stated, in a substance that could only be found in mango seeds.

If they were right, Walter reasoned, this had to be the biggest medical breakthrough since the Salk vaccine. If not. . . ? If not, there were enough desperate and gullible people in the world to give Mangatrile (as the substance was called) a very respectable run for the money. Either way, there was bound to be a considerable call for this unusual fruit. He spent the next three months buying up crop futures from every mango farmer between Mexico and the Indian sub-continent. Sure enough, the Food and Drug Administration eventually declared Mangatrile a fraud and medical dead end, but by that time Walter was home free. He had netted over three million dollars.

In spite of herself, Caro was impressed. It was bold. It was unlooked-for. It was just the kind of nutsy enterprise Catlett would go overboard for. If only she could get a line on what was next on Walter's entrepreneurial menu. . .

'And now of course' – she made a wild stab – 'he's got this deal in Florida going. Microchips, isn't it?'

'Lord no!' Natalie frowned. 'Some kind of property development. I think. I really don't know anything about it . . .' then seeing Caro's sceptical eyebrow, she added crisply, 'and I don't want to know. When Walter was going through that mango business, I nearly had a nervous breakdown. It was a nightmare. We were in hock up to our eyeballs, and I'd go to bed every night sick with worry. I worried about fruit flies and crop blight and whether the monsoons would come in on schedule. I was a wreck. And that was when I decided to opt out of Walter's business life entirely. That briefcase of his for instance. I don't want to know what's inside there. To me, it's the enemy . . . the "other woman" only worse.'

Caro believed her – it was such an impassioned declaration – and yet she was puzzled. 'But don't you want to share Walter's interests with him? Wouldn't it help to ease the burden? Tom and I share all our professional problems. We confide everything,' she added, hoping it didn't sound like a snub.

'Well, you've only been married one day and we've been married sixteen years. Anyhow, I think the biggest help I can give Walter is running his house and keeping my nose out of his business. Which is not to say I don't worry about him. I do! I worry about the crazy hours he keeps, all that white-knuckle flying. Is he getting enough sleep? Is he eating too much cholesterol? I also have four kids to worry about. As far as I'm concerned, that's quite enough worry for anyone.'

Poor Walter, Caro thought. Imagine coming home, all juiced up with adrenalin, head reeling with big deals and big dollars

. . . to what? To a domestic life that offered no greater stimulus than tales of nappy rash and how the TV repairman never showed and you-really-have-to-watch-your-cholesterol-honey! No wonder he jumped up first chance he got, looking for an excuse to get out of the room and make his phone calls.

Bet they weren't all business . . . those phone calls.

As if conjured by her thought, Walter appeared in the doorway chomping on a squat black cigar.

'We were just talking about you, honey,' his wife said.

'Yeah? What's she been telling you, Caro?' He sat down and reached for the cheesecake.

'I was telling her you should watch your cholesterol intake. No! No more cheesecake, Walter. Why don't you have a piece of fruit instead?'

Walter sighed, and pushed the cheesecake away. 'Natalie's turned into a terrible nag.' But his tone belied his words, and even as he spoke to Caro, he was looking at his wife across the length of the table with an expression of . . . of such love, such desire, such piercing intimacy that Caro felt a stab of anguish. She and Tom should be facing each other across the table now, looking at each other just so – with such love, such affection. With lowered eyes she watched Natalie's fingers over the fruit bowl. Hovering. Choosing the most blooming peach, the ripest plums, cutting a cluster of perfect grapes with little silver scissors. Love offerings for her husband. A faint band of sweat glistened on her upper lip.

All this talk of cheesecake and cholesterol when it was clear the two of them could barely wait to be alone. The house, big as it was, seemed suddenly too small to accommodate an outsider.

'You know,' Caro shifted in her chair uncomfortably, 'if you guys don't mind, I think I'll be getting back to New York after all. Maybe your driver could run me to the station.' She gave some lame excuse about catching up on work, countered her host's polite objections, and a half hour later caught the last train in from Westport.

And as the train trundled through the quiet suburbs, she thought about marriage. Other people's marriages. Her own.

'Ours,' Tom had promised 'will be fresh and different. It will be an adventure' – and Caro had concurred. They were urbane people, modern, progressive. But yesterday – had it been only yesterday? – when they had arrived at City Hall, Thea had been waiting on the steps. 'Here,' she handed Caro a brown paper bag, and once inside Caro opened it.

Item 1. A *Keep Cool With Coolidge* button.

    2. A Mars Bar.

    3. A set of housekeys and

    4. A string of lapis lazuli beads wrapped in tissue.

For some moments, Caro stared in bewilderment at the odd assortment, then . . . 'Something old, something new.' Thea laughed, and slipped the beads over Caro's head. 'Only be happy!' And Caro's eyes had welled with tears. In that soulless, brisk and business-like ceremony, Thea's had been the one conventional gesture.

Beyond the window, as the train swept through the night, isolated houses dotted the countryside. It was late. Here and there lights were being extinguished. Married couples were going up to bed at the end of yet another day: to make love, exchange small talk in the dark, perhaps merely to sleep and dream with fingers touching. For that must be what marriage truly was – a feast of unbounded intimacy.

Certainly, Walter and Natalie were in bed now, making love; his look had been as explicit as a caress, and Caro was moved to see that all those years of marriage had not dulled Walter's ardour. That was nice. Yet it was not the kind of marriage she could envision for herself.

That Natalie should divorce herself from her husband's career was something she could understand; Natalie wasn't built to take pressure. But that she should be so singularly lacking in any real life of her own, that given maids and money and energy and health, she should bury herself utterly in domestic life – why, Caro would have gone bananas in a situation like that.

Let alone boring, it was so risky. So fraught with peril. So reckless, putting all that weight, all that emotional investment into something as fragile as marriage. Because husbands die. They desert. Children grow up and leave home . . . and then, then where would Natalie be?

She would have sacrificed everything – youth, career, independence, identity – for no greater reward than the look that Walter had given her across the dinner table. It was a very high price to pay, even for such a look.

And yet. And yet . . . would Tom look at Caro sixteen years from now with all the love and longing of a bridegroom?

All the stress and pressures of the last few days now overflowed, and at that moment nothing in the world mattered so much as hearing Tom's voice, his laughter. By the time the train pulled into Grand Central, she was stricken by a paroxysm of longing. Tom would be at his hotel in London now, sleeping off the long flight. Perhaps not. Perhaps he had been calling her, phoning home to an empty apartment. Wondering. Worrying. 'Please hurry,' she told the cab driver. 'It's an emergency.'

Within fifteen minutes, the best-loved voice in the world was at the other end of the line. They spoke for at least an hour – little nothings, sweet fondnesses – till Tom said, 'Honey, this must be costing us a fortune.' And then they talked a half hour longer.

And when she hung up, finally, reluctantly, she marvelled that the call had seemed so urgent. They had been separated hardly more than a dozen hours, less than if he'd been away on an overnight business trip. And yet it was different.

Different – simply because she and Tom had stood up before a stocky bespectacled man in the Municipal Building and sworn their love.

It was different – because they had pledged.

10

'Think it'll look familiar?' Tom asked as the plane began its descent into Dum Dum airport.

'I doubt it. After all, I was only so big when we left. Probably be as new to me as it is to you.' Yet making their way across the tarmac some minutes later, Caro took a deep breath of the evening air – that pungent mix of dung fires and coriander and diesel fumes and rotting vegetation, of sweat and spice, of heat and dust, then squeezed his hand in a surge of memory and emotion. 'No, it doesn't look familiar . . . but my God! it smells familiar. What a fantastic idea that was, Tom!'

For it had been his idea, and his alone.

The night before they were married, they had promised each other something special, spectacular for the belated honeymoon that still lay some months in the future; and after Tom's return from London, had spent the odd free evening poking through brochures and guidebooks. From the comfort of their East Side living room, they had balanced the merits of skiing in the Andes, camel-trekking across Morocco, or chartering a boat and sailing through the Greek Islands. Wonderful, romantic extravagant journeys all, having but one thing in common – their distance from the workaday world.

Then Tom had hit upon India. 'I've always wanted to go there, all my life, and I bet you're hankering to go back too.'

But why India? she asked. Because, he teased, it was the furthest point from Morristown, New Jersey. But mostly other reasons. All those years while he was slogging away at Harvard, trapped in the academic treadmill, half his generation (or so it seemed) had merrily set out on the trail to Katmandu in search of adventure and oriental mysticism, to say nothing of pot and free sex. To Tom, India signified a kind of liberation. And if he couldn't be carefree during those driving striving years, he certainly could now.

'I'm not saying we should backpack, Caro' he urged. 'We'd go first class all the way.' But she was less enthusiastic. 'It'll be terribly hot.'

'We'll go in the autumn.'

'And you might find it awfully squalid.' In fact, her own predominant memory was one of stolid Victorian villas and mock English lawns, but that could hardly be typical. She'd seen all those WHO posters and TV documentaries.

But the idea bewitched Tom, and the following night he came home with brochures that spoke of maharajah's palaces converted into luxury resorts, storybook settings that boasted an opulence beyond compare. 'We'll drink tea in peacock gardens and swim in marble pools. What's the matter, Caro? Is there some reason you don't want to go?' None she could articulate, merely vague unsifted memories of having been very happy there, very unhappy there. 'No,' she said finally. 'No reason. I was just thinking about the expense.'

'Screw the expense, baby. It's our one and only honeymoon. Besides which, we've earned it.'

Indeed they had. Almost from the day they married, the pace of their lives had perceptibly quickened. Tom was knocking himself out these days, attempting to turn the tide at the magazine, and for once things were going right for her.

Whether it was the offshoot of her happiness or simply a reflection of Tom's unbounded faith in her, she was at last making inroads at the office. Now that she was safely married, she noted with wry humour, the men there had become friendlier, on occasion even mildly flirtatious. And with the completion of *Motel Room 13*, she had cleared her first major hurdle.

Yes, the abominable movie had at last been filmed, although not – God knows! – without exacting its price in anxiety.

'Your baby,' Catlett had called it, and once approval had been granted, Caro flung herself into the project. Overnight, her misgivings had vanished. 'I'm not in the business of making moral judgments,' she rationalized to Tom. 'I'm in the business of making money.' Tawdry as it was, she recognized the picture would be her ticket of admission to 'The Club'. So it was with considerable dismay that, two weeks before the start of filming, Catlett threw a spanner into the works.

'Your picture has occasioned a good deal of anguish in the boardroom,' he told her. 'Some of the directors feel it's a reflection on the company's standing. They think the Grand Old Man of Wall Street shouldn't be putting up money for porn.'

'You mean they want to pull out?' Caro was aghast. 'But you're on the board, too. Do you want to pull out?'

'Me? No – and I'm not so certain the other directors do at heart. Everyone appreciates the financial possibilities. They simply want the thing made to look more . . . palatable. "Kosher" was the operative word, as I recall.'

'Good God, Dan – we're talking about a cheapo blue movie, not *The Sound of Music*. I mean just that opening scene where the girl and the Doberman. . . .'

'I haven't read the script,' he interrupted. 'Nor do I care to. As I say, it's your baby so it's up to you to find some way of making it acceptable to the board, some bit of sugar-coating, perhaps. Don't ask me what. But if you *can* come up with something' – he softened the blow – 'some gimmick that will wash with the powers that be, and still stay within budget, I'll earmark you for a percentage of the profits.'

That afternoon she laid out the problem with George and Albie Liddell. 'We're going to have to trade it up,' she told them 'beginning with the cast.'

'Swell. We'll shoot the opening scene with a pedigree Kennel Club winner. How's that for class!'

'Ha ha, very funny,' Caro retorted. 'Some pedigree girls would be more like it. I've seen the so-called actresses who've been parading in and out of this office, and Jesus, Albie – they're nothing more than hookers.'

'I believe they prefer the term "models". Come on, Caro, these dolls don't have to act. All they need is big tits plus a nice line in heavy breathing where the script calls for it. What can you expect on this budget? Now, on the other hand, if you people want to spend another couple of hundred thou, you can be up to your ass in class. Who'd you have in mind . . . Sarah Bernhardt?'

'Bernhardt had a wooden leg,' Caro said crisply. 'What's more, I'm not giving you another penny. What I want is some name, any name on the marquee that's going to make the whole thing look . . . kosher. A legitimate Broadway actress, say, or a high-fashion model. Maybe a ballet dancer. Somebody prestigious, yet reasonably cheap. We'll cut the production budget by a hundred thousand bucks and allocate that money for a name.' Both brothers groaned. 'Just remember, you guys, that at the end of the day, I'm the one who signs the cheques.'

'Yes Ma'am,' said Albie, suddenly respectful.

For the next week the three of them pared and pushed around the figures, cutting a scene here, a special effects expense there to come up finally with the necessary money. *And* the name.

'Laura Preston,' she announced to Catlett. 'You can inform the board that this film will feature the girl who right now is playing *Saint Joan* on Broadway. And getting rave reviews, I might add. How's that for class!'

'Not bad. Excellent in fact. But would an actress of that stature do what's necessary?'

Which had been Caro's exact question when she'd called Laura Preston's agent. 'I want to make it crystal clear that the contract will call for your client to appear nude and simulate sex on camera. Will she do it?'

'For a hundred thousand dollars' – the agent was already savouring his fee – 'lovely Laura would hunch over for Dracula.'

'Yup,' Caro now assured Catlett. 'Miss Preston is not only ready and willing, but according to all reports, remarkably able.'

'My my,' Catlett marvelled. 'From *Saint Joan* to skinflicks. Is there nothing young women don't do these days?'

For tax purposes, the film was shot in Canada, the chosen location a dreary motel set on a highway some forty miles from Montreal. Given the combination of willing female flesh, horny crew and the absence of all other forms of entertainment, the set quickly assumed the atmosphere of a brothel. 'Do you ball?' the director asked Caro on the first day of shooting, as casually as one might ask 'do you smoke?'. And when Caro glared an angry no, he simply shrugged and assured her that it was nothing personal.

Her initial aim had been to spend as little time on location as possible, merely flying up once or twice a week to crack the fiscal whip and sign cheques. But, she soon learned, everybody had a role to play in the making of the movie, herself included.

'It's up to you to play the heavy,' Albie Liddell explained. 'Me, the director, the camera crew . . . we may have to work with these yoyos in some future picture. So if there are any arms that need twisting – I'm speaking metaphorically – you're the bad guy. Understand?'

She understood. She appropriated the last two motel rooms for herself, turning one into a combination office and complaint bureau; then spent the next three weeks running interference between cast, crew and the outside world. Her duties, she discovered, extended to the bribing of union officials, haggling with caterers, fixing speeding tickets and even sweet-talking a lady from the Canadian SPCA who was nervous about the uses the Doberman Pinscher was being put to. 'Believe me,' Caro assured her, 'That dog enjoys every minute of his work.'

She ventured forth on the set as rarely as possible, finding the tangle of bare bodies distasteful, but when she did, she made a point of dressing meticulously in a tailored black suit, every stitch of which declared 'no nonsense'. She lived on Pepto-Bismol and pizzas, and whenever she could string a dozen free hours together, she'd fly back to New York to meet Tom. To save time, they'd usually rendezvous at JFK, spend the night at the Holiday Inn, and she'd be off again on the early flight next morning. 'My God,' she groaned, 'we've only been married a couple of months and already I have to set up appointments just to make love.'

By the last week of production, she was counting the minutes. All that remained was the crucial scene with Laura Preston, for which two days shooting-time had been allotted.

But within an hour of the noted actress's arrival, Albie Liddell burst into Caro's office. He was ashen.

'You know that light at the end of the tunnel you were talking about. Well, I discovered what it is. It's the headlights of an oncoming truck, name of Laura Preston and it's about to run us down. That bitch has locked herself into her motel room and now she says she won't undress on camera.'

'She *what*?' Caro couldn't believe her ears. 'Goddam it, she has to. I'll sue. Sue her, sue her agent. . .' She reached for the phone to call the company lawyer, but Albie stopped her. 'You can sue OK, but what good'll it do? By the time the case gets to court, we'll be dead financially. Have to break up the set, disperse the crew . . . Christ, six weeks of shooting out the window. The point is, she and her agent want another hundred thou. They figure your company will have to cough it up.'

'The hell we will,' Caro growled. 'I am not about to submit to blackmail. Let me talk to her.'

Talk she did – and the tall husky-voiced blonde talked back. Talked about art and ethics and morals and personal integrity. As for the agent, he only talked turkey. No ticket, no laundry was the sum of it.

Caro stalked back to her office in a fury. This was certainly one professional contingency that had never come up in all those courses at B School. She could, of course, try to sweat Preston out, but every day's delay would cost the company another thirty thousand dollars. And then there was Tom. He was expecting her home on Sunday.

She brooded for a while, then called the director into her office. 'Hank', she told him, 'You know Laura Preston can't do the nude scene.'

'Not can't,' he grumbled. 'Won't.'

'Nope . . . can't.' Caro folded her arms and smiled faintly. 'Now this is a little known fact, Hank, but the real reason Preston can't undress before the camera is – now hold your breath – that she is a he. That's right! Laura Preston is actually a man in drag. Real name, Laurence Preston.'

Hank's jaw dropped. 'You're kidding!'

She gave him a wink. 'Now what I want you to do is spread that little tidbit around the set just as fast as you can. Don't say it came from me, by the way. Then let's see if it smokes her out of her hole.'

Hank slapped his thigh with gusto. 'For an educated woman, you are one smart broad.'

Within the hour, Preston's agent was in her office fulminating. 'You know what they're saying out there? They're saying. . .' he could hardly get the words out in his anger. 'They're saying Laura is a transvestite! Now who would start a filthy rumour like that!'

'I have no idea,' Caro answered coolly. 'Won't you please sit down?'

'Do you know what'll happen if something like that gets around the trade? Not that anyone'll believe it, but still. . .! My God, Laura's scheduled to play *Mother Courage* next fall. For Chrissakes, Harmsworth, do something about it. Go out and tell the crew she's a woman.'

'Is she?' Caro arched her eyebrows. 'You can't prove it by me.' Then, rising slowly from her desk in a cool deliberate motion she had copied from Catlett until she loomed above her adversary – 'Now you listen to me, Byfield. The only way to squelch a rumour like that is have Preston out on the set, all made up and stripped for action within the next sixty minutes. Otherwise, I can assure you that your client – he, she or it as the case may be – is going to be the laughing stock of show business. Do I make myself clear?'

Well before the deadline, Laura Preston – and she was most definitely a *she* – was on camera, heaving and thrusting in a performance that out-Linda Lovelaced Linda Lovelace.

Caro didn't watch her, however. She was collapsed in her office, belting down the Pepto-Bismol.

'Wow, Tom!', she said that Sunday. 'Is it ever good to be home! You won't believe what a bitch I was on location. I can hardly believe it myself.'

'So there it is!' she announced to Catlett the following Monday. 'Wrapped up on schedule, even a few thousand bucks under budget.'

'Good, good,' he gave his quick professional smile, the kind of smile you might bestow upon a competent waiter, then burrowed through some papers on his desk.

Goddamit! she repressed a shudder of annoyance. Here she'd

done a first-class job on a distasteful project, so was it too much to expect a word of praise? Maybe even – God forbid – a pat on the shoulder? Apparently it was, for Catlett seemed more absorbed in his paper chase than running post-mortems on Montreal.

'Aha, here we are!' – he passed her a sheaf of correspondence. 'Now these people have a small manufacturing concern and they've got ideas for a new kind of food processor. Sounds promising, and I'd like you to look into it for me. Company's out in Ohio' – he waved a vague hand. 'Near Sandusky, I think.'

'Could I . . .' she started to say. *Could I be assigned something closer to home? I've only been married a couple of months?* But one look at his impassive face convinced her he would call this special pleading.

'Food processors.' She took the papers. 'That's quite a change from blue movies,' and got up crisply to go, but when she was halfway out the door, he called her.

She spun around to find him regarding her with a quizzical expression. 'I understand you hit a few snags with your leading lady up in Montreal. I had a long chat with your producers this morning.' He paused, and she saw that he was involved in some mental stock-taking.

'You're quite a clever lady, aren't you?' he said finally then burst into a peal of laughter. 'Congratulations, Caroline. That was a nice piece of business. Very nice indeed.'

She left his office walking on air and didn't come down to earth all day.

But Montreal, Sandusky and the twenty-fifth floor of PAGIT were now a world away, and for the first time since their marriage, she and Tom could look forward to two whole unbroken weeks devoted exclusively to pleasure and each other.

They had a day's stopover in Calcutta before catching the plane to the Palace of Chettapur, and passed a glorious morning in the great bazaar, buying lengths of madras, trays of Benares brass, gifts for everyone including themselves. Tom had his hair cut by a sidewalk barber while Caro hoo'ed and hawed, after which they lunched magnificently on pilaf and tandoori. By mid-afternoon, their supply of ready cash had dwindled.

'We better find ourselves a bank and cash some travellers cheques,' Tom said when they emerged from the restaurant.

'There's one just around the corner on Chowringhee Road.' Caro pointed in an untried direction.

'Why Caro, how do you know? We haven't even been down that way.'

She smiled. '*Déjà vu* ' – then shut her eyes momentarily, 'and I can describe it to a tee. There's a big stone lion over the entrance and a lot of marble pillars inside. I used to know an official at that bank. He was a friend of my mother's . . . the man who first interested me in finance. Funny,' she knit her brows – 'I can remember the bank so well, but not the guy's name. Neville? Cyril? Something like that. Must be twenty years since I've thought of him.'

They cashed some cheques – the bank was as she had described – and Caro returned to the hotel to beat the heat. Tom went off on some mysterious errand.

And lying alone in the great brass bed, shutters firmly fixed against the sun, she was still trying to recall the fellow's name.

It had, in fact, not been twenty years since she'd last thought of him. It had been ten – and he had influenced her life in an unforeseen way.

At the end of her sophomore year, Caro had come home from college to be greeted by a pale and angry Gusty. What had provoked her mother's unexpected hostility, Caro couldn't fathom. Perhaps an assignment had fallen through, perhaps she'd been passed over for some award. But whatever the cause, Caro's return was the immediate catalyst.

'I want to know,' Gusty waved a sheet of paper before her daughter even had a chance to unpack, 'just what the hell you think you're doing at college. Look at this report! Just look at it . . . is that what I'm paying good money for?'

Caro was stunned. Her grades were OK. Maybe not Dean's List, but still a reputable sprinkling of A's and B's. Surely nothing to warrant such an onslaught.

'For heaven's sake, Caro, I'm not talking about marks. I'm talking about all this crap you've been taking. Look at these courses . . . Jazz Appreciation!' she spat out. 'French Romantic Poetry . . . How about this one? Interpersonal Dynamics! What's that? A course on how to get laid? What in God's name did you have in mind when you picked your curriculum?'

Nothing. Caro had had nothing in mind except having fun and sharing classes with people she liked. Hardly an acceptable alibi.

'I want to be a well-rounded person,' was the best she could offer her mother.

'Well-rounded, my ass!' Gusty scowled. 'If there's one thing I won't tolerate it's a dilettante. And if you think I'm laying out seven thou a year for you to fool around or discover your identity or whatever it is your generation's always rambling about, you're sorely mistaken. Why, when I was your age, I was already a working photographer on the *Cleveland Plain Dealer*. But you . . . you've had opportunities I've never dreamed of, and you waste your time on this rubbish. What do you plan to do with your life, Caro? I'm entitled to know. Or are you just going to bumble along?'

It was no answer for Caro to say at nineteen that she was guilty as charged. That she had no ambition, no goal other than to be pretty and popular and have nice young men fall in love with her.

Was she interested in photography? Gusty demanded. Advertising? Television? Journalism? 'Then how about the State Department? With your background you'd be a natural. Or you could switch to pre-med. Have you thought about law? Stop being negative, Caro and show some spine for a change. You must have some career in mind.'

Gusty folded her arms and waited in stony silence. Waited for Caro to say she wanted to win the Nobel Prize or run for President or become the first woman to walk on the moon.

'How about Pope?'

'Don't you be snide with me,' Gusty snapped. 'Do you mean to sit there and say there is nothing . . . nothing in this whole wide world you want to do?'

Caro shut her eyes and squeezed her mind. At that moment

she wanted nothing more than to be admired, to be approved of, to be gotten off the hook. From some deep wellspring of memory, an image surfaced. The image of a small child tracing six big noughts into a chequebook, while at her side a handsome sunburnt man beamed down his approval.

'I want,' she said dreamily, 'to go into finance.'

'Finance!' For a moment Gusty was taken aback. Then she considered it, savoured it. 'Yes, I can see it now. Wall Street. Stock-broking. Investment banking . . . God knows what. A tremendous field. Now that,' the blue eyes shone triumphant, 'is what I'd call a career.'

That summer Caro took a job in a downtown brokerage, as combination message-taker, coffee-maker and fly-on-the-wall. Yet from the moment she first walked through those great mahogany doors, she felt she had found her niche. Everything about Wall Street delighted her – the air of money, vitality, the atmosphere that coupled rock-solid power with quick-silver excitement. By summer's end, she was convinced her choice was inevitable, an ambition she must always have nurtured but only now recognized – like a diamond lying in a snowfield, concealed and in plain sight all at once. From that day on, she never doubted her goals, never questioned her motives.

From that day until this – this very afternoon, lying in a bed in a Calcutta hotel room. Only now for the first time did she wonder: was it conceivable that she had shaped her life, chosen her path because a half-forgotten Englishman had once smiled upon a little girl?

She was still pondering when Tom returned, carrying a small packet wrapped in tissue paper.

'For you,' he said. She opened it and withdrew a fine blue woollen shawl, yard after yard of weightless beauty. It was soft as gauze, fine as smoke.

'I spotted it in the market this morning,' Tom explained 'and wanted to surprise you.' He began winding it loosely around her shoulders. 'It's from Kashmir and it's supposed to be the finest woven fabric in the world. The woman who sold it to me said that traditionally, you should be able to slip the whole shawl through your wedding ring. Shall we try?'

Caro, delighted, shook her head. 'I believe it, but no . . . I don't want to take my wedding ring off. Now or ever.'

Tom smiled, and taking the ends of the shawl, pulled her close to him. 'How beautiful you are, darling Caro.' And in his eyes, she could read that same bright message of warmth and love and utter approval that had haunted her for twenty years.

'Nigel.' she murmured.

'What?' Tom's brows beetled.

'For some reason, I just remembered the name of that British banker. It was Nigel Pryce-Jones.'

'Boy,' Tom shook his head. 'Does your mind work in crazy directions.' But later that evening, when they were leaving to catch the plane to the palace of Chettapur, she suddenly flung her arms about him and kissed him on the lips, in full view of everyone in the lobby: 'Thank you.'

'For what?' He was both pleased and embarrassed. 'For the shawl?'

'Thank you for marrying me, John Doe.'

In the garden was a silver swing.

Early morning, even before Tom had risen, she would come down and sit there, swinging gently, watching the sunrise gild the pavilion, irradiate the sapphire lake, awakening the clouds of green parakeets who dwelt in the trees. She would simply sit there, hugging her happiness about her like the blue cashmere shawl.

'You look like a princess in a fairy tale,' Tom said finding her there one perfect dawn. And he, dark-eyed and burnished by the Indian sun, must surely have been a prince in some earlier reincarnation.

Had the palace been inspired, as was the Taj Mahal, by the love of one man for one woman? Certainly, every ornament, every inch of carved ivory addressed itself to the senses. This was the question they asked Jamini, the plump hall porter who sat in a little gilt chair outside their room, a fount of local knowledge.

'One woman? No,' Jamini flashed his toothy smile. 'The

prince who built it loved many women.' The palace had been erected, he explained, to house the rajah's concubines, the greatest beauties in all India. There were three hundred and sixty-five in toto. 'One for every day in the year.'

'For every night, you mean,' Tom laughed.

'The prince was a very great man,' smirked Jamini.

The day before their departure they hired a car and driver to take them to the temple of Arisha, a sight – the little porter assured them – in itself worth a trip to India.

'Let's hope we get some decent pictures,' Tom remarked as they settled into the aging Austin with a packed lunch and the movie camera Gusty had given them for a wedding present.

For two hours, the car bounced over rutted dirt roads, past dusty villages until the landscape emptied out and the world fell silent except for the whirr of insects and the rhythm of the motor. Then they saw it shimmering in the distance, tiered like a wedding cake. The road ended abruptly, and the driver, for whom the scene held no interest, got out and spread his blanket on the dust.

'I guess we hoof it from here,' Caro said. There was no path, only a broad expanse of stony terrain, but as they drew near, details came into view. 'My God, Caro!' Tom stopped short. 'It's an X-rated temple.'

As they climbed the steps the stones came to life – a wild explosion of abandoned sexuality, of human flesh locked in every conceivable act of pleasure. On the temple's broad facade, men and women – now languorous, now passionate – enacted the sixty-four postures of the Kama Sutra with the explicitness of a text book and the radiance of art. Above the multitude of coupling figures, a female divinity surveyed the scene and smiled. Life is good, said the stones. Love is sublime. And sex is its supreme expression.

Nor had the diversity of the Kama Sutra exhausted the sculptors' exuberance, for on the far side of the temple, different and darker embraces could be glimpsed. Here a woman cavorted with a brace of monkeys, there she pleasured herself upon a flowering branch. Each succeeding panel became more fanciful, more lurid. Caro stopped before one. A young girl, clad only in sandals, full-breasted yet so supple as to seem boneless, had wrapped her legs around the huge phallus-like trunk of an elephant. Her head, flung back in joy, spoke of a mindless ecstasy, of sexual bliss untroubled by thought.

'They're all the same,' Caro looked from one frieze to another. 'All the same.'

'How can you say that, darling? The variety is . . . infinite.'

'No, I meant the women.'

For despite the knowledge that it had taken sculptor after sculptor year after year to create this diversity, yet the woman was all the same. Supple, boneless, smooth, ripe, always with that expression of sweet fulfilment.

She touched the statue, ran her hands over the smooth throat, the rounded breasts. Beneath her fingers, the crumbling sandstone was warm and sensual as living flesh. In unconscious mimicry, she slipped her hand beneath the gauze of her sundress and stroked herself, nipples instantly erect.

'Oh God, Tom' she turned to him. 'I'm horny as hell. Let's go straight back to the hotel and make love.'

He had put down the camera and was watching her, and when he spoke his voice was thick. 'No,' he murmured. 'Here. Let's make love here on the stones. Let's do everything the statues do. Let's you and I fuck ourselves into oblivion.'

'That's crazy.' She laughed and slid the dress from her shoulders, her breasts glistening with sweat, then came toward him naked but for sandalled feet and placed his hand between her thighs. For a moment he slid his thumb over the hot swollen flesh of her clitoris, his fingers toying with her pubic hair, while beneath the tightness of his blue denim jeans he grew huge with desire.

'Take me,' she murmured, mind and body reeling. 'Exploit me. No one will see.' But he withdrew his hand from her moistness with a long languid stroke and stepped back.

'Oh, I will, Caro. I will. But first . . . you know what let's do?' He began pulling off his clothes, then stood before her massive and erect. 'First let's film ourselves. Let's capture this moment forever . . . a record of our love, the way we feel, so we can keep it fresh in all the years to come.'

She watched him setting up the camera, her eyes dazzled by the light. He looked black against the brightness of the sun.

How beautiful he was! The body splendid and virile as a god's, the broad chest sweated and gleaming, the slim hips, the muscled thighs, the feline grace with which he moved across the burning stones. He had placed the camera across the top of a plinth and kneeling focussed it upon her body, starting it in motion with a click. Then he came to her, enveloping her buttocks with the broad cup of his hands. They kissed. 'Now!' he roared – and with one great heave of his powerful arms, raised her up off the ground and onto his huge thrusting cock. She was airborne. Weightless. Her knees dug into the high of his back, her arms clung around his neck, and when he entered her – in that moment of supreme fulfilment – they were one. Their love, their passion had merged two separate bodies into a single flesh – no longer Tom and Caro, but man and woman incarnate in a union that transcended time.

They were making love still, long long after the film ran out. They made love against the rough carved surface of the sculptures, on the baking stones of the terrace, in the musty precincts of the inner temple. They made love until the sun subsided and the long shadows of late afternoon dried the sweat of their bodies. Then, bruised, weary, covered with dust and scratches, they stumbled their way back to the car.

The driver was waiting just where they had left him, uncomplaining and incurious. And all the way back to the hotel, they sat quietly, lovers still, not talking, merely touching, his hand warm and caressing beneath her dress while the driver stared pointedly at the road ahead.

As they pulled up before the palace gates, it was Tom who broke the silence with a sigh.

'Well, tomorrow it's back to reality.'

11

'Welcome to the Fun Factory,' Tony greeted her the following Monday. 'How was India?'

Caro looked from Tony to her desk – the unopened mail, the pile of publications, the flood of inter-office memos – then back to Tony again.

'India was. . .' Hell! No point in even beginning to talk about it. In this context, all money and machines, India didn't even exist. 'It was OK,' she said finally. 'We had a good time, a lot of laughs. What's been going on here?'

Tony gave her a quick run down – the Dow Jones down to 830, the Ampex merger looked set to go through, they'd ordered a couple of new Apple computers for the office. And 'by the way, I've been schlepping out to Sandusky on your behalf. Jesus, that plant is a bitch to get to. You sure pick your spots, Caro.'

'I don't pick 'em,' she cast a rueful glance at the corner office. '*He* does, and for all I know he does it on purpose. Speaking of whom . . . how is Simon Legree these days?'

'Who . . . Dan? Oh, he's fine. Just fine.'

For a glum hour or so, she burrowed down into her paper work, and when she finally raised her eyes, it struck her that the office had changed in her absence. It looked emptier. More barren. A desk was missing, her countdown told her. And along with the desk, a body.

'Hey Tony,' she asked *sotto voce*. 'What happened to Ed Griffin. He fall down a hole?'

Tony hesitated, then drew his thumb across his throat. 'Zap.'

Well well, there is a God after all – and if anybody had it coming, it was that suck-up son-of-a-bitch. Still . . . her initial satisfaction soon gave rise to unease.

'Gee, that was fast. I was only gone a couple of weeks. What happened?'

What happened, she learned, was short if not sweet. Griffin had lately become enamoured of some over-the-counter stock and kept hyping it to Catlett for investment. More to get Ed off his back than for any other reason, Dan authorised him to buy in for fifteen thousand shares. Ed must have misheard – at least that was what he claimed – for instead of fifteen, he'd bought fifty thousand shares. No sooner did word get back than Catlett fired him, in full view of the entire department. Everyone was stunned and incredulous, not least of all Ed. It was not his fault, he claimed, it was Catlett's. 'You talk so goddam soft, Dan.'

'Then you should have made it your business to listen goddam hard.'

Caro paled. Improbably, she found herself jumping to Griffin's defence. 'You know, that's a fact, Tony. Christ, you can rupture yourself trying to follow his drift.' That Southern soft-talk, she had long been convinced, was simply another deliberate ploy, designed to keep people off balance. 'Was there a lot of money involved?'

'Beans,' came the reply. 'Penny-ante stuff. Personally I think Dan was just looking for an excuse to give Griffin the axe. Dan never really did cotton to him.'

Caro went back to her work with renewed assiduity, but not before calling the chemist and having a fresh supply of Pepto-Bismol delivered. It was, perhaps, merely a matter of time – weeks, at best a few months – before Catlett trapped her in some petty default, some penny-ante miscalculation, and gave her the boot once and for all.

'Well, honey . . . how'd it feel to be back in harness?' Tom asked that evening. He himself was buoyant, floating in the afterglow of a two-martini lunch. 'Just like old home week, huh?'

'Well,' Caro grimaced. 'It could have been better. Like W. C. Fields said about dying . . . on the whole he'd rather be in Philadelphia. On the whole, Tom, I'd rather be in India.'

'Yeah, that was fun, wasn't it? Listen, honey, what do you say we eat Greek tonight? Bill Jostyn was telling me about this place over on Third that does dolmades stuffed with pine nuts.

If it's OK with you, I said we'd meet him and Alice there around eight. . .'

Caro looked at her husband in astonishment. He had the knack, Tom did, of discarding the past as if it were yesterday's newspaper. Done. Finished. Kaput – whether good experiences or bad. India had been fun . . . sure! It had been super-terrific, wouldn't have missed it for the world . . . but that was last week. All that really matters is now. 'Jam today.' He should have had the motto emblazoned on his tee-shirt, instead of the words *calvin klein*.

Or if not precisely jam, then dolmades stuffed with pine nuts and what's on at City Centre this Tuesday and don't you think we ought to break down and get one of those VCRs?

Or maybe India just meant something different to him.

'Yes, Greek food will be fine,' she shrugged. 'I'll go get my coat.'

'Mind you, I'm not complaining,' she told Sally over lunch some weeks later. 'And of course we had to come back. It's just that it was all so . . . idyllic. I could have spent the rest of my life out there happily – with Tom, of course.'

Sally snickered. 'Sounds like you two never got out of bed all the time you were there.'

'Not that, so much,' Caro coloured, then admitted. 'Well yes, of course that too. It's just that I had time to do a lot of thinking on that trip. Like for the first time in my life it really hit me, I realized how come I went into Wall Street.'

'You wanted to make big bucks.'

'Not really. I think I went into this business because I wanted to win people's approval.'

'Like whose?'

'Oh . . . my mother's for one. And also – now don't laugh – some guy I had a crush on when I was a kid. He was an investment banker in Calcutta.'

'That's about the dumbest thing I ever heard of,' was Sally's instant response. 'And as for winning your mother's approval, listen kiddo . . . you should consider yourself lucky. At least you got encouragement at home. Me, for instance . . . the only way I could win a medal from my mother is with the big Jewish

160

wedding at the Plaza. Seriously, I could be elected Chairman of NBC tomorrow, my picture on the cover of *Time*, and you know what she'd say? "So, Sally . . . why aren't you married?"'

Caro laughed dutifully. She'd heard it many times before.

'It's different for you, Sal. You're dedicated. You love every minute of your job. But I'm beginning to have doubts about mine. There has to be something more to life than just bull-dozing my way to the top. I came back to the office fresh from India, full of the milk of human kindness so to speak, and the first thing I heard was that one of my associates had been given the axe. Ten minutes notice and out. Now logically, I should have felt – hey, terrific! One less competitor standing between me and the corner office. What's more, I despised the guy. But you know what? The whole business made me sick to my stomach. He was a human being, after all . . . a man with a family to support. I tell you, Sally, that dog-eat-dog atmos-phere gets to me every time. I hate it. I don't think I'm suited for it temperamentally. And changing jobs wouldn't solve the problem. At my salary level, the competition's always on. There's no room for Nice Nellies. Maybe I missed my calling. Maybe I should have been a typist or taught nursery school. . .'

'Oh, come off it!'

'. . . or got myself a job in a sultan's *hareem*.' She gave a short embarrassed laugh. 'Yup, I should have been an odalisque lounging around all day on a silken sofa, swathed in rose petals and *hareem* pants.'

'Oh wow!' Sally howled. 'Your Tom must really be a hero in the sack!' and Caro, flustered, changed the conversation. 'I've been reading great things about you, Sal.'

Sally's show had recently made national news. In the midst of an otherwise innocuous interview with a distinguished Sena-tor, Sally had dropped a bombshell, charging her guest with income-tax evasion.

'How do you get the goods on the people you interview?' Caro wanted to know. 'Tom's guess is you get 'em sloshed before the broadcast.'

'Nope,' Sally grinned. 'That's almost impossible. Everyone's so fucking wary these days, they only drink Perrier water. My technique is, I take them to lunch that afternoon, right here at Enzo's, presumably to warm them up. The seafood in this joint is terrific, you know. Me, I always stick to a salad, but I insist my guest have the whole boiled Maine lobster. Now who can resist? But the moment he puts that silly bib around his neck, I've got the upper hand. I mean there is no way you can keep your guard up, stay dignified while you're tackling a lobster. Like the moment my good Senator dropped his little revelation, he was so busy wrestling down a claw, he didn't know what the fuck he was saying.' Sally smiled at her own ingenuity. 'You know, Caro, you ought to try my ploy on that prick you work for. Might give you the competitive edge for a change.'

Catlett in a lobster bib? Caro burst out laughting. 'Oh, he's not so bad. Actually Tom says I should visualize him in polka dot shorts, drinking beer from a can. . .'

'Oh, Tom, Tom!' Sally bristled. 'Why does everything always have to come back to Tom? There are other things in life besides marriage, you know. Like food, for instance. What say we treat ourselves to a couple of big juicy lobsters?'

'Why, Sally . . . after all that, I thought you never ate them for lunch.'

'Well, today doesn't matter,' came the airy answer. 'After all, it's just us girls.'

They lunched superbly, had an amiable quibble about whose expense account to chalk it up to, then headed back for their respective offices. 'See you Tuesday at the Women's Group,' was Sally's last word.

Yet when Tuesday rolled around, the Group was the furthest thing from Caro's mind.

'You go play squash or whatever, darling' she told Tom. 'I'm just going to laze about the house and wash my hair.' But no sooner was he gone than she sprang up and got out the movie projector. Then, lying on the pale silk sofa, the one that Gusty had disapproved of, she watched the flickering figures on the screen. Watched the naked man and woman in the harsh glare of the Indian sun first touch, then kiss, then couple. She played the film five times running, then shut her eyes while the blank white frames flapped over and over into a whir of nothingness.

Her mother, so the story went, had wanted to photograph herself in the act of childbirth. But Caro had done Gusty one better. She had filmed herself in the act of conception.

'I can't believe it!' Tom was pale and shaken. 'I can't believe that an intelligent efficient woman like you could pull such a booboo. In India, of all places. For God's sake, Caro, you couldn't walk two blocks in Calcutta without seeing a poster for family planning, kids running wild all over the place. What do . . . you mean . . . you forgot?'

'I forgot.' She hadn't expected him to be so upset. 'I don't know why, I just did. It was those last couple of days at Chettapur . . . I guess I was so happy I didn't think straight. Please, Tom,' – she was frightened and close to tears – 'Don't rub it in. I feel anxious enough already.'

'I'm sorry, love.' With effort, he reshaped his face into the semblance of a smile. 'I didn't mean to sound like such a shit. I'll make us some tea and we can talk it over like sensible people . . . unless you'd rather have icecream and pickles.'

'Tea will be fine, thanks, and maybe some biscuits. Meanwhile I can do without the jokes.'

She trailed him into the kitchen, watched him go through the familiar routine. First the Twining's Earl Grey; then the water, boiled for thirty seconds; now rinse out the teapot with scalding water; add tea, stir once, let steep for three minutes, but tonight the ritual afforded him no joy. His motions were those of a man in a daze.

Poor bastard, she thought, I really hit him with a ton of bricks. But when he echoed those same sentiments a minute later, she was outraged.

'Ye Gods,' he sighed and poured the tea. 'A man goes out to play a little squash. He comes back and his wife tells him she's gone and got herself pregnant.

'Hold it right there!' Caro snapped. '*I* didn't get myself pregnant. *We* did – the both of us, and don't you forget it, Tom Darius. And the question right now is . . . what are *we* going to do about it.'

In all the time they'd been together, all the hundred . . . no, thousands of hours spent in discussing everything under the sun from Art to Zen, the subject of children had hardly arisen. True, they had touched upon it now and then, in the same way they had talked about buying a condo or making a will. One day. Meanwhile it was too remote to be real, too distant to impinge upon the immediate present. And if along the line a concensus had arisen, the understanding that they would eventually have children (or at any rate, a child), that day was in a distant future. Someday – when they were over the hump, when their careers had crystallized, their short-term ambitions been achieved. When Caro was a partner at PAGIT, maybe; when *Ecology Today* hit its stride. Someday. Certainly not now.

'But how do you feel about it, Caro?' Tom kept asking over the tea, and then again over the second pot. 'How do you really feel?'

She didn't know. She couldn't answer.

Her first reaction had been one of anguish, followed by elation, then fear, then finally a strange light-headedness that proclaimed 'Well, well, Caro Harmsworth . . . how about that!'

But now, watching Tom fidget with the biscuit crumbs, building them into little mountains, smoothing them out into plains – her euphoria, tentative at best, finally vanished. In all likelihood it had never been real.

'I don't know, Tom. I honestly don't. How do you feel? That's just as important.'

'To tell the truth – ambivalent.'

Not much help there, she thought, and for the next half hour they cautiously probed the pros and cons of parenthood. And, when it came right down to it, there were hardly any pros, bottom line. The solution was clear; the word hovered on the tip of her tongue. Yet she was reluctant to be the first to voice it, feeling that Tom – with his biologist's training, his reverence for life in all its majesty and forms – would prefer that nature take its course. Yet ultimately, there was no dodging the issue.

'Of course there's always abortion.'

He rubbed his cheek thoughtfully. 'Is that what you want?'

'I don't know. I don't know anything any more.'

'Well,' he considered, 'if you're at all doubtful about having a baby, maybe it's not such a bad idea. Not that I don't want children, honey – I do some day – just that this probably is not the best time. And, if it makes you feel any better, remember. We're not talking about viable life, honey. Not at this point. We're talking about . . . what? A six-week embryo, technically not even a foetus. Just a bunch of multiplying cells' – he posed his forefinger a fraction of an inch above his thumb – 'hardly bigger than a pumpkin seed.'

She asked 'Is that what you think I should do?' hoping for a hard-and-fast answer. But Tom didn't follow through.

'I can't make up your mind for you, Caro. Whatever you do I'll stand behind you, but I can't take responsibility for a final decision. After all, it's your body.'

She sat silent for a long tortured moment. 'Very well,' she hadn't expected to feel so sad. 'I'll have an abortion. It's no big deal.'

Tom nodded sagely. 'If that's what you want, Caro, then it's probably a wise decision. I'd go along with that.' His choice of words was restrained, perhaps ambiguous; but his face was not. As he spoke, his eyes were bright with relief.

'It's what we both want, I guess,' she murmured. 'Now why don't we call it a day.'

She got into bed, nervous and depressed, but in the dark Tom could not read her mood. 'My God, darling,' he ran his hand over her body in loving inventory – the firm breasts, flat belly, lean thighs – 'You certainly don't feel pregnant. Just as silky and sexy as ever. Are you absolutely sure?'

Never surer than now, she thought, her body newly sensitive, more tender beneath his fingers. 'Yes, Tom, I'm sure.'

The next morning dawned bright and cold, and as they waited in the lobby while the doorman went to whistle up a cab, Tom spun her suddenly around. 'Look,' he said, pointing to their reflection in the mirrored walls. 'Just look at us. Aren't we a stunning couple, you and I?'

And they were. Tom, tall and broad-shouldered with his buccaneer's smile; Caro, lean and elegant in a Saint Laurent suit. Note the maroon and gold braid of the doorman's uniform, the bright yellow of the cab pulling up to the kerb, ready to whisk them off to yet another busy busy day. Why, they might have stepped right off the pages of the current issue of *New*

Yorker. An ad for an airline, maybe – or a terribly expensive scotch. Indeed for anything that was young and fashionable and carefree.

12

The door was painted a cheery green, the brass lion's head sparkled in the sun, and over the fan window a Christmas wreath proclaimed the joys of the forthcoming season.

Just like a very smart townhouse. All that's lacking is the welcome mat. For a moment, she wondered if she had come to the right address.

MANHATTAN MEDICLINIC INC.

Yup, she'd come to the right address.

A piece of cake. Easy as pie. 'Nothing to it,' a girlfriend had counselled. 'And this clinic is the best, the most modern in town. All qualified surgeons. Otherwise, I wouldn't recommend them. They use this new suction method, you won't feel a thing. It's just like vacuuming up a bit of lint.'

Nothing to it. Yet Caro stood on the doorstep, hesitant. For one brisk moment, she considered turning on her heels and walking away, but what would that prove? Only her cowardice. Except it wasn't cowardice. Not really. Certainly not physical cowardice. Nowhere near as painful as having a tooth extracted and she'd always been very brave about going to the dentist, hadn't she? Just think of it as another extraction, then. A bit of lint. A tiny bunch of cells. No bigger than a pumpkin seed, Tom had said.

But getting bigger every day – that's for damn sure.

God knows she had shilly-shallied long enough, putting it off one week, then another. Couldn't imagine why, when everyone she'd talked to had been so supportive. A lot of the women she knew had been down the same road themselves.

And Tom. Certainly Tom had been supportive. 'I'll take the day off and go with you, sweetheart,' he'd said that very morning. But just this once, she hadn't wanted his company.

Poor lamb! He looked so bleary-eyed and miserable, had tossed and turned all night. Hadn't they both, though!

'I'll be OK. There's nothing to it,' she echoed Thea. 'You run along to the office and I'll probably be home before you are.'

'Well, at least let me put you into a cab.' He did, and she had stepped in almost gaily, yet somewhere en route her reassurance had flagged, and she found herself hoping irrationally that the taxi would get bogged down in traffic, or have a blow-out or get lost between her apartment and East 81st Street. Yet the fates deemed otherwise, and the traffic zoomed along depositing her at this bright green door a full fifteen minutes early.

And so she stood there now, shifting uneasily from foot to foot, wondering if she had time to duck around the corner for coffee and a doughnut. Except the instructions had been to arrive on an empty stomach. A passing patrolman eyed her briefly, then moved on. Probably thinking about arresting her for loitering. But could you be arrested for loitering at 9.48 on a Monday morning? On what basis? Loitering with intent not to commit abortion?

She checked her watch for the tenth time in two minutes, and might have stood there indefinitely, had not the door swung open disgorging a brisk young man with the clothes and air of a certified accountant. 'You going in, Miss?' He held the door open, so what could she do? She entered.

Inside, the lobby bore the look of a small but flourishing concern. Recessed lighting, hand-polished plants, a magazine rack sporting everything from *Cosmo* to *Business Week*. Very smart. Very smart, indeed, as was the receptionist who spotted Caro before she had a chance to duck behind the protective cover of a magazine.

'Your name please?'

'I'm early.'

Even to Caro's ears, that sounded a pretty slim answer, so she dug out her appointment card and placed it on the desk. The receptionist smiled, crooned something into an intercom, and Caro found herself whisked away by a young woman in white and ushered into a windowless cubbyhole.

'You can change here,' the attendant pointed to a tall metal locker. 'Leave your streetclothes and bag inside. Then if you'll just fill out the information sheet in this folder, the doctor will be with you shortly.'

'Thank you. What's the name of the doctor I'll be seeing? They didn't say when I made the appointment.'

The woman checked her clipboard. 'You Mrs Darian?'

'Darius,' Caro corrected, slightly annoyed. It was one of those rare occasions when she'd used her married name.

'Darius . . . yes. It'll either be Doctor Santos or Doctor Marks.'

'Don't you know?'

'Whichever one's free. We have four doctors on staff, today. I assure you, they're all absolutely competent.'

Caro thanked her again. Such efficiency, she thought after the attendant left. Just like those downtown barbershops, the ones that had the painted signs in their window: *Four Barbers No Waiting.*

Only they were doctors in this place . . . not barbers. Funny though, the very first surgeons had been barbers. She was sure she'd read that somewhere. Which meant that at one time the skills had been interchangeable.

So please doctor, instead of an abortion, could I just have a quick trim and blow-dry?

Oh for Chrissakes, Caro – that wasn't even funny.

Must be getting light-headed, mind wandering all over the place. Just as bad as the day she'd gotten married.

Only she'd been scared then, really panicky – and there was nothing to be scared of now. A bit of lint. A blob of cells. That's all it was, and as for this flight of craziness . . . well, that's what comes of going without breakfast.

Still . . . didn't hurt to miss a meal now and then. Good for the figure.

Unlike pregnancy. Which was certainly *not* good for the figure.

She hung up her coat, removed a green hospital gown from its cellophane wrapper, then sat down to explore the contents of the folder.

Confidential said the cover. Fine. That was OK with her. She opened it out on the formica table to find a questionnaire inside, a single sheet with two different coloured carbon sets attached.

The top copy was green. A peculiar shade of green. She knew that colour. For years it had poisoned her dreams.

At Harvard there had been a recurring test called the WAC – the Written Analysis of Cases. More than a test, really – more precisely an instrument of torture exquisitely designed to induce maximum stress.

Every other week, students would be handed a bulky case history of some company in the throes of disaster, page after page of the kind of problems that might drive an executive to drink or worse. You had to digest the thousand and one facts, in itself an ordeal, then address yourself to two basic questions. *If you were in charge of this company, what would you do? Why?*

Simple questions calling for labyrinthine answers that must be submitted on a special stock of paper, a paper that stubbornly allowed for no erasures, deletions or second guesses. It was due every other Saturday at a designated place, no later than six o'clock sharp.

That first year at B School, the WAC had stretched her nerves to the limit. The night before it fell due was like the eve of a hanging; even now, so many years later, the memory of that exam was ineradicable – as ineradicable as that peculiar paper stock. Green, it had been – a loathsome, bilious green. The very green that now lay beneath her hands.

She dropped the form as though tainted, and for one brief surrealistic moment, time about-faced. Only slowly did it start up again.

She swallowed, picked up the questionnaire again and inspected it. She was being silly, completely infantile, for what she was now holding was no pass-or-fail do-or-die exam paper, merely a one-page form that posed a dozen simple questions.

NAME.
Caroline Harmsworth Darius, she wrote slowly.

AGE:
29. (There, see how easy it is?)

PLEASE LIST ALL PREVIOUS PREGNANCIES AND HOW TERMINATED (*live birth, stillbirth, miscarriage, abortion*)
None, she wrote.

Epilepsy?

No.

Diabetes?

Syphilis?

High blood pressure?

No, she ticked. Then again no no no no no.

NO!

Caro pushed the form away and lay her head down on the table. No, she had never had any of those problems. No infirmities other than a life-long tendency to nervous stomach, a stomach right now knotted tighter than a lascar's rope. She was a vigorous, healthy woman of child-bearing age – and married into the bargain. Happily married. A woman who would, in all likelihood, bear a healthy, happy baby.

And in that moment, she knew she had to leave.

No good admonishing herself to be logical, because all the logic of that long talk with Tom had fled – routed by some deeper, more inchoate, feeling. No good being logical when every cell in her body, every atom of her being, cried out in rebellion. She could not go against the grain.

The previous summer, she and Tom had gone to a party in Beekman Place, and a very fashionable party it was – full of writers and photographers and women of consummate chic. Toward midnight, their host had brought out a spill of paper filled with a fine white powder. 'Best Colombian,' he announced, then passed it from guest to guest.

Now Caro had no particular views about cocaine; far be it from her to be judgmental. Lots of people she knew snorted coke, including pretty reputable guys down on Wall Street. She was fairly curious herself; yet when the paper passed to her, she instinctively jibbed, and Tom had sensed her hesitation. 'Hey, Jane,' he'd whispered. 'Don't do it unless you want to. Not if it goes against the grain. . . .'

It had gone against the grain, as everything this morning had gone against the grain. She blew her nose and studied the questionnaire again – the list of no no no no no – and suddenly all those no's added up to a great affirmation. Yes! She wanted a baby. Yes! She would have it. No! There was no logical reason, no reason at all other than the pull of instinct, the gut reaction Barney Baker set such great store by. Oh, she'd felt it occasionally in the past, that quick intuitive perception, but never so profoundly as now. And never on an issue that hit so close to home. She picked up the pen, her hand guided by some elemental force there was no gainsaying, and drew a giant X across the face of the form. Incredible, she thought, putting on her coat, that I am being dictated to, pushed around by what. . . ? A bit of lint, a blob of cells no bigger than a pumpkin seed.

'You haven't changed yet,' the receptionist noted in surprise.

'I've changed . . .' her voice broke – 'I've changed my mind.'

The green door safely behind her, she headed straight for the coffee shop as fast as if the law were on her heels. Decision does wonderful things for the appetite, she mused, wolfing down bacon and eggs and hashbrowns. She should call Tom, but it was only 10.30. No point in spoiling his day. As for herself . . . she was going to play hookey for the first time in her life. With a spring in her step, she headed into Central Park, drinking in great gulps of the wintry air.

All about her lay a world she hardly knew. Even in the cold, the park was populated – alive with all the people who didn't work in offices. Just think! You could spend your whole life on Wall Street and never know these people existed. The old and retired, the young and unemployed. Above all, the mothers with children. Unashamedly she peered into baby carriages, watched toddlers squabbling over toys, looked from the children to their mothers. Women pushing strollers with gloved fingers, sitting on park benches in chatty clumps.

Were they happy, these women? Or bored and regretful? Or were they merely cold? Hard to say.

On impulse she ducked into the Metropolitan and found herself walking the marble length of the Italian galleries.

Here too, everything spoke of love and motherhood, indeed of almost nothing else. The Virgin Mary, clapping her hands with delight at the news of the Annunciation. Mary proud and radiant beneath a halo while the Magi knelt in adoration of her Son. Mary, lavishing the smile of divinity on the plump and rosy baby at her breast. Mary dolorosa grieving at the foot of the Crucifixion. It was as if all the painters of the Renaissance had fallen in love with the dream of the Madonna, the image of Woman as Mother.

How come nobody painted madonnas anymore?

Bemused, she went into the museum gift shop and bought Tom a porcelain reproduction of a DellaRobbia angel. It was a charming piece, rather too expensive, but Tom would find it enchanting. He could use it as a paperweight on his desk.

Then she set out again, heading for the little cafe at the zoo.

Yes, she recalled in a glow of affection, there was the table where they'd sat their very first Sunday together – drinking tea, feeding the birds, falling in love.

That earlier day came back to her poignantly now, with all the warmth of last year's golden summer. How young they had felt, how full of themselves. And – truth to tell – how very superior to the mundane crowds milling about them. At one point, Tom had nudged her and she followed his eyes to the next table. There, flanked by two unappetizing children, sat a woman of monstrous proportions. A grotesque. The eyes buried in fat, the ankles dribbling over her shoe-tops, the blouse held precariously together by a safety pin that threatened to yield at any moment and spill those enormous breasts onto the table. The three of them, mother and children, were eating chocolate ice cream out of paper cups. And Tom had whispered into Caro's ear –

'"See the mothers in the park/Ugly creatures chiefly.
Someone must have loved them once/
In the dark and briefly."'

'Oh Tom,' she had giggled. 'You're absolutely awful.'

But she was not giggling now. Was that woman – that obscene travesty of motherhood – herself in some not-so-distant future? Absurd! Caro would never permit herself to grow so fat, slatternly. Yet she sensed that behind Tom's mocking doggerel lay a deeper sentiment – a revulsion from the messiness of life.

'You're so sleek,' he'd say, 'So elegant.' Or 'look at us' in the lobby's mirrored walls. 'What a picture we make!' Yet he did not choose to look behind the picture, to grapple with the bits and pieces that held it together. He didn't want the seams of life to show. Detail bored him; paperwork drove him up the wall. 'The trouble with you,' he occasionally complained 'is you're too pragmatic.' This reluctance to come to grip with life's nitty-gritties manifested itself in curious ways.

Two months after they'd moved in together, Caro was apalled to receive a cut-off warning from Con Edison.

'But Tom, I thought you paid last month's electricity bill.'

'I thought I did, too.'

'Well, don't you have the cancelled cheque?'

He couldn't find it.

'Then how about the cheque stub?'

He'd forgotten to enter it. They wound up rooting through the bottom drawer of his desk and there, unopened, lay the Con Ed bill. Plus a reminder note from his dentist, also unopened. Plus an overdue invoice from Brentano's. And buried further down, an unanswered invitation to his cousin's wedding. 'You know how I hate these family bashes, honey.'

'But Tom . . . not to answer?'

After that, they would both sit down the first evening of every month and do the household accounts together, a routine that made Tom groan. 'Nobody likes paying bills, Tom, but it has to be done.' Ultimately, Caro took over the mechanics, simply handing her husband his share of cheques for signature. 'I shouldn't be doing this, you know,' she said mildly. At the time it had seemed a minor indulgence.

But now, Tom's insouciance took on a darker aspect. He was bright, he was easy and charming; yet beneath his bonhomie lay a stubborn refusal to face niggling realities.

And what was parenthood except an unbroken stream of niggling realities?

For the first time the full impact of what she had done swept over her. She had altered the course of her life, fair enough. But she was also changing the course of his. Was forcing him down a path he had not chosen. By what right? What defence could she offer? A woman's prerogative to change her mind? That was pure sexist bull! She had been thoughtless, selfish, unfeeling.

And yet . . . And yet she could not revoke her decision. How extraordinary life was! You were supposed to feel guilty as hell for having an abortion – and here she was feeling guilty as hell for not!

In any case, she was probably being too hard on Tom. Just because a man forgets to pay a Con Ed bill or quotes some foolish bit of doggerel – that doesn't mean he won't make a good father. Maybe at heart, he wanted children too. And if not. . . ?

If not, he would understand. Who better than Tom could comprehend her actions? Tom – who wrote so movingly about the migratory cycle of birds. The mothering instinct that led seals to return year after year to breeding grounds where hunters awaited them with clubs. The immutable laws that drove salmon a thousand miles upstream to spawn and thence to die. Yes, Tom, so imbued with the wonder of life, would understand the forces that had shaped her action.

You cannot argue with instinct. That was the tenor of her husband's writings. And if so with animals, then how can it be other with people? For no matter how worldly you were, Caro recognized, how clever, how educated, those same instincts were bubbling away beneath the surface. Moulding your future. Determining your fate.

Her pregnancy was no accident. She realized that now. She had not forgotten her pills, she had denied them at some profound unconscious level. The fecundity of India that had so disturbed Tom had spoken to her in another manner, and she accepted the result with a fatalism that in itself was almost oriental.

All that remained was telling Tom. Tom – who didn't even want to own a dog.

'But you're not a Hudson Bay seal or a salmon.' Tom was thunderstruck. 'You're a grown woman. You have a choice. The salmon doesn't. Believe me, darling, I understand what you're saying – the dance of life, the spell of India, the biological imperative. I'm not belittling your feelings, darling. It's just . . . suppose you change your mind again when it's too late? It's not me I'm worried about – it's you. You looked at the madonnas in the Met, you say. Next time you're in the park, look at the real-life mothers. Can you honestly picture yourself sitting there among them? You think there isn't one of them who wouldn't swap places with you in a minute? And what's going to happen to your career, honey? You've worked your ass off getting where you are. You can't just step off the escalator midway. What happens when you want to get back on? You'll probably be back to Square One.'

'Tom,' the tears began trembling. 'There's nothing you can say I haven't thought of ten times over. And I don't have all the answers. All I know is – I can't go back to that green door again. Don't make me. As for the job . . . well, naturally I intend to keep on working. Plenty of other women manage to do it all. Take my mother, for instance.' She brightened. 'Having me didn't slow Gusty down one bit. You know the week after I was born she took that photo that won her the Pulitzer. Tom . . . look! Because I'm the one who's changed my mind, I'll take the responsibility. I'll pay for the child care out of my earnings entirely. It's only fair. . .'

'Oh sweetie . . . it's my child too. I'm not the kind of shit who'll cop out.'

'But it's all my fault . . .' she started to cry again and this time he came over and took her in his arms.

'Please . . . please don't cry, baby.' He pulled her tight against him. 'I hate it when you cry. I only want you to be happy and if this is what you want . . . then it will make me happy too.'

'Oh Tom!' She threw her arms around him and kissed him passionately. 'I know once you're used to the idea, you'll be glad it worked out this way. It won't change anything between us – I promise. We'll just have more of what we have already. You'll be a loving caring father just like you're a loving caring husband. I know. I can feel it in my bones, John Doe.'

'Right!' He wiped first her eyes, then his. 'OK, my Jane. Let's have a baby. You know something?' – he managed a smile – 'I bet it will be kind of fun.'

13

In February, Gusty disappeared.

Conceivably this peculiar event might have taken place weeks, even months earlier, but it was only now that her absence became a cause for concern.

While her daughter was honeymooning in India, Gusty had departed on a project of her own. 'Time is running out,' she told her agent. Not Gusty's time, for at fifty-three she was as lithe and energetic as a teenager. No. Time was running out for the Amazon.

The great rain forest was vanishing, with thousands upon thousands of virgin acres falling yearly beneath the onslaught of developers and mining engineers and foreign industrialists. Vanishing, too, were those once-isolated tribes who inhabited its remotest enclaves. A last chance, Gusty declared before leaving for Belem, to record these stone-age cultures before they succumbed to the twin threats of civilization and extinction.

Yet as it turned out, it was neither Amazon nor aborigines that vanished. It was Gusty.

Ordinarily, her prolonged absence would not have given rise to anxiety, for what indeed was her life but a series of such absences?

True, it was now two months since Caro had heard from her, a Christmas card, but Gusty had never been much of a letter writer, and in this case her chosen locale was not one that afforded the luxury of regular mail and international telephone services. Besides, Caro had other things on her mind.

Then one night Gusty's agent phoned, asking if Caro had heard from her mother. When Caro said no, he sounded puzzled. Gusty had promised him film by February the first; she was usually reliable in business matters. 'I don't want to worry you,' said Shelty Anders. 'I'm just a bit nervous. After all, your mother's not as young as she used to be.'

'Do you think we should notify the wire services, put out some kind of alarm?' Caro asked, but Shelty was opposed. 'Gusty'd hate it if we made a fuss for nothing. You know how independent she is.'

'What do you make of it, Tom?' she asked after Shelty had hung up. 'Do you think something's happened to Gusty?'

No question, the possibilities for mishap were infinite. She might have been kidnapped, caught some tropical disease. Worse. 'You know, some of those tribes are pretty primitive.' And even a broken leg, a twisted ankle in that hostile environment might be a prelude to death.

'Or,' Tom reasoned, 'she could simply be very busy filming. You know your mother . . . she's very capable, so why work yourself up over nothing? The Amazon's getting pretty civilized, by all reports, so it's not as if she were in cannibal country.'

He had said the last ironically, to downplay her anxieties, yet at the word 'cannibal', Caro turned deathly pale.

As a child she had been prone to nightmares – terrifying visions of Gusty being boiled alive and eaten by cannibals inspired by a cartoon she had once seen in *Punch*. She would wake up suddenly, drenched with sweat, convinced the dream was an omen. And the worst of it was not merely that Gusty was doomed to some dreadful fate, but that Caro would remain in ignorance. She had passed large chunks of her childhood in an agony of suspense awaiting news of her mother's return. Never knowing. Always fearing the worst.

'It's not fair!' she now burst out to Tom. 'Not proper! Children shouldn't have to worry about their parents' whereabouts. It's supposed to be the other way around. Goddamit!' – she bristled with anger – 'I bet I've spent more time worrying about Gusty than she ever spent worrying about me!'

'Come on, honey,' Tom soothed. 'You know she always turns up. God knows, she can fend for herself.' His own advice was to cool it.

Caro tried, but with each passing day, Gusty's silence appeared more ominous. By week's end, she felt action was imperative, for her peace of mind if nothing else. In quick succession she contacted the Brazilian Ambassador who put her in touch with the American Consul in Belem who in turn questioned the local chief of police. Nothing.

'Maybe I should fly down there myself and poke around,' she said, but Tom dissuaded her. 'You'd just knock yourself out for no purpose. Besides, you don't even speak Portuguese.'

She finally hired a private investigator who went out to Brazil, spending two weeks and a great deal of Caro's money making inquiries, placing ads in every major paper from Recife to Rio to come up with the same results. Nothing.

'Don't worry, love,' Tom kept saying. 'She'll show up.'

'I don't know. I've got bad vibes. Why did this have to happen now . . .' she wailed. 'Just when everything was going so well.'

More than well – splendidly.

The first stage of her pregnancy had passed like a dream. As for Tom, once over the initial shock, he'd behaved like an angel. 'We're expecting a baby,' he informed everyone during the great round of socializing that marked the Christmas season – with a pronounced emphasis on the 'we'. New Year's Eve they threw a huge party to mark the start of Baby Year.

'How very trendy,' Sally commented. 'Absolutely nobody has babies any more.' And Caro had grinned like an idiot.

Never had she felt so healthy, so buoyant, so full of vitality. Nothing troubled her, not even morning sickness; in fact her chronic nervous stomach disappeared.

'When are you going to tell them at the office?' friends asked. 'When I can't get into my tightest black suit.'

Privately, she hoped to put off the disclosure as long as possible, afraid it might appear as a plea for special consideration, yet she suspected Catlett had some inkling. Once or twice she had caught him watching her with a decidedly odd expression. Maybe her condition showed in her face. Or perhaps he'd noticed her ducking out of meetings oftener than usual to go the Ladies Room down two flights.

But he said nothing, nor did she, until she'd ascertained her legal rights precisely. 'Don't let yourself be hassled,' Felicity Haines advised. 'He can't use this as pretext for canning you. The law is quite specific.'

When she did inform him, shortly before the news of Gusty's disappearance, he looked surprised.

'Why, how very, very nice!' He popped around his desk to give her hand a vigorous pump, and for once his smile extended to his eyes. 'You must be very happy, you and your husband. That's pleasant news indeed.'

'Yes we are,' she beamed. Then gave out a glorious giggle. 'In fact I'm absolutely thrilled.'

They chatted amiably for several minutes with Catlett wanting to know about Tom – what he did, what he was like. He'd never before displayed a shred of interest in her private life, never even asked her husband's name, and under his friendly prodding she responded with warmth.

'*Ecology Today*,' he shook his head doubtfully. 'I hope it's not one of those fringe fly-by-night publications . . . health food and that sort of nonsense.'

'It happens to be a highly respected conservation magazine. Perhaps not quite your cup of tea, Dan' – he'd just returned from a hunting trip and she couldn't resist the dig – 'They take a very strong line about blood sports.'

'Do they? Then I guess I'll have to stick with *Field And Stream*. Tell me, Caroline' – he leaned back and lit a cigarette – 'Does that kind of work pay well?'

His question surprised her. Despite its generalizing cast, the import was personal, probing. *May as well ask what Tom makes*, which, she realized was precisely what he was doing. He wanted to know if Tom earned enough to support a family. If Caro was leaving never to come back.

Oh, what a cool cookie you are!

'It pays all right,' she answered briskly, 'although maybe not much by Wall Street standards. I want to make it crystal clear, Dan, I'm not planning to quit. I'll simply be taking a brief maternity leave and after that, it'll be business as usual.'

'I see. Well, of course that's your privilege.' He obviously knew the law too. 'However when the time comes you may feel differently about it,' and before she had a chance to protest, he went on. 'All I'm saying is don't feel bound by what you just told me. If you want to stay on, the job is yours . . . but should you change your mind, I'll understand. In any event, I don't suppose you want to be dragging out to Sandusky every week. I understand that plant is hard to get to. I think I'll let Marcusson handle the contact end for a while, and I'll see what we can manage closer to home.'

'Why, Dan!' Her claim of not wanting special treatment notwithstanding, she was relieved and delighted. 'That's very sweet of you. I really appreciate it.'

'No trouble at all,' he fluttered his fingers. 'I'll put Tony on it this afternoon.'

Next day, Catlett's secretary came over to her desk. 'Mr C. thought you might find it convenient to have the keys to his private washroom. Please feel free to use it if you don't want to traipse downstairs.' Caro was touched. He was treating her, she noted, with a new cordiality and the first day she turned up at work wearing maternity clothes, feeling self-conscious as hell, he tapped her lightly on the shoulder en route to his office.

'You're looking very nice, Caroline.'

Goddam ironic. For a year and a half she had knocked herself out to win his respect and approval. And now she had won it – but for what? Simply, as Tom had put it, 'by going out and getting herself pregnant'.

Some people!

As winter turned to spring with still no word of Gusty, Caro's despair grew. 'It's something terrible, Tom. I can feel it in my bones' and Tom kept saying she shouldn't worry, it would turn out all right.

Yet inwardly, she began to grieve, for the time had come to accept the inevitable.

Her mother had gone once and for all. Bright, spunky, perky Gusty. Somewhere in the half-million square miles of the Amazon jungle, her body lay undiscovered. Unmourned, except in Caro's heart.

Some years earlier, *Time* magazine had dubbed Augusta Harmsworth 'the tiny Amazon of documentary films'. If so, there could be no more fitting finale than such a death in Amazonia.

And as Tom said, as every kick of her unborn baby confirmed – life goes on.

14

One morning she got out of bed, stood up, looked down and burst into a whoop of laughter.

'What's so funny?' Tom called from the bathroom.

'Me.' She waddled in to where he was shaving. 'Look Tom, no toes.' Her feet had disappeared, toes and all, beneath the bulge of her body and even on second glance, it struck her funny.

'Yeah . . . something, isn't it?' Tom nodded to her in the mirror and returned to his shaving. 'I don't think you should run around starkers like that, Caro . . . you might catch cold.'

For the first time since puberty, her body had become a source of continuing wonder. She could hardly pass a mirror – no, not even a shop window, without sneaking a furtive glance. You're worse than a movie star, she told herself. Yet what she saw pleased and fascinated her – this extraordinary combination of grace and gawkiness. How voluptuous her breasts had become, how enormous her belly and, by contrast, how delicate her arms, her hands, her face. She found a new brightness in her eyes, a new gloss to her hair. And if her springy step had slowed down to a glide, she appeared (in her own mind, at least) to move with the majesty befitting a queen or a priestess.

Not that there weren't nuisances galore: the painful leg cramps, the frequent backache, the never-ending hunger for sleep. She craved sleep, the other pregnant women reputedly craved hot-fudge sundaes, and her first act on coming home after work was to kick off her shoes, stretch out on the sofa and surrender to a delicious lassitude.

Simply to lie there doing nothing, not even thinking, merely submitting her body to the uncharted movements of the life inside her was paradise indeed, and in those moments her face reflected that mindless bliss that had so struck her in the Indian temple.

She stole catnaps like a thief, even in the office; and when Catlett was away she would, with Stella Gibbs' connivance, doze away her lunch hour on his couch. 'Fat and lazy,' she said to Tom. 'I'm getting fat and lazy as a tabby,' which comment evoked his dutiful smile.

Had she a knack for flowery phrases, she might have communicated some of her feelings to him. The joy, the utter awe that the familiar skin and bones that had for twenty-nine years added up to Caroline Martha Harmsworth now housed another human being. But poetry was not her style, and her one sorrow, other than her distress over Gusty, was the subtle change in Tom's attitude.

True, he never said anything negative. Indeed made every effort to be gallant. Yet soon after the first round of announcements, the initial handshakes and comments and good-natured ribbing, the novelty began to wear off. From the start he had never been enthusiastic, merely compliant – Caro recognized that – and as the months passed his listlessness grew in direct proportion to her swelling body.

We never go anywhere, we never do anything: the complaint, though unstated, was implicit every time he turned the page of a magazine or flipped the dials of the TV set. 'Boring, boring article . . . nothing on but the fucking Mets.'

Yet they remained a reasonably active couple. They went places, saw people; it was only the nature of their activities that had changed. Less tennis, more movies; less jogging, more walking – with Tom always half a step ahead of Caro, straining at an invisible leash. And though they continued to eat out six nights in every seven, it was no longer an adventure. You can't order broiled lambchops, Caro noted wrily, at the Szechuan Gourmet. 'OK,' Tom conceded, 'let's go to the Hickory House . . . yet again!'

His restlessness wounded her, and she often found herself urging him to go out on his own – play some squash, hear some jazz, take in a lecture – which he did on a few occasions. But he felt guilty going without her, almost as guilty as she felt on those nights when he stayed home out of husbandly duty.

'You in the mood for a great big party?' she asked him one evening. 'That was Sally on the horn just now, and boy! does she have something to celebrate.'

'Coast to coast,' Sally had crowed. 'Yours truly is going national next October, every week for a prime-time half hour.' It was a show she had dreamed up from scratch, timed to cash in on the flood-tide of the feminist movement. 'Woman to Woman' the programme would be called – each half hour devoted to an exclusive interview with the most powerful women of the day. 'No movie stars, presidents' wives, crap like that . . . I'm going to be talking to the real movers, the women who make things happen.' She had already lined up a formidable season 'The mayor of Chicago, that gal who heads production at 20th Century Fox, the UN Ambassador . . . and if your mother ever shows up, her too. Meanwhile, I'm going to celebrate with some high-style whoopee . . . big party, tons of people. How are you and Tom fixed for next Saturday?'

'Just fine,' Caro said. 'We'd be delighted.'

'Just fine,' Tom said when she told him. 'Ought to be fun. She'll probably have collected half the scalps in New York. What are you going to wear, honey?'

'Oh, I don't know. Have to think about it.' But the inventory of her maternity wardrobe yielded nothing but ample suits, roomy shifts and an abundance of sensible shoes.

The following day she blew a small fortune on a velvet maternity dress at Bergdorf's and a pair of silver sandals. 'Of course,' she rationalized clutching the large lilac box, 'it's not really an extravagance. I can always have it taken in later, or maybe wear it as a hostess gown.' For Tom had always liked her in black velvet and she was determined to do him proud.

Beautiful people! They filled every corner of Sally's huge white apartment – the beautiful, beautiful people. 'Look!' Tom's eyes raked the press of bodies. 'There's Chrissie Evert . . . Al Pacino . . . say isn't that Tom Wolfe?' Indeed yes, and there was the striking Japanese girl who was the cover of this month's *Vogue*; and the latest defector from the Bolshoi, thin as a pin and far more fetching; that English rock star what's-his-name? – and at the hub of the crowd, Sally, resplendent in multi-coloured acres of de la Renta chiffon.

Tom fought his way to the bar, returning with Caro's regulation glass of white wine and a hefty scotch for himself. 'You know who that is standing by the fireplace?' his eyes glittered. 'The new editor of *Harper's*. Listen, honey . . . do you mind if I go over and introduce myself? . . . back in a minute.'

'You go ahead, darling. I think I'll just . . .' but he was gone before she finished her sentence, 'just treat myself to a little caviar.'

Oh screw it! She inched over to the buffet. Wouldn't kill her to go off the damn diet for once. The food looked magnificent and she wondered if she should make up a plate for Tom. She tried to catch his eye across the room – 'Hey, John' she mouthed – but he didn't see her. He was busy moving easily from group to group, laughing, happy, nimble as a fish in water.

He wouldn't be back, not for a while anyhow, and Caro didn't feel up to plunging into the crush. She took a plate, piled it high with forbidden delicacies and found a seat in the corner of the dining room. Next to her sat a plump middle-aged lady, hardly typical of the general run of guests.

'You don't remember me, Caro. I'm Sally's mother. Isn't all this thrilling?'

'Thrilling.' The two women ate and exchanged small talk like sedate chaperones at a high school prom, while disco music screamed in the room beyond.

Caro finished her food, then sat for a while waiting for Tom to rescue her. 'Guess I better go and socialize,' she excused herself and headed towards the music. Above the crowd she could see Tom dancing, hips a-swivel, face aglow, moving feverishly to the beat. Very sexy, her Tom. For a moment she succumbed to a flight of irritation, then gave herself a mental kick.

What the hell! He's enjoying himself. And she wasn't hypocrite enough to deny that, but for her enormous girth, she too would be out there now, drinking, laughing, flirting. Dancing with the best-looking partners.

She hovered at the edge of the crowd. From time to time people chatted with her – and very pleasant they were, too. Always 'Can I get you something? Would you like a chair?'

until Caro finally snapped 'I'm neither an invalid nor a cripple' at a young man who was simply trying to be polite.

In fact her feet were killing her, and as the time passed – the music getting louder, the dancing more frenetic, the guests flying higher on coke and booze and body contact – she grew increasingly miserable.

Shouldn't have eaten that caviar. Always did give her heartburn. By ten o'clock, she had developed a raging headache.

'Would you do me a favour?' She went over to Mrs Klein. 'You see that tall guy over there by the piano . . . the one talking to Meryl Streep? That's my husband. If you get a chance, tell him I've trotted along home and he should stay and enjoy himself.'

A half hour later she was reading in bed when Tom burst in fuming. 'Jesus, Caro, what did you go and disappear like that for . . . without saying a word? You made me look like an asshole. If you wanted to go home all you had to do was tell me. I would have left with you . . . it's no big deal.'

'You were having a good time, Tom. I didn't want to spoil your fun.'

'Is that meant to be ironic?'

'I don't think so.'

'Well, that's how it came out. You make it sound like I was committing some kind of crime. Yes . . . I was having a good time, guilty as charged – but I would have taken you home.'

Suddenly all the injuries, real and imagined, garnered over the last few months overflowed. 'Sure! You would have taken me home. Ginger peachy! You didn't have time to dance with me, to talk to me . . . you didn't spend ten minutes with me all evening, but you had time to take me home. Well, you can stop playing the martyr with me, Tom Darius. It doesn't suit you.'

'Me?' He was outraged. 'I'm not the one who's playing martyr . . . you are. Well, since the night's so young I may as well get some work done.'

'Since the night's so young,' she mocked 'why don't you go back to your party?'

'Oh, for God's sake, there's no talking to you some times.' He stalked out of the room and for the next half hour she could hear the peck peck of the typewriter beyond the wall. Even the typewriter sounded angry.

It was past two when he got into bed. 'Caro?' he tapped her gently on the shoulder. 'Are you awake?'

'I am now.'

'Jesus, I feel terrible . . . absolutely awful.'

'What's the matter?' She switched on the light. 'Too much to drink?'

He shook his head disconsolately. 'We've never gone to bed angry with each other before . . . not since we've been married. What is it the bible says . . . let not the sun go down upon your wrath. I wouldn't be able to sleep with good conscience. Can't we talk things out the way we always used to? Please, tell me what's bothering you. What have I done wrong?'

'Nothing,' she insisted. She was simply tired, work-weary, edgy about Gusty. Then, inconsequentially she blurted out 'you never call me Jane any more.'

'But, baby . . .' He was flabbergasted. 'What an extraordinary thing to say. It was only a nickname . . . I had no idea it meant so much.'

'It's not just the name, Tom. It's . . . everything.' She burst into tears, and with the tears came a flood of accusations, the release of those fears so painfully suppressed the last few months. He found her gross, ungainly, she charged between sobs. He hated her for being pregnant. 'You think I'm repulsive, don't you Tom? No . . . don't bother to lie. I can tell by the way you touch me, the way you look at me. You think I'm grotesque. We're never intimate anymore. . .'

'But Caro, be reasonable,' Tom protested. 'As far as sex goes, well – you're asleep every night by half-past ten.'

'I didn't mean that kind of intimacy, although . . . yes, that too. I meant – we never hold hands any more or really talk or kid about the way we used to. You make me feel like I'm a burden, a millstone dragging you down. . .'

'Simply not true, darling. It's just sheer nerves. And not only on your part . . . on mine too. Like tonight. I guess I was acting kind of manic. I had this compulsion to eat, drink, glut, meet every celebrity, dance with every girl like it was going out of style.' His pondered his admission for a moment. 'I know you'll think this is a crazy analogy but. . . The night before the Battle of Waterloo, there was this fantastic ball in Brussels. Practically the whole British Army was there, from the Duke of Wellington on down . . . all getting drunk, dancing, making out. Because the next day they were going to face Napoleon and nobody knew what the outcome would be. So naturally they wanted to have one last great blast under their belt.'

'Is that how you feel, Tom? Like a soldier going into battle?'

'Well, I suppose that's a very melodramatic way of putting it, but yes! I do. I feel scared . . . apprehensive. I've no idea how I'm going to shape up as a father. All that responsibility – I'm not used to it, honey. My God, even these nine months seem to drag on forever and they're just the beginning. I'm frightened our life is going to change out of all recognition. We'll be so burdened. . .'

'Oh, Tom,' Caro reached out to comfort him. 'Naturally you're anxious, but you'll adjust. I have every confidence. . .'

'Do you? Yes, you do. You seem to have all the confidence in the world – and that's the scariest bit of all. I look at you and you're so assured, so serene . . . so terribly wrapped up in all this that sometimes I wonder if there's going to be enough to go around.'

'Enough what?'

'Enough love . . . enough you.'

'Why Tom!' – she was thunderstruck. 'Are you jealous?'

'I guess I am, Caro. I suppose I'm afraid of losing out.'

'Oh, darling,' her eyes misted over. 'It won't be that way. Love isn't a finite thing, not like money where you've got so much in the bank and no more. I never knew how much love there was in me until I met you, but now there's always more where that came from, always more on reserve.'

'And what if I don't have enough to go around, Caro? What if I fall short?'

'You won't, Tom' – she wrapped her arms around him. 'Not you! You're the best of the good guys.'

'Oh sweetheart . . . such faith!'

He pulled her close, began caressing her hair, her breasts, her swollen belly – and for a while all fears vanished in a seamless act of love. For a long time they lay there, at ease and happy.

Then Caro poked him gently in the ribs.

'I was thinking about the British at Waterloo,' she murmured. 'Because when all was said and done, after all that worry and partying, they went and whipped the ass of Napoleon. You'll be OK, Tom. You'll be fine.'

Caro arrived at the office Monday to find a call waiting for her. 'Good morning,' Walter Lorencz said. 'How'd you like to make a million dollars?'

15

'Good God!' Caro sucked in her breath. 'If I hadn't given up booze for the duration, I'd swear I was hallucinating.'

Spread before her on a specially built table was a scale model of the type favoured by architects and city planners – miniature buildings, inch-high trees, tiny roads and walkways laid out with precision. Of itself the display was enormous, completely dominating Walter's conference room. If nothing else, it proved a triumph of the model-maker's art; yet it was not the size and skill that astonished.

'What is it, Walter? What do you call this thing?'

'You're looking at a model of Worldsville, U.S.A. Take your time, Caro. Have a good look around and then we can discuss it over lunch.'

The model was shaped in a long ellipse; flatland mostly, broken here and there by hilly rises. There were ponds, streams, several ornamental lakes, even a miniature forest. But it was not the topography that grabbed the attention; it was the buildings themselves.

At the near end stood a six-inch high Tower of London with banners streaming; beyond it the Taj Mahal in perfect replica; to the right the Roman Colosseum. Slowly Caro made her way down the length of the room, studying each minuscule building in turn, while Walter sat quietly in a leather lounge chair, chewing on a cigar like a proud father.

Here were the pyramids, complete with Sphinx; the Acropolis; the Alhambra; the pleasure gardens of Tivoli. 'What's this one, Walter?' she asked. 'The Castle of Heidelberg in Germany.' She moved on to the palace of Chapultepec, the great Djemma el Fnah of Marrakech, the elegant curves of the Arc de Triomphe. Over two dozen of the world's greatest landmarks, highlights of the ultimate Cook's Tour, were gathered here in one fantastic compendium. Walter pushed a button. A slender monorail began its journey across the length of the model, stopping here and there at various pavilions.

'What do you have here, Walter?' She finally turned away, sated. 'A World's Fair? Some new kind of Disneyland?'

'Both,' Walter spread out his hands. 'Both and neither.'

He had recently acquired a twenty-thousand acre tract of land, 'in Florida as you so rightly guessed'. The property had been a sensational buy, too far from Disney World to command top dollar, yet accessible by interstate highway. Quite simply a vast acreage of undeveloped terrain, part swamp and part wilderness. On this site, he proposed to erect the greatest theme park on earth.

Within the boundaries of Worldsville, U.S.A., some thirty of the world's top tourist attractions would be recreated, each replica close to the size of the original.

'Just think of it, Caro . . . a tourist could go abroad year after year and never see one tenth of what Worldsville can offer. Besides which, who has the time these days . . . let alone the money? Now, in a single vacation, it's all yours, a trip around the world you can enjoy without leaving the United States. Rather boggles the mind, doesn't it?'

It certainly did. And Caro's first reaction was that Walter's coup with the mangoes had boggled his. Somewhere along the line, megalomania must have set in, for the whole concept was sheerest fantasy. She poured herself a glass of Vichy water, then asked the obvious question.

'What would it take to build something like this, Walter? Five hundred million dollars? A billion?'

'Under a billion,' Walter answered. 'At current construction prices, I've costed it out at a little over nine hundred million. Of course a lot depends on the rate of inflation.'

'Well, Walter' – she could only gasp at his pretensions. 'We're not even in the same ball park, you and I. If we invest a million in any one venture, that's a big decision. Why, there isn't a financial institution anywhere that will put up money that size, least of all on such an iffy proposition. You ought to get yourself a couple of Arab oil sheiks.'

She had said it sarcastically, but Walter nodded. 'Now you're beginning to get the idea.'

There were, he explained, three separate stages in translating the dream into the reality.

Step one: acquiring the site. That he had done partly from his own fortune, partly with money from the Florida banks.

Step two: preparing the site for construction – road building, insect control, drainage, landscaping. Seven million dollars would do the job, he estimated, and it was in this area of 'seed money' that he hoped Caro's company might participate. 'Of course in your condition, Caro you may prefer that I deal with one of your colleagues. . .'

'I'm only pregnant from the neck down, Walter. My brain is still functioning normally. Let's say for the sake of argument, you rustle up the seed money from us and other investors . . . that leaves you just the odd eight hundred and ninety million dollars to scare up. Which is, I presume, step three.'

'Correct.'

'And where is that financing going to come from?'

'We'll get to that presently and when we do, my bet is you'll be able to tell me. First, let's examine Worldsville in depth. You may have noted that each pavilion represents a different country. Now you pick a country included in the model and I'll tell you what a typical visitor might expect in that pavilion. Pick some place that appeals to you.'

'How about England?'

'England . . . Britain. Fine. The British pavilion as you've seen is a replica of the Tower of London. Now picture this. You arrive by monorail. Outside the entrance, maybe there are knights in medieval armour, jousting away. Maybe a cricket match is going on. You cross the moat, enter the building, there's one of those British Beefeaters at the gate, you know . . . with the red uniform and tall fur hats. He greets you, takes your luggage, shows you to your room. . .'

'It's a hotel!' Caro exclaimed.

'More than that – it's a total resort. Your room is British in every detail . . . beamed ceilings, mullioned windows, hunting scenes on the wall. You unpack, go downstairs, maybe have tea in the tearoom – scones, crumpets, that sort of thing. After tea, you might visit the theatre-club . . . there'll be an entertainment centre in every pavilion. Could be anything from flamenco dancers to sword swallowers, but this being England it'll probably be Music Hall acts. Or maybe even a current West End play. Let's say you've got kids. While you're enjoying the show, they're visiting the dungeon, taking rides. Maybe there's an archery court out back where Robin Hood can show them the ropes. Naturally, there's a haunted room somewhere. We'd do it with holograms. Later you have dinner in a typical British restaurant . . . roast beef, Yorkshire pud, then have a couple of pints in the pub. And then . . . and then' – he paused for dramatic effect – 'you go into the shopping arcade. This will be, Caro, the most tremendous range of British merchandise available outside the U.K. Antique shops; cashmeres and Burberrys; china – Spode, Wedgwood and all that jazz. There'll be a gourmet food shop with a selection of English teas, biscuits. All these places take credit cards, naturally. What's your husband's name, Caro?'

'Tom.'

'Right. Now you drag Tom over to the Highland Shoppe to get him fitted out for a kilt. You don't know what clan he is? OK. Right next door there's a genealogist who can plot your family tree for a fee. Meanwhile the kids are going crazy in the souvenir shop. Can you see it, Caro? You have the whole British experience . . . food, sights, goodies . . . and the next day you take the monorail to Singapore or Greece or Mexico.'

She could see it. And in one quick stunning insight, she could see exactly how Walter planned to finance it. It was brilliant. The most dazzling, original, goddamnedest concept imaginable – and Walter had found a way to pull it off. But she kept her counsel. Let him talk.

'You know why most people go abroad, Caro? They don't go for the culture and the scenery. That's peripheral. Sure, as long as they're in the neighbourhood they'll visit the Vatican or pay their respects to the Louvre. But what they really want to do, what they're aching for is to buy. To consume. To go to Harrods or walk down the Rue de la Paix, to visit the flea markets, go crazy in Oriental bazaars, Arab souks. They want to come home up to their eyeballs in merchandise and souvenirs. I'm sure you and Tom are different, more sophisticated. . .' But Caro grinned and shook her head. Why, the very first thing they had done in Calcutta was shop their hearts out in the great bazaar. 'But most people,' Walter continued, 'want just five basic things. One, they want to shop. Two, to eat' – he emphasized each point by raising a finger – 'Three, to drink. Four, to see the night life . . .' He paused.

'And five?'

'Five' – Walter splayed out his hand. 'They want to get back home in one piece. That's the beauty of Worldsville, it's travel without tears. You know you're not going to be hijacked by terrorists, kidnapped by bandits. No foreign cab driver will rip you off. There are no beggars, no muggers, no starving children . . . no grinding slums to offend your sensibilities. In Worldsville everything will be clean, sanitized. It's safe to drink the water. And there's no way your vacation's going to be spoiled by food poisoning or gastro-enteritis or being bitten by a scorpion or catching some tropical disease. Not even a language barrier, because everyone speaks English. Think of it, Caro – Worldsville will be an international showcase, the place where every major country can put its best foot forward.' He stopped triumphant, then folded his arms and leaned back, waiting for it all to sink in. But Caro had already grasped the implications.

'So,' she said. 'You plan to have each country finance its own pavilion entirely. Thirty countries, say, at an average of twenty-five million dollars a throw. You don't have to put up capital beyond the initial investment, and then what, Walter? You sit back and take a percentage of the gross receipts.'

'Me,' Walter interjected with a significant nod. 'And whatever investors get in on the ground floor with me.'

Caro smiled. 'That's a pretty wild proposition, Walter. . .'

'But feasible,' he sprang to his feet. 'Believe me, it is totally feasible.'

'Maybe. But what happens,' she countered, 'if a country decides not to participate . . . a major tourist country like France or Italy? That'll panic the other participants. Something like this, it's either big or its nothing.'

'Believe me, Caro, I've thought this out. If a government doesn't want to participate officially . . . fine! There are plenty of other channels. Manufacturers, Chambers of Commerce, Arts and Craft Councils, hotel owners, department stores that want to get a foothold in the States. . .'

'Restaurants,' Caro said. 'You could have franchise restaurants . . . Maxim's of Paris, say, or Simpsons in the Strand. You know who else might be interested? The foreign airlines, the tourist bureaux. Each pavilion could have a concession where people would plan next year's vacations. You know something like. . . "Now that you've had a taste of Spain or wherever, come see the whole country." You could raise capital on that basis . . . that it will result in increased tourism in the participating countries. . .'

She and Walter spent the next half hour batting ideas back and forth with a growing sense of excitement.

'You do see it, Caro . . . don't you?' Walter was glowing like a thousand-watt bulb – 'the challenge, the potential! It can work and it will! For the last six months I have done nothing but eat, drink and live Worldsville. I get up with it in the morning, I go to bed with it at night. And I know' – he gave his paunch a vigorous thump – 'I know it's going to happen . . . I can feel it in my guts. Within three years, that's how long I figure, I'll have turned twenty thousand acres of swampland into the biggest, most profitable tourist attraction in the world.'

They sat without speaking for several moments, then Caro said 'OK, Walter. Now let's get down to the nitty gritties.'

It was late when she left his office, her head reeling with ideas, her briefcase packed with facts and figures. No question, Walter had done his homework. The growth of tourism in central Florida was astronomical, unique. Much of the groundwork had already been laid: architectural plans, construction estimates. He was organizing a crack international sales team to assist him in raising the money for step three.

But the driving force, the ultimate punch would come from Walter himself – his contagious excitement, his unbounded confidence, his ability to back up vast dreams with hard-and-fast data. 'I'm going directly to the top . . . heads of state, ministers of trade. I've got excellent connections. And you know, I can tell you without false modesty, I am one of the world's greatest salesmen.'

If his presentation to Caro was any indication, he was just that – a spellbinder of the highest order.

Over dinner she unfolded the project to Tom and he, too, was entranced by its scope. 'But wow . . . is that hairy! Do you think your company will go for anything that wild? I thought they were all such hard-nosed business types.'

'Yes and no,' Caro speculated. 'They play it pretty loose up there, especially Catlett. He'll either love it or laugh me out of court. But it's conceivable we'd go for a piece of it . . . a million maybe. Right now, we're sitting on a lot of money. Still, a piece of action in something that size, even a small percentage . . . well, if everything went right, it could be a goldmine.'

'And for you personally, honey? What's in it for you?'

'For me . . .' She stopped and corrected herself. 'For *us* – you, me and the baby – a percentage of that percentage. Oh God, Tom! I don't even dare think about it. Chances are, of course, the whole thing's a pipe dream. But should it come off according to Walter's projections' – she drew a deep breath – 'Honey, we'd be set for life!'

'Touch wood,' Tom said – and Caro rapped on the butcher-block table. 'Only I don't think this is wood, Tom. I think it's laminated formica.'

They both laughed.

'Anyhow, I'm going to broach it to Catlett first chance I get. Tomorrow morning, if he's available.'

He wasn't. And the earliest opportunity Caro had for introducing Worldsville was not, as she had hoped, in a one-to-one talk but at a small staff meeting in Catlett's office. She seated herself on a couch, then looked around to take the measure of the others present. There was Tony Marcusson – well, that was OK. Tony was an aviator at heart. Avery Broome – bad news. He fought any idea he hadn't come up with personally. Gunther Rees – maybe. He'd come up with that screwy petrol-out-of cheese plan. Bill Reynolds – bad, bad, bad. His proudest claim was being down to earth.

And, prowling restlessly between the long white sofas – powerful and problematic – Dan Catlett.

Not, on the whole, a sympathetic gathering and for a moment Caro quavered. Perhaps she should wait to get Catlett alone, but he was a hard guy to corner. Anyhow, she was going to have to run the gauntlet sooner or later; may as well start right now.

'Before we get on to other matters,' she jumped the gun, 'something very urgent has come up.'

'Omigod!' Bill Reynolds laughed. 'Caro's in labour. Is there a doctor in the house?'

Caro, stung, shot right back. 'When I want gags, I turn on the Benny Hill Show. When I come here, I expect to talk business to businessmen.' And before Reynolds had a chance for a topper, she launched into a description of Worldsville. Quickly, concisely, she outlined the bare bones of the plan – its size, its potential, and for once everybody was listening. 'In short, gentlemen, we've been invited to participate in what will be the greatest leisure complex ever built.'

She paused to let the sheer size of the project work its way into everyone's consciousness. For a moment silence reigned, then Gunther Rees whispered 'First you get a herd of cows.' Then Tony tittered. Then Reynolds laughed. 'Worldsville,' Broome quipped. 'Wildsville is more like it.'

Oh God, her heart sank. It was going to degenerate into one of those running-gag contests then and there. They're like goddam schoolboys, she thought angrily. And the worst of it was they were probably right. She looked across the room to where Catlett was lounging against his desk. He too was smiling. Then 'Wait a minute, gentlemen,' he raised an imperious hand. 'Let's let Caroline finish her say. I for one find the idea quite . . . intriguing.'

That said, he ambled over and sat down next to her on the sofa. It was the first time, she noted with satisfaction, that he had ever singled her out for attention. 'Now, Caroline, can you give us some of the details?'

For the next half hour she spelled out the mechanics, aware of his growing interest for he sat there thoughtfully, occasionally rubbing the bridge of his nose with his forefinger. She'd seen him do that before. It augured well.

'Now,' he asked when she had concluded, 'who is this Lorencz fellow? What are his credentials?'

'You know who he is, Dan,' Gunther interjected. 'They call him Mister Mango.'

'Mr who?'

'He's the guy who cornered the mango market a few years back . . . the Mangatrile scandal. Remember?'

'Ah, yes.' Catlett nodded slowly, then smiled. 'That was a nice piece of business as I recall. Have you visited the site yet, Caroline?

Christ! She was in no condition to go mucking about in the Everglades. Instinctively her eyes dropped to her swollen belly; as instinctively Catlett followed her glance. 'No, I suppose not. Well, presumably you have the survey maps available?'

'Yes, indeed.'

'Good. I'm going to call a full staff meeting a week from tomorrow and I would like you and Lorencz to make a presentation at that time. Here's what I want. . .'

He outlined his requirements, more a month's work than a week's, but Caro – elated – could hardly wait to plunge in with both hands. The moment the meeting broke up, she headed for the door when Catlett beckoned her back. 'I'd like to speak to you for a few minutes in private.'

He shut the door, motioned her to a chair then sat behind his desk brooding for a while. She presumed he wanted further information on Worldsville, but when he did gear himself to speak, it was on another matter entirely.

'I understand your mother has disappeared in . . . where is it – Brazil?'

Dumbstruck, she could only nod. In a moment of weakness she had confided her worries to Tony Marcusson and regretted it immediately. 'Promise you won't say anything about it to anyone. I hate being gossiped about, and if my mother does turn up . . . well, she'd hate it too '

Perfectly true. But beyond that was her long-standing distaste for women who dragged their personal problems into the office. Why give fodder to the opposition?

Yet Tony had betrayed her confidence, and now she sat there sullen, resentful that her private grief had become common knowledge. She could imagine how it sounded to Catlett. Given his sense of propriety, it must have struck him as outrageous that one's mother should go traipsing about in the Brazilian jungle. Almost as outrageous as one's wife clearing off for Arizona. In fact she herself found it embarrassing. 'It's a private matter,' she said finally.

'Of course. I just wanted to say that I realize this has been a very anxious time for you, and you seem to be bearing it with a good deal of courage. However if I could be of any practical assistance . . .' – he seemed embarrassed. 'Well, I understand what you're going through.'

'Do you?' she asked sharply.

'Yes, I think so.' He turned and stared out the window and when he spoke again, his voice was hushed. 'My younger brother was missing for a long time . . . over two years. That was in Viet Nam. And in a way the worst part of all was not knowing.'

'I'm sorry, Dan.' Her eyes suddenly misted. 'I didn't know.'

'I'm sorry too. He was a nice boy . . . so much promise. However,' he pulled himself up, 'I didn't say that to upset you. In fact, I don't know why I said it at all. In any event though, your mother isn't in a war zone, so you have every reason to be optimistic. Tell me, what steps have you taken to locate her?'

Caro told him: the consul, the ambassador, the newspaper ads, the private investigator dispatched to Belem . . . 'but nothing' – the tears trickled down her cheeks – 'it's as if she vanished off the face of the earth.'

He made no comment, simply handed her his breast-pocket handkerchief, and waited patiently till she composed herself. Then – 'Have you been in touch with her bank, Caroline?'

'Her bank! What in heaven's name for?'

'Well,' he reasoned, 'from what you say it's possible she's quite all right and simply doesn't realize how worried you are. But where ever she is, assuming she's alive, she needs money to live on. Conceivably, she may have had funds forwarded from New York.'

'Oh my God!' Caro sat up like a startled jackrabbit. It was possible – and it was the one avenue that neither she nor Tom nor Shelty, no – not even that private detective had thought to explore.

'How could I get that information, Dan? That's privileged, I believe, and banks can be pretty close-mouthed. Unfortunately, I don't have power of attorney.'

'Which bank does she deal with?'

Caro told him. He flipped through the Rolodex file on his desk, then scribbled a name on a memo pad. 'Go see this fellow. He's their senior vice president in charge of operations, and he can get you anything you want. I'll give him a ring right now and tell him you're on your way. Of course it's only a longshot but. . .' But she was out the door before he finished his sentence, still clutching the white linen handkerchief.

'Mexico!' Tom's eyebrows shot up. 'What the hell is Gusty doing in Mexico?'

'Beats me,' Caro shook her head. 'Not even mainland Mexico . . . some dinky little island off the coast of Yucatan. This guy Pritchett over at Merchants Trust . . . well, he was very nice about it. Everyone's been very nice . . . Catlett, Tony, the manager of the Mexican bank. Anyhow, to get the sequence straight, I went over to Gusty's bank and everything was laid out for me even before I got here – all her bank records. And you know what? She's had nearly twenty thousand dollars transferred to a little bank in Merida over the past four months. Well, we phoned Mexico, I spoke to the manager and no question it's Gusty. The signature matches, description . . . everything. He even knew her by sight. She comes in every couple of weeks for money. The way we left it, he's going to send a special messenger out to the island tonight, and tell her to get in touch with us pronto. Apparently there are no phones where she's staying, but I guess we'll hear from her within a couple of days. Four months . . . that's how long she's been down there. Four months without one stinking postcard.' Caro burst into angry tears. 'How could she do a thing like that to me!'

Early next morning a cablegram arrived.

CARO TOM DARLINGS. EVERYTHING FINE AND DANDY. NO IDEA YOU WORRIED. HOME IN TWO

WEEKS. PREPARE YOURSELF HUGE SURPRISE. LOVE. GUSTY.

Caro read the message with mixed feelings of rage and relief, then crumpled it and threw it away. Huge surprise. *Well, you're in for a surprise too, old Gusty*, Caro thought, pulling on her maternity skirt. Also huge.

Still, she was thankful the long ordeal was over, and she arrived at the office with an enormous bunch of roses for Catlett, only to find he was out of town for the rest of the week. 'A fishing trip,' Stella explained.

For the next seven days, Caro barely raised her eyes from her desk. When the Worldsville meeting came, she'd be ready.

16

The meeting lasted from ten till after six-thirty and took up every available inch of the conference room.

Walter was on hand for the morning session, accompanied by his ancient briefcase and two smart young assistants. He and Caro had assembled an elaborate slide presentation: charts, figures, projections, graphs, sumptuous architectural drawings of palaces yet unbuilt. It lasted over an hour and was pure showbiz all the way. Then Walter's assistants packed up the slides while he exercised his own distinctive brand of charisma. He was terrific. Talk of selling refrigerators to Eskimos. Walter could have made the sale the other way around. 'I know you'll want to discuss this freely among yourselves,' he wound up, 'and in any case, Caro can answer most of your questions. She's fully familiar with all details. One last matter, however. I plan to move on Worldsville as swiftly as possible. I have appointments next week with the French Prime Minister and Sheik Yamani. Naturally the question of interim financing will arise. It would advance both our interests immeasurably if – should you decide to participate – you arrived at an early commitment. Thank you, gentlemen . . . Caro.'

As soon as he was out of the room, the discussion became general, then heated. A couple of people liked it, most did not. Some of the magic had left the room with Walter. 'Warning,' cautioned Jack Smiley. 'This investment can damage your wealth.'

'I think we ought to take a piece of the action,' Tony said. 'No screwier than the Sonic Jacuzzi.'

'There at least was a product,' Gunther argued. 'Here there's zilch. No patents, no processes, no plant. To me it looks like money down the drain.'

'Down the swamp more likely. Christ, that's alligator country down there.'

'Yeah . . . well, if it bombs we can always go into the handbag business.'

'It's a one-man show.' Caro heard time and again. Sure Lorencz was a helluva salesman, but too much depended on him. 'Charisma isn't collateral – at least not at my bank.' Sporadic laughter. Cries of 'Yeah . . . yeah . . .'

With a shock, Caro realized what was happening. There was a vacuum in the room – a vacuum of power.

Walter had gone.

Catlett was indifferent.

No one was running the goddam meeting! And in that instant she knew if she didn't take charge immediately, chaos would reign supreme.

'OK kiddies . . . here goes.' She picked up the heavy metal water carafe and slammed it hard on the table. The sound cracked through the room like gunshot, followed by stunned silence.

'Gentlemen,' she announced. 'You all had your fun, but recess is now over, and we're going to buckle down to business. If you have questions, I'm the person to ask. I believe I can provide solid answers. If you have doubts, reservations, I'd like to hear them too – in an orderly fashion. May I remind you that this is a meeting, not a free-for-all, and is going to be conducted as such. I'll start by going round the table one by one and hearing from each of you in turn. After which, there'll be a general discussion. All right, Brian,' she nodded to the man on her left. 'We'll begin with you. . .'

It was moving. Sailing. She had the facts at her fingertips, the answers quick on her tongue – and with each question fielded, each objection countered, she felt herself more and more securely at the helm. She could hear a new respect in her colleagues' voices, detect a new confidence in her own.

'Dan,' she pointed down the table, for Catlett's turn had come, 'I'm sure you have questions.'

He smiled and murmured 'I'll pass for now.'

Lunch came. Went. The afternoon wore on. Here and there she could sense a change of attitude. But as the hours spun out, it became apparent that no concensus was likely to emerge. If only Catlett would put his weight down on one side or the other. But he didn't. Simply sat quietly, raising an occasional minor point, but otherwise preoccupied. He looked very tanned and relaxed, with that not-quite-with it air of a man just back from a bang-up vacation. The meeting dragged on and on. Toward seven he left the room and returned some time later wearing a black tie, a dinner jacket and an impatient expression.

'Right.' He rapped his little gold pencil for attention. 'We've heard a lot of pros and cons today, all duly noted. Now I'd like to reach a decision, I've got a dinner engagement in half an hour. So, Caroline, I presume after all this, you recommend Worldsville for investment.'

'I do indeed.'

'How big a commitment did you envision?' He stole a furtive glance at his watch.

Oh shit! She felt a flash of pure rage. All he wants to do is get out of here. He doesn't give a damn about the project. He's just playing games.

Last night she'd told Tom she'd ask for two million, on the premise that she'd be cut down by half anyway, and provided Walter could raise the rest of the capital elsewhere. But now, looking at the weary faces around the table, watching Catlett adjust his cufflinks, she figured – what the hell, may as well shoot the moon.

'I recommend,' she said firmly, 'that we finance it exclusively. The entire amount . . . seven million dollars.'

A few seats down, Gunther Rees tittered, but from the far end of the table came Catlett's soft voice.

'OK.'

At least it sounded like 'OK'. She wasn't sure she'd caught it. Heart beating, adrenalin flooding, she shook her head in disbelief. 'No way.' That must have been what he'd said. The ghost of Ed Griffin reared its chopped head. Ed with his over-the-counter stocks. And that had just been a matter of a few thousand dollars.

'I'm sorry, Dan. I didn't hear you.'

'I said' – he raised his voice – 'OK. Let's go in for the whole seven million. We will, of course, insist on equity proportionate to the size of the investment plus a minimum of three seats on the board of directors. So if you call Lorencz tomorrow, we can begin negotiations. And now if you'll excuse me' – he rose to go – 'I really have to run. Mustn't keep a pretty lady waiting.'

There was a stunned silence, but within a minute of his departure, everyone started talking at once. There was an ugly undercurrent of anger, resentment that so much of the company's assets were to be poured into a single project. And some barely suppressed hostility that Caro – the sole woman, the youngest member of the staff – was to be responsible for the biggest investment the fund had yet ventured on.

'You better be right about this one, sweetheart,' Avery Broome warned, 'or you're gonna be right down there with the alligators.'

But Caro took in none of the rising brouhaha. She merely sat there dazed, staring at what was written on the scratch pad before her.

The figure 7, crossed in European style. Followed by the six big zeroes.

'It's what the French call *folie à deux* – utter madness for two, the kind of thing you read about in novels. We met practically the first week I was down in Belem and' – Gusty snapped her fingers – 'that was that.'

The big West Side apartment was chaos – unpacked suitcases, backed up mail, chairs piled high with Mexican rugs and wickerware. And Gusty herself, bouncier and blonder than ever, in long filigree earrings and a white cotton dress lavishly embroidered at neckline and hem.

'How do you like it? Isn't it beautiful work? I brought one for you, Caro. They're called *ipiles*, these dresses, and the Mayan women wear them year round . . . even when they're pregnant. It's such a roomy comfortable garment. I had no idea it would turn out to be such an appropriate gift. I must say, Caro . . . Tom, it looks as if you've both been indulging in a bit of *folie à deux* as well. My lord, Caro . . . you're big as a house. Why didn't you let me know you were pregnant?'

'And where was I to let you know?' Caro answered with some acerbity.

'Aaah, that,' Gusty sighed. 'I was so sure I'd written you. The mail service in Mexico is simply dreadful . . . lovely people, the Mexicans, but unreliable. The mañana complex, you know.'

Caro swallowed her bile. No point in telling Gusty what anguish she'd caused, what grief, what nightmares. Moreover, she was too consumed by curiosity to waste time in recriminations.

'Tell me about him, Gusty. Where's he from? What was he doing in Belem? And when am I going to meet him, my new . . .' she nearly gagged on the word, 'my stepfather.'

'Well,' Gusty clapped her hands like a child. 'His name is Helmut . . . Helmut Ziegler. He's German, a very fine family in Munich – although I haven't actually met them. Helmut's a lepidopterist, you know, Tom . . . butterflies, and it was the sheerest chance he was in Belem. He'd just finished a field trip in French Guiana, some rare variety he was after. Well, we met, fell in love and the next thing we knew we were honeymooning in Mexico. . .'

This time Caro snapped her fingers. 'Just like that.'

'More or less. The thing is, Helmut speaks very little English so you may have some problem communicating.'

'I speak German,' Tom volunteered. 'Had four years of it at Harvard.'

'Splendid, Tom. Just splendid. I know you two will hit it off. Right now, Helmut's out shopping – poor man didn't have a thing suitable for New York. But he should be back any minute. What I thought is, wouldn't it be nice if we all went out to a Japanese restaurant? Helmut's never had Japanese food. Is that all right for you, Caro? I think raw fish would be good on your diet.' She shook her head in amazement. 'Just can't get over it. You're big as a house.'

'You already said that,' Caro bristled. 'And Japanese food will be fine . . . a damn sight better than Albanian.'

'Oh, wasn't that a hoot,' Gusty giggled. 'You sure were drunk that night.' Then she lowered her voice to a whisper. 'Listen, kiddies, before Helmut gets here, just one thing I wanted to say. His appearance may come as something of a surprise . . . however, we're all mature people and you know you can't judge a book by its cover. The important thing is the inner self, don't you agree? Oops, there's the doorbell' – she jumped up like a jack-in-the-box, primping her hair in a quick frantic gesture. 'Now do try to like him, Caro. He is your stepfather after all.'

When Helmut Ziegler walked through the door, Caro nearly passed out.

'Well, what do you think?' she burst out as soon as she and Tom were alone.

'What can I think? I'm boggled. Your mother is a remarkable woman.'

'I'll say! How old do you think Helmut is, Tom?'

'Hard to say,' her husband equivocated.

'Come on, how old? Take a guess.'

He considered for a moment. 'I don't know. Twenty-four, twenty-five? Of course he could be older, hard to tell with those blond Aryan types, and as your mother said, appearances can be deceiving.'

'He's twenty-four,' Caro snapped. 'I looked in his passport when I went in the bedroom. I can't believe it. What on earth got into Gusty?'

'Not what . . .' Tom laughed. 'Who! I'd say Helmut got in there but good.'

'My God . . . talk about menopause! You know from her description, so goddam cautious, I figured she had lined up some old coot. You know, an aging academic with bad breath and maybe a truss. Jesus, nothing prepared me for Young Siegfried. You talked to him, honey. What was your impression?'

'He seems a nice enough kid. Tell you one thing, he's no lepidopterist. He knows as much about butterflies as a freshman in college, which he was when he dropped out of school. Still, he was engaging in his way, really quite forthright. Not at all pretentious. He told me he quit college when he was twenty and has been bumming around the world ever since, picking up odd jobs. It was sheer accident he met your mother in Belem.'

'Then that was bullshit about his field trip in Guiana.' Caro was settling down into a low simmer.

'No, oddly enough. That apparently was true. He was there looking for something called the *morpho rhetenor*. Now he's a very special butterfly, our *morpho*, the wings are a brilliant blue. There's a special dye made from it, and the U.S. Treasury uses it as an ingredient in the printing of dollar bills. So there are whole bunches of people out in that neck of the wood who try to capture them for re-sale. I think they're paid a flat fee, like bounty hunters.'

'So,' Caro mused. 'He was out there chasing dollars and he finally latched onto the source. Dear God! I've never seen her behave like that before . . . so kittenish. Jesus, she was absolutely fawning him! How could she be such a fool!'

'Don't be an age-sexist honey,' Tom gave a delightful laugh. 'If it were a middle-aged man and a twenty-four year old girl, no one would think anything of it. Besides, if I know your mother, she's getting her money's worth . . . so all I can say is, good for her! Although it is rather bizarre I admit, being five years older than my father-in-law.'

'But why did she marry him?' Caro clenched her fists. 'Why didn't she just adopt him? How long can it last? Anyhow I'm sick of the subject. I'm going to bed.'

But she couldn't drop the matter – it was humiliating, outrageous. The image kept recurring of Gusty's extraordinary behaviour – her absence, and now this new presence. Gusty fawning, flirting, each giggle betraying a new-found desperation. 'Have the lobster, Helmut,' she had urged. Had fed him choice tidbits from the tip of her spoon, while Helmut had smiled and smiled and smiled.

'All my life I wanted a father,' were Caro's last words to Tom that night. 'And this . . . this is what I get.'

17

The little brass ship's clock ticked faintly away on the corner table next the sofa, ticking away the moments. Two more days, it ticked, before she began maternity leave. Two more weeks until what Tom called 'the main event'.

Despite the air-conditioning, it was uncomfortably warm, the midday sun beating mercilessly through two walls of windows. That was the trouble with corner offices. The glare hurt your eyes. If she'd been alone, she would have drawn the blinds, put her feet up and dropped off for an hour or two. But she wasn't, and across the room Catlett sat behind his desk ploughing through the paperwork on Worldsville. 'We better straighten this up before you leave,' he'd said. God knows there was enough of it. The contract alone ran the size of *War and Peace*, and nowhere near so exciting. She'd sweated over every page of it. 'Get as much as you can, give as little as you can,' had been Catlett's orders throughout the weeks of negotiation. Now he was checking out the draft to the last comma, niggling over the dot of every i. It was going to be an all-day job.

Through half-closed eyes she watched him. He was scowling over a paragraph, brows furrowed, reaching now and then to nibble absentmindedly on a chicken sandwich. For a moment she shut her eyes against the noonday glare and relaxed. The silence was total except for the tick of the clock and the occasional rustle of paper.

Then somewhere, something plopped.

No – not *somewhere*. Inside her. Something had gone plop within her, and suddenly her thighs were bathed in warm water. She looked down helplessly, watched the wetness spread across her dress, darken the immaculate white of the cushions.

I've ruined his sofa, was her first reaction – too astonished to think beyond that.

'I don't understand paragraph thirty-eight,' Catlett's familiar drawl floated across to her, 'about who eats the cost of hurricane insurance.'

'I've ruined your sofa, Dan. I'm sorry.'

'What's that?' He rose from his chair, then taking in the scene put down the papers and walked over to where she sat. 'Why, Caroline . . . are you going into labour?'

The first mild contraction cleared her mind like a whiff of oxygen. 'Why, Dan,' she smiled. 'I do believe I am.'

'My God.' It took him a moment to adjust to this new set of circumstances, then he sat down beside her. 'Are you in pain?' She shook her head no. 'Well, in any event, I imagine you want to call your doctor. If you have his number handy, I'll get him for you.'

'It's on my desk in a little green phonebook,' She started to get up but he placed a hand on her arm. 'No no, you just take it easy. Stella's out to lunch right now, but I can find it. Green, you say. Just put your feet up and relax. Don't worry . . . everything's going to be fine.'

When he returned, he not only had her phonebook but her handbag. 'Just in case.'

Doctor Barlow was out of the office. 'It's Wednesday,' the nurse explained. 'He always goes golfing on Wednesday, but if your bag of waters has already broken, then I suggest you nip right along to the hospital. I'll have the doctor paged at the club.'

'I've been given my marching orders,' she handed the phone back to Catlett. 'What's today's date, by the way?'

'The seventeenth.'

'The seventeenth,' she repeated. 'July the seventeenth.' A day to remember. A real birth day. The end of one era in her life, the beginning of another. One year from now, ten years from now, fifty years from now it would always be her child's birthday. Irrationally she began to laugh.

'This is wonderful. I feel absolutely terrific, marvellous.' All the joy, the excited anticipation of the long long wait now at its end spilled into her eyes, her radiant smile.

Catlett smiled back. 'We better get in touch with your husband.'

'Oh, damn!' Caro flung up her hands. 'He's in Washington all of today and most of tomorrow. I've no idea where. We didn't think . . . I really hadn't expected. . .' Her voice trailed off.

'How about calling your mother?'

Instinctively Caro recoiled. 'No no . . . I don't want to bother her at this point. Really, Dan, I feel fine, I'll be OK. I'll just take a taxi to the hospital.'

'You'll do no such thing.' He was adamant. 'Those cab drivers are all maniacs. Now you just relax and I'll arrange transportation.'

She leaned back, feeling glorious except for the occasional nagging spasm. 'No,' she heard him say into the phone. 'I want one of the limos . . . a Fleetwood preferably. Is Ben Hanks around? Fine. . . I like the way he drives. OK . . . downstairs in five minutes.'

'Right!' He swung his chair around. 'We're in business. Is there anything you want before we go?' She combed her hair, put on fresh lipstick – such mundane acts all the while her eyes were dancing with excitement.

'Oh my God!' she surveyed her dress. Soaking wet. 'I can't go out like this . . . I look awful.'

'No,' he said softly. 'You look beautiful.'

'I meant my dress,' she reddened.

'If that's all' – he handed her up off the sofa – 'I have a raincoat here. You can just slip it on over.'

They descended the lift in silence, Caro self-absorbed and dreamy, floating rather than stepping on to the kerb where a long black Cadillac was waiting.

'Thank you, Dan.' She turned to shake his hand while the chauffeur held the door, but he motioned her inside and then got in himself. 'Oh, really,' she protested. 'You shouldn't put yourself out. . .'

'What hospital are we going to?'

'St Andrews.'

'That's way up in the Seventies, isn't it?'

'Seventy-Sixth. I'm sorry,' she giggled. 'When I picked it, I had no idea I'd be leaving from the office.'

'No problem.' He slid open the glass partition and gave the

chauffeur the address. 'Drive carefully, Ben, and watch the pot-holes.' Then reclosing the partition asked 'Do you mind if I smoke?'

'Nope.'

She didn't mind. Didn't mind anything on this glorious day, not even the pains that were coming now at regular intervals, each perceptibly sharper than the one before. She felt like God. The Cadillac swung easily onto the East River Drive – just about a hundred city blocks to go.

'I just realized,' actually she couldn't care less, 'that I'm leaving you with all that unfinished Worldsville stuff.'

'Don't trouble yourself about it . . . just a question of clearing up odds and ends. I'll work it out with Lorencz. Right now, what I want to know is how do we reach your husband? Do you know where he stays in Washington? Which hotel?'

She had no idea.

'Or where we can get hold of him during the day?'

'Well, I know he's gone down to cover some kind of hearing. Senate, I think . . . or maybe it's Department of the Interior.'

'What sort of hearing?'

'It's on the snail darter.' Then seeing Catlett's puzzled frown, she burst out laughing. 'You mean you never heard of the snail darter? And you call yourself an outdoor man. Shame on you.' Oh, she was feeling good, so good. 'The snail darter . . . well it's this itty-bitty fish, ugly as hell by all reports and serving no known ecological function. Anyhow they're building some dam . . . Tennessee, I think . . . and apparently the little beasties are being driven out of their family home. So all the conservationists are up in arms. Tom included.'

'Hmmm. Can't be too many hearings like that going on today. I'll have Stella try and get hold of him.'

For the next few minutes they chatted like old friends.

'Do you have names picked out already?'

Yes she had. Either Nicholas or Alexandra. She hoped they didn't sound pretentious but Tom had a Russian great-grandmother. Besides which, they were very nice names.

Very nice indeed, he agreed.

Oh! she was in heaven, awash with happiness, feeling no pain except physical pain. Every few minutes the conversation would stop short while she braced herself for a contraction. They certainly seemed to be coming thick and fast, but she didn't complain. Welcomed it. The sooner the better.

As they neared Fifty-Ninth Street the traffic which had already slowed to a crawl, now ground to a halt. Even through closed windows, the screech of horns rose in an angry crescendo.

Catlett knocked on the partition. 'What's happening, Ben?'

'I don't know, sir. I think there may have been an accident on the Queensboro Bridge. Nothing's moving.'

'I can see that. Well try to manoeuvre into an outside lane and get off the drive first chance.'

'Yes, sir. I'll do my best.'

Catlett shrugged and leaned back. 'This town! We'd have been better off taking the subway. Are you all right, Caroline?'

She was.

Then five minutes later she wasn't.

'Help me!' she screamed above the shriek of the horns. 'Help me . . . I'm in agony!'

Pain. A great surge of it, so sharp so unexpected that she was being rent in two. She felt the baby pushing, tearing, ripping through her cervix in a desperate struggle to be born. So fast! Could anything happen so fast? It was all wrong – dangerously wrong and in one nightmare flash she envisioned the life within her being jeopardized. The baby dying, choking, strangling on its own umbilical cord. Suddenly the sombre black confines of the Cadillac became a hearse . . . a hearse to house a coffin. They would stay there captive in the deadlock of traffic, trapped in the cacophony of horns while new life died in the very struggle to be born. Pain! Could anyone endure such pain, such naked fear, such sheer unmitigated terror. 'Dying,' she cried. 'I'm dying.'

Then, almost as swiftly as it had come, the convulsion subsided. She gasped for breath, dropped her eyes, expecting to find herself haemorrhaging, clothes drenched in blood. But there was nothing extraordinary to be seen except her hand gripping Catlett's with such intensity that his knuckles were bleached to the whiteness of bone. She relaxed her grip, but he kept his hands in hers.

'Now you hold on, Caroline, and don't worry. We're going to get you in there in plenty of time. Ben . . . I want you to work your way over on the shoulder, that ramp on the left.'

'But sir . . . that's not an exit ramp. It's the wrong way . . .'

'Just do it!' Catlett ordered. 'And let me worry about the regulations. I'll take responsibility. Now, sugar,' he turned to Caro, his tone smooth and soft as Southern molasses, 'you just hang in there, because everything's going to be fine. Just great. Here . . . let me wipe your face. You'll feel better.'

She tried to force a smile through gritted teeth, say something intelligible, but she was too frightened. She rested her head on his shoulder for a moment's reassurance and then the next onslaught began.

The rest of the journey was unrelieved hell – horns blasting, drivers swearing, pedestrians shouting as the Cadillac bull-dozed its way through traffic in callow disregard of every law and red light. By what miracle they arrived without accident, Caro would never know, but arrive they did, the driver pulling up sharp in front of the entrance, then whipping round to help her out.

Catlett on one arm, the driver on the other, she stumbled into the waiting room in a dazed expectation that her entrance would be marked by bells ringing, nurses rushing, doctors running – the whole hubbub of imminent childbirth. One look told her she was mistaken.

Behind a spare formica desk, a middle-aged woman with lacquered hair was smiling into a telephone.

'Please' – Caro broke loose from her escorts and lurched toward the desk. 'Please, I'm in agony.'

The receptionist ran a practised eye over the distraught young woman, then said calmly, 'Take a seat. I'll be with you in a minute. I'm on the phone right now.'

'Then get off the phone,' Catlett's voice came over Caro's shoulder. 'This is an emergency.'

The receptionist gave him the benefit of an icy stare. 'They're all emergencies,' she said sarcastically, then returning to her phone call with a martyred sigh – 'I'll call you back in a minute, Linda. I have to hang up right now. OK,' she turned to Caro, 'What's your name?'

'Harmsworth,' Caro choked. 'Caroline Harmsworth. The hospital was told I was coming.'

The woman checked her daybook. 'I haven't got any Harmsworth here . . .'

'I mean Darius. The name is Darius.' Tears of pain and frustration started down her cheeks while the receptionist looked as though to say what kind of woman doesn't know her own name?

'Here we are. You're Doctor Barlow's patient. Well, the doctor hasn't come in yet. Did you bring your hospitalization card with you?'

Panicky, Caro started grubbing around her handbag. 'Just take a seat over there while you're looking' – the receptionist indicated a bright blue plastic bench where another woman was waiting, equally pregnant and unhappy – 'and someone will be with you shortly.'

With a wave of dismissal she returned to the phone, when Catlett reached over, took the phone from her hand and replaced it on the cradle.

'Now,' he said. 'Mrs Darius needs attention *now!*'

The receptionist glared at him steely-eyed. 'Are you the father?' She had seen it all before, her tone indicated – panic-stricken mothers, hysterical fathers . . . so what else is new? And when Catlett merely narrowed his eyes by way of answer, she turned to Caro. 'When exactly did you begin labour?' But Caro, too numb to think straight, let Catlett answer for her. 'About an hour ago.'

'Is this a first baby?'

Caro managed an affirmative nod.

'Well, my good woman, I can assure you, you probably have six to twelve hours ahead of you. First babies are always slow coming. Now if you'll just take a seat, a nurse will be along soon to prep you.'

Caro, momentarily at a loss, would have gone to join the other waiting women, but Catlett restrained her.

'She is *not* going to wait. She is going to see a doctor right away.'

'Her doctor hasn't arrived yet.'

'Then get someone else.'

'No one else is free.'

'Nonsense! This is a hospital. You have doctors, you have residents. I want someone here on the double.'

The woman's eyes suddenly blazed with anger. 'Don't you dare tell me my business.'

He was silent for a moment. Then 'What is your name, madam?'

'It's on the desk. You have eyes. You can read.'

He studied the plaque, then leaning over the desk, his face barely inches from hers, began hissing slowly through half-closed teeth. 'Miss Rosanne E. Woodely. Very good . . . I've made a note of that. Now I will tell you mine. I am Daniel Rogers Catlett the Third and for your information I am on the Board of Trustees at this hospital. And I am telling you that if a doctor isn't out here in one minute flat, I am going to have your ass in a sling. Is that clear?'

The woman reared back as if slapped, then took it all in. The man. The clothes. The manner. The chauffeur standing to attention. The enormous Cadillac parked illegally outside.

'Yes, sir!' She swallowed and reached for the intercom. 'I'll get a doctor right away!'

Almost instantaneously, a breathless young resident materialized to lead Caro through the swinging doors.

'Good luck, Caroline,' Catlett called after her. But she hardly heard him for the pain.

'It's a girl.'

Even before the umbilical cord was cut, the doctor placed the newborn infant on her abdomen. And with that initial contact of flesh with flesh, they were bonded – mother and child.

One touch, and everything else fell away: the nightmare journey, the pain, the petty insolences, the minor indignities, the chivvying, the non-stop battery of instructions to hold back or bear down or stop or go – all, all fell away leaving only the miracle of life.

As mothers have done since time unremembered, Caro reached out and touched the fine-grained skin still slippery from the passage of birth. Counted the fingers, the toes, memorized each tiny feature, incredulous that her own body had produced such beauty.

It was, to be perfectly clear about it, a very ordinary infant – red and flailing, eyes as yet unfocussed, mouth already groping for the breast, with the soft scratchy mewl of a kitten.

But Caro was not clear about it – she was transfixed, brimming with a joy for which nothing in life had prepared her. 'I created this,' was all she could think. 'Out of my own body, I created this.' She placed her hand on the downy softness of the head, cupped the face in her fingers. Then wept. Wept for sheer happiness.

'A very nice baby,' the resident said. What a dear young man he was! How tired he looked! For a moment she was overcome with gratitude. She wanted to give thanks everywhere – to reward this wonderful hospital, this wonderful doctor, these terrific nurses, to shower them with praise and love. But she was too exhausted to do anything but smile. The resident smiled back. 'Now,' he said 'I'm going to cut the cord and clean her up. Then if you'll bear with me a while longer, I'll have to do a little routine stitching.'

She let the doctor take the infant from her, but by that time it was no matter. The spell had been cast.

It had taken twenty-nine years, yet in a single moment with a single touch, Caro Harmsworth discovered her vocation.

She was a born mother.

Through dozy eyes, neither sleeping nor awake, she saw the door open, could make out a large floating mass of colour – roses, were they? Yes roses – an abundance of them – and behind the moving mass of blossoms . . . 'Tom!'

'Oh, Caro!' He dropped the flowers and swooped to the bed. 'I came as soon as I could.' For a long time they said nothing, simply hugged each other, hearts beating, tears mingling. 'Oh darling, am I glad to see you,' Caro finally managed. She was wide awake now. 'What time is it?'

'A little after ten.'

'She's nearly seven hours old already. Have you seen her yet?'

'Not yet. I came straight here.'

'Go, go, go,' Caro pushed him playfully. 'Go see your new daughter, then come back.'

While he went about his paternal duty, Caro stretched out luxuriantly. Now that Tom was here, her world was complete. Darling Tom. Apparently he hadn't come direct from the airport. He must have gone home first, changed, freshened up, then stopped to buy her all those roses. Well why not! It was a special occasion for him, too.

When he returned, she recounted the sequence of events with relish.

'If only I'd known today was going to be the day,' he groaned. 'I could kill myself for being away.'

'How could you know? I didn't myself till half-past twelve. By the way, where did Catlett find you?'

'Oh that!' Tom tossed his head. 'His secretary had me paged at the hearing . . . and the bitch of it was, I couldn't get a plane out right away. Goddam air controller's strike and the traffic in from Kennedy was brutal. Sorry, love.'

'Doesn't matter. The important thing is you're here.' They talked for a while, small talk, endearments. Caro gave him a list of things she wanted from home, then Tom said 'I'm bushed, sweetie. You must be too. Anyhow the nurse only gave me fifteen minutes.' He kissed her forehead, then rose to go, but when he was halfway out the door, she called him back. 'Oh honey, do me a favour. Look in the closet here . . . I think you'll find a Burberry raincoat. I borrowed it from Dan and in the excitement I guess I forgot to return it. Would you get it dry-cleaned? Better take it to that French cleaners on Sixty Eighth . . . he's very meticulous about his clothes . . . and then return it to him.'

'Sure . . . I'll have the cleaners send it down by special messenger.'

'No . . . not by messenger. Take it down in person and thank him for everything. I'd appreciate it. He really was terrific . . . an absolute tower of strength. I don't know what I would have done without him.'

'Whatever you say, darling – although a messenger would probably be faster.' He paused, then returned to her bedside and pressed his cheek against her hand.

'I love you very very much, Jane Doe.' His eyes were moist. 'Don't ever forget that . . . and everything's going to work out all right.'

'I love you too.' They kissed goodnight, and when he left, the glow of his affection lingered behind like the scent of flowers. But what an odd thing to say, she thought, turning out the light. Everything's going to work out all right.

Of course it was. Why ever not?

18

Advice, runs one definition, is an Eskimo telling a Congolese how to cope with a heat wave.

Advice, Caro discovered the first weeks home from the hospital is what non-mothers offer freely to mothers. Advice by the yard, guidelines by the handful, dire warnings galore – the most frequently repeated of the latter being 'Don't let yourself become a vegetable.' More succinctly, don't cop out.

Somewhere along the line a general wisdom had arisen that parturition led to instant brain death.

Everyone had stories, not stories gleaned from their own experience but winnowed from the biographies of friends, sisters, classmates, colleagues all of whom were a 'horrible example'. Women of talent and promise who had betrayed their gifts and turned into cabbages or – worse yet – crashing bores, merely by the act of reproduction.

'You take Julie Ebers,' Sally referred to a mutual acquaintance. 'Remember what a hot-shot she used to be . . . that swinging mane of hair . . . her own PR agency and all that pizazz? You should see her now. I spent what seemed like a year with her last Sunday, and Jesus – never again. Believe me, Caro, there is nothing more excruciating than hearing about a baby's bowel movements.'

Caro, who had spent an anxious morning on just that matter, reddened and said nothing.

'And she looked like hell, too,' Sally added. 'Something the cat wouldn't even bother to drag in.'

Bev Hutton, who had replaced Caro in the Barney Baker group, came over one evening after work. After some preliminary shoptalk, Bev asked 'You're not thinking of leaving the company, are you?'

Caro shook her head. 'I'm going back next month. Why do you ask, Bev . . . you looking for my job?'

No no, Bev assured her, nothing like that. Simply that she herself was planning to get married and 'the thing is, if you cop out, it points the finger at all us married women'.

Buffie Lewis from her Women's Group had the interesting suggestion that Caro take the baby into the office with her every day. 'You could even nurse it on the job. Lots of women are doing it these days.'

'Not on Wall Street, they're not,' Caro retorted.

Thea came to lunch one day, and the two old friends spent a long, lazy afternoon together.

The past year which had wrought such great changes in Caro's life had altered Thea in subtler ways. She was more disciplined, more confident, than Caro had ever seen her. Obviously the world of work was treating her much better than the world of pleasure had. It was apparent she had found herself in a new metier. She had changed physically too.

For as long as Caro had known her, Thea had waged an unrelenting war against fat on the theory that you can never be too rich or too thin. And though money had never been a problem, the second part of the dogma had only been achieved through constant struggle. Dr Atkins, Dr Tarnower, *Vogue Grapefruit, Calories Don't Count*: Thea had subscribed to each in turn, whittling herself to the *Vogue* model figure that went with the *Vogue* model dresses. But now as she spread butter on a seeded roll, Caro thought she looked better than ever. Blooming, in fact.

'You look marvellous, Thea, with a little meat on your bones. I always thought you were way too skinny.'

'Well,' her friend laughed, 'I decided to be good to myself for a change. For years I used to go to bed hungry most nights, just like a war orphan. And for what, I ask you? So I could end up on the Best-Dressed list like my mother? You know, she hasn't eaten a slice of bread in twenty years. Be beautiful, be thin – that's what I was brought up to believe – because thin is sexy. Now what kind of nonsense is that? You know Victorian women used to force themselves into whalebone corsets till they damn near fainted. So what do we do . . . our enlightened generation?

We squeeze ourselves into skin tight blue jeans or skimpy dresses, and God forbid an inch of blubber shows. And that's supposed to be progress. Really, Caro, I sometimes wonder what's the difference between them and us? I trust you're not going to feed your daughter that sexist bull, although I know you won't. You're far too sensible. Anyhow, I brought a few things for the baby. Hope you like them.'

Caro opened the Bloomingdale box to find half a dozen knitted outfits in bold reds, yellows and greens. 'I thought you'd probably had it with the traditional pink.'

Caro chuckled. Now that Thea mentioned it, no one – no, not even her in-laws – had given anything in little-girl pink. Each gift had been scrupulously unisex.

A new generation dawning indeed.

Gusty's advice was more to the point. 'Don't skimp on household help. Get the best, even if it means paying through the nose. I, personally, have always found Scottish nannies the most reliable.'

She had arrived one morning for a quick visit, wearing three-inch heels and awash with perfume. Uncharacteristically elegant for such an early hour.

'You're looking very snappy, Gusty,' her daughter commented admiringly. 'Any special occasion?'

'Just meeting Helmut at Le Cirque for lunch.' Gusty shrugged off the compliment. 'Anyhow, where's the pride and joy . . . sleeping?'

Caro duly fetched the baby and Gusty held her, making the appropriate ooh's and ah's. 'Me a grandmother,' she clucked. 'Imagine that.' And holding the infant against her cheek posed briefly in the mirror. 'We make quite a picture, don't we?'

They did. And for the first time, Caro was struck with visible evidence of her mother aging. In her own mind, Gusty had always been timeless – youthful, confident, ablaze with energy. But now the mirrored reflection in the harsh morning light played up the contrast between the newborn's tender fine-grained skin and Gusty's older, drier flesh, lined and faintly flaccid beneath the makeup. Gusty must have seen it too, and for one swift moment a look of anguish swept across her face.

Why, she's a middle-aged woman! Caro thought, pity mingling with surprise. A frightened middle-aged woman.

'Here,' Caro said. 'I'll take the baby before she drools all over your dress.' And Gusty had relinquished her young burden with a small sigh of relief.

'So tell me . . . how is Tom enjoying fatherhood?' she asked.

'Very happy, very helpful,' Caro assured. 'We split the chores down the middle.'

'Good, and once you get decent help, that whole problem will solve itself. What you really must keep in mind, Caro, is that in parenthood as in everything else, it's not quantity that counts. It's quality. You don't have to change every shitty nappy yourself, or mix every batch of formula. That's not motherhood – it's martyrdom. Believe me, Caro, I know from experience that wearing yourself out has nothing to do with being a good parent. And if the hours you spend with your child are all happy, creative hours, you'll enjoy a better relationship in the long run. So don't get bogged down in the mechanics. Tom shouldn't either . . . although it's nice, his being such a lamb about it.'

Tom had, in fact, been sending Caro a mixed set of signals. From the start, he pronounced himself proud and happy, showing his good will in the assiduity with which he took on the two a.m. feedings alternate nights. But there was a wry edge to his humour that troubled her.

'Don't think of yourself as losing a studio,' he kidded when he cleared out his books and files from the spare room. 'Think of yourself as gaining a daughter.'

Yet the loss of his workroom bothered him. That room had been his sanctuary, his 'space', and it was with visible pangs he relinquished it to make way for nursery furniture.

'Maybe we should look for a larger apartment, honey . . . three, four bedrooms. That way we'd have room for live-in help.' But even as he spoke, he recognized the impossibility. Who these days short of a Rockefeller could afford a place that size in mid-Manhattan? And how could you even find one, let alone afford it? No one built to that size any more.

But he felt crowded. The apartment that had been big enough for two was just adequate for three, and thoroughly incapable of housing four. There was no short-term solution, both he and Caro knew. 'Anyhow,' he conceded. 'I guess it won't matter that much. After all, we're out most of the time. And who knows . . . one of these days maybe Worldsville will pay off, or the magazine will connect, then our troubles will be over. Meanwhile,' he added, 'I bet you're straining at the leash to be back.'

That the object of all this advice and upheaval should be one tiny baby – weighing rather less than a bundle of groceries, measuring a mere twenty inches tip to toe – never ceased to fill Caro with amazement.

'Alexandra,' she said. 'Such a big name for such a tiny little thing.' They wound up calling her Sasha. Yet for all her small size; her frailty and helplessness, Sasha ran their lives like a tyrant.

It was a tyranny that Caro, for one, enjoyed. For years her life had been governed by external rhythms – alarm clocks, deadlines, phone bells, office hours, curtain times, airline schedules, appointments, meetings. For the first time, she found herself moving to a different rhythm, a more natural one. The rhythm of a newborn baby's needs. There was something seductive about it, for it was no alien and artificial imposition. That rhythm was part of herself. As though the umbilical cord had never been cut, as if their bodies were one and inseparable.

Intuitively she knew when Sasha was hungry, regardless of what the schedule said. She could tell moments in advance when the baby would awake and sound the first tentative cry. Caro sensed it, a kind of heightened pressure in the air, as a barometer heralds a thunderstorm.

Sometimes, when Sasha slept, Caro slept too, for the first weeks were a time of constant fatigue. But often – when friends and advisers and in-laws and yes! even Tom were gone – she would steal into the baby's bedroom and stand over the cot motionless, absorbed in watching the little clenched fists, the tiny rump insouciantly raised. Would simply stand there breathing in unison with the slight rise and fall of the crocheted yellow blanket, waiting for the moment when Sasha would stir and cry. Waiting with a longing that made her fingertips ache for that instant when she could pick Sasha up, cuddle her, caress her, feel the warmth of that body against her own.

She had expected to be bored. She was fascinated. Even the most mundane tasks exerted a peculiar spell – the endless changing and dressing and feeding and burping and bathing.

Sasha was so dependent, so utterly vulnerable – and on occasion Caro would be swept with a surge of protective emotion that made her eyes water, her throat seize up.

It was a sensation unique in her experience. In the course of her twenty-nine years, people had liked her, desired her, wanted her, even loved her. But no one had ever needed her until now. No – not even Tom.

'How was your day?' he asked first thing on coming home in the evening, and she would recount the petty happenings, the miniature non-events of the preceding hours.

'Oh wow!' – Tom assumed she was looking for sympathy. 'You must be going bananas, poor thing. Bet you can't wait to get back to the office.'

She could wait.

For all Gusty's exhortation to hire the best help, it was easier said than done.

Picture-perfect nannies, Scottish or otherwise, were nowhere to be found. 'It's a seller's market,' Caro complained after a week of fruitless interviews. 'This one won't do housework, that one insists on being paid cash under the table, so where's my tax deduction. The woman this morning, well . . . she seemed OK but she won't be available till after Christmas. I'm willing to pay top dollar, God knows. But what it all comes down to is women don't want to do this kind of work anymore.'

'Can you blame them?' was Tom's reply.

By the time Rosita Diaz said she was willing, indeed eager, Caro was ready to kiss her feet.

She was a tiny bird-like woman, Colombian by birth, and the years in New York had done nothing for her command of English; but Caro, thank God, could still get along in Spanish. 'OK, so she's not much in the literacy department,' she rationalized, 'but Sasha won't be talking for a long time yet.' The important thing was, Rosita was motherly, with three teen-age children of her own. She would clean, shop – even cook for Caro and Tom, and could start right after Labour Day. Caro would spend a week showing her the ropes, then return to the office the following Monday.

'Now that that's off our backs,' Tom urged, 'why don't you and I go away Labour Day weekend . . . just the two of us, the way we used to. We can leave Sasha with my parents, they'd love it, and have a little second honeymoon. You know,' he said wistfully, 'I haven't had you alone for a minute these last few weeks. In fact, I haven't had you any way at all.'

Accordingly, Sasha duly disposed of, the two of them drove down to Cape May, and as Tom had promised, it was just like old times. No plans, no worries, no responsibilities greater than the acquisition of a decent tan.

'Let's screw ourselves silly,' Tom said the moment the motel door closed behind them. 'I want you every which way . . . front, back, up, down. I just can't get enough of you.' And they fell upon each other with a vengeance.

Afterwards, as they lay back sweated and panting, Caro asked 'Was it very hard for you, these past months?'

'Mmmmm.' He traced a lazy finger down her spine. 'I guess I just wasn't cut out for the monastic life. Anyhow thank God it's over.'

She got up and slipped on a bikini for the first time in ages. 'Look at me,' she grinned, sucking in her stomach. 'Not bad, huh?'

'Terrific!' Tom ran an admiring eye over her new-old figure. 'Come on. I'll race you to the beach.'

For three days they swam, scrounged for shells, ate lobsters and chips (what bliss after months of deprivation!) and dozed contentedly in the sun. Not since India had their love seemed so total, their days so pleasurable their nights so full.

'But you know something, Tom?' she said that first afternoon on the beach. 'I miss Sasha.'

'Already?' he laughed. 'She'll be there waiting when we get back. Meanwhile, enjoy, enjoy . . . and that's an order.'

'Now wasn't that a good idea?' Tom asked as he loaded the Porsche. It was, and they drove homewards, his hand on her thigh, her head on his shoulder, with a sense of love reborn. But as the car pulled onto the Jersey Turnpike, Caro took a last deep breath.

'You know, sweetheart . . . there's a touch of autumn in the air.'

It was hard to believe she was back. She couldn't get over the fact that her world had changed so completely while life at the office flowed on just as before. Oh, sure there were minor changes. Gunther Rees had quit to go to Frankfurt and they'd brought in some Canadian fellow to replace him. Avery Broome had broken a collarbone sailing. And that Sandusky company had wound up as a write-off, after all that aggravation. In short, business as usual.

On her desk lay the final draft of the Worldsville contract, page after page of technicalities. She scanned it briefly; didn't even look familiar. In her own mind, she had been gone for years. Oh well, she could study it in detail later, she thought, heading into Catlett's office. First things first.

'Listen, Dan,' she said after the congratulations were over. 'I want to thank you so much for everything. If you hadn't been along, I think I would have had the baby right in the reception room. What luck you were on the Board of Trustees.'

He arched an eyebrow. 'You mean you actually believed that cock-and-bull story? I'd never before in my life as much as set foot in that place.'

Caro burst out laughing. 'Well, the key thing is *she* did . . . that Gorgon at the desk.'

'Ah, yes. Miss Rosanne E. Woodely,' he enunciated the name with slow relish. 'God, I detest that sort of woman . . . loud, officious vulgar. I'll tell you one thing, Caroline, if I *had* been on the board at St Andrews, Miss Woodely would be out pounding the pavements right now. No . . . I don't think she believed me. You know what I think? I think she mistook me for the Mafia.'

'You're kidding!'

'Not at all. I suspect she read the whole scene – the dark suit, the chauffeur, the Caddy – and figured I was some sort of Mafia honcho. What do they call 'em . . . godfathers?'

'Honestly, Dan,' Caro appraised him fondly – the fair hair,

the elegant bearing, the well-bred Southern voice – 'No one could ever mistake you for Mafia.'

'Thank you . . . I think. Now' – he switched gears without warning – 'have you had a chance to look over the Lorencz contract, particularly the new termination clauses. . .'

Ten minutes later she was back at her desk, bleak and dismayed. Since Sasha's birth, she had thought of Catlett often and with great affection. He had behaved so beautifully that day, had reached out to Caro in her distress as one human being to another. The pain had long been forgotten, such being the nature of pain, but she could not forget the comfort given and taken, the anxiety shared, the intimacy of that hour – all vanished now beneath a welter of termination clauses and mortgage bonds.

For a while she grappled with the contract, not really comprehending what she read. Catlett had apparently made some changes but right now her concentration was zilch. At ten o'clock, she phoned home – everything was fine, Rosita assured her – then returned to her work biding the time until she might decently call home again.

Leaving for work that morning had been hell, but Tom had seen through her vacillations. 'Tomorrow's going to be no different, honey.'

'Well, what if Rosita doesn't show?' But Rosita did, well before the given hour of eight-thirty only to be instructed for the hundredth time on Sasha's likes and dislikes. 'She always sleeps on her stomach . . . don't forget to burp her after each feeding . . . make sure the baby powder doesn't get into her lungs.' Her last view was of Sasha mewling softly in the cradle of Rosita's arms. For an instant Caro felt a jealous stab. Just remember, she wanted to cry out, that's MY baby.

The scene haunted her all day at the office and she left on the stroke of five to take the subway home. God, the IRT was a stinking inferno, but at least it was faster than a taxi. She arrived just in time to find Rosita giving the baby her feeding.

'But Sasha doesn't like rice cereal,' Caro protested. 'I told you that this morning.'

'Si, si, senora . . . but now she likes rice.' And sure enough, Sasha was lapping it up.

'I'll take over.' Caro threw on an apron, but after Rosita left she could only feel resentment. All of Sasha's quirks, all the individual secrets Caro had garnered so carefully in weeks of close observation were no longer secrets. Rosita had uncovered them all, and it was only a matter of time before the little Colombian knew more about her daughter's likes and dislikes than Caro herself.

That was Monday.

Tuesday she got trapped in an interminable meeting. By four o'clock she was in an icy sweat; by half-past, in agony. At the first lull, she ran to a phone. 'Tom,' she whispered. 'I'm tied up here. Can you get home by six?' But he was in a meeting, too. She phoned Gusty. Nobody home. In the corner of her eye, she saw the men re-grouping in the conference room. As a last resort she called Thea. 'Please, sweetie . . . I'm desperate.' 'Well, all right,' Thea dragged out reluctantly. 'Just tell me what to do.'

Wednesday was fine. Smooth sailing.

Thursday. She would be spending the day at the Worldsville office, she told Rosita, leaving the phone number there just in case. Tom promised to be home by six, no problem, so the whole day was squared away for a lengthy session with everyone who was anyone in Worldsville. Walter's lawyers, PAGIT's lawyers, three bankers up from Orlando – the works.

Mid-morning, Walter's secretary came into the conference room and placed a note in front of Caro.

CALL HOME

The blood rushed to her head. Something ghastly had happened. Why else would Rosita call her there? But what . . . fire, accident, death? Babies choked on buttons, suffocated under blankets, died for no apparent reason in their sleep. Heart pounding like a trip-hammer, she tore out of the conference room and into Walter's private office. By the time she got to the phone, she was so panic-stricken, she could hardly remember her own phone number, and only after several sweaty-fingered tries did she get through to Rosita. 'What's wrong?' she begged. '*Que pasa?*' And Rosita's oddly accented Spanish, difficult to follow at the best of times, now poured out in an incomprehensible stream.

'Slow down,' Caro began crying. 'I can't understand you.'

'She smiled, senora. Our Sasha gave her first smile. A real one . . . not gas, not indigestion. A real smile. I thought it would make your day brighter.'

Caro expelled her breath in one long gasp. 'Thank you,' she managed and hung up.

She collapsed in Walter's chair, shaken and trembling. But as the adrenalin slowly receded, her relief turned to rage. 'For this,' she fumed, 'for this she calls me out of an important meeting. Where's her judgment? Where the hell's her sense of proportion?' But in that tumult of emotions, rage could not endure and she was left with the image of Sasha's smile.

The first smile. She shut her eyes and pictured it, could hardly wait to get home and see for herself. What joy! Yes – and what bitterness too, that her baby's first smile, that first milestone of the spirit, of sociability, that first expression of individual personality, should have been lavished not upon Caro, but on a paid helper. That hurt.

Still . . . there it was. She had missed Sasha's first smile – the moment was gone, unrecoverable. Would she be there to see Sasha's first fumbling step? Would she hear Sasha's first words?

Or would her daughter be cheated, yes, cheated as Caro herself had been all the young tender years of her childhood? The thought was intolerable.

She went to the Ladies Room, bathed her swollen eyes and repaired her make-up, then returned to the meeting. 'Sorry, gentlemen,' she mumbled. 'Some small domestic crisis,' but no one was interested and the Florida banker sitting next to her gave her a stony glare.

That was Thursday.

On Friday there was a downpour and she called home to remind Rosita to check the windows that led to the terrace. No one answered. My God! Was the woman insane, taking an infant out in weather like this? Or had something happened, really happened this time? She kept ringing every five minutes for the next half hour. Should she call the doorman and ask him to gain entry? Or simply get on the subway and shoot on home? She had just about decided on the latter course when Rosita finally answered. 'Where were you?' Caro pleaded. 'I've been calling and calling.' But Rosita had merely been down in the basement doing the laundry.

'I don't think I can handle it,' she told Tom that night. 'I'm a nervous wreck.'

'But everything turned out all right,' he soothed. 'Sasha's doing fine and Rosita is obviously very capable.'

'Yes, she's capable,' Caro agreed – although it was Rosita's very competence that troubled her. Yet she could hardly admit that she was jealous. That was so petty. 'As you say, Rosita's fine, Sasha's fine. I'm the one who's not fine.'

'Did you ever think,' Tom offered cautiously 'that you might be suffering from post-natal depression? It's a common phenomenon.'

'I'm not depressed . . . I'm anxious. There's a difference. I keep having these anxiety attacks. I sit there in the office and all of a sudden, for no apparent reason, I break out in a nervous sweat. I've ruined two good silk blouses already this week.' She gave a self-deprecating laugh.

'Well, maybe if we went out more,' Tom said 'it would help take the pressure off. How about tonight? Let's call a sitter and go out and have a bang-up dinner. I'm getting pretty tired of rice and beans, anyhow. We could be back in time for Sasha's ten o'clock feeding. And you know, pretty soon she'll be sleeping through the night, so we could resume some kind of normal social life.'

'But then I'd never see her at all on weekdays. My God, honey, I see little enough of her as is.'

'I know it's rough right now,' Tom rumpled her hair affectionately, 'but give yourself time to adjust. What you're going through is a transition period, almost like a pilot moving from one time zone to another. Emotional jet lag, so to speak. Could be you went back to work a few weeks too early.'

'Could be,' she said. 'I never should have gone back to work at all.'

'Oh, Caro!' Tom blanched. 'You don't mean that!'

'No . . . I don't suppose I do.'

Up to a point, Tom was right; the passage of time gradually eroded the sharpest edge of her anxiety, the work once again exerted its fascination. There was, of course, no question of her quitting. No conceivable way she and Tom, to say nothing of Sasha, could begin to manage on a single salary. Why, the rent alone would devour two-thirds of his earnings. And the comfortable cushion she had acquired over the years had been considerably depleted: furnishing the apartment, the trip to India, chasing after Gusty – and now Rosita.

'Isn't it incredible,' she remarked one woebegone first-of-the-month 'that on a gross of more than eighty thou a year, all we manage to do is stay afloat?'

They embarked on a brief spurt of economy, deciding after much soul-searching to sell the Porsche. It had never been a practical car. When she was pregnant, Caro could hardly fit into it and now with all Sasha's gear, keeping it on was sheer indulgence. 'But I've never been without wheels,' Tom complained. 'Not since I was sixteen.' So they sold it for half what it had cost, then spent the same amount of money on a station wagon.

Even Tom, who rarely worried about finances, was growing anxious.

'Maybe you're the one who should quit,' Caro suggested, 'and try for a more lucrative job.'

'But I'm making decent money. We'd be out of the woods if it weren't for Sasha. Just give me another year, Caro . . . that's what I figure it'll take to turn the magazine around. In the meantime . . .'

In the meantime, he would start hustling – picking up extra income where he could, giving lectures, free-lance writing, the odd consultancy job. She'd be seeing a little less of him in the future, but that couldn't be helped. At least no one could fault him for not trying.

So Caro bowed to the inevitable, and the terrors of the first week were not to be repeated. Yet increasingly she felt she was leading a Jekyll and Hyde existence; two sides of her, constantly alternating and mutually exclusive, waged a perpetual war. All the qualities needed at the office – toughness, suspicion, aggressiveness, the never-ending quest for personal aggrandizement – fought with those nurturing qualities called upon at home. There she must be tender, soft, pliant. And unlike Jekyll, she had no magic potion, one sip of which would affect instant transformation. Bits and pieces from one life kept dribbling haphazardly into the other. The emotional fall-out was constant.

Sometimes in the office she would catch herself stroking the polished surface of the crystal ball, caressing it unthinkingly as though it were Sasha's smooth cheek. She yearned for touch, for affectionate contact with a craving as intense as sexual desire. Its absence was a deprivation, a source of permanent low-level pain.

You never saw children around Wall Street, she realized. It was an unnatural society – only adults, working adults. But on occasion, even in this artificial environment, a mother and child would stray into the area, fugitives from the new housing projects springing up to the north. And at the sight of an infant, Caro's nipples would tighten, her uterus contract. It was instinctive, and as instinctively she would turn away.

Frequently, the spillover was the other way around and she would come home, her mind and briefcase brimming with unfinished business. 'Don't bother me with trivia,' she snapped at Rosita one night upon learning that Sasha wouldn't eat carrots. 'I've got about ten million dollars worth of problems on my mind.'

She was afraid of missing Sasha too much, of not missing her enough. She couldn't find the balance. Had the job been boring and routine, there might have been no problem. Had she been a checkout girl or a file clerk, she might have whiled away the hours in daydreams. But she was not. The work was engrossing, and now that the novelty of her motherhood had worn off, she was given no special quarter.

There was one client, a woman with a mail-order business in White Plains, herself a mother, from whom Caro had expected a measure of sympathy. But one morning when Sasha came down with a cold, Caro cancelled an appointment. Mrs Thesiger hit the roof.

'Don't you have a housekeeper?' she demanded.

'Well, yes. . .'

'Then you can goddam well let the housekeeper wipe the baby's nose.'

Next day, Catlett summoned her to his office. 'That woman out in White Plains has been raising hell. She wants you off the account.'

'But Dan. . .'

'I told her no. I said every member of my staff has the same high level of competence, you included, and she can either work with you or go find capital elsewhere. However, if you're going to break appointments, find a better excuse. People like to feel they're dealing with professionals.'

The next time she found a better excuse. Yet Thesiger had been right. As Gusty said, you don't have to change every nappy, and Caro needed little reminding that she was being paid, very well paid, to do one kind of work, while Rosita was being paid to do another.

Yet still she worried. The marathon meetings that had so fascinated her continued to fascinate, and she always arranged for extra domestic help on those days. But when Rosita's quitting time rolled around, she could feel the panic rising. Had the sitter shown up? Was she reliable? Honest? Drunk? Crazy? Why didn't the agency ever send the same sitter twice? Every extra hour of the meeting was an hour on the rack, and she would sit there as the conference-room clock showed six, then six-thirty, seven, wondering what to do – whether to slip out quietly or sit there and suffer. Sometimes when meetings ran very late, Catlett would say 'If anyone has to leave, go ahead.' He never used to say that, and she felt it was said for her benefit. Sometimes she stayed, sometimes she went home. Either way, she felt guilty.

Felicia Haines was aptly named – a happy, contented woman. Not just smart – smart was what you'd expect from some-one who, still shy of forty, was heading up a major law firm. The felicity was pure bonus.

A handsome, big-boned Texan with a laugh redolent of wide-open spaces, Felicia seemed to have it all pulled together in a way Caro both admired and envied. Her office was a mixture of the professional and the personal. Alongside the usual trappings of law books and public-service awards were photos of her husband, of her teenage boys in school uniform, of herself wearing cut-down denims atop a catamaran.

'I don't know why businesswomen are so reluctant to put family pictures on their desk the way men do,' she once remarked. 'We're not machines, after all.'

Caro had met her at the women's group, and had once or twice consulted her professionally, always meaning to get to know her better. Caro had long been curious how the lawyer managed to juggle so many different roles, and finally decided to satisfy her curiosity by asking the older woman to lunch.

'I'd like your advice, Felicia,' she now confided over aperitifs. 'I'm having trouble with my balancing act. Between Sasha and Tom and the office and all, there just doesn't seem to be enough of me to go around. I keep thinking I should pull a Wonder Woman number . . . you know, you whip off your glasses, whip on your star-spangled cape and *vroom vroom* . . . you're all ready to wrestle down tigers.'

'Yeah . . . and her soufflés never fall either.'

Both women laughed.

'You do it though, Felicia . . . the Wonder Woman bit.'

'Me? I couldn't bake a soufflé to save my life.'

'I mean, you've got it all together . . . the big career, good marriage, nice kids. By now, I suppose, your kids are pretty self-sufficient. But how did you manage when they were babies? Or did you have a star-spangled cape?'

'Yup, I had that cape,' Felicia conceded, 'and his name is Terry Haines. You know that old cliché that every successful businessman needs a good wife behind him? Well, every businesswoman needs one too.'

In her case, the 'good wife' had been her husband. The couple married when Felicia was in law school and Terry just setting up as an architect. By the time she passed her bar exams, she was already pregnant with the twins. No, it wasn't an oversight. They both wanted children and felt the time to do it was when they were young, while their careers were as yet uncomplicated. Then, just before the twins were due, she was offered a great job in New York.

'Literally, they made an offer I couldn't refuse. And my God! I wanted it.'

So she and Terry worked out an arrangement. He would take

a sabbatical from his own career and be the full-time parent for a couple of years, at least until the children were old enough for nursery school.

'And it worked?' Caro was surprised.

'On the whole, I'd say yes. It was pretty sticky at first but . . . Terry's a very loving guy. It's not inscribed in stone tablets, you know, that women must do this and men do that. More a matter of temperament, I'd say. And temperamentally that suited us. Of course if the circumstances were reversed, I'd do the same for him. If, for instance, he got the offer he couldn't refuse. I think that what matters in the long run is knowing what you want to do most. Ordering your priorities.'

'I wish I knew what mine were,' Caro said. 'But from the day Sasha was born I've felt ambivalent. Every now and then I'm tempted just to up and leave PAGIT and make Sasha my full-time job. My mother was a professional, you know, and frankly I felt short-changed when I was small. I'm afraid of history repeating itself. And then I think . . . well, that's crazy. I've worked so hard to get where I am . . . am I going to throw it all away just to change nappies? To say nothing of the money involved.' She picked up the lunch cheque and rolled her eyes. 'Tell you one thing. There'd be no more of these expensive lunches.'

She related the conversation to Tom that night who found Felicia's solution 'interesting . . . though not exactly my bag.'

For Tom had his priorities, too, and though he helped with Sasha when he could, Caro was reluctant to lay more on him.

And so she worried about Sasha and Tom and the job and herself. Then worried that maybe she was worrying too much.

And behind everything, adding fuel to the fire of her unease, lay the nagging question of Worldsville.

19

'Listen Walter, we have to get together – soon.'

'Can't talk now, Caro. Got a noon flight to Tokyo. Look, why don't you come with me as far as L.A., we can talk on the flight and then you can take the next plane right back?'

'Oh Christ, Walter. We did that last week.'

He was so elusive, so hard to pin down, yet with the complexity of the Worldsville situation shifting almost daily, it was vital she be kept up to date.

She had twice visited the site in Florida. The first time, her heart had sunk to the pit of her stomach. Walter was correct in calling his acquisition 'the mosquito capital of the world'. The place was dismal – a stretch of swamp and wilderness unappetizing even to nature lovers, and had she seen it prior to their presentation, she doubted she would have been so sold on the idea. In fact, she had been appalled at the depth of the company's commitment, privately agreeing with the appraisal that Catlett must be out of his fucking mind and certainly her first view of Worldsville had done nothing to allay those fears. Yet why blame Catlett? It was she who had done the research, had made the startling recommendation. Responsibility, blame or credit, rested on her head alone.

The second Florida trip was more reassuring. The company's money was everywhere visible – in bulldozing, roadworks, landfill. Even the mosquitoes were getting under control. But it took a giant leap of the imagination to project what she saw before her into the gleaming model world that lay on Walter's table. From here on, everything was dependent on Walter – his contacts, his charisma, his ability to raise foreign funding.

God knows he didn't lack for energy. Riyadh one day,

Madrid the next, then double back to Riyadh – the Madrid deal in hand – before catching the plane to Bangkok.

He didn't lack for faith either, for, as he occasionally reminded Caro, he had put everything he owned on the line.

'Listen,' he told her half jokingly. 'If this thing bombs, you guys will be picking me over like piranhas – everything from my polo ponies to my signet ring. I'll be lucky to wind up with my briefcase, so just remember – you're not the only ones taking risks.'

Like a dealer in a gambling casino, he constantly shuffled and reshuffled the prospects. 'It's a poker game,' he said, but to Caro it sometimes seemed a house of cards. At the first sign of weakness, the first major defection, the entire structure threatened to tumble down.

For despite all his high-priced staff, Walter was essentially a loner; he had a secretive streak, a reluctance to volunteer information or delegate authority, with the result that even Caro – closer to the project than anyone – rarely had a clear idea of precisely where matters stood at any time. She was, therefore, constantly breathing down Walter's neck. As Catlett was breathing down hers. As, she had no doubt, the President of PAGIT was breathing down Catlett's.

'Look, Walter' – she now said – 'I can't go chasing after you. It's up to you to keep me informed. We've got an awful lot of money at stake.'

'OK, tell you what.' Walter proposed that she come and spend the weekend at Westport. 'Bring Tom, bring the baby,' and there they could talk business to their hearts' content. Maybe get in a little tennis to boot.

The last thing she wanted was to surrender her Saturdays but she went and it proved such a successful arrangement it soon became a regular feature of their lives.

Tom and Walter hit it off right away, Tom always liked dynamic people. And he loved the Westport house, with its go-go atmosphere and the amenities of a top-flight country club. Once the business end of the weekend was over, usually by Saturday afternoon, the two men would embark on a non-stop routine of vigorous activities; tennis, snow-shoeing, jogging, handball. Walter kept horses, and Sunday mornings would find them galloping off across the wintry meadows only to return, happy and exhausted, in time for lunch. After which Walter would immediately fall into the phone ('Get me Hong Kong . . . Manila . . . Get me Rio.') while Tom unwound in the luxurious sauna.

Caro was pleased for him, that he should find such an outlet for his energies, happy for herself and Sasha. Business, sports and phone calls notwithstanding, the Lorencz house was primarily a home. Large though it was, you were never very far from the clatter of children. Laughter echoed down the halls. Even Sasha, though two years younger than the youngest Lorencz child, responded to the easy atmosphere. The house was informal, familial, a place where you didn't have to apologize when a baby cried or dribbled or dropped a bottle on the floor.

'Don't bother to bring anything,' Natalie had said before that first weekend. 'I've got it all – crib, playpen, jungle gyms . . . the whole bundle.'

Funny when she thought about it, that of all the people she and Tom numbered among their friends, there were no families in the conventional sense. True, she knew a handful of women who had children, but they were for the most part single parents – divorced, separated, unmarried. And all of them worked. Natalie alone was a full-time mother.

Thus in its way the Lorencz household appeared exotic, a focus for legitimate curiosity.

'How do you manage?' Caro asked that first Sunday sitting over coffee with her hostess. 'I mean, Walter's always away. Just this past week, Tokyo, Singapore, London . . .'

'Don't I know!' Natalie sighed. 'He chalked up twenty thousand miles in the last ten days alone. Thank God at least for Concorde! Last night was the first time we had dinner together since New Year's Eve. It's been awfully rough on him, poor dear.'

'I bet,' Caro concurred. 'But what about you? How do you cope with being alone so much?'

'Alone?' Natalie laughed. 'Believe me, with four kids you're never alone. Yes, sure I miss Walter and I wish like hell this Worldsville business were over, although if it hadn't been

Worldsville it would have been something else. Walter's pretty compulsive, you know. He has to do, he just can't be. Still,' she added thoughtfully, 'it's not as bad as it sounds, and I get a lot of *naches* from the kids.'

'What's that?' Caro asked. 'Sounds like some kind of kosher food . . . potato pancakes, isn't it?'

'No, that's *latkes. Naches* is . . . well, I don't think there's an English word that has the same exact meaning. *Naches* is a kind of joy, a very special pride you can only get from your children. Like last week, for instance, when Josh tied his own shoelaces for the first time. That gave me *naches*. And the older they get, the more *naches* they give you. Do you understand?'

Caro understood.

'What I can't figure out,' Natalie went on 'is how you manage. All that juggling . . . business, husband, baby. I think it would drive me up the wall.'

'Oh, I manage,' Caro replied, 'although it makes for a very full life.'

Yet riding home that evening, she kept recalling the conversation with Natalie. Her earlier presumption that Natalie must be secretly dissatisfied and restless, she now knew to be false. She had a swift picture of Natalie at the dinner table that afternoon, surrounded by her children, bathed in love, proud and happy. Then a swifter vision of Caro herself. Yes – Caro, with her arms full of children, loving children. And the intensity of that vision made her gasp.

The following morning, Rosita didn't show.

20

'Godalmighty, Tom. It's nearly nine and she's always here by quarter past eight.'

'Well, try her house again.'

'I've been trying, every five minutes and there's still no answer. What am I going to do? I've got a nine-thirty meeting downtown. As it is, I'm running late. Could you. . . ?'

No, he couldn't. 'Sorry sweetie . . . gotta run.'

She waited another half hour, then phoned to say she'd be delayed, and spent the rest of the morning biting her nails and swallowing black coffee.

Toward noon, Rosita arrived, haggard and red-eyed in a thin black coat and threadbare gloves.

'What's the matter?' Caro was shocked by her appearance. 'What's wrong?'

Emilio, the woman answered in a flood of tears. Her oldest boy, her first born. He had been arrested the day before on a Bronx street corner and charged with dealing in drugs. She had just come from a juvenile detention centre, the hearing was set for next week. No . . . there was nothing Senora Darius could do; it was very kind of her to offer financial help, but money wasn't the answer. 'I can't work here any longer,' Rosita wrung her hands. 'My children need me.'

So, fond as she was of Sasha, much as the money had helped, there was no question in her mind. How could she – 'I ask you as a mother' – bring up someone else's child when her own children were running wild in the streets? 'I'm sorry,' she wept, giving Sasha one last affectionate hug.

'Me too,' Caro said.

The next day the agency sent up Mrs Schrecker. In volume, she equalled two Rositas – a bulky middle-aged Swiss with starchy white uniform, starchy grey hair, a thin smile and vast bosom. The bosom was the only motherly thing about her. She exuded an aura of Lysol.

From the start, Caro disliked the woman, and even Tom – usually so amiable about newcomers – couldn't resist the occasional dig. 'Frau Gruppenfuhrer,' he used to call her behind her back. 'Now Caroline,' he would bark in hoarse imitation. 'Eat your greentz. That iss an order. You don't eat your greentz, you don't heff no puddink.'

'Jawohl, mein fuhrer,' Caro clicked her heels.

That Caro harboured an aversion, that Tom poked fun was quite irrelevant, but Sasha herself did not respond to the new regime.

'She misses Rosita,' Tom observed, and Caro agreed. 'But maybe it's just as well,' she rationalized.' Sasha was getting awfully attached, and at least Schrecker can speak some English.'

Yet her unease dogged her in the office, lending a nervous edge to her days till one afternoon, on nothing more than impulse, she went home without warning after lunch. Even from the outside corridor, she could hear the deafening roar of the television. My God! A miracle the neighbours hadn't complained. She opened the door to find Schrecker, blouse unbuttoned, feet up, lounging on the sofa engrossed in *General Hospital*. The volume was up to the limit. So loud, in fact, that Caro's entrance went unnoticed.

'What the hell is going on here?' Caro strode across the room and snapped off the set. Behind the closed bedroom door, she could hear Sasha screaming.

'Sasha!'

She tore into the room and swooped the baby up in her arms. Sasha's face and hair were covered with snot and tears. Everything – vest, kimono, blanket, even mattress were drenched. She must have been crying for hours. Caro froze, then wheeled back into the living room and for an uncertain moment the two women glared at each other speechless.

'You spoil that child.' Schrecker was the first to find her voice. 'Always picking her up. Spoil, spoil, spoil. Iss no gut.'

'Get out of here!' Caro flung herself headlong upon the

woman. With Sasha clutched to her breast, she began pumelling that starched bosom with her clenched fist. 'Get out, you bitch. Get out . . . get out!'

For one hideous instant. the confrontation threatened to end in mutual violence, but Mrs Schrecker jumped back, whey-faced.

'I'm goink,' she began shoving belongings into a huge plastic bag. 'Don't you vorry, I'm goink. But you heffn't heard the last of this.'

The moment she left, Caro collapsed onto the sofa, cradling the hysterical Sasha in her arms. 'Baby . . . lambchop . . . Sasha darling,' she wept. 'I'm sorry . . . I'm sorry . . . it's all my fault.'

Next morning she called up the employment agency prepared to give them hell. 'And this time send me someone reputable.'

'I've very sorry, Mrs Darius,' came the icy reply. 'We won't be sending anyone at all, not after yesterday. Mrs Schrecker tells me you assaulted her.'

'I what?'

'She happens to be a fine woman with excellent references . . . we've never had any complaints about her before. You're lucky we persuaded her not to bring charges. In the future, I suggest you find an agency more to your specifications.' Click.

'You find the next one,' Caro told Tom that night. 'I'm sick and tired of chasing will o' the wisps. And if you don't come up with somebody pronto, I'll quit my job and look after Sasha myself.'

'Is that a threat?'

'Nope, just a statement.'

He came home next day, fingers raised in a victory sign. 'Now it's only a temporary arrangement, but at least she'll stay a few months.' By good fortune, a girl had turned up at his office that very morning, trying to sell some magazine articles, and finally admitting she was broke and willing to take any kind of work that was going.

'But is she suited?' Caro frowned.

'She seemed a nice enough kid. Twenty-two, twenty-three maybe . . . a college graduate. A little flaky, maybe, but kind of sweet. . .'

'Oh Jesus!' Caro groaned.

'Look,' Tom bristled. 'You told me to find somebody and I found somebody. What the hell do you expect on twenty-four hours notice . . . Mary Poppins?'

No, not Mary Poppins, Caro thought the moment Jennifer Wilkes walked through the door. But, as Tom said, kind of sweet if terribly ethnic, with scads of Indian bangle bracelets, Mexican huaraches and a head of hair that had never seen the inside of a beauty parlour.

'What have you got in there?' Caro watched Jennifer take mysterious packets out of a brown paper bag.

'It's my lunch.'

'Oh, I provide lunch,' Caro said. 'There's a ton of stuff in the refrigerator . . . steaks, chops. Help yourself to whatever you want.'

'I only eat organic.'

'I beg your pardon?'

'I only eat organically grown food, Mrs Darius.' She began unwrapping packages of wheat germ, alfalfa sprouts, a large dripping square of tofu. 'Do you know how much synthetic preservative there is in one pound of hamburger? Enough to cause cancer in twenty-four rats.'

'Well,' Caro sighed. 'Eat what you like . . . provided you feed Sasha according to my instructions.'

'Oh, you can rely on me,' Jennifer said fervently. 'I adore babies.'

She did. And Sasha adored her too. All in all, Tom's 'find' was working out remarkably well, until one Sunday evening, when she called to say she wasn't coming back. 'I'm up in Kingston,' she explained. 'I've just joined the Inspirational Church of the Ramakhrishna. You see, my karma. . .'

'Fuck your karma!' Caro exploded. 'What about me? What about Sasha?'

'I'm sorry, Mrs Darius.' In her new state of grace and divine forgiveness, Jennifer could not be roused. 'I will always remember my time with your family as a period of inner spiritual growth.'

Gusty found the next replacement, and this time there were no grounds for complaint. MacPherson, her name was – the proverbial Scottish nanny – clean, sober, knowledgeable, with more references than the *Encyclopedia Brittanica*. Trouble was, MacPherson proved frightfully expensive and her wages did not include any cleaning, cooking or laundry other than that required in looking after her charge. So they had to hire a cleaning woman as well.

'Money, money, money,' Tom wailed. 'Where's it all going to come from?'

Definitely not from *Ecology Today*.

Some months previously in a change of tactics, Lucinda Weeks and Tom had decided to revamp the magazine, to liven it up and broaden its appeal in hopes of reaching a wider public. Paradoxically, however, the greater their success, the greater their deficit, with each extra copy sold leaving them that much deeper in the hole. For a while the general public had responded to the new look, advertisers had been slow to follow suit. 'Maybe you should look for a merger with another magazine,' Caro suggested, 'or try selling off your circulation.' But Tom wouldn't hear of it. 'The medicine's working,' he insisted, 'so it's only a matter of time before the advertisers get on the bandwagon. *Ecology Today* – the magazine of tomorrow. That's our new promotion slogan by the way. In the meantime. . .'

In the meantime they had a cash-flow problem, and Lucinda had offered Tom a sizeable equity in the publication in return for what she deemed a 'modest investment'.

'Well that's not "modest" by my lights,' Caro balked. 'That's practically every cent of our savings.'

'Oh, come on, honey. Where's the Wall Street plunger I loved and married? You've invested in screwier things than this. What about that porno movie . . . what about Worlds-ville?'

'That's different. That's company money, and even so I lose sleep over it. You're talking on two different levels, Tom. For PAGIT, half a million is a moderate investment. For us, one tenth of that is heavy . . . very heavy, even given a piece of the magazine.'

'A sizeable piece,' Tom emphasized. 'Lucinda's prepared to give us a good chunk of the business.'

'It's not a question of how big a chunk,' Caro argued. 'You

know a hundred per cent of nothing is still nothing.'

In the end, however, despite deep-seated misgivings and a gut feeling that it was money down the drain, Caro went along. Tom might or might not turn the magazine around. On the whole she was doubtful. The history of business was studded with cautionary tales of magazines that had gone bankrupt at the height of their circulation.

Yet the fact remained that Tom was staking his entire future on the magazine – not just time and effort, but all his own savings, too, and Caro didn't have the heart to say no.

As she anticipated, their contribution (for that was how she saw it – a charitable contribution rather than an investment) did little to staunch the floor of the magazine's lifeblood, like putting a band-aid over a haemorrhage.

But she had done it willingly, if not happily, first because she loved Tom.

And also, because she wanted something in return.

'You're kidding!'

'I'm thirty.'

'That's a non sequitur if ever I heard one. For Chrissakes, Caro, you make it sound like you're on the brink of menopause. Here I am at the most critical point of my career, up against the wall, and you talk about having another baby. How can you sit there and say such a thing?'

'You asked what was bothering me, I told you. Believe me, I've thought it through,' she rushed on before he could raise further objections. 'It wouldn't make much difference in our lives. We already have MacPherson . . . she could look after two children for the same money and the kids could share a room, so the additional expense would hardly be worth mentioning. Or maybe we could find a cheaper apartment.'

'Whoa!' Tom roared. 'Hold it right there. It's not that I'm against having more children . . . *in theory*, but you certainly picked a helluva time. My God, Caro. . .' – he stopped abruptly – 'you're not pregnant already, are you?'

'No,' she was indignant. 'I wouldn't do that without consulting you. The thing is, Tom I'm thirty. . .'

'So you keep saying. . .'

'And if we put it off, if we keep waiting for the ideal time . . . well, there's never going to be an ideal time. I'll be thirty-one anyhow when. . .'

'Be reasonable. What's the hurry? Lots of women have children at thirty-five, forty even. Take Ursula Andress, she was forty-two. . .'

'You take Ursula Andress!'

'I'd love to take Ursula Andress, but that's beside the point. Look at it another way . . . you're only thirty. You've got Sasha, you've got me, you have a beautiful apartment, a fantastic job. What more could you want?'

'I told you – another baby.'

'But why the big rush to have another so soon . . . or for that matter, to have another at all? You know what Mies van der Rohe said, about *less is more*.'

'Yes, and small is beautiful and Zero Population Growth is the greatest invention since sliced bread and who am I to clutter up this already overcrowded planet? I've heard all those arguments, Tom, I've said them to myself in the past . . . but that doesn't alter my feelings. I want another baby, and who knows? After that I may possibly even want another.'

'Caro!' Tom was horrified. 'Why stop at three? Why not have twenty? You sound like an article out of *Readers Digest*, vintage 1950, rather than a modern educated woman. We're not even on the same frequency, you and I. I just don't understand what you want . . . what you're looking for?'

'*Naches.*'

'What's that supposed to mean?'

She gave him a long cool look. 'It's a special kind of kosher food.'

'Well, fuck you! I ask a serious question, I get a smart-ass answer.' With that he stalked out of the room. They didn't exchange another word that night and slept in opposite corners of the king-sized bed, each nursing a private injury.

For once the sun went down upon their wrath.

All next day she was miserable. Each time she replayed the conversation it was with a growing sense of guilt and anguish. She and Tom had had arguments before. Sure. But in the past their disagreements had always ended in compromise and kisses – kisses all the sweeter for being laced with salt. This, however, was more than a lovers' quarrel, more than a tiny crack in the veneer to be pasted over and forgotten. It was a rift, and a rift can become a chasm. The depths of Tom's rancour – and of her own – had stunned her, and she was uncertain what to do next.

Somehow she got through the day and toward quitting time popped into Catlett's office for some papers.

She caught him leaning back in his chair, feet on his desk, contemplating an unopened bottle of champagne.

'Oh,' she remarked. 'Looks like you're celebrating something. That Cleveland deal finally come through?'

'Nope.' He languidly lowered his feet. 'It seems that today's my birthday.'

'Seems?'

'To tell the truth, I'd forgotten all about it,' he gave a self-conscious grin. 'But Stella remembered . . . hence the bubbly. Although I don't know that turning forty-two is anything to celebrate.'

'Certainly better than being forty-three. Happy birthday, Dan.'

'Thanks.' He motioned her into a chair, then tapped the bottle with a little gold pencil. 'Veuve Clicquot . . . the best of the best. Nothing but the best of the best for old Dan Catlett.' For a few moments more, he contemplated the bottle with rapt absorption. 'You know when I was in law school, Maddy and I used to celebrate practically everything with a bottle of champagne. Birthdays, law exams . . . when the home team won . . . when the home team lost . . . practically everything. I had this scruffy little room in Chapel Hill and we used to sit around guzzling champagne out of paper cups. Not Veuve Clicquot, mind you, but some stuff from New York State that used to sell for about three bucks a bottle. It was probably awful by any civilized standard, but my God. . .' his eyes went soft with memory – 'it sure tasted good.'

'I imagine it was the company rather than the vintage,' Caro said.

He looked up at her and smiled suddenly. 'I guess champagne isn't champagne unless you can share it with a pretty woman. Will you join me, Caroline . . . that is, if you're not in a terrific rush?'

She was, rather; but in that brief exchange of glances, she had caught something fragile and tender within him, and it had touched her.

'With pleasure. Tell you what, Dan. You open the bottle and I'll . . . ummm' – there was a sizeable array of crystal on his bar – 'I'll go get some paper cups from the water cooler.'

They sat and sipped and talked about nothing very much – Broadway shows, office gossip – for a pleasant half hour. He had recently returned from a trip to Saudi Arabia.

'How was it out there, Dan?'

'Weird.' He shook his head. 'There are no women there. Oh there are women, of course, but they keep 'em pretty much under lock and key, and the few that you do see are dressed from head to toe in those big black tents. Even the secretaries are men, you know. You can't imagine how odd it is to spend an entire week without seeing a woman's face, a woman's smile. No booze there either, for that matter.' He poured out the last of the champagne. 'This is much much nicer.'

They touched paper cups and drank it off.

'And now, sugar, I'm afraid it's back to work for me. Hope I haven't kept you too late.'

'Not at all.' She crumpled their cups into the wastebasket. 'And thanks for the champagne. It was lovely.'

'Thank you for keeping me company.'

He rose to open the door for her, when suddenly, on impulse, she leaned over and kissed him on the cheek.

'Good night, Dan. Take care.'

Poor bastard, she thought fondly, getting into the taxi. Going home, God knows when, to an empty house, a solitary dinner. And lucky me! – the wine had made her feel heady, buoyant – going home to a real home, a loving husband, a beautiful baby.

Last night she'd been a fool – no doubt about it. Here she was a woman with everything – well, practically everything – and still asking for more. Who could blame Tom for being pissed off?

'Driver,' she called. 'Let me off at the florist shop on the corner,' and when she did arrive it was with an armful of roses.

The first thing she saw on entering the apartment was a huge glass jar filled with cinnamon hearts atop the living room table. The second was Tom feeding Sasha in the kitchen.

'Oh sweetheart!' She dropped the roses and swooped across to him. In a moment they were in each other's arms. 'Let's never have an argument like that again. Let's talk it over calmly.'

Which they did, long into the night, Caro finally agreeing to wait until Sasha was a year old 'and then we'll see how things shape up. Promise?'

She promised.

Yet the vision of herself, content and serene, her arms filled with children – that vision persisted. Flourished, till it became more than a vision, but a need. And Tom's resistance in no way modified it.

He was not cut out to be a father – that was the long and short of it. True, he played the role with a certain flair, usually managing to put a bright face on it, but his heart was not behind his smiles.

'You never talk to Sasha,' Caro once complained. 'Even infants like to be talked to from time to time.' But Tom, so graceful in chatting up strangers, such a master of delightful banter, became tongue-tied with Sasha. 'I guess I'm no good at one-way conversations,' he remarked, and even his choice of endearments was stilted, mocking. 'The National Debt' he would call the baby, or 'The Tsarina' and on one occasion when they had to leave a party early 'Gotta split. His Master's Voice is calling.' Perhaps on another man's lips the words might have been affectionate, but Tom's wry tone didn't quite mask the darker undercurrent of resentment. 'Every time Caro and I get going in the sack,' he regaled a dinnertable full of guests, 'damned if the party-pooper doesn't wake up howling. I swear to God that baby is psychic.' Everyone roared but Caro. In fact it had happened exactly twice when Sasha was cutting her first tooth.

No, Tom had not found himself in parenthood as Caro had.

Yet somehow it was she, not Tom, who was the odd one out. Increasingly she felt herself to be a loner. A maverick.

Why was it, she wondered, that motherhood was held in such low esteem by almost everyone they knew? To be a woman lawyer or broker or biochemist – that was admirable, the route to social approval. But to be a mother, to raise a family? Why you were hardly better than a mindless vegetable, contributing to nothing but the overpopulation of the earth.

With few exceptions, the people she knew viewed child-bearing as, at best, an interruption in the serious business of career. At worst, an act of pollution, on a par with chopping down sequoias. Only recently there had been a convention of a group dedicated to non-parenthood, with awards being given left and right for those sterling men and women who had refused to muck up the planet with offspring. Caro found the televised proceedings absurd. 'Why just think, Tom . . . what if their parents had felt the same way? Then . . . where would they be?'

Not that she was one of your Right-to-Life diehards, mind you. Abortion was every woman's right, she couldn't agree more. But what of that other right . . . the right to procreate, to mother, to follow one's instincts and leave the business of achievement to others? She didn't understand why, for that matter, everyone equated achievement with career, for what was Women's Lib all about if you couldn't choose the tradition-al role without being made to feel a traitor to your sex? Yet those women who did always seemed to wind up as either figures of fun or objects of pity.

Only a mother.

Only a housewife.

Only a social leper.

Something had gone awry somewhere, and what Caro had not confided to Tom, what she could scarcely admit to herself was that she wanted to quit – just chuck her job and cop out. In her own mind, she had reached the limits of her ability to cope.

Tom had written a very moving article for the latest issue about the ecological changes taking place in the Baltic Sea. Over the years the ocean floor had silted up, forcing the salt waters of the Baltic into the sweet waters of the Swedish rivers.

The change was raising havoc with the marine life, and species that had thrived for millenia in the sweet-water environment were now faced with extinction. For once the balance of nature had shifted, they could not adjust. They died.

Yet was this not what was being asked of her – to adjust to a mixture of sweet and salt? She couldn't do it. The strain of the past few months had taught her that much, and now she too was suffocating in a netherworld that was neither sweet nor salt.

I – she wanted to cry out – I! Not the snail darter, nor the Swedish river carp, but I am the endangered species.

She had believed herself a new breed of woman, infinitely capable, equipped to compete and achieve and blaze her name in glory. Superwoman. And should she choose to marry and mother as well – why not? Who says you can't have it all?

But what if you didn't want to be Superwoman? What if the price of success was too high, the consolations too meagre, the burden of guilt too great? What if your values shifted somewhere en route to the top – and that given brains and education and opportunity, you discovered your greatest gift happened to be a talent for loving . . . nurturing? What if the balance sheet didn't balance? She knew what her choice would be.

Yet there was no conceivable way she could say such things to Tom. Had he wanted a conventional housewife, he would have found himself one. They had married with the firm understanding that they would continue as independent people, self-sufficient; that she was as willing to pay her own way as he was his.

That had been the deal from the start.

Yet that reasoning afforded her scant comfort.

The fact was – she had changed. Circumstances had changed her.

She would hold Sasha, look at her, studying her more closely than she had ever studied any textbook, any contract. Here were Gusty's bright and inquisitive eyes. Tom's humorous mouth, his broad cheekbones. Here too was Caro – and in those still-small features, Caro could trace her own smile, her high colour. Sasha had even inherited Caro's characteristic big toes.

Sasha changed from day to day, and every morning there was something new. The start of a tooth, the first taste of plums, the triumphant closing of a fist about a toy.

How evanescent every moment was. Memorize the tiny dimples on the back of her hand, now – before they vanish. Feel the vulnerable softness of the fontanel closing beneath your loving fingers.

One evening Caro brought out the cassette and recorded the sound of Sasha in her bath – funny, silly, meaningless burbles, but they too changed from day to day. Would soon vanish utterly, routed by the advent of speech.

It was a never-ending pattern of change – wonderful, astonishing, infinitely various – a thousand transient moments to be caught and stored for future memories.

Had Caro once filled Gusty with that same sense of wonder? She suspected not. And her own recollections of childhood were bathed in a dark wash of loneliness – a loneliness she could not bear passing to Sasha. She yearned for Sasha to have what she herself had never known: roots, continuity, a family that consisted of something more than isolated people going separate ways.

Yet for all her reluctance to bring the matter up again with Tom, her feelings did not alter. They merely deepened. She wanted more children. She wanted more time for the one she had. And though she wouldn't speak of it to Tom so soon (for she had promised), yet she knew he read the message in her eyes.

'Let's make love.'

'Not tonight, honey. I'm bushed.'

'Really?' She ran her hand down his torso into the tangle of his pubic hair; beneath her fingers, his penis grew instantly erect. 'See, Tom . . . you aren't that bushed.' She climbed on top of him, rubbing her breasts gently against his chest. 'How about like this?' she said. 'You always liked it with me on top.'

'You know what I really want, baby?' He placed his hand on her shoulders and began pushing her down. 'I want you to take me in your mouth.'

But instead, Caro locked her legs firm against his hips and

254

guided him deep inside her, moving in and out slowly, erotic-
ally, until his excitement matched her own. Then, abruptly, in
one shuddering spasm, he broke the grip of her legs and
pushing her from him, spewed a warm bath of semen onto the
flesh of her stomach.

She was momentarily confused. 'What's the matter?'

'I'm sorry . . . I couldn't control myself,' he gasped.

But he had controlled himself very well, it struck her, pulling
out just that split second short of orgasm.

'Why did you do that?' she demanded. 'Why didn't you wait
for me?'

'I said I'm sorry.' He lay back panting for a few moments
then offered to get her a towel.

'I don't want a towel.' She was tense and unhappy. 'I want
. . . for God's sake, Tom, doesn't my pleasure matter any
more?'

'Of course it does, darling.' He kissed her, then placed his
hand between her thighs and began masturbating her with deft
sure strokes. 'Now you just relax.' Deep inside her, those strong
broad fingers began to exert the magic, alternating soothing
and arousing, now rhythmic, now unpredictable. God, he was
an artist. But at the very moment of her climax, beyond the
sound of blood rushing in her ears, beyond her quick sharp cry
of pleasure, she heard him murmur 'Oh, baby, that's a little
time bomb you've got in there.'

The words landed with the shock of cold water on a hot body.
With a violent jerk, she pulled away from under his hand and
sat up in a rage.

'What did you mean by that!'

'What?' he sounded bemused.

'A time bomb.' She snapped on the light with a vicious swipe.
'What's going on here? Why don't you want to make proper
love any more. Oral sex, funny sex . . . everything but old-
fashioned sex these days.'

He looked weary and bloated in the lamplight. 'I don't know
what you're talking about. As far as "proper sex" – whatever
that is – I never knew you were such a prude. You didn't used to
be. We've been happy in lots of different ways.'

She gave him a long simmering look. 'You think I'm trying to get you to knock me up, is that it? Like some high school kid on the hunt for a husband?'

'Please, Caro . . . you sound very hostile.'

'I feel hostile, goddamit. Tell me, is that what you think? Don't you trust me anymore?'

For a moment, his lips hardened into a thin white line. 'OK . . . since you brought it up, yes! That's what I think. I looked in the medicine chest last week, there was a lot of stuff there . . . aspirin, band-aids, a lot of stuff . . . but no birth control pills.'

'I don't . . . .' She started to say *I don't keep them there. I keep them in the night table*, but she was too outraged to give him any such assurance. 'I don't owe you an explanation. I'm on the pill . . . you'll have to take my word for it pure and simple. All I can see is you're behaving like a selfish shit. You don't trust me . . . well, that's just dandy. But when you wanted something, Tom, I trusted you. I trusted you to the tune of fifty thousand dollars for your goddam magazine, but you don't even trust me to keep my word.'

'Oh, come on, babe,' he tried to mollify her, but his words added sting to the wound. 'Don't call me babe,' she snapped back. 'You already have a baby, remember?'

'How can I forget?', he said wearily.

21

It was an ordinary Saturday, rather pleasanter than most. Caro and Natalie sat in the sunroom drinking coffee. Sasha was babbling to her teddy in the playpen. The Lorencz kids were tossing frisbees on the lawn. The cook was in the kitchen peeling potatoes. Tom and Walter were riding in the fields behind the house. In the distance you could hear the Lorencz dog barking. At a squirrel probably. That dog went crazy over squirrels.

'Such a glorious day,' Natalie remarked. 'We really should be out of doors.'

'We really should,' Caro smiled contentedly, then poured herself another coffee.

Somewhere a door banged shut.

'Judy!' Natalie shouted, then shook her head. 'How many times have I told you not to slam the front door.'

But it was not Judy Lorencz, it was Tom who burst into the room, scratched and bruised, splattered with mud, like an apparition at a Hallowe'en party.

'Quick! Walter!' He was shaking so hard he could barely articulate. 'Walter . . . he. . . .'

'What!' Natalie sprang to her feet. 'Was there an accident? Did he break something.'

'Yes . . . no . . . he fell off the horse, but I don't think he broke anything. He looks terrible . . . all red, can't breathe. I brought him as far as the stable, couldn't carry him any further.' Tom gasped for air. 'I think he's had a stroke.'

'Oh my god!' Natalie's hand flew to her throat. 'Tom, quick, call an ambulance. Caro . . . get the children inside. I don't want them to see.'

*

Walter Lorencz died of a massive coronary ten minutes after arriving at the Westport hospital. According to Jewish ritual, he was buried before sundown the following day.

The morning of the funeral, two men arrived from the undertakers to get clean clothes in which to dress the corpse; and Natalie, mute and pale, went through the motions of collecting a suit, laying out shirt, shoes, socks, his favourite tie. But as the undertakers were leaving, she shouted 'Wait a minute!', then darted from the room to return some minutes later clutching Walter's black Hungarian briefcase. 'Take it!' she cried. 'Take it and bury it with him. I never want to lay my eyes on it again.'

'What a nightmare!' Tom said on the drive back to Manhattan. 'Most hellish two days I ever spent. You know Walter never even had a history of heart trouble that anyone knew about. At least that's what the cardiologist said. I guess the riding did him in.'

'Walter worked himself to death,' was Caro's grim reply. They drove for a while in silence, then Tom asked 'What do you suppose will happen with Worldsville?'

'Worldsville?' she said. 'You just went to its funeral.'

'That seems to me a pretty hasty judgment. Don't the financial backers take over when something like this happens? I should think your company would be in a position to step in and appoint a new manager.'

'Probably. I hadn't thought about it.'

'You know, hon, maybe it can be salvaged. Couldn't you take over, maybe step into Walter's shoes, at least for the time being? It's a fantastic opportunity. After all, no one's closer to the project than you are. You've said so yourself plenty of times.'

Caro recoiled in horror. 'What should I have done, Tom? Should I have jumped into the grave and grabbed Walter's briefcase and been on the morning flight to Paris? What's the matter . . . isn't one corpse enough for you? You want me to kill myself too?' She burst into huge uncontrollable sobs that set the baby off crying in the back.

'Jesus, Caro. I'm sorry,' Tom put a tentative hand on her knee. 'It was only a suggestion.'

She reared back – 'Don't touch me!' – and spent the rest of the journey weeping hot tears against the cold car window.

That night she couldn't sleep and saw the dawn in huddled in the kitchen over endless pots of tea, sorting out the implications of the tragedy.

Worldsville was dead, interred in the coffin with Walter, and with it all her dreams of wealth and freedom.

Perhaps she should have seen it coming, bowed to the warnings raised that day in the conference room. A one-man band, someone had called it. Certainly she of all people should have anticipated what the doctors had not, that no one could maintain that pace – the travel, the pressure, the worries – and still survive. It was a classic case of self-destruct.

Burnout, to use the fashionable term.

And as for her? True, Worldsville hadn't cost her her life and perhaps something could yet be salvaged from the impending disaster. For despite her shocked protest, Tom had not been so crazy in suggesting that Caro step into the dead man's shoes, that she grab the helm, keep the project afloat at least until the storm blew over. And Tom was certainly correct in saying no one was closer, more knowledgeable about Walter's affairs than she.

Yet assuming she could. Assuming she had the nerve, the guts, the single-mindedness; assuming that by dint of a near superhuman effort she could stave off the worst of disaster – did she want to? At what cost? Or would Walter's fate in one form or another be hers?

Tom's suggestion had infuriated her, but now she realized that it was not Tom alone who had provoked her rage. It was Walter. By what right had Walter widowed his wife, orphaned his children? How dare he? Had he not, by the very act of dying, betrayed the family that loved him and needed him? Every day obits like his appeared in *The Times*, in the business papers – sad paragraphs that had you shaking your head and murmuring 'How tragic! Such a young man, too!'

Then there were the stories the newspapers never ran, but if you had eyes you saw them unfolding all around you. Broken marriages. Emotional crackups. Bill Reynolds at the office belting down furtive slugs of Chivas from the bottle in his bottom drawer. Tony Marcusson nursing a peptic ulcer. Sally popping a pair of valiums before each broadcast. Caro herself and the eternal Pepto Bismol.

Men had no monopoly on burnout in these new egalitarian times; those tensions, those pressures that had once been exclusive male prerogatives were now on offer to women as well. The new equality.

As for Worldsville, let it sink without a trace. Sell it off. Liquidate it for whatever it would fetch. It wouldn't bring Walter back to life and there were worse things to lose than mere money. Or jobs. And she knew hers was on the line. For if what Catlett wanted was an all-male sanctuary, she had given him his opening. Laid her head on the chopping block and handed him the axe.

If so, it might spell the end of her career. Very well. She could accept that. For unlike Catlett she had another life to turn to – a rich and private life – and it had never seemed so precious as now.

She was still shaken and red-eyed when she went into the office that morning, with that peculiar resignation of a prisoner under sentence of death. All she wanted was to get it over fast, just break the news to Catlett and take her medicine. But when he arrived, it was clear he already knew. 'Caroline,' he said tight-lipped. 'I want to see you right away.'

She trailed, heavy-hearted, into his office and sat down while he rooted about in his desk for cigarettes. He was very pale.

'Terrible,' he said finally. 'A terrible thing. Lorencz was only forty – just a little younger than I.' He brooded for a while over his cigarette and Caro was struck that he was visibly more upset about the death of a contemporary than the imminent collapse of Worldsville. Yet was it surprising? They were so much alike, he and Walter, their lives so similar despite the differences of style and surface. Walter had painted in broad bold strokes, Catlett preferred to work in pastels, but the picture was the same nonetheless.

'Terrible,' he repeated. 'You're friendly with the wife, I understand. How is she bearing up?'

'As well as could be expected. Her family came in from

Pittsburgh, Saturday night, and they've kind of taken over . . . very helpful, very comforting.'

'Well, that's what families are for. And of course she has the children.'

Curious. That's what Natalie had said in the hospital corridor when word had come of Walter's death. 'At least I have my children.'

'Four of them,' Caro swallowed back the tears. 'The oldest is only thirteen. I don't know how she's going to manage.'

'Let's hope he carried a lot of insurance,' Catlett sighed, then buzzed for Stella who brought in coffee in delicate Haviland cups.

'Now,' he said when she had gone 'to business. As you know I renegotiated some points in the contract when you were in the hospital, and now with Lorencz's death, control of the company passes to us – his liabilities and his assets. That was covered in the final revision. Now, my own personal feeling is that Worldsville *per se* is a dead issue, so the big question is – what next? Have you given it some thought?'

'I've been up all night thinking about it,' – she geared herself for the crunch – 'I believe we should sell the property immediately, take whatever we can get for it and eat the loss. Otherwise, we'll just be throwing money out the window. The banks in Florida . . . they may want to foreclose. Of course I'll do whatever is necessary. That's first of all. Second, I accept that I'm responsible for what has turned out to be a major error of judgment. If you want, my resignation will be on your desk this afternoon.'

He studied her at length, his own face expressionless, then lit another cigarette. 'To take your first point, let's not panic. I'm off to Florida in a couple of hours. As for your second point . . . you're being unnecessarily hard on yourself, Caroline. This is a high risk business with a built-in failure ratio. That's something you're going to have to live with at all times. However, as far as responsibility goes for Worldsville, you didn't make that decision . . . I did. I liked that property the first time I set eyes on it.'

She had a swift flash of memory: Catlett, the day of her presentation, tanned and tuned out, scratching idly on an insect bite. Just back from a fishing trip, Stella had said. Of course – he'd fished the same waters as Walter.

'Your mind was made up before you ever walked into the conference room, wasn't it, Dan?' He nodded, and she didn't know whether to be angry or relieved. 'So my whole presentation was just an exercise . . . makework.'

'No. Not at all. You did a brilliant job, made a first-class presentation. First class! I myself was very impressed. But you didn't really think I'd give you that kind of leeway – you or anyone – to commit us to an investment that size. No. Ultimately the decision was mine, and so is the final responsibility.'

The day after she had told him of Worldsville, he had flown to Florida. What intrigued him was not Walter's dream of a tourist paradise – he'd always seen that as iffy – but the site's proximity to a proposed base for an expanded space-shuttle programme. Should that come off, the land would be a natural for an industrial park and housing development. He'd spent a hectic week chasing down NASA officials, Florida politicians, friends in Washington, family connections – all the good-old-boy network he had cultivated over the years.

'To me it was first and last a real estate deal, and I'd never done any big-scale real estate before.' His eyes glittered suddenly. 'I think I fell in love with the challenge. Anyhow, we're going to hang in there, keep developing the site. Everything hinges, of course on the NASA base being built . . . in any event, it's going to be a long, slow haul. But as I say, that's my problem, not yours. In the meanwhile, as you pointed out, we're faced with notes falling due to the Florida banks, and frankly I'm reluctant to dip into the company's pocket any further. Fortunately, however, along with Lorencz's liabilities, we also have title to his assets.' He began scratching figures on a memo pad. 'Mmm . . . that office of his . . . polo ponies, ought to be able to get something on that. . . .' He totted up the figures and frowned. The minuses clearly offset the plusses. 'And then of course, there's the house.'

Caro knew it was coming but it hardly lessened the shock. 'The house,' she echoed numbly.

'Yes, the house out in Westport. That's a very valuable

property, you know. It was appraised last year at one million two . . . I imagine it's worth even more today. So I think the first thing we should do is get the house on the market, and that'll give us some money to play around with. . . .'

'I can't. . .' She turned to the wall, unable to meet his eyes.

Can't. The word floated across the room, the word that wasn't supposed to exist in these precincts, in her vocabulary.

'I can't,' she began to weep. 'I . . . I've been a guest in that house, I've spent happy hours there. These people were my friends, almost like a second family. I don't even think Natalie realizes. . .'

'I'm sorry,' he said gently. 'Nobody likes it but it has to be done. Frankly I thought Lorencz had no right going out on a limb like that. He should have made the house over to his wife a long time ago. He never should have used it as collateral. He knew he had a family, responsibilities. But I have responsibilities too, Caroline, and I'd be remiss in my job if I hadn't pressed for every advantage. I'm sorry,' – he reached over and took her hand – 'I had no idea you were so close. But business is business.'

He was right of course. By every guideline he was right. Maybe it was the business that was wrong.

She dried her eyes with a crumpled tissue.

'I understand. But don't ask me to do it, Dan,' she pleaded. 'Just don't ask me to be the one who wields the knife. Because I can't.'

He was silent for a moment.

'No,' he sighed. 'Clearly you can't, and I wouldn't ask you to. I'll do it myself – and try to make it as easy for Mrs Lorencz as I can. Meanwhile, why don't you run along home and get some sleep? You look absolutely exhausted.'

Too distressed to go home, too wound up to sleep, Caro wandered uptown and before long found herself in the gallery district of SoHo. On impulse she decided to drop in on Thea, wanting nothing so much as to sort out the events of the last harrowing days with a friendly but disinterested party. She found her old classmate in the small back office of the gallery checking through a stack of invoices, and for a moment Caro had the strange sensation that their roles were reversed; that it was Thea now who was all brisk and businesslike, and Caro who was confused and uncertain.

'My God!' Thea rose in alarm. 'You look like death warmed up. Sit down and I'll get you something to drink. All there is is this godawful sherry we serve at openings' – she poured her friend a generous tumblerful – 'but have a swallow and tell me what's wrong.'

Caro complied to both orders and when she finished her story, she felt marginally better.

'Well, I've still got a job,' she concluded. 'I suppose that's some small consolation. And as far as Worldsville goes, it seems in the last analysis it wasn't even my responsibility. And you know something? Much as I'm ashamed to admit it, I'm relieved. I can't bear the idea of being a hatchet man.'

'Nobody likes it.'

'Mmmm,' Caro nodded. 'That's what Catlett said.'

Thea was silent for a moment, then said thoughtfully 'Why do you think he did it . . . got you off the hook like that? From what you say, he didn't have to. Do you think he wants something in return?'

'Like what?' Caro was puzzled.

'Like you, for instance.' And before Caro could protest, Thea went on 'I've never known a man to do me any favours without expecting something in return. Maybe he's interested in you.'

'No way!' Caro shook her head vigorously. 'Absolutely no way. Number One, he's got a thing against businesswomen, and Number Two. . . .'

Number Two. A while back she and Tom had been at Lincoln Centre and in the intermission Tom had nudged her. 'You want to feast your eyes on something gorgeous? Take a look at that woman at the bar.' Caro turned. There was no mistaking the object of Tom's admiration. She was unspeakably elegant, perfect features, great clouds of magnificent blonde hair. And beside her, whispering in her ear with a proprietary air was none other than Dan Catlett, too absorbed to notice he was being observed.

'See the guy with her?' Caro said. 'That's my boss.'

'So . . .' Tom grinned. 'The famous Catlett. Lucky bastard. Want to go over and say hello?'

But Caro shook her head. 'No. He's on his own time and so are we.'

'And Number Two' – she was shaking her head now at Thea 'He's got the pick of the most beautiful women in New York. No,' she insisted. 'He's definitely not interested.'

'You're so emphatic,' Thea looked at her shrewdly. 'You find him attractive, don't you?'

'I admire him.'

'That's not what I asked. Be honest.'

'Honestly?' Caro pondered a moment. 'Yes, I suppose in a way I do. Not so much physically, although he's quite a nice-looking man. It's something else. . . .'

'Money?' Thea asked. 'I'm not being snide. Money is very sexy stuff.'

'No. I don't know. . . . He intimidates me in a lot of ways. He's so tough, so sure of himself, so . . . powerful. Yes, that's what it is. He reeks of power. That's pretty sexy stuff too.'

'Oh wow!' Thea whistled softly. 'I didn't expect that coming from you. You sound like I did ten years ago. That's what knocked me out about Brooks when I first met him. He was so dynamic, driving – and it made me feel sweet and feminine and helpless. And what a trap *that* turned out to be! The oldest trap in the world. You know what Sylvia Plath once wrote? "Every woman adores a Fascist." And look what happened to her – she killed herself. Those kind of relationships are always murder one way or another, and in a certain sense I'm glad I caught Brooks screwing around. Because otherwise we might have gone on indefinitely, with me becoming more and more passive, and him becoming more of a pig. As it was, I wound up with an ego the size of a peanut. And you know what helped me pull myself out? You did, Caro. You were a kind of role-model for me, living proof that women can make it on their own. This job, for instance. It's such a joy for me to realize that I'm competent, that I can think for myself, make decisions. For the first time in my life, I really respect myself. Last week my boss asked me if I were interested in running a gallery for him – he wants to open a branch in Dallas – and my first instinct was to say no. That would really mean being out on my own. But my second reaction was – someone like Caro would jump at the chance. What I'm trying to say is . . . I've profited by your experience, Caro, and maybe you should profit from mine. Don't let yourself get involved with these macho types. Men like Catlett swallow women alive.'

'It will hardly come to that, Thea' – the conversational turn was making her writhe. 'He's not up for grabs and neither am I. After all, I'm a happily married woman.'

But was she? She was no longer even sure of that.

The admission, so painfully extracted, that she found Catlett attractive conceivably surprised Caro more than it had Thea. Or perhaps 'attractive' wasn't the proper word. Lots of men were attractive, from Clint Eastwood to the new Greek waiter at the Athena Cafe. And who didn't occasionally speculate – in a purely theoretical sense of course – on what it might be like to go to bed with this one or that?

But the sentiments he evoked were far more complex.

From the start, Catlett had fascinated her, occupying a disproportionate share of her thoughts. Tom used to tease her about it when she started working for him. 'Really honey, I should be jealous,' he kidded her. 'From the way you go on and on about him, I sometimes think you have the hots for the guy.' To which she'd retorted 'Don't be absurd.'

Yet she would be hard put to describe her feelings for Catlett, for their relationship was one of constant flux. There had been, on her part, a distinct element of fear. But every now and then she would get a glimpse, unguarded, of his softer side, and respond with a surge of affection. Always, always she had sought his approval. Praise from him was praise indeed, invigorating her like a whiff of pure oxygen. Conversely the slightest criticism cut deep. And had she been forced to sum up this strange conglomerate of emotions in a single word, that word would surely be – respect.

Yes, she respected him. In some ways more than she respected Tom, for Catlett had about him a tensile strength, an unflinching grace when the chips were down. Grace. Grace

266

under pressure. Wasn't that the classic definition of courage?

God forbid Caro would ever have to cross him in business, but for the rest. . . . ?

For the rest, she would have trusted him with her life.

Tom went to California for a story on the medfly and returned in a quixotic mood.

'Yup, everything went fine. Solid story, good interviews. Had some terrific Chinese food out there, better than anything you can get in Manhattan. And I met a lot of people. Oh, by the way, your dynamic, brilliant, talented husband has been offered a job by – of all people – Akron-Holt.'

'The chemical firm? What is it . . . lab work?'

'Nope. They want me to head up their publications department – technical reports, trade-press releases, that sort of stuff.'

'Really!' Caro was impressed. 'That should pay good money. What are they offering?'

'Close to double what I'm making now' – Caro's heart skipped a beat, but Tom seemed to find the proposition droll. 'Akron, Ohio! How's them apples! I thought you'd get a boot out of that. Naturally I told them I'd think it over, didn't want to appear rude, but. . .'

'But what, Tom? You're not going to turn it down. My God! It's a lifesaver.'

'Oh come on, honey, you don't think I'd seriously consider it.'

'Why the hell not?'

'Well, for one thing . . . I'd be out there, you'd be here. We'd only see each other weekends.'

'I'd come with you of course.'

'And do what? It's not much of a financial centre, you know. . .'

'Tom, we'd manage on your salary. I'd run the house, look after Sasha. Please . . . please don't turn it down out of hand. You know, you're not giving me reasons . . . you're giving me alibis. What's the real reason you don't want it? Come clean.'

'I'm surprised you even ask that. Don't you realize what it would mean? I'd be just another corporate man, a nobody, a cipher. And Jesus, Caro . . . Akron! It's the boondocks, a million miles from nowhere . . . what would we do with ourselves? I'd hate it. I'd hate the place. I'd hate the work . . . goddam boring.'

'Lots of people do work they hate, Tom.' Her voice began to tremble. 'They do it because they've got families to support. Miners . . . garbagemen . . . shoe clerks. *Me*, Tom. I do work I don't want to. I go into that office every day with my stomach in knots. Well, I've contributed my fair share to this menage . . . more. Maybe it's your turn!'

'Please, Caro . . . don't pressure me. I feel cornered enough as is. If you're unhappy on Wall Street, I'm sorry . . . but that was your chosen line of work. Allow me mine. I know you feel you've made all the compromises and things haven't worked out as planned. But I've made compromises too. Be fair, Caro – you were the one who wanted the baby, not me.'

'You never said no,' she burst out.

'I never said yes, either. I went along, honey . . . that's all. I went along because I love you, I wanted you to be happy. But it was always with the understanding that I wouldn't have to shoulder the burden alone . . . that you'd pull your own weight. Now all of a sudden, you want to change the rules in mid-game. If you'd told me when we got married, if you'd come to me and said – Tom, I want to quit my job and stay home and have babies . . . well, I think I would have called a halt right there. But you said no such thing. Never. You said – funny, I can recall your very words – that nothing would change between us. You promised, in fact.'

'I didn't know I was going to feel this way, Tom. I couldn't read the future. Neither can you for that matter. Who knows what'll happen with the magazine? It could collapse tomorrow, it might hang on for a year – but you can't pin your hopes on it. That much I know, so all I'm asking is that you don't turn down the Akron job outright. Sooner or later you're going to have to consider alternatives, and who knows . . . you might be happy doing something else.'

'Yes,' Tom said thoughtfully. 'I might.'

All week long she brooded about the Akron offer, convinced the time had come for Tom to rethink his career as she had re-evaluated her own in the harsh days since Walter's death.

Since childhood, assumptions had been made about her, assumptions she had only lately begun to question. Follow the yellow brick road and you reached Emerald City – an Oz for every Dorothy. Only this Dorothy wasn't going to stop off en route to collect cowardly lions or helpless scarecrows. Let the men fend for themselves, just as you fended for yourself, because winning was all, and nothing succeeds like you-know-what.

But what end did it serve, this ceaseless scrambling? What was the purpose, the price? So you could wind up like Walter, dead and buried? Like Catlett, alone and remote? The hell with it.

For if those days of panic had proved one thing, it was that Caro was not cut out for competition. It was a matter not of talent, but of temperament. The hard, incisive edge, the coldness of nerve, the inner steel that made for ultimate achievement – all were alien to her inmost nature.

She wanted . . . well, yes, to love and be loved. OK, she loved Tom and knew he loved her. But even that was not enough. She yearned for more – to be cherished, protected. To have her husband stand between her and the harshness of the outside world. Let someone else win the battles, slay the dragons, stand at the head of the crusade. Let Tom do all those things on her behalf. For herself she ached, quite simply, for what most women have always desired: a home, a husband, children. And if that were an admission that smacked of weakness and defeat, so be it. And just as she accepted this new reality, so Tom, too, would have to face up to it. They'd move to Ohio, raise a proper family and that was that. It was essentially a question of talking Tom around, appealing to his sense of honour. His love for her.

Friday on the way home she picked up the Akron paper at a newstand, and spent the subway ride scanning the property ads. Compared to New York, rents were pretty reasonable. Maybe they could even buy something in a nice suburb. A proper house to go with a proper family. She hadn't lived in a house since she was a kid.

That night, Tom worked late and when he came home, bleary-eyed with fatigue, it was to find Caro scented in his favourite Calèche, wearing the black negligee that had always constituted an invitation.

'Did you have dinner yet, Tom?'

'At the office.'

'Then how about dessert?' She twined her arms around him and for a moment he rested his head on her shoulder. It felt heavy. Deadweight.

'Poor Tom!' His mood was contagious. 'I gather you had a bad day at Black Rock. Would a little loving help?'

He disentangled himself gently.

'I think tonight I'll pass up your offer and settle for a pot of coffee instead.' With that he threw his jacket on the sofa and loped into the kitchen.

'Ah that place, that place. . .' he grieved. 'We had to let two people go today. Old Lucinda clumps around the office poking through waste baskets, retrieving pencil stubs. "Oh, look, Tom, this one's three inches long",' he mimicked Lucinda's eager tone, '"and there's hours of life in it yet." What does she think . . . that Citibank is going to accept a bunch of used Eberhardt-Fabers as repayment for debt?' He made a noise between a laugh and groan. 'Well, let's hope the medfly issue marks a turning point. It's going to be a good piece.'

Caro ground the beans, brewed the coffee – the clean pungent aroma filling the kitchen, routing out that other scent, the scent of failure. By the time the coffee was on the table she was feeling more cheerful.

'You know, honey,' she sat down across the butcher block table, 'Maybe we should both accept the fact that the magazine is really a dead issue.'

'Is that a pun, Caro?' He looked up wearily. 'You seem to forget we've got fifty thousand dollars of our own tied up in it. Maybe you're willing to write off that kind of money, but I'm not – not yet.'

'In my own mind I wrote it off a long time ago, and I think it's time you did, too. Look' – she took his hand in hers. 'You mustn't take this as a personal failure. Businesses go broke every day, yet people pick themselves up, launch out in new directions. The magazine served its purpose, Tom. It's helped build your reputation so it's not a total loss. I think we should look upon the whole situation as an opportunity to start out afresh, make a whole new life. I don't think these last few months have been very satisfying for either of us, so maybe this is a blessing in disguise. You know, I've been thinking it over and I'm convinced you should take the Akron job. A corporate post can be very challenging, honey, give you plenty of scope. You might surprise yourself and love it. We could get a house . . . it's dairy country around there, by the way, probably quite green and pretty, and I think that would be lovely for Sasha. For me too. I want to quit anyhow. I'm not married to the job, Tom; I'm married to you. I don't really crave the big career any more . . . I don't know if I ever did at heart. I think it was just something that was expected of me. But you know in my whole life, the happiest I've ever been were those weeks after Sasha was born, making a home, being a private person. That's what I want now – to make a real home for Sasha and you. And I want more children. I hate the thought of Sasha being an only child like me . . . I want her to be part of a family. Please, Tom, take the job and we can settle down, start another baby. . .'

'We agreed to shelve that discussion until Sasha was a year old.'

'That's only a couple of months away. Besides, I may not get pregnant straight off, so it would hardly make any difference. You said. . .'

'I said, if you remember, that we could talk about it in July, Caro. Just talk . . . not necessarily do anything.'

'But you promised. . .'

'No, *you* promised.'

'Tom, darling' – her voice flooded with anguish – 'when you wanted money for the magazine, I gave it to you. I gave you your chance, now I'm asking you to give me mine. I've never asked you for anything before, but now I am. Tom. Please don't deny me this.' She put her hand on his arm and beneath her fingers could feel his muscles tense.

'Don't, Caro. Please . . . I . . .' He stopped, his eyes suddenly welling with tears. 'All right, let's talk,' he said hoarsely. 'I've had something ripping at my guts all week. But first, I could use a drink. How about you . . . a little brandy or Scotch or something?'

Without waiting for her answer, he rose and fetched a bottle of Hennessy and two brandy snifters. He poured hers to the brim, then sat down gingerly at the edge of the chair.

'I know this is going to be very painful for you to accept,' he whispered into his drink. 'I've done nothing but agonize over how to say it. There aren't going to be any more children, darling. Not now . . . not ever.'

She stared at him open-mouthed.

'Don't you grasp what I'm telling you, Caro? I've had a vasectomy.'

She dropped her glass in horror. For a moment her ears froze shut and she could hear nothing but the blood pounding in her head and muffled words, coming as though from a great distance. '. . . last week in California. I should have told you right away, but I guess I was a coward. I just didn't have the heart, and frankly, I didn't think the question would arise so soon. At any rate, what's done is done. Here . . . you've spilled your drink. Let me get you another. I'm sorry' – he wiped his eyes with the back of his hand. 'Truly sorry.'

'But if you're sorry' – she couldn't take it in. It was too big, too indigestible. 'If you're sorry, that means you've changed your mind. I mean, can't the operation be reversed? I read somewhere . . .'

'I'm not sorry I did it, Caro. I'm sorry to cause you so much misery.'

'But why, Tom, why?' She began weeping. 'How could you take such a step without consulting me? By what right?'

'By the same right that you had Sasha. Did you consult *me*? Did you really give me a choice? Oh, I went along, OK, your heart was set on it anyhow. And at the time you told me that was your right, your decision. It was your body, you said. Well, this is my decision, my body. I'm not trying to be cruel, Caro . . . simply trying to be fair. We were going to be fifty-fifty all the way, remember? I'm entitled to make decisions, too.'

'But where would have been the tragedy, Tom?' she blurted out. 'Your parents raised three children, and you – you're the youngest. You should thank God your father didn't feel the same way. What is it . . . is it the money? Do you begrudge the expense?' Her rage overtook her anguish. 'You could always make a living. We wouldn't starve.'

'No,' he said miserably. 'It's not the money. It's something else . . . it's the space. Please, Caro, hear my side.'

Around his parent's house in Morristown there grew a box hedge – high and handsome and trim, precisely marking the boundaries of the family domain.

When Tom was small, too small to see over the top, he would try to peer through the leaves to the street beyond. But the hedge was dense, impenetrable. It had a close, dark smell. What he came to think of as a prison smell.

His mother used to joke about it. 'Well, Tom, one of these days you're going to be just as tall as that hedge. Maybe taller.'

He grew. But so did the hedge. And somehow the hedge always managed to be one up.

The day Tom left home for college, he and his father had stood in the shadow of the hedge, chatting, smoking farewell cigarettes, and his father had said 'Tom my boy, the world is yours for the taking. And by God, I envy you!'

Now most people might look at Everett Darius and see nothing but a pleasant suburban doctor with a neat toothbrush moustache, getting a bit paunchy about the middle. But Tom's father, too, had once been young. Had nurtured dreams, heroic fancies of going out to Africa and joining Albert Schweitzer, selfless visions that had been vanquished by the reality of a wife, a family, children. And now his horizons ranged no further than the box hedge; his ambitions were no nobler than breaking ninety on the golf course and being elected president of his club.

'I could have forgiven him . . . no, I would have applauded him' – Tom told Caro – 'if he'd run off with his nurse or embezzled hospital funds or joined the communist party. If only once he had burst out and grabbed life with both hands. But he didn't, of course. He was always afraid. I guess that's what I admire about your mother, Caro . . . she has the courage of her craziness.'

In his way, Tom loved his parents, was grateful to them, yet his affection was tinged with faint contempt, tempered with real fear – a fear of history repeating itself. For to live as they did, knowing what each day would bring, to see the path roll out unchanged and unchangeable year after year – that, that was the real craziness.

Because just beyond the box hedge lay another world. A bazaar, a vast and multicoloured bazaar stretching to the horizon, offering an infinity of roles, of choices, of possibilities. And suddenly everything was spread out before you to be sampled, explored. If what you tried pleased you – fine. Wonderful. Then by all means take it and hang on to it. If not, you simply moved on.

'Just think, Caro, our generation – yours and mine – has been the first to transcend the barriers, to venture out beyond the box hedge.'

You could smoke pot or build computers or enter EST or splice genes or play the sitar or run for office or join a sex club or paint pottery or fly a jet or change the shape of your nose. You could opt for any of it, all of it. And so you moved through endless space, trying things on here and there, like garments in a cosmic dressing room, until you discovered which items fit, which did not. At least for the time being.

For that was the beauty of the world beyond the box hedge: nothing was final.

No. Nothing. Not even the old institutions. Marriage, for instance. Marriage wasn't final anymore. Not necessarily. Why, he and Caro had discussed it the night before their wedding, had spent hours probing the 'what if's; then gone ahead secure in the knowledge that if their marriage didn't work – and he hoped to hell it would! – at least there was the consolation that it needn't be final. Indissoluble. For if it truly were, who then would marry? Caro herself had said as much.

And so you went ahead and got married anyhow, on a tide of hope and good faith. You exchanged promises, you undertook to love and honour so long as you both shall live – yet all the time knowing that you were dealing not with vows but with wishes.

You loved each other on that wedding day. You loved each

other now – this night. But who could swear that you would love each other still in twenty years? In fifty years?

Indeed it was the knowledge that those vows were not really binding that made marriage possible, that gave you space to live and breathe and grow and change.

All his life Tom had craved space, emotional elbow-room. All his life feared confinement.

Funny when you think of it, but 'confinement' was the old-fashioned term for childbirth. The Victorians had hit it right on the button.

Yet it was not Caro who had been confined by Sasha's birth. She had found in it a curious freedom. It was he, Tom, who was confined. Confined. Restricted.

Because children were final.

They were the one item in the great bazaar that could not be exchanged, revoked or denied. They would put down their roots, grow, hemming you in closer and closer. Like the box hedge.

Sometimes when he held Sasha, she would close her fist around his finger, and in that tiny feeble grip, Tom felt the weight of shackles.

'It's not that I don't love her, Caro. In my way, I do. But I fear her, too. She threatens me. Even before she was born she came between us. It was as though you were having a love affair when you were pregnant, a love affair between you and your body. And it crowded me out, pushed me into corners.'

He had hoped with Sasha's birth his feelings would alter. That the child would touch some deep instinctual chord within him, release some emotion as yet unplumbed. But she did not. Perhaps the chord was never in him, for he had no doubt the fault was his. And that knowledge burdened him with guilt. He had looked into himself to find a new depth of love and had found instead emptiness and fear.

What could he say of those first few months? He missed the pleasures he and Caro had once shared. The impulse trips, those delicious Sundays spent in bed, the spontaneity that had marked their lives. Those were short-term losses, and he could accept them – even as he bristled. After all, Sasha wouldn't be an infant forever. If the demands to be made upon him were merely physical, temporary, he could cope. Changing nappies might be smelly and boring, but it was a finite task. What Tom feared were those other demands, demands that would only increase with the passage of time. Demands for strength, for support, for solidity, for continuity of purpose. For love.

Sasha's need lay across his future like a shadow, blocking his choices, restricting his space. And all the time there was Caro clamouring for more children.

'I need to have freedom, Caro – including the freedom to fail. To change directions, to feel unencumbered. A little while ago you said we could remake our whole lives. That's something I've always believed in – passionately. But what happens when my need for freedom conflicts with Sasha's need for stability? That Akron job, for instance. You may be right. It's conceivable that I might go out there and find I enjoy the corporate milieu. Conceivable, though highly unlikely. Still, I'd be willing to take the chance if that's all it were – just a chance on a job. But you're asking for more than that, Caro. You're asking me to commit myself to a way of life, and I'm not ready to do that. Suppose after a year or so out there, I want to pull up stakes. Go back and get my Ph.D., maybe, or write a book or do research. . . .'

'What are you saying, Tom?' Caro was aghast. 'That you're thirty and still don't know what you want to do in life?'

'Did you know?' he countered. 'Did you really know what was right for you until after Sasha was born? Perhaps, looking back on it, you might have been happier in a different type of marriage, but neither of us realized it then. You were the one who was so afraid of being tied down. Don't lock me up in a house in the suburbs, you said, and I promised I wouldn't. Your goals have changed and I respect that. But would you deny me the opportunity of changing mine, too? So don't lock me up either in a house with a box hedge and a twenty-year mortgage because I'm not sure I can handle it. I want us to stay married, Caro, but out of love – not obligation. I refuse to be like my father. I don't want you to wind up like my mother – heavy, leaning. Oh God, Caro, don't you see? I can't take the weight.'

'The weight?' she echoed.

'The weight of having you, you and Sasha dependent on me for everything, looking to me to make every hard decision, provide every basic need. Everything – the roof over our head, the clothes on your back, every scrap of food we eat . . . doctor's bills, dentist bills . . . a whole lifetime of it, Caro. If Sasha goes barefoot, hungry, it'll be my fault. All mine. It'll be Tom, the bad provider. And who will I have to turn to for help? No one. The idea of all that responsibility, of everybody's welfare resting on my shoulders is simply more than I can endure. I'm not Samson – I never pretended to be. I don't want . . . I don't want. . .'

What was it he didn't want? To grow up? To grow old? But the sentence remained unfinished, for Tom suddenly laid his head on the kitchen table. Laid his head down among the coffee cups and saucers – and wept.

And at the sight of him – defeated, desperate – her own anguish took second place. She came over to him, placed her hand on his cheek. And with her hand, her heart too reached out to him in his misery. He was like another child, another Sasha. 'Oh Tom . . . whatever is going to happen to us?'

'I don't know,' came the muffled answer. He raised his, blew his nose on a paper napkin, then kissed the palm of her hand. 'I don't know. The thing is, I feel so fucking guilty about everything – you, the baby, the vasectomy. Oh God . . . maybe I'll take the Akron job after all. Maybe it's the answer. Just give me time to think it over. Meanwhile I'm so tired . . . so tired. . .'

He moved off to the bedroom, collapsing fully clothed across the bed. A minute later he had fallen into a deep, leaden sleep. For a long while Caro watched the rhythm of his breathing, stertorous, heavy. Then opening the drawer of her night table, removed a small packet of pills and dropped them into the waste basket. She would need them no longer.

Tom's action had shocked her to the core.

'What's done is done,' she told herself repeatedly. 'Some people never have children.' – there was that consolation – 'At least I have Sasha.' But the sense of loss haunted her, and often she would sit at her desk, going through the motions of work, yet all the while entertaining fanciful schemes. Perhaps she would leave Tom and take a lover. Perhaps he would have a change of heart and get the operation reversed. Perhaps they might adopt a child one day. A war orphan maybe. There were always war orphans somewhere in the world.

Pure woolgathering, she knew, for Tom would not reconsider. Nor would she, for her part leave him. He had acted not out of malice but in response to his own anxieties; for all his faults, his flights of panic he was still her husband. Still Sasha's father. In a curious way, the revelations of that night had brought them closer together. Too much love had passed between him and Caro for it to be jettisoned like so much ballast.

Nor could she deny the justice of Tom's case.

He was not Samson. Nor had she ever asked him to be. Never, till now, expected him to play the role of old-fashioned he-man, to assume the stance of the strong, protective male. His charge that Caro had tried to change the rules in mid-game was abundantly true, and her bitterness was as much directed against herself as against him.

Yet the irony of it all was devastating. She had advertised herself as free and independent and successful, and by the display of those very qualities had liberated Tom from the exigencies of manhood.

How ironic that the prime beneficiary of the women's movement should not be women like herself, but men. Men like Tom.

'My my, don't you look thin and interesting!' Sally opened the door and welcomed her in. 'Some new kind of diet discovery?'

'Yeah, it's called the High Anxiety Diet – ten pounds in two weeks. I wouldn't recommend it.'

'Well, don't stand there like you're Avon calling. Come on in, Caro. I've had the place redecorated since you were here last. Personally, I was getting fed up with that white-on-white Joan Crawford shit. You could never put your feet up. Anyhow, I've decided the most contemporary thing you can have these days is Early American, a sort of country cottage on Park Avenue. What do you think, Caro?'

'Stunning. Looks like the new wing at the Met.'

'Cost like it, too. Jesus, sweetie, you ought to quit high finance and get your ass into the antique business, it's where the bread is. In braided rugs, New England samplers. Take this sideboard, for instance. I won't tell you what I paid for it – a fortune. It's a Shaker piece, the genuine article. You mean you never heard of the Shakers? They were this sect that flourished in the Eighteenth century. No – flourished is hardly the word for it. Funny geezers, the Shakers. They didn't have children on the theory that mankind was so inherently evil the best thing they could do was refrain from begetting more sinners for Satan. If you had kids, you were drummed out of the corps.'

'They're extinct, I presume.'

'Yeah . . . but they left behind some beautiful furniture. Still, you didn't come over for a course on cabinet-making. I know you, toots. When you visit Aunt Sally, there's always something wrong. What is it this time?'

'Man trouble.' Caro slumped into a Boston rocker. 'Is there any other kind?'

'Yeah . . . there's career trouble, tax trouble (I'm having it right now), money trouble, health trouble . . . man trouble should be at the bottom of the list. What happened? Tom do something stinko?'

Caro gave a bitter smile. 'He's joined the Shakers.'

'Oh?' Sally's mouth formed a perfect circle. 'Do tell.'

For the next twenty minutes she sponged up the details of Caro's story – the unhappy turn in their marriage, the problems with Sasha, Tom's vasectomy, her own difficulty in coming to terms. Sally didn't interrupt, but when the recital was over, she shook her head perplexed. 'You know, I've never really understood you, Caro. You always thought you could have it both ways – the happy family number plus a seat on the board of directors, and now you sound surprised that everything hasn't materialized on cue. Yer pays yer money, yer takes yer choice, I've always said – and I took mine. But you – you wanted it all. Honestly, I can only be sympathetic up to a point. What the hell did you expect? You have such a prehistoric view of marriage – home . . . babies . . . fidelity. . .'

'Fidelity?' Caro's ears pricked up. 'I've always been faithful. What are you trying to say, Sally – that Tom has been screwing around? Do you know something I don't?'

Uncharacteristically, Sally reddened. 'All I'm trying to say is, maybe he's not the plaster saint you thought he was.'

'You do know something. Then for God's sake tell me. I wouldn't say it came from you.'

'Nothing. Believe me, Caro, that was just a passing remark. One, I'm not a private detective and two, even for the sake of argument if he does screw around now and then . . . what's the difference? At night all cats are grey . . . speaking of which' – she dismissed her friend with a peck on the cheek – 'I've got to get dressed . . . going out in fifteen minutes.'

Caro had to run too, she said. Tom was baby-sitting and she'd promised to be back before eight.

But in the taxi home, she puzzled over Sally's cryptic remark. Did Tom or didn't he? Despite his casual flirtations, she had always assumed he didn't – not even on his sacrosanct 'free Tuesdays'. Was he a liar? She thought not – and on those occasions when she'd caught him embroidering the truth, he was so transparent, motivated by nothing more than the desire to make people happy or spare their feelings. 'You'd make a lousy businessman,' she once chided him fondly. 'You're much too honest.'

No, Tom didn't lie. Nonetheless, there was a difference between outright falsehood and withholding of painful information; and no question, Tom had a nasty habit of suppressing unpleasant facts, ferreting them away like Con Ed bills or unwanted invitations.

If Tom's predilections did lie in that direction, Lord knows he had ample time and opportunity. What man did not! The seminars, the conventions, even lunch hours (when she and Tom first met, they had whiled away many a lunch hour in hotel bedrooms).

It was possible, all too possible, and as for Sally – well, that woman had an unerring instinct for uncovering misconduct, like a pig nosing for truffles.

Had she caught Tom literally with his pants down? But with whom? Someone in his office – but then how would Sally know? For a wild sick moment, she had an image of Tom and her mother. Impossible! – yet Tom had always been fascinated by

Gusty, and Gusty herself had a penchant for young men. 'Good thing I didn't see him first,' she'd once said. But the image was too distasteful even to be harboured. Thea? Far more possible. 'If they gave out Nobel prizes for lookers' – he'd once said, his tongue practically hanging out – 'that girl would get it. She is absolutely sumptuous.' Caro had a swift vision of Tom's head buried in Thea's magnificent breasts – his lips, his hands doing all the things he'd done with Caro. Yet Caro couldn't believe Thea capable of such treachery. No, nor Sally either – and anyhow Tom had always poked fun at Sally's appearance. 'Would you rape this woman?'

No, the likelihood was some girl Tom had met at one of Sally's parties – the *Vogue* model perhaps, maybe that lovely Russian ballerina – the prospects were infinite. Sally had opened a bedroom door and found Tom. . .

Of course the greater likelihood was that there was no one else. After all, even seasoned reporters get their facts wrong now and again; and by the time the cab pulled up at Xanadu Towers, Caro decided to settle on the greater likelihood. What was marriage if not a matter of trust? Riding up in the lift she was already brimming with guilt for even having entertained such notions.

'I'm home, honey,' she called.

Tom trod into the living room, eyes hard, jaws set, clutching a sheaf of crumpled papers.

'Why Tom, is something wrong?'

'You're goddam right something is wrong.' He rattled the papers like a tamborine. 'Three weeks work down the fucking drain . . . all the notes on the goddam medfly. All I did was step away from the desk to answer the phone . . . Jesus, go look in the bedroom. The stuff's all over the floor like confetti.'

'I'm sorry, darling.' Caro threw up her hands in dismay. 'Sasha didn't mean it. It's just that she likes to explore things, she's into paper right now. The thing is, Tom, she creeps so fast you really have to keep your eye on her.'

'What am I?' his eyes were wet with impotent rage. 'A goddam prison warden?'

'Now, Tom' – she tried to placate him. 'It's probably not as bad as it looks at first glance. Nothing ever is . . . that's what you said to me about Worldsville. Look,' she stepped into the bedroom. 'Let's calm down and see what we can salvage.'

For the next half hour they rummaged around on the floor, hunting for missing index cards, scotch-taping bits and pieces of manuscript. In fact, the damage had not been as extensive as Tom had feared, but when the mess was reassembled, he jammed the papers into his briefcase and snapped the lock shut with an angry click. 'I'm going down to finish up at the office. At least there I can work in some kind of privacy.'

'I'm sorry, Tom. . . .'

'You're sorry, you're sorry. A lot of good that does!'

In her cot, Sasha slept the sleep of the just.

But the medfly issue was never to appear, for shortly after, *Ecology Today* breathed its last.

Tom had come home whey-faced and gone into the bedroom without a word. A few minutes later, Caro followed him in and sat beside his prostrate form on the bed.

'What is it, Tom?' she prodded gently. 'Chapter Eleven? Did Lucinda file for bankruptcy?'

He nodded mutely into the pillow and after a long while murmured in a voice so low Caro could scarcely hear 'OK, you win. I'll take the goddam job in Akron.'

She made an effort to mask her relief. 'Oh Tom,' she leaned over and kissed him. 'You won't be sorry. I'll make you very, very happy . . . I promise.'

The following day he made arrangements to begin the new job in six weeks time. He needed the interim, he explained, to preside over the last rites of his beloved magazine.

A week later, Caro asked Catlett out to lunch.

'No wild duck today, it's not hunting season yet. However I think you'll enjoy the quenelles. And George, how about a nice blanc de blanc?'

She had an eerie sense of *déjà vu*. The flowers on the table were June roses, not hot-house carnations; the girl in the green dress no longer graced the corner table – today Caro was the only woman in the room – yet the place itself projected that same hushed aura of privacy and privilege.

'There's Wriston of Citibank,' Catlett nodded to a man who had just entered. 'If you'll excuse me for a moment, Caroline . . .'

She watched him make his way across the room, cool and immaculate in his pin-stripe suit and white shirt. He looks like a priest, came the fugitive thought – a high priest of money, custodian of a thousand dark secrets. When he returned to the table, he seemed preoccupied.

'How was the Coast?' she inquired politely.

'Interesting I'm developing a very sweet deal out there.'

He did not amplify, nor did she press. He was not in the giving vein. The wine arrived, was duly uncorked and sampled. He lit a Dunhill with the familiar gold lighter. 'Stella tells me you had something in particular you wanted to discuss?'

But his mood was so cool, so aloof, she decided to delay her news. Instead she would first satisfy herself on a matter she had puzzled over innumerable times.

'I want to ask you a question, and not such a hypothetical one.' She smiled in reference to their earlier conversation in this room, but he did not smile back. 'I want to know how far I can expect to go in the company.'

'How far do you want to go?'

This time she knew the correct answer. 'All the way, Dan. Straight to the top.'

He regarded her with narrowed eyes. 'Indeed. And do you think you'll make it?'

'That's what I'm asking you, Dan.'

He didn't answer, simply lit another cigarette with a close-to-the-chest expression, and for a moment she had a sense of repeating that elaborate pavanne of their first lunch together – the guarded questions, the cautious replies – but it was so stupid in light of how long they had known each other. Was this, could this conceivably be the same man who had held her hand and wiped her tears the day Sasha was born, who had given her sweet words and comfort when she needed them.

'You can speak bluntly, Dan. I'm not going to make a federal case out of it. I just want your opinion.'

He considered for a minute, then met her open glance. 'Yes. You could make it. If that's what you really want, I have no doubt you can make it given time. You've got a good mind, an exceptional grasp of business – better than most of the men in my group, I might add. But I'll tell you something else – you'd hate it at the top. You'd just be stockpiling misery. And you know why?' He flashed a quick and unexpected smile. 'Because it hurts you to go straight for the jugular. You lack killer instinct, Caroline – and you can take that however you choose . . . as an insult or a compliment.'

She wavered for a moment, then reached across the table and squeezed his hand. 'I take it as a compliment, and thank you Dan. Now I'll tell you what I really wanted to talk about. I'm going to do something today I've wanted to do for a long, long time. I'm quitting. You can consider this as one month's notice. My husband has been offered a job in Ohio, and we'll be moving out there, starting a whole new life. I'll get a chance to be with my daughter. Aaaah,' she lit up the room with her smile. 'You know how I feel? Like someone who's just been let out of prison.'

'Well, well, well.' He squeezed her hand in return, then signalled the waiter. 'I think this calls for some champagne, Veuve Clicquot at the least, then we can settle down and have a totally social lunch.' And when the waiter had taken his order, he turned to her with a face free of constraint. The high priest had been banished, or at least taken the afternoon off. 'But tell me, who am I going to kick around when you're gone?'

'Oh, you'll find somebody.' They kidded amiably for a few minutes, and with the popping of the champagne cork, they ceased to be boss and subordinate, priest and acolyte, warriors in the battle of the sexes – merely two old friends having a pleasantly bibulous lunch.

'Tell me, Dan' – she now voiced what she had long suspected – 'I was promoted to your group as part of an affirmative action programme, wasn't I? The token woman?'

'I always supposed you knew that.'

She shrugged. 'I guess so, I just didn't care to admit it, even to myself. Not very flattering to the ego. You must have resented it terribly, my being fobbed off on you like that.'

'I fought it from the outset but it was a Board decision,

completely out of my hands. I thought you were too young, too inexperienced, not aggressive enough . . . you were being promoted for all the wrong reasons.'

'But what if I had been really tough and aggressive. . . . ? What if I had killer instinct? You know, Dan, not that it matters any more, the first time we lunched here I asked you if you were prejudiced against working with women and you never gave me an answer.'

'No.'

'No . . . meaning, no you're not prejudiced, or no . . . meaning no, you never gave me an answer.'

'No, I never gave you an answer.'

'And is that your answer?'

He laughed. 'To change the subject, your husband must be delighted about this turn of events, and now I imagine you'll be raising a proper family. . .'

She almost dropped her glass. Of course! He assumed she was pregnant again; it was a perfectly natural conclusion and he must have taken her embarrassed lurch as confirmation for he rattled on. 'You're very wise not putting it off, the way Maddy and I did. Looking back, I think it was the greatest mistake in our marraige.'

He had only mentioned his wife once before and with great bitterness, but today – perhaps it was the champagne, perhaps the lowering of barriers between him and Caro – the words began to flow freely, uninterrupted by the arrival of food.

He had met his wife at Law School when they were both students and had fallen head over heels in love. The day they married was, he said, 'the happiest day of my life', and after graduation the newlyweds have moved to New York with the understanding that Madeleine would practise law for a couple of years – it seemed a shame to waste a good education – until he was established on Wall Street. After that, of course, they would settle down and have children. 'It never occurred to me that we wouldn't. I was raised to be a family man.'

But time had a way of slipping through Madeleine's fingers. There was always something beckoning on the near horizon: the chance for promotion, the next fascinating case, the unique opportunity that could not be ignored. And so the years slipped by, and then she was thirty. And then thirty-five. 'And then we both were forty, and Maddy left. She traded in fifteen years of marriage for a Vice-Presidency. And you know what I had to show for all those years, Caroline? A list! A list of just about every caterer and take-away food place within delivery distance of Gramercy Park. Fifteen years! . . . imagine, fifteen years of marriage and I don't think she ever cooked me one proper dinner with her own two hands. Not one real dinner.'

Clearly it rankled all out of proportion, and to Caro it seemed a very trivial symbol of what must have been a long and difficult marriage.

'You know, Dan,' she said softly, 'You can always pay someone to cook and clean.'

'You can pay for any service in the world, sex included, came the tart reply, 'but it's not the same as something freely given. You should know that as well as anyone.'

His rebuke brought her up short. Indeed, who should know this better than Caro, raised by paid helpers, dreading to repeat the same loveless pattern with Sasha.

'I'm sorry,' she apologized. 'You're right . . . it's not the same.'

He pushed his food away untasted – 'restaurant meals' his gesture seemed to say – then lit another cigarette.

'When she actually left, I couldn't believe it,' he was talking half to himself, half to her. 'I felt betrayed, humiliated. It was the first time in my life I'd ever been faced with failure. I'm not talking about the little ups and downs of business, but real failure. Personal failure. Looking back, I know a lot of the fault was mine. I was too driven, too wrapped up in my own career to really see what was happening. But at the time, my God! was I angry. I guess I may have taken some of that out on you, and if so, I'm sorry – but it was a terrific blow to my pride. So you know what I did? I made a bet with myself. I wanted to see if I could sleep with a different woman every night for a month . . . not bimbos, either, but attractive, respectable women. After fifteen years of being the faithful husband, I figured I owed it to myself.'

Caro stared at him in astonishment. The last thing in the world she had expected to hear was a blow-by-blow description of his sex life. Why was he telling her all this? Had he no one else to confide in?

No, she realized, probably not.

'And did you win your bet?'

'It was extraordinary,' he mused. 'Not one woman ever said no. In fact, most of the time I didn't have to ask. It was automatic, served up along with the nightcap. The odd thing is, they were quite nice women . . . pretty . . . desirable.'

For a moment she thought he was boasting, but there was no vainglory in his voice. He was merely stating an observation. 'I reckon I could have won the bet if I persevered, but I gave it up after a couple of weeks. I felt it had nothing to do with me. I could have been anyone, any man with reasonably decent table manners and no symptoms of venereal disease. Besides, I don't like to think of myself as a performing seal.'

He brushed an invisible bit of lint off his sleeve with a disdainful hand, thus dismissing the memory of his brief career as a swinger.

He was a fastidious man, Caro realized – not just in his dress. He was a morally fastidious man.

'Then why don't you remarry . . . some nice young girl?'

'I'm forty-two, Caroline. Young girls bore me, they have nothing to say. I much prefer women.'

'Very well, then – some nice not-so-young woman. There's an abundance of them around, you know. I'm sure you could have your pick, Dan. You're attractive, successful, you have connections . . . what they used to call a catch. Come on,' she teased. 'I bet you're the darling of every hostess on Park Avenue.'

He gave a silvery laugh. 'You've been reading my mail. Honestly . . . every night I go home and have to wade through about a dozen invitations. I'm that rarest of all commodities, the spare man at every dinner party, the eligible male. Everybody's got just the right woman for me. This one's a doctor, that one's a professor at Columbia – they're all introduced with the highest credentials. Well, let me tell you, I average twelve hours a day at the office and the last thing I feel like hearing over dinner is someone else's professional problems. I had fifteen years of that.'

Yet he had twice flirted with the idea of remarriage. For a while he had lived with an actress, and from his description, Caro recognized the elegant blonde she'd seen at Lincoln Centre. 'Eve was terrific,' Catlett said fondly. 'Beautiful, smart . . . and God, she could make me laugh. But she was never there. I'd come home from the office, she'd be leaving for the theatre. We had Sundays together, that was all.' He'd then become involved with a bright and charming woman, a divorcee with a teenage son. 'I said I'd marry her if she gave up her career, that I could afford a full-time wife . . . and you know what?' – the memory amused him. 'She called me a dinosaur. "Dan," she said, "you're the last of the dinosaurs." She was probably right, but who wants to get into bed every night with an Appeals Court judge? Not me!'

Unwittingly, Caro giggled. 'So you gave up the quest?'

'Pretty much. Still, I have my consolations, my hobbies. I cultivate orchids, you know.'

No, she didn't. 'You mean those little white orchids you sent me . . . you grew them yourself?'

Yes, a rare hybrid variety. Orchids fascinated him, his eyes glittered as he spoke, and after his wife had left he had rebuilt the entire top floor of his house, turned it into a glassed-in orchidareum where every element could be controlled – heat, light, humidity. 'They require infinite care you know, I suppose that's what's so engrossing. They're very sensitive, very delicate . . . you have to nurse them every step of the way.'

He might have rambled on indefinitely had not the waiter come to clear away.

'Oh my God,' – he checked his watch. 'It's after two. I have to take a meeting in twenty minutes.'

'But Dan, you haven't eaten anything.'

He took a roll from the silver breadbasket. 'I can eat in the taxi, however you go ahead and have some dessert. You're looking a bit on the thin side. Now you're leaving' – he stood up, suddenly all business – 'I'll send a memo as to who will be handling your projects, so please see that everyone's properly briefed. I have some very busy weeks ahead, but maybe we can get together again before you leave. If not – good luck in your new career.'

And he was off.

She lingered on over coffee. What a curious man he was, so mercurial, so unbuttoned one minute, so businesslike the next. The last of the dinosaurs. She smiled at the epithet, looking for some nice lady dinosaur to cook him hot dinners.

Still, he knew what he wanted and . . . what the hell! it was probably what most men wanted deep down, including Tom once he gave up tilting with windmills. Her bet was when they settled down in Akron they'd both be all the happier for it. She would make him a wonderful wife. What was that motto Mrs Darius had put up in her kitchen, all done in cross-stitch embroidery?

Kissing don't last. Cookery do.

Not that Tom would lack for kissing she promised herself. Or Sasha either. She would make them both happy, be careful not to lean, and Tom would accept their new circumstances with his customary grace. Perhaps he already had, for he had been exceptionally tender and thoughtful these last few days, despite the fact that his magazine was in its death throes.

Meanwhile, she had a lot of things to do, such as going home right now and giving Nannie MacPherson her notice.

'You understand, Mac,' Caro dandled Sasha on her lap, 'we've been very satisfied with you, the baby too, and I'll be happy to give you excellent references.'

'Thank you, Mrs Darius, that's very kind. I don't expect I'll have any difficulty finding a new position.'

'No, I'm sure not. Anyhow, you have four more weeks here and I'll give you one week's severance pay.'

'I have two days' vacation money due me as well.' MacPherson wasn't a Scot for nothing.

'And vacation money,' Caro said. They were two business-women concluding a deal. 'You can leave early today, however. I'll give Sasha her dinner.'

'Very good, Mrs Darius. She's to have a lamb chop, creamed spinach and stewed pears. It's in the fridge.'

'Thank you. That's all for now.'

From the kitchen where she was feeding Sasha, she could hear Tom fumbling at the door.

'Hi sweetie,' she let him in. 'I tried to get you at your office but your phone was busy all day. My God, you look wiped out. Here . . . let me take your jacket.' But he lurched past her wordlessly and collapsed into the wing chair, exhausted.

'Wait a sec,' she whispered. 'Let me just put Sasha in the playpen and then we can talk.'

When she returned she handed him a double Scotch, then curled up at his feet. 'You want to tell me about it?'

'What's to tell? You must know what it's like, Caro . . . you're such an experienced businesswoman. Jesus, this last week has been sheer hell. It's a madhouse up there, creditors calling every ten seconds . . . printers, photographers. Like a fucking pack of hyenas fighting over the kill. We wound up taking all the phones off the hook.'

'It's not the end of the world, honey,' she tried to soothe. 'Bigger businesses than yours have gone bankrupt . . . there's no blame or shame attached. And anyhow, it's not as if you didn't have another job all lined up.'

'Thanks a lot!'

'Look, Tom. You're too wrought up to talk right now. Why don't you drink your drink and have a good hot shower. You'll feel better, then we can have some dinner. I'll send out to the Mandarin. . . .'

'I'm not hungry.' But he took a swallow of his Scotch and headed into the bathroom. For the next half hour she heard the water running furiously.

Poor Tom! It had all been rotten, not the less painful for having been expected. Still, perhaps seen in perspective it was all for the best. The magazine had been a millstone around both their necks.

She was dressing Sasha for bed when he came into the baby's bedroom, freshly turned out in a LaCoste sportshirt and clean jeans. His anger had dampened down to deep sadness.

'I'm going out for a walk, get some air. I'll be back about nine. In the meanwhile,' he paused and chewed his lip, 'there's something I want you to read. It's on the living room table, and we can talk about it later tonight.'

She kissed Sasha goodnight then went into the living room. On the coffee table lay a sealed white envelope, a letter by the looks of it. There was nothing on the outside to indicate contents. She opened it and removed three sheets of paper. It had been written on Tom's office typewriter. She recognized the type face. Yes, a letter. Undated.

My darling Caro,
In all the time we've known each other, nearly three years, I've never before written you a letter. We've exchanged phone calls, birthday cards, wedding rings, presents, caresses – but never letters. How curious then that this love letter should be the first time I've ever written you.

For that's what it is above all things, dear Caro. A love letter. I loved you from the moment I saw you standing there at the Kips Bay Racquet Club in that sassy little tennis dress of yours. You smiled at me, I remember, and I thought that smile the most beautiful thing I'd ever seen, brighter than sunshine.

I love you still, Caro, though of late I have come to miss that beautiful smile. And part of me will love you forever. Always, *always* remember that, my darling.

I wish this were only a love letter, but it is not. It is also a letter of farewell.

Dear Caro, I am leaving. . . .

She put the letter down and shut her eyes. Even shut, she could still read that sentence.

Need a drink.

Tom's half-empty Scotch was on the table, but suddenly the thought of drinking from something his lips had touched made her shudder with revulsion. Instead, she got up, poured herself a tumbler of brandy, then walked onto the terrace and laid her head against the cool glass of the door.

Thirty stories below, traffic hummed imperturbably, accented only by the occasional honk of a taxi, the toot of a barge ploughing lazily down the East River in the thickening twilight. From the terrace adjacent came the strains of a Mick Jagger record and a glissando of laughter. Someone was having a party.

Familiar sights, familiar sounds. Unfamiliar emotions.

The end of the world as we know it.

Wasn't that the phrase they used in every two-bit science fiction movie when the Martians invaded or a nuclear holocaust destroyed Times Square? Great line. Always good for a laugh when she and Tom watched the Late Show in bed.

Yet here it was – the end of her world as she knew it. Gone, shattered, cut away from beneath her feet without warning. Nothing would ever be the same. You'd think there would be some physical evidence of a change so monstrous – thunder, lightning, tremors in the earth, plagues of locusts – some gross and outward manifestation of catastrophe. But no. She looked around. Everything was neatly in its place.

The ficus tree, she noted, needed watering.

The end of her world as she knew it, and the ficus tree didn't give a damn. Kept right on growing, seeking sunlight, demanding water, oblivious that but a few feet away three sheets of white paper lay on a coffee table. Foolish tree!

She swallowed half the brandy and poured the rest into the dry earth of the pot. Serve it right for not knowing the world had ended.

She went back inside, noting as she passed a white-faced stranger in the mirror, then picked up the letter again.

'I've never before written you a letter.'

'No, he never had. They had always faced each other, always talked, eyes meeting.

Coward!

She found the spot where she'd left off.

I am leaving. I know you recognize the impossibility of going on as we have this past year, without happiness or pleasure or laughter. I'm sure you feel this break as necessary for your survival as for mine. Believe me, Caro, I love you. There is no one else.

Liar!

It is simply that we are what we always have been, two separate and independent people who, for a while, grew with each other but now have only grown apart. I neither blame myself nor blame you. . . .

Hypocrite!

She began skimming, skipping through the carefully wrought prose. It was double-spaced, cleanly typed, like the final draft of one of his articles. She paused only long enough to cull the few facts that lay hidden among the underbrush of words.

He discovered he could not bring himself to go to Akron. It would have only made him miserable, and he was afraid he would take his resentment out on Caro and Sasha. Instead he was moving to California. Something had come up very suddenly – a fellowship at one of the universities out there. He planned to work on his doctorate. Maybe write a book. It was something he'd always dreamed of doing. As for Sasha. . . .

As for Sasha, I accept my share of responsibility for her welfare and will contribute financially insofar as I am able. However, Caro, as I'm sure you know, academic salaries are indecently low and housing in California very expensive. Still I will do what I can.

I know on your own part you would not want to accept money from me, even if I were able to give it. You once told me that you never wanted to be dependent on a man, that you thought women who lived off alimony were leeches. I know you would not wish to become one yourself. You of all people – so capable, so proud, so fiercely independent. . .

Traitor!
Cheat!
Deserter!

I hope we can work out the details like the two civilized people we are, and that looking back you and I will only remember the good times. For there were good times, darling Caro, and I will always treasure them, those moments shared, those memories born of love. The weekend we met. The time we went sailing off Block Island. Those crazy midnight rendezvous at Kennedy airport. That trip to Sugarbush when we got snowed in. That lovely drunken dinner at Windows of the World. Kansas City. Amagansett. India. . . .

Bastard!

There was no point reading further, though the letter went on, each betrayal obscured by a sugar-coating of words. Like putting a dog out of its misery by burying a poison pellet in its favourite dish. Nonetheless the dog died.

Bastard!

Rage paralyzed her. Rage, hatred, contempt. He had not written that letter in a single afternoon. She knew his style too well for that. It had been written and rewritten, worked and reworked during furtive hours at the office. Secretly, like a bank clerk embezzling funds.

Every bit of it was planned. The California job. That hadn't turned up in an afternoon either. She might be naive about the academic world, but not so dumb as to realize fellowships didn't materialize out of nowhere. They had to be applied for, interviewed for.

Bastard! He had planned his escape over·what? . . . weeks, months, . . . with the cunning of a prisoner of war.

She had no tears, no grief, for anger had consumed every other human emotion. She had been lied to, betrayed. And now abandoned. Three years of love obliterated, murdered in a single moment.

She was still sitting, rock-motionless, when he let himself in. Softly, timidly, a mourner at a family funeral. He must have expected to find her weeping and hysterical for his expression upon seeing her was one of surprise and yes! relief. For a moment he hesitated in the doorway, then gliding towards her, hands outstretched called 'Caro.' They were going to talk like civilized people.

But before he could touch her she found her voice, low and venomous, alien even to her own ears.

'*Bastard*!' Her mouth tasted of bile. 'You goddam fucking son-of-a-bitch lying cheating bastard. Don't touch me.'

He recoiled as though stung, paused, and then began adjusting himself to this changed set of circumstances.

'I'm sorry, Caro' – he made a choked effort to be reasonable. 'Truly sorry you feel that way, but getting abusive isn't going to make things any better. I had hoped we might talk this over like civilized people.'

'Civilized people don't desert their wives,' she hissed. 'They don't abandon their children.'

'Desert . . . abandon.' Tom leapt to his own defence. 'Those are very melodramatic words. Why do you have to make me out to be such a shit? People get married and sometimes it doesn't work out . . . that's all. It's nobody's fault. Anyhow, I'm going to get a drink. You want one?'

She didn't answer. She was in complete control, disciplined as an actress, able to stand outside herself and distance her feelings from her words and her actions. It was the only safe place to be – outside herself. She watched him pour a Johnnie Walker with uncertain hands, but by the time he sat down facing her across the table, he was cool and remote. He had found his own distance too.

'Come on, Caro. Let's behave like grown-ups. I can't believe this comes as a total surprise.'

'Who is she?'

'Who is who?'

'Don't bullshit me. There's a woman in this somewhere pulling the strings. I know you. You've never made an un-assisted decision in your life. So who is it . . . the beneficiary of your favours these days?'

'Oh, come off it, Caro. There's nobody . . . I told you in the letter.'

'That letter' – she stirred the fragments with her foot – 'is nothing but a pack of self-serving lies . . . a bunch of shit. *Dear Caro . . . darling Caro*. Why don't you be a man and face up to the truth for once in your life?'

'Because I wanted to spare your feelings. Is that a crime?' His voice was dark and angry. 'I may as well have saved myself the trouble. You want the truth? OK . . . I'll tell you the truth. I'm leaving because I'm sick and tired of being made to feel like a heel, of being the bad guy while you're the martyr. Oh, you never said it in so many words, but the message comes through loud and clear. Be a man, you say . . . well, you don't think I'm much of one, do you? I'm a lousy father, I've deprived you of children. I can't even run a fucking magazine successfully. Goddamit, I'm fed up with being the villain of the piece, with eating guilt every morning at breakfast. I resent it . . . . I resent it like hell. Everyone else thinks highly of me . . . I like to think well of myself on occasion. Does that surprise you?'

They glared at each other across a frozen sea.

'Who is it? Is it Thea?'

'Jesus . . . talk to the wall!' He snorted and folded his arms. 'You don't even hear me. You just can't accept the fact that I haven't fallen into the clutches of some fantastic babe.'

'I know you, Tom. You don't jump ship without a liferaft. Who's going to balance your chequing account? Who's going to pay the electric bills?'

'Boy,' he shook his head in wonder. 'You sure are one tough cookie. I came back thinking I'd find you in tears, needing comfort. I was prepared to give you that comfort, but what do I get? . . . cheap sarcasm and trashy accusations. I don't know who put these ideas in your head . . . your boss or whoever. . . .'

'Catlett?' Her eyes narrowed. 'What does he have to do with any of this?'

But Tom drove on. 'You've got to find a scapegoat, don't you? It's easier to blame it on another woman than take the heat yourself. What do you want . . . a name to drag out in divorce court? OK . . . have it your way. The cleaning woman, Lucinda, Mrs Schrecker. Take your pick. You're so perfect. Well, I may not be the greatest monk since Saint Augustine but I'll tell you one thing. At least I don't fuck total strangers in elevators.'

For a moment she didn't know what he was talking about and then it hit her – that incredible night of the blackout.

'I never . . . I never never told you that.'

'Oh yes you did.' But his denial came too swiftly.

'Never!' She never had. She had confided that dark episode to only one person, and there was only one place, one situation where such a confidence could be betrayed. Two lovers giggling in bed.

'You and Sally!' She clutched her stomach. 'You've been banging Sally all the time.'

'It's not what you think.' Tom was suddenly flustered.

'Don't lie to me, Tom. This is truth night. All cats are out of the bag. My God, you owe me this.' For the first time that night a tear coursed down her cheek. This second betrayal was somehow too much to be borne.

'I'm sorry,' Tom turned from her gaze, momentarily contrite. 'I didn't mean it to happen.'

Sally had seduced him, he swore to God. She had stalked him, staked him out and 'You know me. I have a tough time saying no.' It had been during Caro's last month of pregnancy; she had been gross, unwieldy, physically unattractive and Tom had felt resentful. Then there was Sally – glamorous, aggressive and chic. 'It was her fault as much as mine,' he said. 'More. She was always envious of you, you know. You had the good looks, the nice husband, and now you were going to have the nice baby. Yes, Sally was envious and I was weak. One more thing for me to feel like a shit about.'

It had never been much of an affair – more of a roll in the hay. And it was over and done with long ago.

In Caro's mind, the pieces began to click together, like tumblers in the combination of a safe.

'It was in Washington, wasn't it . . . the day Sasha was born.' She remembered. Recalled Tom coming to the hospital that evening, muted and apologetic, wearing different clothes from those he'd had on in the morning. The last tumbler clicked into place.

'And Catlett found you out there, didn't he? How? . . . calling round the hotels and then what? Don't tell me,' she gave a bitter laugh. 'You were registered as Mr and Mrs Tom Darius.'

Something like that, Tom mumbled.

She poured herself another brandy and they sat for a long time in silence, each buried in disparate thoughts.

'I quit my job today,' she said finally. It was something dimly recalled, an event that had taken place a million years ago, before the end of the world as she knew it.

'I quit,' she added, 'so I could stay home, lover, and be a good wife and wonderful mother. How's them apples, as you like to say?'

'Then you'll have to unquit it.' She shook her head no.

'You'll have to,' he repeated. 'Because there is no way – *no way* – that I can afford to support two households.'

'Then you'll goddam have to find a way or I'll haul you up in court so fast you won't know what hit you.'

'Money!' he shot back. 'All you ever think about is money. You sure are a ball-breaker, sweetheart. Well, don't try to push me, Caro, because I'm not going to take it lying down. I had hoped we might work out something amicable, be friends even, but I'm not going to be crucified for having made one lousy mistake.'

'Get out!' – all that careful control was beginning to slip away. 'Get out of my house . . . now! Out of my sight. This minute. There's the door . . . now get the hell out!'

They exchanged looks of pure vitriol.

'In case you forgot, Caro, this is my home as much as yours. I've paid my share of this month's rent and you're not going to turn me out on the street at midnight. What is this . . . some fucking soap opera? I'll leave when I'm ready, not before. Probably the week after next . . . I've got a lot of things to clear up in the meantime. And you can quit your job or keep it, I don't give a rat's ass, but don't expect me to spend the rest of my life in sackcloth and ashes. Because I am goddam tired' – he shouted – 'of being the heavy around here. You can have the bedroom. I'll sleep on the sofa. That should spare your sensibilities.'

'Die!' she said. 'I wish you were dead.' Then she went into the bedroom and shut the door.

All weekend long, Tom was busy around the house, making phone calls, packing, sorting, shipping. He worked up elaborate lists of what was hers, what was his, what to sell, what to keep. 'Look, I'll take the car, you never use it anyhow and you can have the living room furniture including the TV. I'll take the stereo, it's mine anyhow. That seems to me about fair.'

She didn't answer.

'This Mahler First, is that mine or yours? I don't remember.' She remembered. They had played it the first time they made love. She said nothing. 'Look, Caro, you're not making it any easier with the silent treatment.'

But why should she make it any easier?

She tended Sasha, went about her chores wordlessly, and watched him go about his. If the place had burst into flames, she would not have yelled 'Fire!'

In fact, she never spoke to him again.

22

Monday she talked.

'Felicia Haines says you're the best divorce lawyer in town.'

Through his moustache, Mr Wilcox smiled a routine acknowledgment. He was a portly balding man with unshockable eyes and an air of Father-knows-best. 'I do what I can for my clients,' he said. 'Too bad about Felicia.'

Actually Felicia had been Caro's first choice of attorney. The previous night, she had phoned the lawyer at home to ask for a rush appointment, only to be confronted with unsettling news.

'I'm sorry,' Felicia had said, 'but I'm not taking on any cases. In fact I'm in the midst of selling my firm. We're moving to Spain next month.'

Spain! Caro couldn't believe her ears. What business did a hot-shot New York lawyer have in Spain?

Felicia explained. Years ago, when she got her first big break, her husband had made considerable sacrifices. She owed him one. Now Terry's big break had come along – a commission to design and build a new government centre in Madrid. It was the chance of a lifetime. Felicia had dithered, doubted, then finally decided. Her marriage came first. And despite some regrets, she was now looking forward to the experience with gusto. 'It'll be a whole new life for all of us.' Naturally, she was sorry to hear about Caro's troubles, heartily recommended Herb Wilcox. 'He can get blood from a stone.' And so the women had wished each other good bye. And good luck.

Blood from his clients, too – by the look of things.

Caro took a swift inventory of the surroundings: Barcelona chairs, spit-and-polish panelling, a view of the U.N. 'Is that a

Utrillo over there?' she asked, and he fluffed with pride. Yessir – business must be booming.

'Shall we get down to cases, Mrs Darius?'

In these precincts time was money, and Caro rapped out the facts one, two, three: Tom's adultery, his impending desertion, the question of Sasha.

'Do you think it likely your husband will contest the child's custody?' Wilcox asked, and for the first time in days, Caro laughed. No, she assured him. Definitely not.

'That simplifies things. So what precisely do you want, other than a divorce?'

'What I want,' came the grim reply 'is to see him drawn and quartered, but since I understand that's no longer legal, I'll settle for every penny I can get. The point is, he's abandoning both me and his daughter and if I have to take full responsibility, raise her all by myself ... well, by my lights that's a full-time job like any other. So I want enough alimony to live on...'

'Technically speaking, it's not termed alimony...'

'Then maintenance, support ... whatever it's called. Let's not quibble about words. Plus ... I think I'm entitled to damages' – at that, Wilcox raised an eyebrow – 'well, some sort of compensation. After all my husband has admitted to adultery with my best friend. I'm the injured party,' she wailed.

'Dear lady,' the lawyer clucked in sympathy. 'I'm sorry to disillusion you, but while adultery may still be a no-no in bible class, it carries no weight in court. We have what in lay terms you might call no-fault divorce, it's considered a great advance. So even if you caught your spouse in Times Square at high noon being indelicate with a female chimpanzee, it wouldn't affect the financial settlement. Just give me the figures – what you earn, what he earns, the value of your communal property...'

And when Caro told him, he scowled. 'You out-earn your husband substantially. You were working when you married, you worked both before and after the child was born ... frankly there isn't a judge in this state who'd award maintenance to a Harvard MBA making sixty thousand dollars a year. If you'd been financially dependent on your husband, we'd be in a different situation...'

'But I'm dependent *now*,' Caro protested. 'I've quit my job. In four weeks I won't have a penny coming in – not even unemployment insurance.'

'And you know what your husband's attorneys will say to that? That you've quit out of spite, to hold him up.'

'You mean the court can force me to keep on working?' She was aghast.

'They can't force you, but they won't find for you either.' He paused to let this reality sink in.

'Then what's the bottom line?' Caro felt nauseated. 'My husband can walk away from everything, free as air, and I get nothing?'

'Your child will be entitled to some support, based on his ability to pay, although if he's moving out of state you may have a hard time collecting it. And, of course, you get fifty per cent of communal property.'

Great! Terrific! Fifty per cent of a subscription to City Centre Ballet and half the food in the freezer. Plus a hundred per cent of the headaches.

'You know, Mr Wilcox,' she pulled on her jacket. 'I'm beginning to wonder if I can even afford your fees.'

'So am I,' he smiled amiably. 'I'll turn your case over to one of my junior associates. I'm afraid it will be routine.'

But as she rose to go, she gave a bitter smile. 'Where is the justice in all this?'

'Justice?' The word sounded archaic on his lips. 'There is no justice . . . there's only law. As Dorothy Parker once said about divorce, the screwing you've had isn't worth the screwing you get. I'm sorry, Mrs Darius.'

She returned to her office thoroughly shaken.

Money. Tom had charged her with thinking of nothing but. Yet at the moment, it was a paramount concern, and for the next hour she hunched over her desk pushing about the figures and not liking the results. Her cash reserves covered barely two months' expenses, and she'd have to allow for legal fees. The solution, of course, was near at hand – sitting in the corner office. All she had to do was march in to Catlett, tell him she'd changed her mind. A woman's prerogative. Maybe instead of quitting she should hit him up for a raise, for even if she stayed put, running that household was going to eat up every penny she earned.

'If only it weren't for Sasha,' she found herself thinking, then recoiled in horror. My God, she was beginning to sound like Tom. Because if it weren't for Sasha, she would have nothing – no purpose in life at all.

Quit she must – yet the consequences were frightening. Was it possible that this upheaval in her life, this cataclysm would be marked not just by the death of her love for Tom, but the surrender of all those comforts and pleasures she had for years accepted as her due?

What was life without money? She couldn't imagine. She began to weave a scenario: her living with Sasha in a city housing project – tiny rooms, cement floors, a view of the air shaft – collecting welfare, applying for food stamps, a case history in some social-worker's file. Could you even apply for welfare with a closet full of Geoffrey Beenes and St Laurents? One thing for sure, she'd be a helluva lot better dressed than the social worker. The whole image was absurd. Nothing in life had prepared her for a marginal existence.

For the rest of the afternoon, she raked her mind for alternative solutions, everything short of remaining on Wall Street.

That morning, Tom had informed her he would be moving out within two days, apparently finding her silence more unbearable than any amount of screams and invective. But now the prospect of going home and shutting herself in the bedroom while he packed was too depressing. Instead she called a sitter and arranged to spend the evening with Thea. So she wouldn't see Sasha at all tonight, but what the hell – they'd be seeing plenty of each other in the future.

'Oh sweetie, I'm so sorry.' Thea's eyes turned moist. 'And Tom, of all people! I always had him figured for one of the good guys. Men are such shits, aren't they? But I must say, you're being terribly brave about it, the old stiff upper lip. When it happened to me, I was bawling my eyes out for months.'

Caro didn't even try to explain her reactions, that remote unreal sensation that everything – Tom, the lawyer, even

303

sitting here amid the familiar clutter of Thea's loft – wasn't happening to her at all. She might have been watching figures up on a screen, the dispassionate observer of some curious melodrama glimpsed from a distance. And yet she knew that once the tears began, they would never end. She would weep into infinity, and only anger could keep her grief at bay.

Control. Control was essential. That and a way out of the immediate predicament.

'I was wondering, Thea, now that you're moving to Dallas if you'd be interested in sub-letting your loft. I'm trying to cut down my overheads.'

'Omigod!' Thea sat down heavily. 'If I'd only known a couple of weeks ago. But I've sold it, Caro . . . I'm buying a condo in Texas. Do you need any money? I'd be happy to. . .

Caro answered with a vigorous shake of her head. She wasn't reduced to beggary – not yet, at any rate.

'No . . . I'll manage.'

'I know you will,' Thea patted her hand. 'You'll line up something, another job. Maybe even something better. Meanwhile,' she roused herself briskly, 'you and I should do something about dinner. You look as if you'd blow away in a strong wind. So supposing you make a salad and I'll put on some chops.'

For the next half hour, the two women busied themselves in the kitchen. Thea set the table with care and taste, and Caro sat down gratefully. Thea was right about one thing: calories were comfort.

'This is how everything ends nowadays, isn't it?' She watched Thea lighting the candles. 'All the novels . . . all the new movies. With women alone.'

'No,' her friend answered, softly. 'With women together. We're the tough ones, you know. The real survivors. Sometimes I wonder if we really need men any longer, except for sex, and even there, they're mostly disappointing. Men aren't an economic necessity these days, thank God. We women can support ourselves. I tell you, the longer I live, the more of a feminist I become. We women put our emotions on the line every time and what do we get in return? Heartache and clap. That's all I ever got out of Brooks. You know, when I first discovered he was playing around, I felt terribly guilty, so sure it was all my fault. And then I looked around at the other married people I knew and asked myself – where are all the happy couples we're supposed to emulate? Do you know any personally? I don't. My guess is we could walk down the street, stop any woman at random and hear stories very much like yours and mine. Worse, probably. Not just betrayal, infidelity, desertion – but rapes, beatings, criminal abuse. Looking back I can honestly say the best things that have come my way have come to me from my work and from my friends – not from lovers. Take us, Caro. Fifteen years of unbroken friendship, and we've never had a real argument. Not even a harsh word. Yes . . . friendships and work. I'm really looking forward to setting up shop in Dallas. It'll be the first time in my life I've ever been self-supporting, and you can't imagine what that means to me. I'm only sorry to have to leave you in the lurch at a time like this, but you'll be OK, Caro. You'll be just fine.'

They finished the meal in amicable small talk, then made their farewells. 'Don't worry, Caro!' – Thea hugged her in the last embrace. 'You'll find a way to work things out.'

Caro went home profoundly depressed to find Tom shoving books into cardboard cartons. Echoes of Howie Bernstein. Only worse. For Caro was losing a husband. And Sasha would be losing a father. With eyes averted, she headed for the bedroom and shut herself in.

At the age of twelve, Caro had become obsessed with the idea of discovering the identity of the man whose genes she carried. She knew his name and nothing else. But what did he do? Where did he live? Above all, what did he look like? For there was little of her mother in Caro's appearance, and as she entered adolescence the differences between them became more pronounced.

'Almost five foot six already,' Gusty measured her one evening. 'You're going to be very tall and willowy when you grow up. . .'

Just like your father, Caro completed the sentence in her mind.

Often when she was alone, she would pull her hair back, suck in her cheeks and glance in the mirror quickly, hoping to catch her reflection unaware, and thereby glean some vision of what *he* might have looked like. And sometimes, when she was wearing jeans and a man-tailored shirt, she would be rewarded with a fleeting impression – high cheekbones, lithe body – that just might have characterized the mysterious Harmsworth.

There was little to be gained from asking Gusty, who declared she could scarcely remember the gentlemen in question. 'As far as I'm concerned, he's just another face on the cutting-room floor.' Yet it was that remark that gave Caro a lead.

Throughout her career, Gusty kept a large and scrupulously indexed file of still photographs, housed in fireproof metal cabinets. The collection was so extensive as to require a small room of its own, and that room had been declared off limits. But now, the forbidden files assumed a magic aura for within them, Caro was convinced, lay the secret of her parentage.

She bided her time until Gusty was off in the field, then began her assault on the sanctum. She began with the H's. *Haiti, Harijans, Hassidim* but no *Harmsworth*. Next she tried the P's. P for *Personal* P for *Private*. No entries under either heading. M for *Marriage*. W for *Wedding*. Still nothing.

It was inconceivable that Gusty – who viewed all life through the camera's lens – should have let her own existence slip by unrecorded. Well then, Caro would begin at the beginning, check out each item from A to Z. Halfway through the files, she hit pay dirt. *Misc & Pers* read the caption on the huge manila envelope. Miscellaneous and Personal – perhaps to Gusty they were synonymous. Caro spilled the contents out on the table. Pictures by the hundreds, photos of every size. Gusty as a school girl in Indiana, Caro as a baby. Glossy prints of her mother posed with the great and near-great. Photos – untitled, undated, unsorted – of friends, lovers, housekeepers, neighbours, colleagues and total strangers.

Methodically, Caro set about her task, eliminating first all photographs of women, then those of men whose identity she knew. Next, photos of fair-haired men on the assumption that her own dark hair had come from *him*. Finally, pictures of men she considered too old, too young or simply too unattractive. One candidate was weeded out because he wore glasses, another because his tie was too loud. This one had a sneaky smile, that one a bad complexion. For hours she edited with a ruthless hand, eliminating all but two photos.

The first, taken in a nightclub, showed a very young and happy Gusty seated next to an Army officer. No . . . not Army. Air Force. Caro could just make out the wings on his jacket. The man was heart-breakingly handsome, but he had dark hair and high cheekbones like her own. Was he tall enough? He was sitting in the picture – rotten luck! – so Caro could only guess about height.

The second photo offered even thinner grounds for conjecture. Just a snapshot, badly overexposed, of a tall clean-cut young man in tennis whites. Little could be gleaned from the face; even under the magnifying glass the features were blurry. Yet there was something suggestive in his stance, a certain grace, a distinctive conformation of bone. He was willowy, this tennis player, decidedly willowy.

She placed the pictures side by side on the light table, scouring them for further insights, convinced one of these men was her father. But which? Then it struck her. The men were one and the same! True, the tennis player was clean shaven, but that proved nothing. Lots of military men shaved off their moustaches when they became civilians.

For months after, she brooded about her discovery, weaving intricate fantasies from the meagre clues. Flight Lieutenant Harmsworth, USAF (the Korean War, she figured, plotting the chronology from the Book of Knowledge), had been a fighter pilot. He had met Gusty on leave, married her after a whirlwind courtship, left the service with honours and settled down to become. . .

To become what? A tennis pro? No – too frivolous. More likely an airline pilot or – better yet – a rocket engineer stationed at Cape Canaveral. That would explain the sunshine that infused the second photo.

During her mother's absence she signed up for tennis instruction, began playing daily, even inquired about how old you had to be to take flying lessons. And when Gusty returned, Caro flaunted her new-found enthusiasms in hope of eliciting some clue, some chance remark. *Just like your father*. But Gusty observed nothing, other than that Caro had become listless, a condition she attributed to puberty. Finally, Caro could bear the suspense no longer, and when her mother asked if there were anything she wanted before Gusty returned to the field, Caro responded by bursting into tears.

'I want to see a picture of my father,' she pleaded. 'Just one . . . I beg of you' and Gusty, stunned by this emotional onslaught, reluctantly conceded. 'That's assuming I even have one. It was ages ago.'

So back into the file room, and from Gusty's absorption it was clear she hadn't opened the *Misc & Pers* envelope in years.

'Oh, look at this' – she seemed to have forgotten the object of their mission. 'Me and Golda Meir. Here's that house in Nairobi. Oh – and Nigel. You remember Nigel, don't you?' she babbled, while Caro waited in agony. At least she saw the edge of the night-club photo peeping out. But seconds later, Gusty passed it over without comment and was rattling on about something else.

'Who was that, Gusty? With you in the nightclub a couple of pictures back?' Gusty reversed her tracks. 'This one?' And Caro, too choked with emotion could only nod. Her mother studied the picture for a moment, then shrugged 'Damned if I know.'

Caro was devastated. No photo of her father existed. All her fantasies were *just* that – fantasies. Perhaps the man himself had never existed except in her imagination, and Caro had sprung from nowhere. A test-tube baby. The fruit of an immaculate conception.

'Aha!' Gusty pounced triumphantly. 'Here we are. Not a very good likeness I'm afraid. It's only a snapshot. . .'

Only a snapshot. A blurry overexposed snapshot of a tall willowy man in tennis whites. At the sight of it, Caro broke down.

'You see,' said Gusty. 'I was right. I knew it would upset you. Now get some Kleenex and blow – don't snuffle.'

'Was he . . . a tennis pro?' Caro said through her tears.

'Good lord, no! Nothing so raffish. He sold advertising for a newspaper. Now don't ask me which one, don't ask me where, because I don't want you trying to find him. He's probably remarried by now, with kids of his own . . . so if you have some romantic notion of looking him up one day, I advise you to put it right out of your mind. It would only pain you, pain him . . . me too, for that matter. Just remember, Caro, men come and go in this life. You can't rely on them for anything. Anyhow, we girls always have each other.'

For some months, Caro kept the picture by her bedside, but during the next move it got lost in transit and after that was totally forgotten. What was it, after all? Just a snapshot of an unknown man with a tennis racket.

Funny though, now that she thought of it – she had met Tom on the tennis court.

All that night, she brooded about Gusty, shuffling and reshuffling ancient memories. 'We girls always have each other.' But Caro had never had Gusty. She had had other things: years of loneliness, years of lovelessness, an eternity of coming home to empty houses, of broken promises and forgotten birthdays and half-hearted apologies. Now she felt that Gusty owed her – owed her everything. And the time had come for Caro to collect her debts.

23

Helmut answered the door. Gusty was just putting on her makeup he explained in quite adequate English (he certainly was a fast learner, that lad). Would Caro like a cup of coffee while she waited?

He waltzed into the kitchen whistling *Queen of Hearts*, the brief terry cloth robe setting off his tan to beach-boy perfection.

Jesus, she watched him contemptuously, doesn't he do anything but sit around under the sunlamp? Nine-thirty on a weekday morning and he's not even dressed.

'Why don't you get a job, Helmut?' she began riding him as he set cups out on the coffee table. 'Why don't you join the rest of the working world?'

'I have a job, Caro.' And when she arched an eyebrow, he added 'I work nights,' then burst out laughing.

Christ, she'd asked for that one, she thought, burying her eyes in the coffee cup. Even with the language barrier removed, she could never think of anything to say to him. She could hardly discuss her mother. But if on her part the silence was embarrassing, Helmut seemed to be finding a quiet amusement in her discomfiture. He sat on a footstool, legs crossed, chin in hand, contemplating her with a smirk.

'You have good legs, Caro.'

'I beg your pardon?'

He didn't repeat his statement, however, just sat sipping his coffee and surveying her as though she were meat on the rack. Gusty finally made her appearance, dressed to the hilt.

'How are you, dear?' The two women exchanged casual pecks. 'And what brings you here so early? Nothing wrong, I hope?'

'I'd like to speak to you alone, mother.' She emphasized the 'mother'; it was a term Gusty had always discouraged.

'Yes, of course. You run along now, darling' – she rumpled Helmut's blond hair affectionately – 'while Caro and I have our little chit chat.' When he left the room, she consulted her watch. 'I'm afraid I don't have too much time, Caro. I have a meeting at CBS in an hour.'

'I'll be brief.'

And Caro was, telling her tale simply and coherently with Gusty nodding in appropriate places.

'Well I must say, Tom has behaved abominably . . . just abominably.' Gusty frowned in condemnation. But to Caro there was something ironic in her mother's stern disapproval. For what had Tom done, in actuality, that Gusty herself had not done so many years ago – abandon a spouse and leave behind a letter?

'Abominably!' Gusty repeated. 'So you'll be staying in New York after all. I must say, I always did think that idea of your moving out to Akron was crazy – but of course that's all academic now. Do you think they'll reinstate you at PAGIT?'

'Probably. But I'm not going to ask. I'm finished with Wall Street, Gusty. That's over.'

'Then how on earth are you going to manage?'

And when Caro explained, Gusty gaped at her incredulously.

'You're not seriously suggesting you and Sasha move in with us?'

'Yes I am, Gusty.'

'I can't believe my ears,' her mother marvelled. 'Now I'm awfully sad about this business with Tom, but these things happen every day. And it's no reason to throw up a perfectly good job, a first-class career and come running home to mama like a kindergarten kid. You're thirty years old, Caro, a healthy young woman. You should be capable of standing on your own two feet. If you need a little money to tide you over, that's one thing . . . but to move in here? You must think I'm made of money. My God, Caro, when I think of what I've spent on you over the years. All those nannies and cooks and housekeepers. The best private schools . . . college . . . Harvard. I paid your bills for more than twenty years, Caro, and let me tell you it cost me a fortune. Frankly, Caro, without those expenses I would have been a rich woman today. And why did I do it? So you could make something of yourself, that's why. My generation fought all those battles so that your generation would have it made. Now I ask you . . . is this what I put you through Harvard for . . . so you could push a baby carriage in Central Park? Not bad enough you quit, but to top it off you actually want me to support you in a life of leisure. Well, that beats everything!'

Gusty concluded her speech with an impatient shrug – a slight restless gesture that seemed to say – be done, get on with it, I have more important things to do.

And in that shrug Caro read the sum total of a thousand slights, a thousand humiliations, of petty neglects and major omissions without number. A lifetime's resentment now boiled up in her throat, spilling over uncontrolled.

'Why shouldn't you support me!' the words tumbled out. 'You support Helmut, goddamit! You buy him his clothes, his food. Why not me? I'm your own flesh and blood! You owe me this Gusty. You owe me everything, because I've had nothing from you from the day I was born. Nothing! You robbed me of my childhood, of ordinary love and security. You even robbed me of my father! When have I ever had your respect, your whole-hearted approval? Name me one time when I ever came first in your life. Did you ever fuss over me the way you fuss over Helmut? It makes me sick – sick and jealous to see you fawning over him. My God, in one year you've lavished more kisses on that fucking stud than I've had from you in thirty years. And don't give me that shit about your sacrifices – how much it cost to bring me up, what a rich woman you could have been . . . blah blah blah. Because I've heard that a thousand times. Well, money is the cheapest currency in the world, Gusty. It's what you give when you're incapable of giving anything else. So keep your goddam money . . . spend it on Helmut. I should have known better than to expect anything from you!' She got up, trembling with rage, and lurched toward the door. 'I wash my hands of you, Gusty, once and for all. Why not? You washed your hands of me the very day I was born!'

She couldn't face the office after that, phoned in sick for the day. Not that it mattered. The waters there were already closing over her. They'd even taken her name off the *Confidential* memo list. Nor could she bring herself to recall that scene with her mother. It was too hideous – Gusty's face blazing with fury, speechless for once in her life. Too awful to think about.

Instead she went to the movies and sat through three showings of *Superman II*. It was better than brooding or feeling. Better than facing the fact that all the doors were shutting against her.

24

On her way out next morning, Tom said 'Today's the day, Caro. I'm leaving. The movers are coming at ten. I thought you might want to part on a more pleasant note.' He held out his hand but she swept past him. 'OK, have it your way,' he called after her. 'I'll leave an address in L.A. so you'll know where to forward my mail.' She walked out without looking back.

That evening, she came home to find Sasha and Mrs Mac-Pherson waiting in a half-empty apartment. The place looked naked, unfamiliar. Tom's books, bookcases, desk, chairs, records, odd bits of furniture – all gone. White squares on the wall marked the spots where his bird prints had hung. The carpet was strewn with tag ends of cardboard boxes and cigarette butts.

'I told the movers to clean up after themselves,' Nannie MacPherson pursed her lips. 'But they didn't. The cleaning woman didn't turn up either. No one's interested in doing a proper job these days.

'Thank you, Mac.' Caro picked up a piece of paper on the coffee table where the Buddha figurine used to be. It was an address in North Hollywood. Care of a woman's name. So what else is new? 'That'll be all for today, MacPherson.'

Six o'clock, feed Sasha. Six-thirty, put her to bed. Seven, turn on the news, then watch *The Muppets, Mr Merlin, Nurse, Love Sidney, Shannon*, more news, *The Late Show – Blume in Love* starring George Segal. She'd seen it, but what the hell. Too much effort to switch channels. One-thirty, turn in. Another day tomorrow. She fell into bed fully dressed.

'Won't you come in, Caroline?' He smiled and shut the office door noiselessly behind him. 'You look tired, sugar, very tired. Come . . . lie down here for a while.'

She did as he said, spreading her dark hair against the white cushions of the sofa, while he drew the blinds against the bright summer sun. Then he came to where she lay.

Cool elegant fingers smoothing her hair, sliding down her throat, undoing the tiny silk buttons of her blouse until her breasts lay bare and aching beneath his hands. 'Beautiful Caroline.' He kissed her lips and she could feel the fine cashmere of his suit brushing against her naked nipples. She opened her mouth to him and he began making love – sensual, erotic, in total command of both her mind and her body, while from beyond the window came the vague rumble of traffic. She lay helpless beneath the soft rain of his caresses as he stroked her, undressed her, entered her. . . .

Caro awoke drenched in sweat.

The bedside clock read 3.42. She switched on the light. The first thing to meet her eyes was Tom's closet door ajar, empty and gaping as an open wound.

My God, what a dream! Catlett of all people!

Yet the dream had been seductive, full of comfort and sweetness and pleasure. If only you could walk out of reality, as through a door, and into the dreams of your choosing. Yet the reality was everywhere in this room: the empty closet, the four flattened rings in the carpet where Tom's desk had stood, the gouged-out plaster over the bed where a reading lamp used to be. Son of a bitch had taken one of the reading lamps. They were a pair, for Chrissakes. Wonder he didn't take the bed while he was about it. His half, anyway.

For the first time the absoluteness of Tom's departure came crashing down on her. He had gone. Escaped to where her wrath could no longer touch him. The wretch! For if there had been any pleasure during these last few days, it had been watching him writhe beneath her contemptuous silence, but now he had even robbed her of that.

Coward! To deny her the power of wounding him as he had wounded her. She had a momentary urge to run out onto the street, collar perfect strangers and end the long silence. 'My husband has left me,' she would tell them. 'Tom Darius has deserted his wife and child.' Then she'd spell the name to make sure they'd got it right. But what was the use of that . . . he'd never know. Better idea. First thing tomorrow, she'd call up *The New York Times*, place a classified ad. *Tom Darius is a Son of a Bitch*. Why limit herself to *The Times*? She'd phone the professional journals, write anonymous letters to the President of UCLA, The Harvard Almuni Association. *Scientific American*.

Beautiful! She could picture his face when he read his name in the Letters column of *Scientific American*. 'Dear Sirs, Know ye by all present that Tom Darius is a cheat and a bastard. . .'

It was only fair that everyone should discover the kind of person he was – the kind who abandoned his family, then fled from taking his punishment like a man.

Where was he now . . . the fucking bastard? Lying in the arms of some woman in an arty Greenwich Village apartment? Or with Sally? They could both roast in hell. Fast asleep, alone and dreaming carefree dreams in a motel en route to California? How dare he be happy? How dare he get off scot free while she and Sasha were left behind to suffer. Oh God – there was no justice! It was all too corrosive, too painful to be borne. Easier by far to shut her eyes and slide back into the sweet comfort of her own dream, flee to the beckoning safety of Catlett's office, his arms – for the dream had been a happy, loving one. She switched off the light and recaptured the image. In the darkness, Dan Catlett possessed her again and again.

She arose early, and began putting on makeup with far more than usual care. What to wear? No, not one of the grim dark suits that had constituted her uniform the past two years – he liked women to look feminine. But nothing flashy or obviously sexy either – he despised vulgarity. She threw all her clothes out on the bed, settling finally on a soft silk dress the colour of ripe apricots. Then slipping it on regarded herself with faint satisfaction.

Thin, yes. But thin was interesting, and he himself was slim and fine-boned. Not that she was going to do anything so crude as to seduce him, mind you. Merely put herself in his way, look fetching and play the rest by ear.

In the meanwhile she would confide her plight to no one at the office. Her revelations would be for his ears only.

Catlett didn't arrive till after lunch, and when he did it was amid a cluster of Japanese businessmen whom he ushered into his office without so much as a glance for anyone else. Next day, he didn't come in at all.

All weekend long Caro attended to her chores, but even as she shopped and pottered and took Sasha to the park, her mind was elsewhere, locked in the stranglehold of fantasy. Why torture herself thinking of Tom when for the same mental outlay she could be soothed and caressed and beloved?

Odd that she had never considered Catlett's true merits before. Not realized, in all this time, that as near as the corner office there lay a safe harbour. Protection. Refuge. For Catlett was everything that bastard was not: strong, powerful, enduring. Responsibility rested easily on his shoulders. Had he not always been there when she needed him – rock solid in times of crisis? When Gusty had pulled her disappearing act, Catlett had helped find her. When Walter died, Catlett took over. When Sasha was born. . . .

How could she ever forget that day? He had been there, Tom had not. You look beautiful, he'd told her. He'd held her hand, wiped her brow, fought tooth and nail for her in that godawful hospital. Sugar, he'd called her – which she'd found amusing and quaintly southern, yet he was not a man given to casual endearments. She raked her memory seeking fuel for her fantasies – the kind word, the thoughtful gesture – and with each passing hour it became more and more obvious that the man was inordinately fond of her. No. Fond was too mild a word. He desired her, coveted her. For all she knew, even ached for her as she was now aching for him.

And what a splendid man Dan Catlett was. No quitter, no coward like Tom. He was a man who knew how to treasure what was his.

Very well, then. She would be his. She would become his proudest, most cosseted possession – to be cherished like his fine porcelains, to be nurtured like the fragile blossoms of his greenhouse, protected eternally from all that was cold and harsh and ugly.

She would become his mistress, perhaps even his wife! Mrs Daniel Rogers Catlett III. Wouldn't that frost everyone! Gusty.

Sally. But most of all that bastard Tom, who was probably right this moment screwing himself silly with some. . . But better not to think about that. Better to replay for the thousandth time those dreams that had burgeoned into full obsession.

Monday, no Catlett. Tuesday, ditto. By Wednesday she was in agony. 'Do you know where Dan's got to?' she asked Tony with smothered anxiety, only to hear he was away all week in Texas, waltzing some people with oil-drilling patents. . . Tony rattled on, but all Caro registered was *Texas* and *week*. Damn it to hell! Didn't he know time was running out?

The next day she spent prowling the streets that surrounded Gramercy Park, trying to guess which of those handsome old houses was his. This brownstone, that redbrick Federal? There would be a greenhouse at the top, but from street level she couldn't make out the roofs. Rather than jump to an erroneous conclusion, she decided to wait. Time would tell.

Friday was spent behind the red door at Elizabeth Arden getting 'the works' – everything from hair-styling to foot massage. Cost a bundle, but what the hell . . . it was an investment. And she'd look sensational come Monday.

When people called at home – Tom's friends, mutual friends – she was cold and abrupt, resenting the time stolen from daydreams. 'Tom Darius doesn't live here any more,' she would announce. 'He has left his wife and child.' That said, she'd hang up. They rarely called twice. Well, screw 'em . . . screw 'em all. She wished to see no one she and Tom had known as a couple. She only wanted to see. . .

On Monday, Catlett passed her desk with a mumbled 'good morning', then closeted himself in an all-day meeting. The remainder of the week he was either in conference or on the road.

If only she could reach him, talk to him, find him after hours. Perhaps there was some particular bar where he passed the odd evening and she might happen to drop in. 'Why, Dan, what a coincidence.' But she didn't think he frequented bars. Men's clubs were more his style.

Or orchids. Maybe he belonged to some association of orchid fanciers that met regularly. She checked out the phone book: an

Orchid Garage, an Orchid Italian Restaurant, but nothing even close to her requirements.

One night when he was out of town, she stayed late and after everyone had gone, let herself into his office with the key Stella had given her the year before. He had a luxurious bathroom with a small dressing room attached, and though she had used the amenities now and then during her pregnancy, she had never lingered. But now she entered with a sense of frenzied expectation.

First she examined his medicine chest – unrevealing for the most part. Electric razor, toothbrush, deodorant, aftershave. An immense bottle of aspirin, half empty. My God, he must have monstrous headaches. But nothing of real interest – no signs of drugs or sexual proclivities. His shower: the usual soap, washcloths, towels. The dressing room was more rewarding and she passed a delirious hour, her head buried in the contents of his wardrobe. Here were the familiar black pin-stripe suits from Dunhills, the immaculate pile of Sulka shirts, Countess Mara ties, cashmere socks, underwear. All his shoes were English. Here too were dinner jackets, black tie, white tie, shirt studs, silk scarf: everything for glittering evenings on the town.

She stayed till nearly ten, simultaneously rapt and terrified, then left quiet as a thief, the clean scent of his shirts in her nostrils. Quick! Before the cleaning woman comes.

Yes, Catlett lived his life from that office; it was the core of his existence. He was there early mornings, late nights. Only now, when her need for his presence was so desperate was he absent. Always on the road. Or in meetings. Remote. Unavailable. A nod and the occasional smile came her way. Nothing more.

And so each day passed, born in an agony of expectation, dying without a word or a touch. And so each night passed in unbounded and increasingly lurid fantasies.

She wasn't aggressive enough: that had always been her failing. Another woman, the hateful Sally for example, would have had no qualms about cornering him, throwing herself across his path in the most explicit manner. Yet for all her yearning, Caro could not. Despite the shamelessness of her daydreams he remained an aloof and elusive figure.

By her last day on the job, her dreams lay in ashes. Ten

o'clock and no Catlett. He was probably off on the road again. She would never see him again: fate had ordained it.

With a heavy heart, she began cleaning out her desk, then she would make the rounds of goodbyes. Leave him a brief and friendly note. Nothing too personal, for Stella read all his mail, maybe just. . .

'If you're free for lunch today, Caroline. . .' – a light touch on her shoulder, and there he was standing before her with a cheerful smile, deaf to the violent thud as her heart bounded wildly against her rib cage. 'Today's your last day here isn't it, so if there's someplace special you'd enjoy eating . . . Chez George, Oscars, anywhere reasonably nearby. . . .'

By sheer triumph of will, she managed to get out the sentence she had rehearsed so often in mental scenarios. 'What I'd really like to do, Dan, if it's agreeable to you, is just have a quick bite and . . . ummm . . . see your orchids. I've heard so much about them, and I love flowers. That is, if it's no trouble.'

Please God – if there is a God – will him to say yes. How could he deny her this last request?

'My orchids!' He blinked in surprise. 'Really! I didn't know you were interested. I'm always afraid of boring people with them. . .'

'No,' she breathed. 'I won't find it boring.'

The prospect seemed to amuse him. 'Well then, orchids it shall be. Personally, I hate these big midday meals. I'll call my housekeeper, ask her to make up a couple of sandwiches and pick you up at your desk around twelve.'

25

Yes, it was one of the houses Caro had singled out, a fine, weathered red-brick Federal with fan windows and wrought-iron grills. The woman who opened the door – short, stout and fiftyish – allayed any fears that 'housekeeper' was a euphemism for resident mistress.

'Would you like me to stay and serve, Mr Catlett? It's only sandwiches and fruit salad.'

'That won't be necessary, Mrs Lacey. I can find my way around the kitchen.'

He ushered Caro into a long, light living room – parquet floors, oriental rugs, Chinese chippendale polished to the colour of dark honey. The room was full of pretty things. On a corner étagère, Caro recognized the peachbloom vase he had been so proud of, along with other porcelains, delftware, Japanese netsuke. Each item chosen with a connoisseur's eye.

'Can I get you a drink . . . a glass of sherry perhaps?' As he poured the drinks, the outside door closed. The housekeeper leaving for the day. Caro stifled a sigh of relief.

'Do you live here all alone, Dan?'

'Uhuh. Ridiculous, isn't it? The place is much too big for one person, even for two. Madeleine always used to say. . .' She shut out the rest of the sentence. She hadn't come to hear him dredge up the past. 'Everyone keeps telling me I should get an apartment up town, one of those new condominiums,' he went on, 'but I don't know. I hate the idea of living sandwiched between strangers. Anyhow . . . cheers.'

'Cheers.' She drank off her sherry.

'If that will hold you for a while' – he took her glass – 'then I suggest we see the flowers first, have lunch after. You don't mind if I take off my jacket, Caroline? It's pretty hot up there.'

No, she didn't mind. She removed her own, then followed his shirtsleeved figure up a flight of carpeted stairs past closed doors (which one was his bedroom?), up another flight to the top of the house.

'Welcome to my sanctum.'

He opened first a wooden door, then another of heavy glass leading onto a captive jungle. Sun came dappling through the skylight, spilling beads of brightness over flowers of every size and colour. Orchids everywhere, undisciplined. Some were beautiful, some savage, some delicate, several grew gross and obscene. They were ranged in tiers, in planters, hung languorously from baskets, exuding moisture to the touch. The heat was womb-like. A trailing tendril brushed Caro's cheek with faint suggestive fingers, while from a corner a bank of carnations lent their suffocating sweetness to the air. There was a gleam, a sudden flash of colour so swift she could scarcely make out the contours. Then a tiny hummingbird, all jewelled wings and enamelled eyes, plunged headlong into the depths of a purple blossom.

Taut and silent, she stood motionless, drenched in the sheer sensuousness of the room, turned to him trembling, hunger in her eyes.

He loosened his tie, then advanced slowly to where she stood. 'Caroline' – he placed a hand on the bare moist flesh of her arm while she waited hushed and expectant for his embrace. He came no closer, merely searched her face with questioning eyes. 'Do you want to tell me what's wrong?'

'Wrong!' she cried. The humming bird, alarmed, took flight in a whir of wings. And now drunk with anguish, half-stupefied by the scent of flowers, she flung herself at his feet, arms twining round his legs and pressed her lips against his shoes.

'Please . . . love me. I want you to make love to me . . . here . . . now.' Her words came out in stertorous gasps. 'I want you to take me, possess me . . . tell me sweet lies. Please . . . I beg of you. . . .'

For a stunned second he remained paralyzed, then leaning over, gripped her by the elbows and prised her off him with sudden force. 'For God's sake,' – he yanked her to her feet –

'Don't *ever* do that again, Caroline. Don't *ever* throw yourself away like that . . . on me, on anyone!'

Stricken, she raised her eyes to his, and in his face there was no trace of love or desire, only shock. Shock and *pity*.

Oh my God, I disgust him!

She turned away, straining for flight, but he tightened his hold, and when next he spoke, his voice was low and composed.

'Did your husband leave you, Caroline? Is that it? Is it Tom?'

She tried to shape an answer but could only manage a hoarse, inchoate croak, and when the words did come, they were the words she had dreaded, feared most, had tried to bury these many weeks behind the scrim of fantasy.

'He broke my heart.'

There it was – articulated at last. No calling them back, those words so long held at bay like a ravening animal, the grief so cunningly dodged and denied.

'He broke my heart!'

And with a scream, she tore free of Catlett's grip, stumbling past him through the double doors, toward the precipice of stairs, blindly, drunkenly, until her legs gave way. Halfway down the steps, she collapsed like a puppet with broken strings.

'He broke my heart,' she wept – and all the tears she had so steadfastly refused to shed in front of Tom, in front of everyone, now raged uncontrollably, here in a strange house before an outsider who had no real part in this drama except the role to which her diseased fantasy had assigned him.

For Tom had broken her heart. That was the truth of the matter. He had left her because she was worthless, selfish, contemptible. A wretched failure. Everyone recognized that – Tom, Gusty, Catlett – everyone. They could hardly despise her more than she despised herself. A vile, foolish, unlovable woman with nothing to offer anybody, least of all this man now sitting patiently beside her on the staircase handing her tissues out of a bottomless box.

How insane, degrading to think that Catlett, of all people, would be content with another man's discards. Stupid Caro, lacking even the sense to spare herself this final humiliation – for Tom was surely right.

Yes, Tom had taken her measure, sized her up, seen her for

what she was – and run like hell. It was no less than she deserved.

And so she sat weeping, until the tearducts rebelled, until her eyes were swollen half shut. And only after an eternity of pain, did she stop and mumble to the man sitting beside her on the steps 'I've made a fool enough of myself for one day.'

She got up to go, but he took her hand and guided her into a large marbled bathroom.

'Now, Caroline, you wash up and comb your hair and then we'll have something to eat.' He began running water in the basin while she stared at herself in the mirror. The face was an apparition: blotchy, swollen, red-eyed, streaked with mascara. She set about washing the face away, while he stood in the doorway contemplating her with a wary and tentative expression.

Why didn't he go? Just close the door and leave her alone. Couldn't she even go to the bathroom in privacy? In the mirror their eyes met.

'I'm not going to slash my wrists, if that's what you're thinking.'

He paused. 'No – of course you're not. I'll go make some coffee.'

They sat at a small table in a kitchen so sunny it stung her eyes.

'Eat a little.' He put a roast beef sandwich on her plate. 'You'll feel better.'

She ate a little and felt better.

'I'm not usually such a crybaby,' she said, then to her embarrassment began weeping again, not the hysterical spasms of a half hour earlier, but the tears of ultimate sadness. 'I'm sorry . . . it's . . . I feel as if someone has died.'

'Mmmmm.' He hummed an assent. 'Don't apologize, Caroline. There's absolutely no call for it. Yes, it is like death . . . a death in the family, but it might help if you talked about it, tell me what happened.'

And so, wet-cheeked and snuffling, she bumbled through an incoherent narrative . . . Tom's letter, his UCLA job, his admitted infidelity. 'But of course you knew about that long before I did.'

Catlett listened attentively, with occasional sympathetic murmurs, but when she had done he asked 'How did your husband leave you?'

She gaped at him. Had he understood nothing of what she had said? 'How? He put on his coat and walked out – that's how!'

'No, no.' It was Catlett's turn to be embarrassed. 'I meant financially. Did he leave you well provided for? Do you need a loan to tide you over?'

But after that humiliating scene in the greenhouse, she could not bring herself to ask him for anything. By now her sole desire was to leave this place with some atom of pride, some vestige of dignity intact.

'That's very decent of you Dan, but I'm all right in that department. I've been lucky in the market lately . . . pretty comfortable, so what I think I'll do is just take off a couple of years and be a mother to my daughter. Sasha . . .' at the mention of the name, she began weeping again. 'That's what it was all about anyhow, Sasha. She's all I have to live for.'

'Your husband is a damn fool, Caroline.' Catlett handed her a linen napkin and she blew her nose. 'But it's not the end of the world, believe me. I know you'll think I'm fatuous for saying this but . . . you're still a young woman, you have most of your life ahead of you. Sooner or later I'm sure you'll meet someone who's more appreciative of your qualities, someone more deserving. And as you say, you have a daughter. I know things look pretty bleak at the moment, but give yourself time. You're a very nice lady, Caroline.'

'And you're a gentleman,' she blinked through her tears. They sat a while long in imperfect silence. In the hall a grandfather clock struck the hour.

'I have to leave in a few minutes,' he murmured. He was awfully sorry, but he had a meeting with some fellows at Morgan Guaranty and they were a pretty prompt bunch down there. Already she could see him retreating into his own world – the real, disciplined all-male world of money and business and power. 'I think the best thing for you to do would be go home and get some sleep. I'll have my girl clear out your desk and send your things over by messenger.'

On the street he hailed a cab. 'This young lady is going uptown,' he told the driver, then extended his hand for a farewell shake. But instead she placed her palm on his chest. 'Your tie is crooked, Dan.' She straightened it, patted it down, then forced a smile. 'I couldn't have you going over to Mr Morgan's bank looking like that.'

'Thank you.' He held the cab door open. 'Goodbye, Caroline.'

'Goodbye.'

Through the rear window, she looked back, saw him getting into another taxi heading downtown and ride out of her life.

26

Profit and loss, profit and loss. At the end of each business month, it was the prudent practice of most going concerns to draw up a balance sheet, a statement of profit and loss. It showed where you'd come from and precisely where you stood at this moment.

That afternoon, Caro drew up her own appraisal.

Losses. She had lost her husband. Her mother. Her closest friends. Her self respect. Her capacity to escape into day-dreams. Even the ficus tree had died on her, each brown withered leaf bearing mute testimony to her failure. So much for losses.

Profits? None she could think of offhand. But then it was entirely conceivable that Caro Harmsworth was no longer a going concern.

Shortly before six, a messenger arrived with a large card-board box. God it was heavy; for a moment she couldn't fathom why. Listlessly she began emptying its contents. Phone book, desk diary, digital clock, rain hat, umbrella, Tampax, sun glasses, Pepto-Bismol, a half empty box of Godiva chocolates. At the bottom her groping fingers closed about a large dead-weight object, packed in corrugated paper.

With both hands she drew it out, then unpeeled the wrappings. The crystal ball.

How many times had she gazed into its depths, anxious, hopeful, seeking revelations and finding within it bright promises of riches and glory, success and happiness? She placed it carefully on the coffee table and gazed at it once more. But today the crystal ball was bleak and empty. Like her life. Like her future. For once the damned thing hadn't deceived.

She left it lying there, for there was nothing further to be read, now or ever. Anyhow it was Sasha's dinnertime, a tugging at her skirt reminded her.

'It's you and I against the world, baby,' she made a mock stab at humour while Sasha shovelled down carrots and spinach and hamburger. 'Christ almighty! Does everything have to go on the floor!' She cleaned the mess up and wept.

Once the baby was in bed, she went back to pass another night slumped in front of the TV set. My God, what did people do with themselves before the idiot box was invented? Stayed married probably, for lack of other diversions.

The Seven O'Clock News. 'I'm Brooke Shields for Calvin Klein.' 'Take the Pepsi challenge.' *Family Feud.* 'Clorox adds freshness to your wash.' 'Dristan got me through the night.' *NBC Magazine.* 'You're going to like us – TWA!'

'And now, stay tuned for *Woman to Woman*, that super talk show starring our own super gal. . .'

And there she was! Wearing a couple of thousand bucks worth of Galanos spangles, smiling her little chipmunk smile straight at Caro.

'Good evening, America, this is Sally Klein. Tonight I have a very special guest – an extraordinary woman whose curiosity and courage and camera have taken her to the remotest corners of the world – from India to Iceland, from Bali to Brazil. In fact, she's been called the little Amazon of documentary film-making. And now it's my pleasure to introduce. . .'

But Caro needed no introductions. In fact she never heard the end of the sentence, for she had seized the crystal ball and, with all the force and might of her being, in one final burst of fury hurled it through the smiling faces on the television screen. It exploded with the impact of a bomb. Broken glass, smashed tubes, splintered wood flew everywhere as Caro rose to her feet screaming. Screaming at Sally, at Gusty, at Tom, at the whole world beyond this room.

'You broke my heart, you motherfucker! You broke my heart!'

Like the crystal ball, her life lay in ruins.

328

27

Long after, she would look back upon those nightmare weeks with the certain knowledge that Sasha had saved her from herself. But at the time – frightened, lonely, whipped – she longed only to take to her bed like a figure in a Gothic tragedy, pull the sheets up over her head and never arise again. Escape! There were so many forms of it. Madness, drunkenness, drugs, suicide – such tempting alternatives to life.

Yet Sasha would permit none of it. With all the selfishness, the unblinking tyranny of a year-old child, she was perpetually blocking Caro's way, insisting her mother stop this nonsense immediately, dry her eyes, get up, get on with the mechanics of living.

Sasha – wondering what everything in the world tasted like from housekeys to the contents of those funny bottles and cans under the kitchen sink. Sasha – trying to squeeze through the terrace railing for a closer look at the traffic thirty floors below. Sasha – exploring the fascinating possibilities of electric outlets, gas jets, kitchen knives, pop-up toasters, ever curious to discover how hot is fire, how cold is ice, and how come walking is such a hard and treacherous business. Sasha – crying or babbling or laughing or dirty or hungry or bored, but always demanding. 'Look at me. Help me. Watch me. Feed me. Play with me. I need, I need, I need. . .'

Sasha never let her up, not for a single waking moment, yet those needs were the glue that kept Caro from falling apart.

'You dear, sweet, crazy, funny girl,' Caro said when Sasha trailed into the living room, hair damp and smelling like a whorehouse. 'That was about a hundred bucks worth of perfume you just dumped. What am I going to do about you?' To which Sasha answered sagely, 'Ba ba gla.'

Yet when the baby slept, the hours were long and lonely, with the memory of Tom lingering in her mouth like the taste of bile.

Every so often, someone would call, that handful of casual friends who had yet to hear that her marriage was over. But though Caro hungered for the conversation of intelligent adults, things never worked out quite right.

'Can you and Tom come to dinner with us next Saturday?' an acquaintance called to ask.

'Well, Tom doesn't live here any more, Liz, but I'd be delighted to accept.'

'Oh!' There was a heavy pause at the other end. 'Well maybe you and I could have lunch together instead. One of these days. I'll call you.'

'Don't bother.'

Ultimately, the only phone calls were wrong numbers and – one midnight – a heavy breather. Caro listened to about thirty seconds of obscene whisperings, then hung up. Yet later she laughed to herself, 'Best proposition I've had in ages.'

Once you reached a certain age, the world was made for couples. That much was plain.

One Saturday night out of sheer loneliness, she hired a sitter and headed for a local singles bar. She'd never made that particular singles scene before, not even when she'd been truly single, dismissing it out of hand as 'the meat rack'. But what the hell . . . no harm in dressing up for a change, having a few scotches, maybe meeting some tolerable guy. She had no one to be faithful to anymore, and Jesus . . . she was human, too.

The place was mobbed. Talk about investments! – what a business for some smart fund to get into. Had to be a goldmine, customers practically swinging from the rafters, drinks at four bucks a throw.

She squeezed through an asparagus patch of bodies to a freshly vacated barstool. Somebody'd scored. On the next stool sat a self-proclaimed Adonis, resplendent in sun-lamp tan and custom-made biceps. They inventoried each other swiftly. Another Helmut was her bet. Thanks a lot, but no thanks.

Furtively, she scanned the crowd. Lots of girls, cute and *young*, talking loud and mock-happy to everyone and no one in particular. Lots of men, too, though the good-looking guys were beating 'em off, and the few who weren't, looked so hungry.

That guy in the corner, for instance, with the bright pink shirt. A thatch like Robert Redford, thick and blond, but the eyes beneath were pouchy and tired, restless. She swivelled her head so he wouldn't think she was studying him, sized up a group of men at another table. Dressed to the nines, they were. Gays. Why didn't they go down to Greenwich Village where they'd be more comfortable! Now there was someone really attractive – L. L. Bean shirt, broad shoulders, mid-thirties was her guess.

He smiled and Caro smiled back, then he stood up, hands extended, to greet a long-haired girl in a skimpy tee shirt. Christ – she was a kid! He must be nearly twice her age. Well, fuck it. The last thing she needed was some guy with a Brooke Shields syndrome.

She looked down the bar to catch the bartender's eye when a hand clamped down on her shoulder. 'Hiya, doll. You all alone?'

Why, if it wasn't Mr Pink Shirt! Close up, she could see the hair owed more to Clairol than genetics, still – she was no chicken either.

'I'm alone.'

He wedged himself in between her and the Adonis, managing to rub his genitals against her hip en route.

'You looked kinda blue sitting there. Whatsa matter . . . have a fight with your boyfriend? Young guys these days . . . no finesse.'

He leaned forward to signal the bartender, and she had a glimpse of a pale band of skin around one finger. He must have stashed his wedding ring in a pocket, just for the occasion. Adorable!

'Yeah . . . what can I do you?' the bartender asked.

Caro placed a ten-dollar bill on the counter. 'Give my friend here a drink' – she slid off the stool – 'and nothing for me. You don't have what I want in this place.'

Ten minutes later she was back in the apartment.

'You're home early, Mrs Darius,' the baby sitter commented. 'How was the movie?'

'Lousy. I walked out halfway through.'

Her bring-'em-back-alive days were over, that was the long

and short of it, and anyhow she had more pressing problems than the rounding up of suitable bedmates.

A few days after Sasha's first birthday, her monthly bank statement arrived. Talk of anti-aphrodisiacs!

'Hey, lovey,' she remarked to her sole companion. 'Did you know we have just enough money to last another twenty-two days at this rate? As your beloved father used to say, how's them apples?'

'Ba gla. . .'

'Ba gla indeed, You're a lot of help, Sash. Well,' she sighed, 'it looks like I'm finally going to have to get up off my ass and do something. You don't happen to have the number of *The New York Times* handy, do you? No, I didn't think you would.'

Hhshld Sits Wtd-Female

HOUSEKEEPER/BABY SITTER Live in with year-old child. College educated. Good driver. Sober. Responsible. Seeks post in family with young children.

28

'Welcome to Mount Kisco.'

The man who handed her and Sasha down from the train gave an audible sigh of relief. He looked as his wife had described him – 'nice' – an easy-going, baldish man, sociable eyes behind horn-rimmed glasses, the start of a Saturday beard. 'We were half afraid you wouldn't show up. That's what happened with the last one. Car's parked right over here.'

'Very good of you to meet us, Mr Gerber.'

'Please call me Dave.' He began loading suitcases into the rear of a cluttered station wagon. 'We're very informal out here as you can see by the condition of the car. Barbara's home waiting with the kids. They're very excited about meeting you. By the way, what would you like them to call you?'

'They can call me Caro . . . everybody does. And this is Sasha.'

'Hello Sasha.' He gave the baby an experienced and fatherly tweak. 'Anyhow, Caro . . . I want you to know how delighted we are that you accepted our offer. I imagine you had a lot of opportunities to choose from.'

'A lot,' Caro agreed. 'I felt like the belle of the ball.'

She had anticipated her ad drawing a lively response, but nothing had prepared her for a veritable torrent. For a delirious week, she permitted herself to be flattered, cajoled, lunched, implored and in one case, even wept over. 'I'll give you more money' was a constant of the litany.

Colour TV, separate phones, private bath: those were perks scarcely worthy of mention, for among the prospects dangled were maid service, summer in the Hamptons, swimming pools, opportunities for foreign travel. She was besieged with offers. And why not? She was that rarest, most valuable of commodities: the responsible mother-substitute. The very woman for whom she herself had searched so frequently and with so little success.

Yes, she had her pick of situations, and oftener than not it was she who conducted the interviews, stated the terms. Among her prospective employers were several high-powered career women in whom Caro recognized those tensions and anxieties that had scarred her own working life. She gave them wide berth. There was an abundance of single parents (not all of them female, either), but Caro was wary of getting into a narrow situation. She ruled out anyone who pried or seemed overly friendly, families with problem children, people who gave off vibes of strained or failing marriages. In her mind it was vital that Sasha be provided with some semblance of a normal happy home, a proper family with a proper father. Let the child learn that there were responsible men in the world.

Although the offer she accepted didn't bring top dollar, it had other merits. Barbara Gerber for one. Her employer was a bright and unpretentious woman in her mid-thirties, a pediatrician with a practice in Westchester County. Her husband of whom she spoke with companiable affection was a lawyer. They'd been married twelve years, had three children – two girls in grade school and a boy slightly older than Sasha, lived in a big rambling old house – nothing fancy, but Caro and Sasha could have two rooms and a bath of their own. A handy man came in occasionally to do the heavy work and Caro would have the use of a car. 'It's just a beat-up Volkswagen, but it gets you there,' Barbara explained. Most nights off, and the weekends to dispose of as Caro saw fit.

'I don't pretend to be a cook,' Caro warned.

'Do your best,' the other woman shrugged. 'We can divvy that up. What worries me is if you're used to Manhattan, you may find the suburbs pretty small potatoes. It's beautiful country up there, but still it's a good fifty miles out of New York.'

Yet it was precisely this distance from the city that appealed to Caro. To be where no one knew her, to cut herself off from the past, from the risk of chance encounters and unwanted memories. . . 'I can come out next weekend,' she announced, and the women shook hands on it.

The following day, Caro began dismantling the apartment. A few prized possessions went into storage, the rest were sold to a used furniture dealer. She paid off the utilities, gave her old clothes to a thrift shop and closed out her bank account. After much soul-searching she decided to take along some mementos of her marriage, including half a dozen pictures of Tom. For herself, she didn't care if she never set eyes on the man again, but the day would come when Sasha would ask what her father looked like. And Sasha had a right to know.

Otherwise, the move was to be a total amputation. She informed the lawyer handling her divorce and no one else, and departed, leaving no forwarding address behind.

Who would care to get in touch with her anyhow?

Moreover, who was there whom she wanted to see?

29

'Does it bother you living with strangers?' Barbara Gerber once asked.

'I grew up living with strangers,' Caro replied.

Yet it had bothered her, especially at the outset, this peculiar situation where she was neither friend nor family, nor yet conventional employee.

The first few nights, after the children were put to bed, she ate off a tray in her sitting room, but toward the end of the week, Barbara rapped on her door.

'We were wondering if you'd join us for dinner – that is, if you have no other plans. Actually' – Barbara gave a diffident laugh – '"joining us for dinner" sounds terribly grand. It's just meatloaf in the kitchen, nothing fancy, but you're certainly welcome.'

So Caro joined them, somewhat ill at ease, and throughout the meal the conversation, though polite, remained stilted. In fact it barely progressed beyond the wasn't-it-warm-today? and please-pass-the-breadsticks stage. With each bite, Caro grew more unsure as to her role. Was she a dinner guest expected to make pleasant conversation? Was she a servant with corresponding obligations? Should she excuse herself the moment dinner was over and return discreetly to her room?

At the end of the meal an uncomfortable silence fell, then she and Barbara rose in unison and reached to clear away the serving platter – Caro grasping one end of the dish, her embarrassed employer grasping the other. For a moment both women stood motionless, feeling awkward, then simultaneously burst into laughter.

'Isn't this ridiculous!' Barbara exclaimed 'Us standing on silly formalities. In this household everyone does everything – including him' – she nodded to her husband. 'So come on,

Dave, make us some coffee and we can all sit around and relax.'

The little incident cleared the air, and after that, the three of them shared informal suppers, easy and companiable meals with the conversation ranging from the general – news of the day, local issues – the specific. Much of the talk centred about the children, naturally, and household problems; much of it about the Gerber's particular interests. Barbara was active in half a dozen neighbourhood organizations, Dave was heavily involved in civil rights. They were decent, compassionate people, both of them, and Caro looked forward at the end of each day to some time and talk shared with other adults. Only one topic remained off limits: Caro's own history. No doubt the Gerbers were curious about the newest member of their household, but aware of Caro's reticence, they never made direct inquiries. And when, on one occasion, Barbara remarked 'Harmsworth . . . that's an unusual name. Are you related to that woman who does those marvellous TV documentaries?", Caro replied simply 'Nope.'

The closing days of summer were spent mostly out of doors, trotting the children around to the local pools and playgrounds, but once school started, she found herself with odd snippets of time on her hands.

'You know, Barb, the paint is peeling in the upstairs john.'

'Yeah . . . awful. I suppose I should call in a decorator.'

'I'll paint it,' Caro said. 'I don't mind.'

So she painted the bathroom, then reorganized the cupboards, cleared out the garage, taught herself to make some decent casseroles. One rainy afternoon, she tried her hand at a chocolate souffle, and damned if it didn't turn out just fine.

Once a week, Caro would drive the Gerber's older daughter to her piano lesson. The music school – actually a small frame cottage on a side road – reverberated with a montage of sound. From the open windows on the upper floor came the harmonies of a wind ensemble while scales were duly being hammered out on a ground-floor piano. The first time she dropped Debbie off, Caro sat in the car for a while listening to the cheerful cacophony. The next week she went in and introduced herself.

'I understand,' she said to Debbie's teacher, a slight energetic woman still in her twenties, 'that you and your husband know all about the musical life in these parts.'

'Sometimes,' Sarah Russo laughed, 'I think we are the musical life in these parts. Piano, violin, chamber music . . . you name it, we teach it. Why, are you interested in lessons?'

'What I'm interested in . . .' Caro began –

In high school and throughout college she had sung in glee clubs and student chorales – of course that was ages ago! – yet she recalled it as a deeply satisfying experience. 'I always meant to keep it up, but somehow never found the time.' Now, however, she had relative leisure and was wondering if there were anything in the neighbourhood she might join.

'I'm not a great voice,' she said, 'but I do sing in tune and I was considered a good sight-reader.'

'What are you?' Sarah asked. 'An alto?'

Caro nodded.

'Oh, wow!' Sarah said. 'Have you come to the right place!' She conducted a group called the Northern Westchester Choral Arts Club that met every Tuesday evening. 'All the members are amateurs, but pretty good – and we're very ambitious. And as it happens we're desperately short on good altos. So why don't you come around to the next rehearsal and give it a whirl?'

'Thank you,' said Caro. 'I'll do that.'

The Choral Arts Club met in the high school, and Caro – who had trouble locating the auditorium – arrived just as the members were settling into their places on the lighted stage.

She doffed her coat, slipped through the darkened rows of seats and made her way noiselessly into the alto section. Someone handed her music. It was a Bach motet she had sung years ago in college – serene and ethereal.

Jesu meine freude . . .

She joined her voice to the others dissolving it seamlessly into the close mesh of sound. Rapt now, and forgetful of the world beyond the music, there existed only the ravishing texture of the harmonies, the white tip of Sarah Russo's baton. The work ended simply, softly; and in the hush that followed, Caro felt all breath suspended.

Then somebody sighed, the end of a sublime moment shared.

'Well,' said the conductor finally, 'We have a new alto with us tonight. Welcome aboard Caro – glad to have you. Now let's get down to some honing and polishing.'

The two hours of rehearsal passed in a moment, and at the end of it, Caro, elated, walked over to Sarah Russo. 'I don't know when I've enjoyed myself so much – not since college, I don't think. I'd almost forgotten what a marvellous feeling it is. So, thanks for letting me join.' She went to fetch her coat and leave when Sarah called after her 'Hey! Don't go!'

It had become the custom, after each rehearsal, for all the members to go out together and have hamburgers and coffee at a local roadhouse. 'That's half the fun of getting together,' Caro was informed, 'so don't go running off.'

Her fellow-singers, Caro soon discovered, were a cross section of local life. There were housewives in the group, students, a local builder, the man who ran the cheese shop, a few business people who commuted to New York – in short, a thorough rag bag of residents with nothing more in common than a zestful pleasure in making music. Yet oddly enough, that sufficed. And by the time the evening was over she had made acquaintances, exchanged phone numbers, felt herself for the first time in years to be part of a larger community.

She drove home happy, whistling snatches of Bach and looking forward to next week's rehearsal with gusto.

And so summer turned into autumn. The leaves began falling and Sasha and Mordecai (what a name! but he was a sweetheart of a kid) rolled ecstatically in the pile of heaped-up leaves while Caro raked the path. She made the children acorn necklaces.

'No, not in your mouth, Sasha.'

Gradually her life assumed different patterns. Often the days were dull, the work tiring and repetitive. There was no particular pleasure to be gleamed from sorting laundry or mopping spilled orange juice off the floor for the umpteenth time. Yet equally often she found herself called upon to exercise all her imagination and ingenuity and tact – arbitrating squabbles, dreaming up rainy-day pastimes, making snap decisions on how best to cope with every emergency from scraped knees and broken dolls to bathroom floods and flat tyres. In its way the job was as varied and demanding as the one at PAGIT, only the rewards were different.

There was the profound satisfaction of watching Sasha settle down, grow up. The little baby-fat bracelets were disappearing, small fingers grew more deft, more assured.

Among Sasha's toys was a set of graduated plastic cylinders that could be stacked to form a Christmas tree. For weeks Sasha fiddled with the toy, stacking the brightly coloured circles every which way, never quite getting the hang of it. Then one day she put it all together and announced her triumph in a delighted squeal. And Caro's pride was a match for the little girl's own. 'Why!' she suddenly realized with mixed joy and nostalgia, 'she's not an infant any more.'

The once stumbling steps and pratfalls were fast becoming a cock-of-the-walk swagger, and from the constant babble of infancy the outline of real language was emerging.

'Dada,' she greeted Dave one day, in imitation of Mordecai, and Caro bit her lip. 'No, darling,' she whispered, 'that's not your daddy.'

Both the Gerber girls were mad about fairy tales, and sometimes in the evening Sasha would sit with them while Caro read of princes and dragons. Funny little Sasha – not comprehending a word, yet clearly relishing the sense of belonging.

As for Caro she was neither happy nor sad. Time passes. Wounds heal. Scars remain.

Over dinner one evening, Dave mentioned that he had been solicited by a salesman for a mutual fund. It sounded attractive, he said.

'I wouldn't invest in Woolett if I were you,' Caro said. 'They're a very poorly managed company. If you're looking for performance, you'd be better off with Oppenheimer Target or Sherman Dean.'

The Gerbers stared at her with astonishment. 'Really Caro – I didn't know you followed the market.'

'I worked in Wall Street for years.'

'Were you a secretary?'

Unaccountably, the question rankled. 'No, not a secretary. I happen to have an MBA from Harvard.'

'Really!' Barbara echoed. She didn't ask the next question though it hung implicit in the silence. 'Then what on earth are you doing here!' Nor did Caro add to her statement, though it had given her a brief twinge of pleasure to flex a professional muscle for a change.

Undoubtedly, the Gerbers concluded that she had taken this job to hide out from some personal disgrace. Probably assumed she was an unmarried mother, for they always scrupulously abstained from asking any questions about Sasha's parentage. OK with Caro if they thought she was single. No big deal.

A couple of days later, a letter from the law firm of Wilcox and Havens informed her she was now truly single. The divorce had gone through without a hitch, and Tom, if she could find him, was responsible for contributing a modest monthly sum toward Sasha's support.

Fuck it. Let him keep his money. It was hardly worth her letting him know where she could be reached. For that was over. Over. Son of a bitch, she thought routinely, she would never forgive him.

Yet that night in the cool of her room she was surprised to find that some of her bitterness had vanished, unnoticed, while she had been looking the other way.

It wasn't his fault; he couldn't help himself. And now she realized that the man who had deserted her was essentially the same man she had married: charming, immature, good-natured, afraid of giving or receiving pain. A man who, despite certain virtues, had been woefully ill-equipped to cope with the pressures of parenthood. A lightweight.

Who knows – he might make some other woman a perfectly adequate husband, although she was inclined to doubt it, for he suffered a fatal flaw. He was the victim of his charm.

Charm kills, she had read somewhere – and it was true. Tom's charm had killed. It had cut him off from the real business of life, had been the screen he erected against encroaching reality. He would never make a father because he could never truly love. Love costs. Love calls for hard decisions. So perhaps in the long run, his leaving had been all for the best.

341

No – no more lightweights for Caro. That mistake she wouldn't make twice.

She could survive without him. He was no great loss. Except these cold October nights she missed his warmth.

She climbed out of bed and put on a pair of socks. There . . . that was better. Maybe she'd even drop her mother a line one of these days. Well, why not . . . Gusty was what she was, too!

The next day, as she and Barbara sat in the kitchen shelling peas, Caro mentioned in an offhand manner that she was now divorced. 'You didn't even know I was married, did you?'

Barbara smiled and shrugged. 'Well, you obviously didn't feel like talking about it so I didn't want to pry. What difference does it make really? In either event as of now you're a free woman.'

'I always was a free woman,' Caro mused. 'In fact that was the heart of the problem.' Then, because she and Barbara knew each other well enough, because Tom was so nearly exorcised from her life she began to confide the story of her marriage, her career, her conflicts, Tom's unexpected desertion. 'I came here, frankly, because I had no place to go. Not that I regret it, but you should know my reasons.'

'Do you ever think about remarrying?' Barbara wondered.

'Oh, I don't know. . .' Caro dragged out a sigh. 'I can't say my experience with men has been so terrific that I want to set myself up for a repeat performance.'

'Oh, marriage is OK,' Barbara drawled. 'You know the story about the cat that jumped up on a hot stove and got so burnt it wouldn't even jump up on a cold stove after that. History doesn't always repeat itself.'

'Mine seems to.'

'And what about going back to Wall Street? Do you ever think of that?'

'That' – Caro said firmly 'is even less likely. I suppose when Sasha's old enough to go to school, I'll get my own place and some sort of job, but at this point I can't see that far ahead.'

'Still,' Barbara said, 'it seems a shame to have all your skills go to waste. Maybe you'd enjoy doing some volunteer work. You know I'm a consultant at the Westchester Boys' Home. . .'

'Whoa . . . I'm no social worker.'

Social workers they've got, Barbara assured her. But the Home could use Caro's expertise. The place was a shambles financially, no one knew from beans about good business management, but if Caro would give them a couple of hours a week. . . 'The people are nice, too,' she added.

So Caro began getting involved, first with the Boys' Home, then with the United Fund Drive. She made a few more friends locally, and the Gerbers would usually include her in their dinner parties. All the men she met were married, but that was OK. She wasn't in the mood for further commitment.

'Nothing heavy,' as Howie Bernstein used to say.

The weather got colder. First frost. She went behind the house one windy day and collected over a bushel of windfall apples.

'What'll we do with them all?' Barbara wondered. 'They'll go rotten.'

'I've got a receipe for apple butter somewhere,' Caro remembered, and the two women spent all of Saturday in a kitchen fragrant with apples and cloves.

The last of the leaves fell. The first of the snows came. Veteran's Day. Caro's thirty-first birthday, an event she let pass unnoticed. Bitter cold. The ponds were freezing up. Thanksgiving next Thursday.

The day before the holiday, Barbara stayed home and began preparing for a family party – brothers, sisters, in-laws. 'You'll join us of course, won't you, Caro? Unless you've made other plans.'

What other plans? 'Thank you, that's very kind. Do you want to do the desserts, Barb, and I'll do the vegetables?' Caro began rinsing cranberries, cleaning brussel sprouts, chopping celery for stuffing while Sasha darted in and out among the pots and pans.

'What's that you're whistling, Caro? It's a catchy tune.'

'Oh, was I whistling? I didn't realize.'

30

'I'll get it.'

Dave Gerber struggled out of the easy chair, letting fly a cloud of pie crumbs, and went to answer the phone.

'There's someone asking for Caroline,' he called across the room. 'I didn't know anyone called you that' – then clapping his hand across the receiver, added 'He sounds southern as pecan pie.'

Her heart turned over.

'I'll take it in my room if you don't mind.'

'Hello, Caroline,' came the once-familiar accent. 'Happy Thanksgiving. Oh, this is Dan Catlett,' he added as an afterthought.

'Yes,' she said hoarsely. 'I know. You're the only person who calls me Caroline.'

His voice stung like salt on an open wound. It came from another world, another life best forgotten. Why now? Just as she was burying the past. She sat down weakly on the edge of the bed, while he chatted airily about Thanksgiving and turkey and the weather and God knows what else. All she could think of was – What does he want? How did he know where to find me? Somewhere in her confusion she picked out the words 'good news'.

'Good news?' she echoed numbly.

'Yes, first-rate. If you don't mind, I'd like to break it to you in person.'

He was going upstate for the weekend, ice-fishing, passing practically through Mount Kisco; so if was convenient for her, he'd stop off en route. Was nine o'clock too early? He could only stay a half hour or so.

'Yes, that would be very nice, Dan.' She gave him directions to the house. 'I'll see you tomorrow morning.'

After he hung up she sat for another ten minutes, nervous and upset. The memory of the last time she'd seen him, that humiliating afternoon in Gramercy Park, now returned in full force. Even after six months, it hurt like hell, and she had made a point of never looking back upon that day, editing her recollections as ruthlessly as a Moscow censor suppressing news of a Polish uprising.

Finally, she freshened her lipstick and went back into the living room. Not that she owed the Gerbers an explanation, but God forbid they should think her caller had been Sasha's father.

'That was my ex-boss. He's going to be in the neighbourhood tomorrow and said he might drop in. That is, if it's all right with you.'

She had never invited anyone over before. After all, this was not her house; but Dave answered, feel free. They were going to be away anyhow.

And Caro, so perturbed at the prospect of seeing him again, let the mention of 'good news' slip her mind entirely.

From eight o'clock on, she kept an eye on the window, on the lookout for a black Cadillac or maybe a Rolls. More likely a Rolls. He had a passion for things English and expensive. Dunhill suits. Church shoes.

Just before nine, a perky green Volvo station wagon poked its nose in the drive, hesitant, and for a moment Caro thought it was a passing car looking for a place to make a U-turn. But no, the car proceeded down the driveway, pulling up next to her Volkswagen.

She went out to greet him, if indeed it was he, for the man who stepped out seemed a total stranger. Knitted wool cap, worn sheepskin coat, thick foul-weather boots.

'Hello Caroline!' He waved a cheery hand, then reaching back into the car, pulled out something bulky.

She came toward him smiling. 'You know, for a minute I didn't recognize you, Dan.'

'Yes,' – he looked to where she stood shivering in jeans and a tattersall shirt. 'I guess we've never seen each other in civilian clothes before. You better get inside. It's freezing out here.'

He followed her jauntily into the house, toting a big box from F.A.O. Schwartz. 'Something for your little girl.'

'How very thoughtful!' Caro flushed. 'She's playing in the kitchen. You want to come in and have a cup of coffee? Sasha, puss, here's someone who's brought you a present. Take your coat off, Dan.'

Sasha zeroed in on the box like a dive bomber, more fascinated by the ribbons and wrappings than what might lie inside. But when Catlett opened the package, she was wide-eyed. 'Here.' He pulled a black-and-white panda, soft, cuddly, nearly as big as Sasha. 'And look, sugar, here's how it works.' He was squatting down beside her on the floor. 'You pull this little metal thingummy here . . . that's right . . . pull it out.' He guided her hand and a little recorded voice sang out 'My name is Andy Pandy and I belong to Sasha.'

Sasha let out a squeal of pure rapture.

'Why, Dan!' Caro had watched the proceedings astonished. What a delightful toy. And he must have gone to some trouble to have the recording custom-made. Imagine – a busy man like that. Even remembering the baby's nickname. Then she turned away, afraid he might catch her moist-eyed. 'That was a lovely thing to do. You really shouldn't have. . .'

'Why not? I got one for my nephew a couple of months ago and he's crazy about it. Anyhow . . . you promised me some coffee.'

'Of course.'

She set about making a fresh pot, when the thought occurred that he must have left his house very early this morning. Such a bitter cold morning too. 'Have you had breakfast, Dan?'

'I had some orange juice.'

'And that's all? You shouldn't go fishing on an empty stomach. Would you like some pancakes . . . some bacon and eggs?'

'Please, don't bother. I can stop at a diner.'

'It's no bother,' she insisted.

'Well, if you're sure. . .' he was hesitant.

Yes, she was sure.

In that case, he relaxed, he'd like some bacon and eggs. 'Bacon not too crisp, two eggs, please, the yokes set, the whites

346

just this side of runny, very dark toast and black coffee.'

She cooked the breakfast with a smothered smile – that order was pure vintage Catlett – then served him, pouring a cup of coffee for herself. 'Mmmm,' he wrinkled his nose appreciatively. 'Is that apple butter? Haven't had it since I was a kid.'

He alternately ate and fired questions about her new life. Did she like the country? Did she miss New York? What were her employers like? She answered in moderate detail while Sasha rolled around the floor with the panda. As for Catlett, he made no comment, merely listened.

'Now,' he said, drawing a manila envelope from his pocket. 'To business. As I mentioned, I've good news for you. You have a sizeable sum of money coming. There seemed to be some question as to whether you were entitled to it, since you're no longer with the company, but I felt you were. So let's say it's in the form of an *ex gratia* payment.'

'Worldsville!' Caro's eyes lit up. But Catlett pursed his lips. No, afraid not. Damn thing was still in limbo. NASA couldn't make up its mind. May wind up taking a bath on it after all. No, it was. . . 'that movie of yours. *Motel Room 13.*'

'You're kidding!' The picture had gone clear out of her mind; she'd never even heard if it had been released. But he was assuredly not kidding.

After a slow start, the movie had taken off like a rocket, especially overseas. Japan. Europe. South America. 'They seem to favour that sort of thing in South America . . . strange people those Latins. Anyhow, here are the figures. I'll go over them with you.'

He fished in his breast pocket and came up with – glasses. Now that was new. He never used to wear glasses. He acknowledged her surprise with a shrug and a muttered 'too much fine type lately,' then began going through the papers. Exhibitors' gross receipts, Japanese rentals, conversion rates, cruzeiros into dollars . . . but she hardly listened.

She couldn't get over how changed he was. It wasn't merely the glasses or the unfamiliar clothes. He seemed softer than she remembered, easier. Almost boyish in a way.

'So anyhow,' he wound up, 'you're approximately eighty-seven thousand dollars richer than you were this time last week. That's a before-tax figure of course.'

'I can't get over it.' And she didn't mean just the money.

'Yes, it is nice, isn't it?' he grinned. 'Not a fortune, but still . . . enough to afford you some independence.'

She was silent for a moment, then said something that had been troubling her from the moment he called. 'You must find it very odd, my taking this kind of job.'

'Not at all,' he framed his answer cautiously. 'You used to work for me and now you work for somebody else. Everybody works for somebody – me included. Nothing particularly odd about it.'

'You know what I mean,' she persisted. 'I'm a housekeeper, a glorified baby-sitter. Why should I be euphemistic about it? I'm a servant, Dan, pure and simple. And how many MBA's can say that? I suppose you think I'm a terrific coward, hiding out in the sticks like this. But it was the only way I could think of to be with Sasha.'

He took off his glasses and rubbed his eyes, as though to view her afresh. And when he spoke there was none of that old-time irony in his tone.

'On the contrary, Caroline,' he said finally. 'I take off my hat to you. I think you've shown great courage, real guts. You knew the kind of life you wanted for your daughter, what you felt was right, and you achieved it in a very practical manner. It couldn't have been easy.'

'Thank you.' She was too moved to say anything more.

'And thank you' – he jumped into the momentary breach – 'for giving me breakfast. Well, if I'm going to be upstate by noon, I should be leaving now. Ice fishing,' he laughed. 'A bunch of guys from Warburg have a cabin in the back of beyond. Apparently you go out on the ice, cut these little holes in the lake and hope the fish have the good sense to bite. Well, might be fun. A chance to make some contacts, anyhow. About your money, the cheque should be ready on Monday. Do you want me to open an account for you in the city or just send it here? Think about it and I'll call you next week.'

She threw on a sweater and walked him out to the car. The cold was brutal, intense, and it was starting to snow. What would it be like out there fishing on ice? He'd freeze to death. She could picture him, blue and shivering, blowing on frost-bitten fingers. And as he started the car, she leaned over to him, her feet dancing against the cold.

'Dress warmly, Dan.'

The moment the words were out, she could have bitten her tongue. Who was she to tell Dan Catlett what to do? He was a grown man, for God's sake. But he smiled and said 'Thank you. I shall.'

Sunday evening, while she and the Gerbers were in the midst of a Scrabble game, he dropped in on his way back to New York, with some trout in a brown paper bag. Just passing by, he said standing in the doorway, thought he'd leave them off – but Dave Gerber insisted he come in for a drink.

No, nothing alcoholic, thanks. He still had an hour's driving ahead of him, but if Caroline would be so good as to make him a cup of coffee. . . .

Yes, of course.

He took a chair in the living room, folded his arms and turned to Dave. 'Caroline tells me that you're a lawyer, Mr Gerber.' Then he went on to ask Dave's opinion about a recent and controversial Supreme Court ruling.

Caro went into the kitchen, wondering if a political argument would develop. Catlett had a tendency to sound off when he held the floor at meetings and on certain topics he could be . . . well, insufferable. But when she came back the two men were chatting amiably, and the moment she entered, Catlett sprang to his feet. A long time since a man had risen for her. There was something to be said for old-fashioned manners, she thought.

'Mr Gerber and I have agreed to disagree,' he gave a gracious smile, and Caro had the notion that the pair of them had been interviewing each other in some circumspect manner, with Barbara as onlooker.

He drank his coffee, didn't linger, and when he got up to leave, Caro pressed a jar of apple butter on him.

'How very kind. I'll have it with my breakfast tomorrow.'

She went into the kitchen and began putting the fish away when Barbara came in with a pensive air.

'He's very interested in you, your Mr Catlett.'

'I doubt it.' Caro could not credit the idea seriously. He was a man who hired housekeepers; he certainly didn't socialize with them. Nonetheless, Barbara's remark intrigued her. 'Why? Did he say something when I was out of the room?'

'No. He talked about politics and fishing.'

'So there you are,' Caro said, but Barbara continued 'He didn't just drop in, you know. He told me where he'd been fishing – the other end of the state. Well, all I can say is no man drives fifty miles out of his way in weather like this simply to deliver a couple of fish.'

Possible, but unlikely, was Caro's conclusion.

Had he been truly interested in her . . . well, God knows she had handed herself to him on a platter. Nothing could expunge the memory of his face, filled with disgust and horror. He had plucked her off him as though she were some type of loathsome parasite. OK. He'd felt sorry for her, in fact been rather sweet afterwards – but that was no basis on which to build. Once before she had fallen into the trap of making him the focus of her fantasies, with disastrous results. She wasn't going to make that mistake twice, either.

Better to think about the money. Money was real, tangible. Even after taxes it was enough to get her a modest place of her own, tide her over until Sasha was in nursery school. Then, perhaps, she could find a decent job. Not that she didn't like the Gerbers, but the thought of being under her own roof exerted a powerful attraction. After much soul-searching, she suggested to Dave and Barbara that perhaps they should start looking for a replacement for her. No rush. Maybe some time after the first of the year.

As for Catlett, he would surely call about the cheque – he was meticulous about that sort of detail – but her private guess was she had seen the last of him.

He called Monday morning and she asked him to put the cheque in the mail. He called Tuesday afternoon to ascertain if it had arrived. Wednesday he phoned from O'Hare in Chicago.

350

He was in between connections, had a half hour to kill. Was she free to talk?

She was, but in fact he did the talking – almost all of it connected with business. How the new prime rate was killing everybody. That Sonic Jacuzzi company – remember? – it was going public. How Bill Reynolds had this terrific drinking problem and he wasn't sure about the best way of handling it.

'What do you think I should do about him, Caroline?'

'Me?'

'Well yes. I value your opinion.'

There was more in that vein. Only when his flight was called did the conversation take a more personal bent.

'How are the roads out there . . . still so icy?'

'Terrible.'

Did she have snow tyres on? Did she keep chains in the trunk? Plenty of sand? 'I don't like to think of you driving around in this weather in that dinky little Volkswagen.'

'The car's fine. I'm fine. Honestly, Dan.'

'Mmmm . . . well, they're boarding my flight. Take care. Best to Sasha.'

Thursday he didn't call at all, and Caro went to bed feeling depressed, but the next morning he phoned to say he'd been invited to a house party in Pound Ridge that weekend, 'practically next door'. Could he take her to lunch on Saturday. Had she ever eaten at La Cremaillère? He understood it was the best French restaurant in the area. Sasha was welcome too, of course.

'Well, Dan, I don't think her manners are quite up to French restaurant standards. I'll leave her with the Gerbers for the afternoon.'

'As you wish. I'll make a reservation for two, then. And would you do me a favour?'

He remembered her turning up at the office once looking very handsome, then proceeded to describe her apricot silk dress in detail. Would she wear something bright and pretty? She looked terrific in rich colours.

'You were right,' Caro told Barbara. 'He's definitely interested.'

'And are you?'

'I don't know.'

On the whole she decided she was, and that night, steaming out the apricot dress, she permitted herself a brief cautious fantasy. They would have a splendid lunch, lots of wine, and over brandy, looks would be exchanged – then smiles, murmurs. It was highly probable they would wind up the afternoon making love in some country inn. Nothing lurid, as in the sickly daydreams of last spring, and she would certainly make no advances. But should the opportunity arise . . . well, it had been a long time since she'd slept with anyone and he was so terribly attractive.

He arrived on the button, apparently sharing her sense of occasion for he brought her a spray of flowers and some wooden beads for Sasha.

'You look very festive in that dress,' he nodded approvingly.

The restaurant, too, had a festive air – crisp linens, sparkling crystal – and as he ordered, she felt a glow of anticipation. But no sooner had the cocktails arrived than he began to talk about business. His eyes danced, his face grew animated. It was clearly the water he swam in, the air he breathed, though hardly the prelude to an afternoon's dalliance. Yet Caro was riveted, for what he proceeded to do, over three elaborate courses, was pick apart every member of his staff. There they were, all her former colleagues, spread out as on an operating table, innards exposed, flaws revealed. With relish, he confided which ones had domestic troubles, which ones lived beyond their means, who was cheating on expenses, how the way to get results out of Healey was flattery and sweet talk, while Broome and Marcusson responded better to threats. Which men had the stuff, which didn't. He'd decided to fire Reynolds right after Christmas. The man talked too much at parties. Maybe fire Linderfors too. He'd have to think about that.

Caro listened with growing fascination, for these were the men she had worked with, practically lived with, and in many cases his judgments jibed with her own. Yet the intimacy of his dossiers surprised her, for his office stance had always been one of distance and impartiality, screened by a curtain of cigarette smoke. Now she realized the curtain was camouflage, and all the while he had been studying the men, exploring each one's strength, seeking the Achilles heel, probing for the wind-up key in every case.

So, too, he must have spent long hours analysing and dissecting Caro, forming his conclusions and keeping his counsel. He was not keeping it now, and halfway through the meal, she accepted the fact that they would not finish the day in the bedroom of some country inn. He had a need to talk, to confide – a need more urgent, at least on this occasion, than the need for sex. And in Caro he had found the ideal audience: knowledgable, intelligent, discreet, someone who would neither babble nor blackmail.

In fact, she was enjoying the afternoon hugely, although not in the manner anticipated, and since his mood was so open, she began asking him questions. How had he arrived at certain decisions? Why he had employed certain tactics? His answers were usually complex, his reasoning Machiavellian.

'Crazy business we're in, Caroline,' he remarked at one point, as though she were still in it with him. One deal in particular had always puzzled her, an instance where she felt doubtful ethics had won the day. 'Was that legal?' she now asked. He made a circle of thumb and forefinger. 'Just!' Yet a few minutes later he astonished her in answer to another question.

'You mean those metallurgist fellows who'd found a way to cut the cost of handguns?' How could Caro imagine he'd back some company that could put a Saturday Night special into the hands of every nut who managed to scrape twenty dollars together? Appalling.

'But you keep guns, Dan.'

'Hunting rifles, Caroline. I shoot ducks. I don't shoot people. Yes, I know there was a lot of money to be made on that one, but if I couldn't permit myself the occasional moral luxury, I'd get into some other line of business.'

This from a man who'd financed a porno movie.

She laughed. 'You know, Dan. I don't think I'll understand you in a million years.'

'Oh, you will,' came the airy reply. 'And long before that. Let's go for a walk and then I'll run you home.'

He called for the bill, found a fifty-cent discrepancy, then asked the waiter to put a strawberry tart in a box for Sasha. After which, they went for a stroll in the woods.

'Are you warm enough?' He put an arm around her shoulder. 'You really should have a fur coat living up here.'

He phoned on Tuesday, asking her out for dinner and a movie that night, and this time there was no pretence of his happening to be in the neighbourhood. She was about to say yes when she remembered it was her choir-practice night. They'd be doing the Christmas music from Handel's *Messiah*. Rather a treat, that.

For an instant she wavered, then told him no. 'I'm sorry' – she explained the situation – 'but this is important to me.'

'Oh.'

There was a prolonged hush at the other end. Was he angry? Offended? Was he still there?

He finally broke the silence by asking when the rehearsal was over. If it didn't run too late, perhaps he'd pick her up and they could have a bite afterwards.

'The thing is, Dan, we all go out together after and socialize for an hour or so. You're more than welcome to join us, of course . . . it's just, I don't know if you'll find the people interesting.'

'Maybe some other time then,' he drawled. 'But give me the directions anyhow.'

She left for the rehearsal with mixed emotions, certain she had wounded his pride. God! Men's egos were such fragile concoctions. And Dan, of all people – so used to the limelight, so accustomed to getting his way in matters both great and small. Still, if his interest in her was at all serious, then it was time he recognized that Caro too had particular tastes, private pursuits.

Nonetheless, when she arrived at the high school, she looked around for his Volvo in the parking lot and registered a faint disappointment at not finding it.

Five minutes into rehearsal, however, and the whole business was completely forgotten – lost in the glorious affirmation that was *Messiah*. Whether it was the coming of Christmas, the nature of the music or some imponderable factor that begged definition, tonight the chorus took fire – and from its ranks joyous peals of sound rolled back to the farthest corner of the darkened auditorium. They sang for nearly two mindless hours, ending inevitably with the entire group rising as one man for the great *Hallelujah Chorus*.

'Oh, wow!' Sarah Russo put down her baton and wiped the sweat from her brow. 'Terrific!'

From the pitchy blackness of the back row came the sound of someone clapping. And there was Catlett, slim and smiling, gliding forward into the light.

'I hope you'll forgive a gatecrasher,' he walked up to Sarah and shook her hand. 'One of your members was so kind as to invite me. I enjoyed it enormously. Hello, Caroline.' He turned to where she stood beaming 'May I join you all?'

Later, after everyone else had dispersed, they sat alone at the deserted table drinking coffee.

'You're full of surprises, Dan Catlett,' she confessed. 'I never expected you to come.'

'Why not?'

'Oh . . . I thought you'd see this all as very provincial . . . life in the boonies, so to speak.'

'Me?' He arched an eyebrow. 'I'm the original smalltown boy, at least by New York standards. Charleston isn't exactly a metropolis, you know – although I like it,' he added defensively. 'Well, you surprised me too, Caroline. I hadn't a notion you were interested in music. I watched you up there singing and you looked so different . . . transported, almost. I could hardly take my eyes off you.'

Funny, he mused – you could deal with people year in, year out and only see one aspect of their lives: the professional. This one's in municipal bonds, that one's an airlines analyst or a commodities broker. It was so easy to pigeonhole them; to adjudge them good or bad, smart or dumb – all on the basis of this narrow view.

His grandfather, the original D. R. Catlett, had founded a bank in Carolina that specialized in loans to market gardeners. And the old man's proudest claim was being on a first-name basis with all his customers. Not just the customers either. He knew their wives, their kids, their problems, their peculiarities.

'But those were different times,' Dan conceded. 'Nowadays who can afford all that energy? Everything's so big, so depersonalized. I guess that's why I enjoyed myself so much tonight, hearing you sing and all. Tell me, were you ever interested in it professionally?'

'No,' Caro grinned at the idea. 'Just something I do for fun, for personal satisfaction.' She looked at him shrewdly. Such an odd question to ask. 'Why, Dan? Did you want to be something else when you were young?'

He shook his head no, but she didn't believe him.

'Oh, come on,' she coaxed. 'You weren't born wearing a pin-stripe suit. Didn't you ever want to . . . run away to sea or join a circus? Do something wildly implausible?'

He considered for a moment, then reddened and looked away.

'Funny, I hadn't thought of it in years . . .'

'What?'

'You'd laugh if I told you.'

She promised not to, so he told her anyway.

When he was in college he wanted to write detective novels, had even dreamed up and fleshed out a hero. Sam Jethro was his protagonist's name, a Deep South Perry Mason. 'They're a special breed, Southern lawyers, sort of folksy, but very shrewd, very wily.' For the next ten minutes he outlined a convoluted plot that included beautiful blondes, embezzled trust funds, mysterious corpses in the Cypress Gardens.

'Did you actually write it?' Caro asked.

'I started to, but . . . I guess the real world intervened. Speaking of which,' he checked his watch, 'I really must go. I have a breakfast meeting first thing tomorrow morning. Can I run you home?'

But her own car was outside, so instead he followed her home in his Volvo, waiting in the road while she pulled into the Gerber's driveway. Then he dipped his lights twice and drove off.

After that, he drove up two or three nights a week, sometimes straight from the office in a company Cadillac. A hundred mile round trip at the end of a long, hard business day. Usually with something for Sasha.

They talked, went out for dinner occasionally, played gin rummy. But mostly talked. Increasingly the conversation became personal – about his family (a large and close one), about his ex-wife, about growing up in the South. And Caro found herself opening up too. The childhood adventures and travels that Tom had found so glamorous, Catlett saw as appalling.

'I don't care for your mother very much,' he declared.

'That's not quite fair. You've never met her.'

'Oh yes, I've had that pleasure.' And seeing Caro's startled expression, he explained. The day she'd come to see his orchids, he had been alarmed about her and that evening – business over – had visited Gusty. 'I thought at a time like this, a domestic crisis, your mother would naturally want to be with you. . .'

His eyes glittered coldly, and Caro had a swift vision of an acrimonious scene – Gusty for once getting as good as she gave.

'What happened?' Caro asked breathlessly.

He gave a curt laugh. 'Let's just say she's not the Number One member of my fan club. Intractable woman!'

Another time, he asked her if she missed being married. Not too much, she replied. Certain things, though. Which particularly? She giggled. 'You'll probably find this ridiculous, but I can't seem to get warm these winter nights. I go to bed with socks on.' She was about to ask what about you, Dan? What do you miss? when he said 'Come on, let's play some gin.'

Dead stop. About face. He was always doing that in conversations. Talk always had to be of his own choosing. She went to fetch the cards.

'What stakes do you want to play, Caroline?'

'Penny a point all right?'

'I guess I can afford that.'

She laughed and began dealing.

'You know, Caroline,' he said casually. 'I'm over a million dollars in hock.'

'You're joking!' She laid down the cards.

'I wish I were. Last year I got involved in a pretty funny venture ... too speculative for the company but just crazy enough for yours truly, and it's literally milking me dry. You remember that proposition of Gunther's ... about turning cheese into gas.'

First, you get a herd of cows. . .

Dear God! It was the original office gag line. How could he take such a flyer?

But the idea intrigued him – like Rumpelstiltskin's flax into gold. He'd bought a farm in Connecticut, installed a herd of cows that were right now eating him out of house and home, hired three engineers and purchased half a million dollars worth of specialized equipment. It was maximum risk, but held the promise of maximum profit. To finance it he had sold his boat, his summer place, his Bentley, taken out a second mortgage on his home. Just last week, his porcelains had gone under the hammer at Christie's. 'You were right, Caroline. They were a good investment.' Though he recounted all this with humour and no trace of self-pity, the loss of his collection must have hurt.

'I'm sorry Dan,' she placed her hand over his. She had never seen him vulnerable before. 'I'm sure it will all work out. I have every confidence in you, but if I can help in any way . . .'

'You can help,' he grinned. 'You can deal the cards and give me a chance to win that seven dollars you took me for the other night.'

The nature of their new relationship puzzled her. That he craved a confidante was clear; that she qualified superbly for the role, equally so. Beyond that she could only conjecture. Was this elaborate courtship – not just of her but of Sasha – simply a prelude to a sexual advance? She doubted it. He was by nature an aggressive man, prone to swift and pre-emptive decisions – and Caro was no dewy-eyed virgin.

Yet for all his verbal frankness, his behaviour toward her remained sexually circumspect. He made no effort to place himself in a romantic light, indeed she sometimes wondered if his tales of personal troubles and professional machinations were not a deliberate campaign to alert her to his least attractive aspects. 'I reckon you don't find me an idealist,' he told her. 'But I am what I am, and I have no patience with those men who are out to save the world, full of fine talk and good works, while they run roughshod over their own families.' It was a pointed reference to Tom. But if he wished to take Tom's place in Caro's bed, he was going about it with great caution. And, as he had previously remarked, there were willing women galore in Manhattan.

Yet sometimes, particularly when he phoned long distance, she would detect a note of longing. Wistfulness.

Calling her once from Seattle, his first question had been 'What are you wearing?' and she knew he wanted to conjure her image three thousand miles away.

Another time she complained about a strange crackling on the line. 'What's that funny noise, Dan?'

'That's me. I'm eating popcorn.'

'Don't they feed you on the plane any more?'

'I can't eat that airline swill.'

'Then why don't you go into the airport restaurant and have a decent meal before the flight?'

'I can't do that either.'

'Why not?'

'Because I'm busy talking to you.'

As confused as she was about his feelings, she understood her own even less. She wanted to have an affair with him. Why not? He was attractive, considerate, unfailingly kind to Sasha. Amusing in his own wry way. Yet she feared it, for love affairs were, by their very nature, tempestuous and finite things. She was afraid of jeopardizing a valuable friendship for what might prove to be a one-night stand. Then Catlett, too, would join the ranks of men who come and go.

He was the only person she could really talk to; his company, even his phone calls fleshed out her life, gave colour to her days. Sasha adored him – that was good, that was bad. And Caro wished there were some way she could restrain her daughter, restrain herself from falling into the trap of dependency.

For dependency scared men shitless.

The Sunday before Christmas he came up for the afternoon with boxes from Saks and F.A.O. Schwartz.

'I won't be seeing you for a while, Caroline,' he announced. 'But anyhow, here are a few presents for under the tree.'

Her heart sank. Presents. Was this his way of saying goodbye, pretty boxes and wrappings, his equivalent of Tom's three-page letter? To do with money what Tom had done with words?

'You're going away, Dan?'

Yes. He was off to Charleston first thing in the morning for Christmas with his family, after that to the Bahamas. A week-long house party thrown by The Purple People Eaters. Had Caro ever heard of them?

'The British rock group?' She blinked in astonishment. 'I wouldn't have thought they were quite your style.'

Probably not, but he couldn't always be choosey and this particular group had more money than the Bank of England. Right now, the pound being what it was, they were on the prowl for dollar investment opportunities, and with a little luck and a lot of hustle, he figured he could pry them loose for a couple of million. Show them how to turn cheese into gas. Could be a lifesaver.

It would have been fun if she and Sasha could have come along for the ride (they looked like they could use some sun), but business was business.

'What are your plans, Caroline?'

'Nothing much.'

In fact her plans had revolved around spending Christmas with him. The Gerbers were off for a week's skiing, she'd have oceans of time. Only last night she'd found a recipe for Christmas goose.

Her disappointment escaped in a sigh.

'I'm sorry, sugar, but business is business,' he repeated.

So it was, and she had needed this reminder that he led a life apart from her – a demanding, dynamic, exciting life. Still . . . 'That means I won't see you again till next year.'

'Only a couple of weeks. Tell you what' – he brightened – 'Get Sasha dressed and we'll all go for a drive, have a bite of lunch somewhere.'

'Sasha,' she called. 'Time to suit up.' She went into the bedroom began wrestling Sasha's arms and legs into a nylon snowsuit. 'I don't know who designs these things,' she muttered to herself. 'Men probably.' For the garment was diabolically intricate: toggles and zippers, flaps and snaps. 'Please, Sasha, stop wriggling.' She got down on the floor and began extricating a squiggly left leg from a right-hand sleeve in a routine worthy of the Marx Brothers. 'Come on, darling, co-operate. Dan's waiting.'

Suddenly she looked up to see him leaning in the doorway watching her. She had caught him unawares and . . .

He was radiant! There was no other word for it. Smiling. Beaming. Radiant. The grey eyes, usually so cool and guarded, were dancing now, flooded with warmth, aglow with wholehearted admiration. And yes – with love.

For in that instance, his face had been a declarative sentence. I LOVE YOU. It was written big and bold in every feature, every muscle. Might as well rent a billboard in Times Square and let the whole world in on the secret.

He didn't say that, however. Simply smiled and said 'You're very graceful,' then knelt down beside her and Sasha. 'Here, let me help you with that contraption.'

They drove along the Hudson, stopping for hamburgers, and after a while he pulled over to the side of the road.

'I want to show you something.'

They got out, walked up a gravel path to a look-out point with a metal guard rail. Far below, in the broad sweep of the Hudson, a vast armada lay at anchor.

'The mothball fleet,' he said.

Ghost ships. Hundreds upon hundreds of them, the remnants of America's World War Two Atlantic fleet. Battleships, destroyers, minesweepers, cruisers, stretching as far as the eye could see, all painted grey as the December sky. The decks were bleak and empty now, silent except for the wail of the wind, but if you stood there long enough and listened hard, you might still hear shouting and gunfire and the cries of young men. Caro heard it. And so too did Catlett, for after a long while he turned away and said 'Life is so fragile.'

He had lost a brother in a different war, and Caro recalled the day he had told her of it. It had been the first time she'd seen the softer side of him. It had been a time her own mind had been haunted by thoughts of death. That same day he had put her on the track of finding Gusty.

'We'd better start heading back' – he took Sasha's hand. 'It's getting late and I have a lot to do tonight.' As they walked back to the car, Caro said 'Can I ask you something Dan?'

'Anything.'

'How did you find out where I was living? And don't say through my bank in New York. I closed my account.'

He smiled. 'But you kept your credit cards.'

'You're very good at finding people, aren't you?' And when he shrugged, she went on. 'You found me . . . my mother. You found Tom the day Sasha was born. Where did you locate him, Dan? What did he say?'

'I don't remember.'

It was a lie, of course. He had total recall, was practically a walking memory bank, but now he turned to her and fixed his eyes on her face. 'Why, Caroline? Does it matter?'

'No.' And the moment she said it, she knew it was true. It didn't matter any more – not in the least. She had nothing left for Tom, not even curiosity. 'No,' her eyes met his. 'It doesn't matter a bit. Now let's get out of this place . . . it gives me the creeps.'

They drove back in deepening twilight, and when he got out he left the motor running. 'I can't come up, have to get home and pack. . .' Suddenly he threw his arms around her and kissed her – a long, hard, passionate kiss that left her breathless. Then burying his head in her hair, he murmured 'I'm absolutely crazy about you, Caroline . . . you know that, don't you? Head over heels . . . simply head over heels.' Having said which, he jumped in the car.

'I'll call you,' he shouted through the window. 'Merry Christmas.'

It was absurd, of course. Impossible. How could she conceivably love Don Catlett? He was the antithesis of everything she had been brought up to value in a man. He was – and made no bones about it – tough, manipulative, domineering, possessive, proud, autocratic. His attitudes on many things, women included, appeared to have been formed somewhere back in the eighteenth century. But beyond the professional man she had discovered the private man, and that was of a different order. For he was that mixture of sweet and salt that she herself could never be, capable of swimming in both waters.

In the years past she had feared him irrationally, idolized him unduly.

And now she loved him. Desperately. Passionately. Head over heels – he had taken the words right out of her mouth. She loved him for many reasons, not the least of which was the love he bore her. He cherished her, admired her in a way that Tom had never done. He loved her for what she was rather than for what she had accomplished.

To Tom, she had always been a status symbol 'My wife, the Wall Street executive.' To her mother, a mark of achievement 'My daughter, the Harvard MBA.' To almost everyone she knew, she had been little more than the sum of her accomplishments. 'Caro Harmsworth – The First Woman Who. . .' The token. The symbol. The vanguard. And when she ceased to be those things, she had lost value, become an outmoded and degraded currency, worthless in everybody's eyes, but Catlett's.

Christmas Eve she waited until a minute after midnight, then tore open the large Saks box with her name on it. Inside was a long robe of purest cashmere, faced with silk.

'Darling Caroline,
Always be warm. I only wish it could have been sable.'

He phoned from the airport en route to the Bahamas.

How was Charleston, she asked.

'Fine. Terrible. I did nothing but mope about the house and think of you.' His flight left in fifteen minutes but meanwhile – Did she have a good Christmas? What's the weather like there? Put Sasha on for a minute. Was the robe all right? Did it fit?

'Beautiful, Dan. Warm as toast. I'm wearing it right now. Listen . . . . you're going to miss your plane.'

He paused and she could hear the airport PA system echoing in the background.

'Caroline, there's a late night flight into Kennedy. Say the word and I'll be on it. So which will it be . . . New York or the Bahamas?

'But Dan . . . what about your British investors?'

'Fuck 'em!'

She laughed – he so rarely used profanity – and said the word. Three of them in fact.

'I love you.'

A huge intake of breath, then 'I'll see you tomorrow.' All at once he was bubbling, full of plans. She should bring her prettiest clothes, they'd spend the weekend at his house, he'd fix up a room for Sasha, get a sitter, they'd do the town – opera, ballet, whatever she wanted. He'd be on her doorstep first thing in the morning.

'No, darling,' she said. 'Let me come to you.' For some reason it seemed terribly important.

31

'The last time you were in this house you offered yourself to me.'

Once again, they sat in his living room. But this time the porcelains no longer sparkled in the corner étagère. The dappling summer sun had given way to the fading light of a winter afternoon. In an upstairs bedroom Sasha lay napping. Flames leapt and crackled in the fireplace. It was a time to talk, to share, to make love. Not a time, Caro felt, to dredge up painful memories.

'It's not an incident I'm likely to forget, Dan, although I had hoped you would.'

'Yes, you offered yourself to me,' he repeated, 'for a lot of reasons – all of them wrong. Out of anger, bitterness, revenge. Out of wounded pride.'

He let the matter drop, and went to poke the fire, but she knew it was not a random remark. He was not given to random remarks, and when he returned, he chose to sit opposite her, on a tapestry chair facing the sofa. His face was grooved with solemnity, and in that moment she knew he was going to propose. But what a sad and curious preamble.

'I've been a little in love with you for a very long time, even before I fell a lot in love with you these past few weeks. Were you aware of that, Caroline?'

No, she shook her head, she was not. For how long?

Ever since – he reached into memory – one day nearly two years ago. He had come into the office one morning, and found her sitting at her desk, daydreaming, eyes turned inward, smiling over some secret joy. With precision, he described what she'd been wearing – a narrow black suit with velvet revers, and now she too remembered. It had been in the early months of her pregnancy, and she had worn that suit, already pinching at the waist, with the knowledge that it would be a long time before she wore it again. She had been pleased, excited. But had she been smiling? She didn't recall. Catlett did.

'Yes, you were smiling.' And to him it was more than a smile, it was a revelation. He had never seen her like that – private, glowing, full of intimate joy – and he had envied her husband. What a lucky man! – that unknown Tom – to come home each night to such love, such warmth and happiness.

Naturally, he suppressed his feelings, said nothing, for Caroline was a married woman and he himself, for better or worse, a gentlemen. Yet the image lingered and grew. Later, after Sasha was born, he would watch her at meetings. She was so softened, vulnerable, sometimes visibly suffering and his heart had gone out to her. Not out of pity, but out of a desire to protect and cherish, for by then he had taken Tom's measure.

The day she had come to his house, he had ached to take her in his arms and make love to her, to possess her in fact as he had done so often in fantasy. Yet he could not bring himself to do this, for it would have been the rankest exploitation. He would have possessed her for all the wrong reasons. 'I may be a male chauvinist, Caroline, but not – I hope – a pig. I couldn't bear the thought of your calling someone else's name in my bed.'

And so he had waited. He had always known where to find her, might have picked up the phone at any moment and heard her voice. Yet he had waited, biding his time. Waited for her to shake free of the past. And now she was free.

'And now I want you to come to me for all the right reasons. Marry me, Caroline. You, as your own woman . . . me, for the man that I am.'

He was waiting now for her answer, yet despite the foreknowledge that he would propose, she felt confused, anxious. Why did everything have to happen so swiftly? Why now, when she was only just free – a fresh survivor from the agonies of one marriage – must she be asked to enter the same hazardous course yet again?

'I love you, Dan,' she answered slowly – 'with all my heart. But marriage? I don't know.'

'What don't you know, Caroline?'

'I don't know what you want out of marriage. Tom and I, we were very sure we wanted certain things when we married and as it turned out, we couldn't give them to each other. You, too, Dan. You may want something from me that I can't give, and marriage is a very expensive proving ground. What do you want of me besides my love? Please, be totally honest.'

There was no immediate answer. Instead he began marshalling his thoughts behind a screen of smoke, frowning, framing his words. At last, he squashed out his cigarette and spread his hands on the table.

'I want it all. Everything. One hundred per cent. Your love – yes, that goes without saying. I want devotion, too. Loyalty. Trust. I want all the little services – hot dinners and clean shirts – and all the big ones as well. I want you to kiss me goodbye every morning, be here waiting for me every night. I want you to laugh at my jokes, share in my victories, console me in my defeats. I want you always at my side, supporting me in public, letting me know in private when I get out of line. I want you to fill my life, to bear my name and my children. I'm a greedy bastard, Caroline, and I want it all. The whole elaborate structure.'

Each day he battled chaos, walked tightropes, lived on nerves, played roles. He wanted to come home each night to a haven of warmth and love and family. He was starved for intimacy. For the affectionate life. And when he died he wanted to leave something more behind him than an obituary in the financial pages. He wanted to leave a heritage of children. He wanted Sasha too. 'For when you are my wife, she will be my daughter – in name, in prospects, in my affections. But most of all, I want you. No – not want.'

He paused and clenched his fists. Then

'I need you, Caroline.'

So there it was. He had asked her for everything. One hundred per cent. Asked her to give and give and give. Asked for the things no one else had cared for, the very qualities others had rejected. He had called upon her greatest talent: the gift for giving.

He lit another cigarette with unsteady fingers, then smiled self-consciously. 'Well . . . that's my shopping list,' he gave a nervous laugh. 'You asked me to be honest and I was. Now you tell me, darling. What do you want out of marriage?'

'You,' she whispered. 'Only you.'

She stretched out to him and in a second he was in her arms, burning with happiness. 'Oh my darling,' he murmured. 'My own sweet darling, you'll never regret it. I'll make you happy. I'll be good to you . . . my lamb, my darling.'

They began making love – there on the soft velvet couch in his living room – his hands in her hair, his lips on her breast, all the caresses and endearments she had once lived in fantasy now all the sweeter for being real. She shut her eyes in the anticipated joy of surrender.

My name is Andy Pandy and I belong to Sasha.

'Oh, for God's sake!' Caro groaned. 'Sasha's up.'

But he kissed her with good grace and began doing up the little buttons on her blouse.

'I've waited for you a long, long time, Caroline. I can wait until tonight.'

He was effervescent, full of plans. All she could think of was *he is so happy*. Where would she like to get married, Dan wanted to know. In church? at home? Anywhere but City Hall, she replied. Good, they'd get married from his parents' house in Charleston. She'd love his family and vice versa. Next week. No problem. He'd arrange everything. Where did she want to go for their honeymoon? He was partial to Montego Bay this time of year. Was that OK? Fine. Montego Bay it would be. What did she want for a wedding present? A fur coat? Diamonds? If she pierced her ears, he'd buy her diamond earrings.

'Really, Dan' – she began to laugh. 'I don't need or want anything.'

'Well, you should have something splendid. I must say, I picked a helluva time to ask you to marry me, when I'm in such a precarious situation. For all I know, we may wind up living on a farm in Connecticut, milking that goddam herd of cows.'

'I'd live with you in a hut.'

'Well,' he laughed. 'I'm sure it won't come to that.'

They began dressing for the opera, all ease and gaiety, falling unconsciously into the little preening gestures of marriage while Sasha played on the bedroom floor.

He did up her zipper, brushed her hair. She fixed his cufflinks and straightened his tie, all the while thinking – *he is so happy*.

The housekeeper arrived to sit for Sasha, and they got ready to leave for Lincoln Centre.

'What opera are they singing tonight, darling?'

'I don't know. My secretary got the tickets.'

MADAMA BUTTERFLY
An opera in three acts by Giacomo Puccini

'Oh good.' Caro opened the programme. 'I've never seen it.'

The setting is Nagasaki in the early 1900s. As the curtain rises, young Lieutenant Pinkerton of the U.S. Navy declares his love for a Japanese geisha. On this day he will marry her for 'nine hundred and ninety-nine years. . .'

As the lights dimmed she settled back, and the gold curtain parted to reveal Lieutenant Pinkerton – handsome, ardent, immaculate in crisp white uniform, black trim – awaiting the arrival of Cio-Cio San, his little Butterfly. But Caro was finding it hard to concentrate, conscious only of Catlett's presence beside her, of his hand resting lightly on her wrist. *He is so happy*, she thought. They exchanged smiles. He murmured something into her ear, but the people behind them began shushing, and reluctantly, she forced her gaze back to the stage.

Ah . . . there is Butterfly. How charming she is. Fragile. Arms filled with wedding blossoms. She embraces her beloved Pinkerton. For him, she sings, she has given up her family, her home, her religion. From now on, he will be her whole world. The couple swear their love, glorious voices rising in a rapturous duet. . . .

Caro, entranced, let the music wash over her. *Viene la sera*, the lovers were singing. *The night is coming*. . .

'Gorgeous, isn't it?' Caro turned to Catlett.

'Yes,' he glowed. 'You are.'

'I meant the music.'

Viene la sera. She squeezed his hand. Their night of love was coming, too.

ACT II. *Some years later. A little house above Nagasaki harbour.*

Pinkerton has sailed away and the curtain rises on Butterfly and the child of their love. With her faithful servant Suzuki, she awaits his return. . .

Un bel di. The soprano's voice floated across the hall with piercing intensity, wrapping Caro in its beauty.

Un bel di. One fine day he will come back, this man she waits for with love and longing. One fine day his ship will return and he will hold Butterfly again in his arms. But listen! What's that? A cannon shot. Yes. Run to the window. Look – there below in the harbour. At last . . . at last his ship! Soon he will be with her. This very night. Butterfly dons her wedding dress again, and begins decorating her tiny house with cherry blossoms. . .

Inadvertently, Caro's throat muscles tightened.

'I'd love something to drink, Dan,' she said the moment the lights went up. 'I'm simply parched.'

'Me too. Plus I'm dying for a cigarette.'

Hand in hand, they made their way through the crush that circled the bar, and he managed to order some champagne.

'Here's to us, darling. . .' They clinked glasses, when across a sea of heads, somebody waved.

'For heaven's sake,' he swallowed off his drink. 'There's Hartzberg of Goldman Sachs. Do you mind if we just nip over and say hello?' He ushered Caro through the mob to a middle-aged couple, a short balding man, a plump fur-bearing wife.

There followed a flurry of introductions – 'This is my fiancée, Mrs Darius. Darling, I'd like you to meet . . .' an exchange of handshakes, a murmur of congratulations. Then the older man said 'Can I talk to you for a few moments in private, Dan?'

The men moved off to a quite corner, leaving the women behind to make small talk. 'The men and their business!' Mrs Hartzberg rolled her eyes, and they began talking of other things: of the opera, the weather, their children. 'That's a delightful age,' Mrs Hartzberg said of Sasha. 'Of course our boys are grown now . . .' But Caro only half-listened, for she was surreptitiously watching Catlett.

A year ago she too might have been there in the corner talking business with the men. OK. No regrets. But now as she watched him – his brow furrowed, his eyelids lowered in concentration – he seemed suddenly the old Catlett, remote and aloof. Even the black dinner jacket and white shirt struck her as a reincarnation of his office uniform. He was utterly absorbed. If only he would raise his eyes and look at her, smile, give a complicitous wink. Perhaps even blow her a kiss. But no – he was wrapped in his own cocoon.

Not until the bell announced the start of Act III did he return to her side. 'We better hurry, darling' – he took her by the elbow. 'Curtain will be going up any second. . .'

ACT III Dawn, the following day. Butterfly has waited through the night in vain.

Riveted now, Caro sat bolt upright in her seat, with eyes and ears for nothing except the drama being played out on stage.

Dear God! Please make him come, that heartless Pinkerton. Come now to the woman who has trusted you, loved you, borne your child. Aaaah . . . There is his music. At last. At last Pinkerton comes. But what's this? He is not alone. Who is the woman with him? His wife? Yes, his new wife, his real wife. And now he has come to claim his child and say goodbye. You brute! Traitor – to have seduced Butterfly, won her with vows and love and now to abandon her without mercy. He has broken her heart. Her life is over. Her wedding dress will this day serve as her shroud. Goodbye. *Addio*. She kisses her little boy for the last time, gives him a toy, a tiny American flag. She sends him away and now is alone. From the low table Butterfly picks up a dagger. She steps behind the screen. . .

Caro began weeping. Was weeping still as the curtain fell.

'Here, darling.' Catlett handed her his handkerchief, unembarrassed by her tears. She wiped her eyes and blew her nose. 'Yes, that certainly is a terrific tear-jerker, Caroline. Very affecting.' Yet he was unaffected. *He was so happy*. 'What would you like to do now, sugar? Go dancing? Have some late supper?'

'Let's just go home.'

'Of course.'

Out on the street the snow was beginning to pile up. 'We could sure use some of those Japanese cherry blossoms right

371

now,' he remarked cheerfully as they pulled into Gramercy Park. 'Do you want to make us some tea, darling, while I put Mrs Lacey in a cab?'

Caro was in the kitchen, poking through unfamiliar shelves when he returned.

'The tea's over here,' he showed her. 'Teapot's in the same cupboard with the glasses.'

He perched on a kitchen chair and watched her go about her woman's work. He was not happy anymore.

'No secrets, Caroline,' he announced when she was done. 'I want to know what's troubling you.'

She poured the tea and smiled thinly. 'It's just . . . well I've been wondering Dan, if maybe we're not being overhasty. I mean getting married . . . next week. That's awfully soon. You know we really haven't thought it through. . . .'

'I've thought it through.'

'Well . . .' she hesitated. 'I haven't. You kind of swept me off my feet this afternoon. I need some breathing space I've just begun thinking it through for myself and . . . it's such a big decision, such a huge commitment. What's the rush, after all? We might not get along. You may change your mind and want out. . .'

'I won't change my mind. Why, have you changed yours?' And when she didn't answer he burst out 'My God! It's that damned opera! Is that when you started "thinking it through" . . . somewhere in the middle of Act II?' She still didn't reply and he shook his head in amazement. 'Well, of all the ridiculous . . . For God's sake, darling, it was just chance that they happened to be doing *Butterfly* tonight. It might just as easily have been *Carmen*, where the girl drives the loyal man up the wall or . . . supposing we'd seen *Samson and Delilah* . . . would that have been better? . . . where the woman cuts off the man's hair or his balls or whatever? It amounts to the same thing as I recall. In which case we wouldn't be having this talk right now. Caroline,' he pleaded. 'You're not Butterfly, I'm not Pinkerton. That was art . . . theatre . . . not real life.'

'You're wrong, Dan. That was real life.'

He was stunned.

'I . . . I don't know what to say to a statement like that. I

372

don't know how to counter such fears. You seem to think that every man is a Tom Darius.'

'In my experience – yes.'

'In your experience,' he echoed. 'OK. You've had some pretty rotten experiences. But all men aren't the same. You've simply known the wrong ones. The wrong women too, I might add. You've been crammed full of nonsense all your life, I grant that. But I'm not Pinkerton or Tom or anybody else. I'm me – Dan Catlett – who loves you and wants to marry you. See me for myself – that's all I ask. You know me. We go way back, you and I. We've known each other at our absolute worst and at our best. The only thing we haven't done is go to bed together and we can remedy that right now.'

'Yes, let's – by all means. Let's be lovers. Let's live together for a while, a sort of trial period, see how it works and then we can talk about getting married.'

'No.' He was categoric.

'Just no? Does everything have to be so black and white with you?'

'No. We're not children, Caroline, we're adults. And it's time we got on with the real business of living. I don't want an affair. I didn't make all those trips to Mount Kisco simply to get you into bed, much as the prospect delights me. I won't settle for anything less than marriage. It won't work otherwise.'

'How can you be so sure?'

'Because there'll be no real commitment on either side. What happens when we have our first serious argument? And we will have them, you know, we're both people with pretty lively tempers. What's to prevent either one of us from simply walking away. Why stick it out? Why negotiate? Where's the incentive when it's so much easier to drift apart, to drift into other affairs. We could have had an affair a long time ago and I didn't want it. I can't believe it's what you really want either, for yourself – or for Sasha. Can you seriously want her to have a different "uncle" every few months?'

'That's unfair,' Caro began crying.

'It may be unfair, darling, but it's realistic.'

'And you think marriage is some sort of guarantee . . . happy ever after?'

'I don't know. But let's you and I live every day on that assumption. Let's get up every morning with the firm understanding that it's not just for now. It's for always. That we will always be together as long as we live, that we share the same hopes, the same dreams. Come on, darling' – he wiped a tear from her cheek – 'I won't pull a Tom on you. You know that in your heart of hearts. So what is it you're so frightened of? Tell me,' he implored.

'I'm afraid' – she met his eyes – 'that your life will swallow me up.'

That afternoon he had asked her for everything and she would give it. Gladly. But what would be hers in return? His odd hours, the small change left over from his work, hurried calls from airports. Her life would be shaped to his needs, contoured to his career. She would be there for him – but would he always be there for her?

'You'll own me, Dan,' she said – and when he didn't protest, continued.

He would lead his life, a life that wracked her with anxiety: the crazy hours, the stress, the missed meals, the 'white knuckle' flying. Would he be there for her when she needed him? She doubted it, for she had seen the high price exacted by pressure. The student who'd committed suicide at B School. Walter Lorencz's death. Tom's desertion. The pressures had been different, the responses varied, yet each had proved wounding. Self-destructive. She feared – no not him. But for him. And for herself as well.

'You'll own me and perhaps that's all right. But I won't own you. Yes. I'll be here waiting every night for you to come home, but where will you be? In a meeting? At a business dinner? On a plane to Seattle? Your real life will be somewhere else – away from me.

'*No!*'

He leaned across the table and grasped her hands in both of his. 'This is my life – feel it.' He gripped her harder until the fingers ached, the knuckles blanched. 'Feel my hands on yours, my bones, my flesh. This is what's real. Everything else – business, money – it's just a game. Just theatre, like that opera tonight. That's something you never quite realized. You took it too seriously. Still . . . it's a game. A very exciting, seductive one, granted, and I adore it. But my real life will always be here with you.'

He pressed his thumb hard into the pulse of her wrist until she could feel her blood pumping beneath his grasp. 'Flesh and blood. Flesh and blood. That's what everything comes down to bottom line. All that matters. Flesh and blood. Yours. Mine. Ours.' Then loosening his hold he brought her hand to his lips and kissed the tender throbbing wrist.

'I love you, Caroline. I can't be happy unless you are too. But do you know what I'm offering you? Freedom. For you'll have more freedom married to me than you ever had working for me. You'll be free to do the things you've dreamt of and never had time for. I don't want one of those Saudi Arabian wives, all shrouded and hidden from view. I may be selfish, darling, but I'm not crazy. Everything I have is yours, you know that. Not fifty-fifty, but a hundred-hundred. That's how I see us. Believe me, I want you to do the things that give your life meaning. You tell me you enjoy being active in music. Fine. Be more active. Sing. Become a sponsor at the Met. Raise funds for the Philharmonic. We don't live in a vacuum – we're both three-dimensional people and I want us to stay that way. So do what gives you satisfaction. Read, think, cultivate friends, cultivate your voice. Cultivate orchids, if you like' – they both smiled – 'and children. You'll find no lack of worthwhile occupations.'

'But you know,' she said softly, 'children don't stay small forever. Everything you've mentioned – yes, that's how I want to live now, and very likely may want to live that way forever. But who can say? Conceivably, some time in the future – ten, fifteen years from now, I may just want to pick up my career. What then?'

'Ten, fifteen years from now,' came the answer, 'I may want to quit and write detective stories. Your guess is as good as mine. We'll grow, we'll change – I have no doubt of it – and possibly in ways we've never foreseen. But the one thing that won't change is you and I. That stays. That will endure. I can't predict how much my life will alter. I'm an ambitious man. I can only say I'll try. Don't be afraid I'll swallow you up for you have influence over me, too. Do you have any idea how much?'

He looked at her with his heart in his eyes. 'Oh Caroline, you can make mincemeat of me with one of your smiles.'

'Can I?' She blessed him with one of her smiles. 'Can I really?'

He gave a happy nod – for her smile had told him everything – then leaned back to light a cigarette.

'My darling, Dan' – she looked at him, perplexed. 'I don't think you'll ever change your ways. You're you. Why, you can't even give up smoking.'

He got to his feet, picked up the pack of Dunhills, the heavy gold lighter, the ash tray and dropped them into the garbage.

'I just did – permanently.' Then he came to where she sat, knelt and wrapped her in his arms. 'Now, Caroline, will you marry me?'

She began laughing. 'How can I make a rational decision while you're kissing me?'

'Don't make a rational decision. Make a gut one.' He cradled her to him, all strength and love and will.

Yes yes yes yes yes. 'Yes,' she whispered. 'I'll marry you and live with you forever.'

They went to bed, undressing slowly and with a sense of ritual, touching, kissing, full of discovery and wonder. Only when she came into his arms for the ultimate act of love did she remember. 'I'm not on the pill, darling.' He laughed and kissed her. 'Neither am I.'

They made love, tentatively at first, tremulously, and finally with that passion and freedom that expressed the depth of their love and their commitment. They lay for a long time, bodies intertwined, talking, caressing, just being content and happy. 'Isn't this nice?' he said. And now his voice was soft only for her.

At last he got up and picked the quilt off the floor, pulling it warm about them.

It was an extraordinary quilt – every inch of it appliqued in beautiful Victorian needlework. It was a garden full of improbable flowers and fanciful birds – a hundred different shades of greens and lilacs.

'I've never seen anything like it before,' Caro held it against her cheek. 'It's like the Garden of Eden.'

'My great-grandmother made this quilt for her trousseau.' he told her. 'She handed it down to my grandmother and my grandmother gave it to me when I first married. Tonight you and I will sleep under it. Tonight and for many years to come. Past . . . present . . . future.'

He turned out the light.

In the dead of night, something woke her with a start. A street noise? Had Sasha fallen out of bed?

She slipped out and went into the next room. No, not Sasha, for the child was sleeping heavily, her head nestled into the plush of the panda bear. The noise must have come from outside. Just a car backfiring.

She looked out the window. Still snowing. A foot of it at least. In the lamplight, Gramercy Park lay white and timeless. How quiet the house was now. Nothing but the tick of clocks, the occasional creak of a floorboard as she tiptoed back to bed.

He was sleeping lightly, restless. Muttering something she couldn't quite catch. *Benches*, it sounded like.

She leaned close, straining to hear the words.

'Debentures,' he mumbled. 'Fourteen and a half per cent.' Whatever his dream was, it was not a good one.

Debentures.

She climbed back into bed.

How can I possibly marry a man who dreams about debentures the first night we spend together?

But she could. And she would.

She reached over to him, touched him gently to break the thread of the dream. And at her touch he moved toward her, even in sleep seeking out the curves of her body, burrowing into her softnesses, settling against her until he fit like a second skin. Then, his hair brushing against her lips, he sighed and fell into a deeper peaceful sleep.

'Close to Dan.'

That had always been the game at the office. Everyone hustling, manoeuvering to get 'close to Dan'. But no one would ever be closer to him than she was now. She had never in her life belonged anywhere, but now she belonged with him. She had never before been certain of what she was, but now she knew.

Woman. Wife. Mother. The trinity was complete. Thea's parlour game solved at last.

No regrets.

What a curious mixture he was, this man. A mixture of strengths and needs. She, too, was the same mixture. The last years had revealed all her needs, her failings. She knew them well. But only now had she discovered her strength.

Her power.

For she had power. Lying in the darkness, she remembered his face in the theatre, alight with love. *He was so happy.* It was a happiness she had created – for she had that power.

Yes, she could create happiness, evoke love. In Dan. In Sasha. And that was real power indeed. A greater power than buying and selling little bits of paper, than squeezing more dollars out of contracts.

She had the power to conceive life. To bring it forth, nurture it, shape it. And *that* was real power, too. A power almost divine.

Even now, this very moment, a new life might be growing within her, a life drawing its nourishment from her body, its strength from her own. A life that would be welcomed and loved. The vision filled her with joy.

What was it, she tried to recall, that line of John Maynard Keynes? 'In the long run we are all dead.'

Well, Maynard, baby – you were a great economist but a lousy philosopher. In the long run we are all alive.

We are alive in our children. And then in their children. And so on into the infinite future.

And knowing this, Caro shut her eyes and went to sleep.

Contemporary Romances

Once a Lover   £1.95   **Diana Anthony**
Set in New York and San Francisco, *Once a Lover* is the
moving love story of Lainie Brown, a young artist, and
Jean-Paul Vallier, a blinded sports superstar. Then he
regains his sight and Lainie fears she will lose his love. But
she learns painfully and joyously why she is so worthy of
Jean-Paul's enduring devotion.

Celebration   £1.50   **Rosie Thomas**
Bel Farrer, a wine columnist, was a high-flying career girl.
But beneath her glittering professional appearance was a
vulnerable heart. Both the titled aristocrat bound by an
ancient code of honour, and the reckless, carefree playboy
claimed her heart and she had to make a choice.

Perfect Dreams   £1.75   **Carolyn Fireside**
The world of high fashion, Hollywood and the jet set is
the backdrop for this rich love story. Gabrielle Blake, a
photographer's model, is independent, intelligent and lovable. Among the rich and famous men who fall in and out
of Gaby's life is Terry Baron, a young journalist who
finally rescues her when her career collapses. But is it too
late for them to rescue their love for each other?

Perhaps I'll Dream of Darkness   £1.35   **Mary Sheldon**
In this compelling and beautifully written story of love and
obsession the lives of a teenage girl and a burned-out rock
star entwine fleetingly — with disastrous results. Probing
deeply into her characters' lives, Mary Sheldon creates a
portrait of frustrated passion that leads to tragedy, and
captures both the grace and terror of obsessive, idealistic
love.

FONTANA PAPERBACKS

Catherine Gaskin

'Catherin Gaskin is one of the few big talents now engaged in writing historical romance.'
Daily Express

'A born story-teller.' *Sunday Mirror*

THE SUMMER OF THE SPANISH
WOMAN   £1.95
ALL ELSE IS FOLLY   £1.65
BLAKE'S REACH   £1.75
DAUGHTER OF THE HOUSE   £1.50
EDGE OF GLASS   £1.50
A FALCON FOR A QUEEN   £1.75
THE FILE ON DEVLIN   £1.50
FIONA   £1.75
THE PROPERTY OF A
GENTLEMAN   £1.75
SARA DANE   £1.95
THE TILSIT INHERITANCE   £1.95
FAMILY AFFAIRS   £2.50
CORPORATION WIFE   £1.75
I KNOW MY LOVE   £1.75
THE LYNMARA LEGACY   £1.95
PROMISES   £2.50

FONTANA PAPERBACKS

Belva Plain

– the best-loved bestseller –

Evergreen   £2.50

A rich and tempestuous story of Anna Friedman, the beautiful, penniless Jewish girl who arrives in New York from Poland at the turn of the century and survives to become matriarch of a powerful dynasty.

Random Winds   £2.50

The absorbing and poignant story of a family of doctors – Dr Farrell, the old-fashioned country doctor who dies penniless and exhausted, his son Martin who becomes a brilliant and famous brain surgeon, but is haunted by his forbidden love for a woman, and Martin's daughter Claire, headstrong, modern and idealistic, whose troubled romance with the unknown Englishman provides a bitter-sweet ending.

Eden Burning   £2.50

A romantic saga set against the backdrop of New York, Paris and the Caribbean. The island of St Felice holds many secrets, one of which is the secret of the passionate moment of abandon that threatened to destroy the life of the beautiful fifteen-year-old Teresa Francis. A story of violence, political upheaval and clandestine love.

FONTANA PAPERBACKS

Fontana Paperbacks

Fontana is a leading paperback publisher of fiction and non-fiction, with authors ranging from Alistair MacLean, Agatha Christie and Desmond Bagley to Solzhenitsyn and Pasternak, from Gerald Durrell and Joy Adamson to the famous Modern Masters series.

In addition to a wide-ranging collection of internationally popular writers of fiction, Fontana also has an outstanding reputation for history, natural history, military history, psychology, psychiatry, politics, economics, religion and the social sciences.

All Fontana books are available at your bookshop or newsagent; or can be ordered direct. Just fill in the form and list the titles you want.

FONTANA BOOKS, Cash Sales Department, GPO Box 29, Douglas, Isle of Man, British Isles. Please send a cheque, postal or money order (not currency) worth the purchase price, plus 15p per book (maximum postal charge £3.00).

NAME (Block letters) _____

ADDRESS _____

_____

_____